LADIES WHOSE BRIGHT EYES

FORD MADOX FORD

LADIES WHOSE BRIGHT EYES
A Romance

Towered cities please us then
And the busy haunts of men,
Where throngs of knights and barons bold
In weeds of peace high triumphs hold,
With store of ladies whose bright eyes
Rain influence and judge the prize.

—L'Allegro

THE ECCO PRESS
NEW YORK

Copyright © 1953 by Ford Madox Ford
All rights reserved
Published in 1987 by The Ecco Press
26 West 17th Street, New York, N.Y. 10011
Printed in the United States of America
Library of Congress Cataloging-in-Publication Data
Ford, Ford, Madox, 1873-1939.
Ladies Whose Bright Eyes:
(Neglected books of the twentieth century)
Reprint. Originally published: Philadelphia:
Lippincott, 1935.
I. Title   II. Series
PR6011.053L3 1987   823'.912   86-4452
ISBN 0-88001-088-6

PART ONE

M<small>R</small> S<small>ORRELL</small>, <small>JUST LANDED FROM</small> N<small>EW</small> Y<small>ORK</small> <small>AFTER AN AL-</small>
most too pleasant voyage, was accustomed to regard himself
as the typical Homo Sapiens Europaeus. He was rising forty;
he was rather fair, with fresh, brown hair; he was by profession a publisher and at the top of the tree; he had a vigorous
physique, a drooping moustache and a pink, clear skin. He
owed no soul a penny; he had done his duty in the war; he
rose usually at eight, voted Conservative and had been given to
understand that he might be honoured with a knighthood at
a near date. So his eyes which were clear and blue were slightly
threatening—as if with an expression of being ready militantly
to assert at once his right and his rectitude. He stood just six
foot.

He stepped out into the swaying corridor from the compartment into which he had gallantly accompanied Mrs Lee-
Egerton. He wanted to smoke a cigar and now that he was
off the boat, to reflect whether he had not made a fool of him-

self. The carriage was swaying very much, the train travelling at an unusual speed. This pleased Mr Sorrell. If he was not responsible for it he was at least a friend of its author, Mr Makover of Pittsburgh. He himself had gone with the Pennsylvanian to interview the driver. Mr Makover had offered that amiable mechanic a fiver if he got them up to town in time to dress, dine and go to the Empire before the ballet began. Thus Mr Sorrell took pride in the speed at which they travelled.

His left shoulder struck with violence the outer window; his right pained him when it hit a brass handrail of the inner one.

"Oh, steady," he exclaimed.

He had been bending down in order to peer into the compartments to discover one in which he could smoke. He saw the spotless expanse of white of a nun's headdress and at the same moment he was thrown violently against the outer window. For a moment he had a panic. He thought he had just missed breaking it and going through.

He exclaimed: "This won't do!"

He set his feet hard against the outer wall of the corridor. He was not going any farther. He got out a cigar, pierced the end of it and began to smoke. Then he took another peep at the nun.

She excited in him an almost unholy curiosity. He could not remember ever to have been so near a nun before. It seemed odd that one should be seated in a train. It was still more odd that she should be coming back from the United States. You would have said that America with its salutary emigration laws would not permit one of them to enter its territories. He would have thought that Catholicism had died out.

But there was still a Pope. There had been one four years ago. When Mr Sorrell had still been proprietor of the *Four-*

penny Magazine it had published an article with illustrations on a day's work in the Vatican. He had then commissioned the editor to try to get for him an article by the Pope even if it cost him a couple of hundred pounds.

That was modern life. Today a subject seemed of enormous importance; in a month you would not touch it as any sort of publishing matter. . . . Keen intelligences those of today!

And he was in the movement. He had agreed to pay the Theat Publishing Company of New York $15,000 for the English Claflin rights. Mr Claflin, the aviator, had flown completely round the earth, over both North and South Poles, non-stop, and never deviating by more than a mile from the 90th Parallel. . . . Or perhaps the lines that went from North to South were not parallels. The earth bulged and they met at the Poles. It was a good thing that they had encyclopædias to cold-store that sort of knowledge for them. The modern man had to know so much that he could not carry it all round in his head. Yet there was some mediæval fellow who was said to know all knowledge. Shakespeare, no doubt. Trust Shakespeare! But perhaps Shakespeare was not mediæval. Mr. Sorrell wished that he had a better head for dates. And of course Shakespeare had not known that Bohemia was not on the sea. . . . At any rate Mr Sorrell could be proud that he had published so many encyclopædias. That was a public service. They were knighting him for it. A pestilential fellow called Bunter who wrote salacious memoirs had told him that his encyclopædias atrophied the brains of the public. The little wasp! That would teach him. They would never knight *him*. His books sold though. But did you ever hear such a thing? The public brain atrophied! What did that mean? . . .

At any rate the intrepid Mr Claflin had written a book about his intrepid exploit—or had had it written for him so that it had been awaiting him when he got back to New York. And now, well out of the contagious atmosphere of that city, Mr Sorrell was inclined to wonder if he had not promised to pay too much for that work. But he had put his back into it. All the way over from New York he had occupied himself after lunch, whilst Mrs Lee-Egerton took her siesta, in writing a sixteen page pamphlet about the Claflin book. In it the words *intrepid aviator* occurred fourteen times and there were other repetitions. But McCrackan would see to that. Lean, dark, shining-haired McCrackan was invaluable. And cheap. He was running Sorrell, Son & Nephews all off his own bat at the moment. For not five hundred a year. And absolutely to be trusted. Like a feudal vassal!

He had now to get the pamphlet, the book, the illustrations, the preliminary puffs and the advertisements out as soon as possible. You ought to be able to do that in a fortnight. The American plates of the book were by now out of the hold of the Eurytonka. They would be in London that night and delivered to the printers next morning. That would give the reporters seven days in which to write their reviews and his travellers to get orders from the libraries. So Mr Sorrell could look forward to an exciting and pleasurable spell of work. By devoting himself with furious energy to the task of obtaining publicity from the halfpenny papers, and with that devotion to the team of his whole staff which is the cricket of publishing, Mr Sorrell imagined that he would score another immense success: And it would have been done in record time. It was only three weeks since the day when, in London, he had received from Theat and Company of New York the cable announcing that they had secured the full rights in Mr Claflin's book. Mr Claflin had arrived the day before in New York with his memoirs in his hand-grip.

Bending down to peep again at the nun, Mr Sorrell felt satisfaction at the fact that he lived in the present day. It was the day of rushes. There was no saying how many deals you could not get through in all sorts of fragments of time. He was even proud that he felt exceedingly tired. Except for the few hours that he had spent in the society of Mrs Lee-Egerton, he did not think that he had really had any leisure whatever in the five days that the journey from New York to Southampton had cost him. He was, too, proud of his profession. In the old days a publisher had to consider what was Literature. It had been uncommercial. Publishers had worked in a kid-glove sort of way, trying to establish friendly relations with authors. Now it was just a business. You found out what the public had to have and gave it them. And Mr Sorrell held up his head with pride. It was he, more than anybody else, who supplied the sort of printed stuff that the suburban season-ticket holder must indispensably have. In his day Mr Sorrell had done to this end many curious things. Yet he had started out in life as a mining engineer.

He had not begun with the least idea of publishing. He had rather remarkable mechanical talents and a still more singular gift of tongues. He used to say that he could pick up any South American dialect in ten minutes and drop it completely twenty minutes after he had no more use for it. In his career as mining engineer this had been to him of great use. He would be sent off at any minute to inspect any mine, whether in South Africa, in Galicia, or on the Klondyke. And without having to rely on the representations of the Anglo-Saxons or Semites who might be trying to sell a mine, he had been able to pick up nearly always tidy little bits of information from native miners and the hangers-on at bars. So that he had not limited himself to his mechanical and mineralogical efforts. He had had a finger in a pie or two of his own.

Thus he had been already a warm business man when his cousin, William Sorrell, had died. His uncle William Sorrell, senior, of the firm of Sorrell and Sons, the publishers, established in 1814—his venerable uncle, William, had offered him a share in the business direction of the ancient and august house. The literary side Old William had intended to maintain in his own hands.

Mr Sorrell had gone into the matter carefully. His uncle, by methods as antiquated as those of the builder of the Ark of Noah, contrived to extract from the business an income of between six and seven thousand pounds a year. As his uncle's sole heir, now that his cousin was dead, the business would ultimately fall to him. Mr Sorrell had accepted his uncle's offer. It had, indeed, only taken him five minutes to consider it. He had remembered that the business was old and not much supervised. There must be innumerable screws that could be tightened; there must be innumerable economies that could be effected. Half the staff could probably be kicked out. The site of the snuffy old Georgian house that the firm owned could be converted into a veritable gold-mine by building modern offices upon it. And "William Sorrell, Son and Nephew" could be floated as a public company.

Mr Sorrell had imagined that he would practically limit his energies to the floating of this company. Publishing had then struck him still as something connected with Literature— as something effeminate. But books, if you got hold of the right sort of book, were something that the city clerk must have. The right sort of book was as indispensable as a season ticket, a clean collar, or a radio set. At the same time Mr Sorrell had been not so obtuse as not to see that it would be difficult so to modify the old-fashioned publishing traditions of William Sorrell and Sons—they *were* worth between six and seven thousand a year—as to make them square with publishing what the city clerk would want. The long standing reputation of the house was an asset that Mr Sorrell did not at all want to depreciate. It had cost him a great deal of thought, but at last he had achieved the happy medium. He had begun with encyclopædias. He had gone on to cheap editions of the classics originally published by Sorrell and Sons. After all, had not they brought out works of explorers like Speke, Burton, Grant, and Livingstone in solid quarto volumes? So what was there against their publishing gentlemen like Mr Car K. Claflin. Exploring by aviation had replaced the old-fashioned and tiresome footslogging of the earlier travellers. It was all in the very tradition itself. It *was* the tradition. It was perfectly true that you had to print Mr Claflin upon heavy glazed paper so that his reproductions from photographs should come out well. You had to publish him in fortnightly parts, so as to appeal to the pockets of season-ticket holders and commuters. But the old flag flew where it used to fly. The Firm was still the Firm, though just every now and then Mr Sorrell chafed at his traditions and wished that he had been born an American citizen. His old uncle was actually alive at Reading. There he insisted on perusing all the manuscripts that were sent in to the firm. He discussed them with his two maiden cousins of incredible ages who kept house for him. Nevertheless today Mr Sorrell was able to think that he had accomplished the smartest bit of publishing that had ever been known since the makers of books began to move their offices from Paternoster Row.

He peeped again at the nun. She sat perfectly tranquil and

self-possessed. She moved a little in her seat and he obtained through the small windows a good view of her face. She had very red cheeks, as if she had been much in the open air, blue rather hard eyes. Her large teeth imparted to her face an air of rustic and rather hoydenish good health. She looked to Mr Sorrell's eyes like a prosperous market woman. He had expected that she would appear pale and dark and ascetic. With all the traces of suffering! His cigar drew well, and, propped between wall and wall of the corridor, he felt, upon the whole, comfortable. He had come out to think whether he had not made a fool of himself with Mrs Lee-Egerton. But having the kind of brain which is able to cut off its thoughts into hermetically divided compartments, he was determined to leave the subject alone until he had come much more clearly to the end of his cigar.

What a bully time he might have had if with all his present faculties and knowledge he could be thrown right back into the Middle Ages—when the world had been full of nuns. What would not he be able to do with those ignorant and superstitious people! He would invent for them the railway train, the electric telegraph, the aeroplane, the radio and its developments, the machine gun and the gas bomb. Above all the gas bomb! He would be the mightiest man in the world: he would have power, absolute and enormous power. He could take anything. No king could withstand him. The walls of no castle and of no mint could keep him out. And he felt in his physical being a tingling, impatient sensation, an odd emotion of impatience. It was as if just at his right hand there must be suspended an invisible curtain. Could he but see it, he had only to draw it back to enter the region of impotent slaves over whom he could be lord of wealth as of life.

It was, of course, the sight of the nun that had aroused in

him this train of thought. When he once more looked at her she was, with an expression of enjoyment, eating a sandwich out of a paper bag. And Mr Sorrell laughed. It seemed to him as absurd that a nun should eat sandwiches as that she should travel in a Southampton-to-London express. He did not know how he ought to consider that nuns should subsist any more than how he should consider that they ought to travel. He rather imagined them consuming myrrh and hyssop, drinking the tears of affliction, and gliding in their stiff black skirts, without ever touching it, over the ground; quite close to it. This Mr Sorrell was accustomed to do in a recurring dream that he had in common with most of the rest of humanity. The nun brushed the crumbs off the wide expanse of linen over her breast. Becoming aware of Mr Sorrell's eyes she frowned slightly at the thought that he must have seen her eating and moved over to the other corner of the vacant compartment. Mr Sorrell did not see her again. And as if it were a signal to him to resume thinking upon whether he had made a fool of himself, Mr Sorrell thrust his right hand into the deep pocket of his long grey ulster. He drew out a leather jewel-case that had "L. E." stamped upon its slightly domed top in gilt letters of a German-Gothic character.

2

HE WAS PUTTING ON WEIGHT. HE WISHED NOW THAT ON THE
voyage he had spent more time on the mechanical horse and
at the punching-sacks in the gymnasium and less beside Mrs
Lee-Egerton on the deck in the sunshine. He regretted to think
that soon he might have to say farewell to his physical excel-
lence. In his day he had been a strong man with a keen eye.
It was not all gone but if he were not watchful it might go.
As liaison officer to Allenby's cavalry, riding anything from
a camel to a thoroughbred Arab stallion beneath the torrid
suns, he had run himself as fine as a man could. At the military
tournament that had celebrated the surrender of Jerusalem
he had been pretty high up in the Turk's head and tentpegging
gymkhana. . . . Pretty high up! He could do most things
that could be done on a horse at full gallop. . . . He *had* been
able to. And with his knack of picking up languages he had
been pretty useful to that Army. He had loved his days in
Palestine where he had got a nodding acquaintance with

Hebrew along with the two local Arabic dialects and at the end of the war he had been as lean as a rake. And as hard.

Yes, he had regretted his Palestine days. That after all had been a life: in a country without a telephone where on a horse in the shadow of an olive tree beside a great rock you could imagine yourself anything—a Mameluke: a horseman of Godfrey of Bouillon. . . . Anything with a horse and a spear. . . . And, yes, no damned telephone!

Good Palestine days. . . . A good war too, it had been, as far as he had been concerned. He had never been afraid of roughing it and a spice of danger—even quite a lot of danger —opened your lungs. It made you breathe deep, which was the best thing life had to offer you.

No doubt today was better than yesterday. The world was more full of the wonders of the machine age. Human intelligence had no doubt progressed.

All the same. . . .

There had been the time when he had been prospecting in the Caucasus for the Tsar's Government. . . . Unheard of untouched mineral wealth in those old mountains. It was no doubt there still. He did not suppose those Soviet fellows would have done more than scratch the ground. There would be still every thinkable mineral. Undoubtedly in paying qualities. He had worked it out that it must be the Soviet Republic of Darghestan by now. . . . And Prince Diarmidov's little castle, on its grey spur on the range between Novorssusk and Iékhaterinodar. You did not forget *those* names. 1913! Good years!

The Prince had done him well. More caviare than you could eat, and silks, and cigars. But there were hardships too. No white bread. No roads. . . . All the same he had got a crushing mill to work. It had been good at night to hear from up above the stamps pounding on. A good honest sound. Crushing hard ore. None of your purring dynamos that made telephones drill like hell.

And those Tcherkess raiders. . . .

He squared his chest. He supposed he was one of the few men of today who could say that he had been wounded by a flint arrow head. . . . Every damned kind of metal those fellows had used. The prince had got a bit of pot-lid in his behind. From a blunderbuss.

No wonder the prince had cooled off to the whole project and had reported that the crushings had not panned out so well. Of course he had not been nursed by Elizaveta Dionovna . . . Dionitchka! With the high head-dress that hid her hair. It was golden. Like a good washing from one of those rivers. As fatalistic as any Oriental. Absent even. And fair as the girls of Lewes or Salisbury. With Circassian blood no doubt. . . . And her apron of green and white chequers. . . . There were things that you did not forget.

It was of course sentimental, but he imagined that if the Soviet Republic of Darghestan would offer him the chance. . . . They needed gold those fellows. . . .

But Dionitchka would be forty. Or murdered or married. And he was in deep enough already. . . .

Still he would like before he died or got really fat to have one more stretch of roughing it. In a rough land with a horse and a gun. And possibly also with no woman . . . that mattered!

He supposed he would some day learn to be more circumspect with respectable women. He had been nearly married twice and he had had one or two affairs of the heart that he did not care to think about much. In one case he had burned his fingers rather severely. His rival in the affections of a married lady—an erratic one—had persuaded her to give up to him Mr Sorrell's letters to her. Afterwards to save his own skin the rival had handed those letters over to a remarkably injured husband and it had seemed to Mr Sorrell that he had had to sweat blood and fire before he had come out of that scrape. It had been a warning and nothing but the laxness of shipboard would have made him have anything to do with Mrs Lee-Egerton.

It was not that anyone knew anything against her—but her husband was the sort of man who was always shooting in the Rockies. He was indeed shooting in the Rockies at that moment. That made it all the more remarkable that Mrs Lee-Egerton should have appeared anywhere as near him as New York. Lee-Egerton was the son of a peer of so many descents that Mr Sorrell would have been glad to know him. To know Mrs Egerton was not nearly so remarkable. It was extraordinarily easy to come across her, attended, as it seemed always, by a band of laughing cavaliers. On the other hand Lee-Egerton, whom few people ever saw, was said to be a happy, dangerous person. He might descend upon you at any time with a magazine rifle or worse. Nevertheless, with the idea of this rather thunderous personality at the back of his head, Mr Sorrell had felt himself quite remarkably soothed by her frequent companionship on board. He had not been soothed by anything or anybody quite so much for a long time. It was not that she was in her first youth. She had a son, as Mr Sorrell had reason at that moment to know, actually at Cambridge. There he had got himself into scrapes, all the more damnably complicated in that he was the heir-presumptive to the title, though his uncle could not be got to speak to any of his relatives. But Mrs Egerton had a sort of haggard. pale, passionate repose. She was very dark and very tall and very aquiline; she was, moreover, exceedingly thin. Mr Sorrell imagined that he had found her restful because she was exactly the opposite of himself. For, whereas he was exceedingly optimistic, she was oppressed by a great grief. The great grief was her confounded son. And to him, feeling as he did, large, and protective, Mrs Egerton had confided her almost unbearable sorrow. She had started for the United States, intending a campaign of social pleasures and triumphs. That was to have begun in New York, to have ended in Washington, and culminated in a scandalous book of which, with immense success, she had already written two or three. But in New York itself, before she had had time to get her foot really planted, she had received a most lamentable letter from her son at Cambridge. This she had shown to Mr Sorrell on the second night out, whilst after dinner they had reclined side by side in arm-chairs in a pleasant nook on the upper deck. Mr Sorrell had taken it to a porthole to read. Young Egerton would be in the most damnable scrape in the world if he could not have two hundred and fifty pounds at the very moment that Mrs Egerton landed at Southampton. Mr Sorrell had returned to Mrs Egerton in a frame of mind as grave as it was consolatory. He said that she might be quite sure that it would be all right, though it was quite certain that young Jack must be in as disgusting a hole as it was by any means possible for a young man to be in. And Mrs Egerton, the enormous tears in her enormous eyes plainly visible in the Atlantic moonlight, had declared to him that he could not by any possible means imagine what a mother's feelings were like, or what a good boy her Jack really was. And at the thought that he might have to go to prison she shuddered all over her long and snake-like body. Mr Sorrell said of course it could not possibly come to that.

Next evening, they had been sitting side by side at dinner in the *à la carte* restaurant of the upper deck. She had suddenly thrust over his plate of *hors-d'œuvres*, whilst the select band played, and the waiters appeared to skim through the air, a marconigram form bearing the words:

"*Bulmer pressing. All up if necessary not here by eight to-morrow. God's sake help. Jack.*"

"Oh well," Mr Sorrell had said cheerfully, "you must radio your husband's solicitors a message to wire the money to him."

Mrs Egerton stared at him with huge eyes. She swallowed an enormous something in her throat. She ate nothing else during that meal and Mr Sorrell's dinner was completely spoilt. She disappeared before he had finished it, and Mr Sorrell went to pace in solitude upon the comparatively deserted deck. Although they were only two days out and were not yet past the Banks, he had acquired the habit of expecting to find this charming lady there. It was not, however, for at least an hour and a half, which in his impatience seemed interminable, that, through the moonlight, she came to him and, exclaiming "I can't do it!" burst into tears.

"You can't do what?" Mr Sorrell asked. And then there came out the whole lamentable story. Mr Sorrell imagined that he must be the only man in London, or in the space between London and New York, who really understood what Mrs Egerton was. So he was the only one who would be able from henceforth to champion her. . . . Her husband allowed her the merest pittance—not twenty pounds a week—for her private needs. His solicitors were instructed in the most peremptory manner never to advance her a penny of this pittance. She had come out expecting to exist upon the hospitality of the United States, so she had upon her hardly more than her return ticket. The real stones of her jewellery were all in pawn and replaced by imitations; she could not anyhow in the rest of the world, although she was surrounded by seeming friends, raise anything like the sum of a quarter of a thousand pounds. Her husband was fourteen days' journey beyond the nearest telegraph station in the middle of a savage region.

"And oh," she said, with a glance at the heaving bosom of the sea, "I couldn't *live* if anything happened to Jack. Once he was an innocent boy saying his prayers at my knee." And after a good deal of hesitation and stammering Mr Sorrell got out the offer to lend the lady the required sum.

She said, of course, she could not think of it; as her son had made his bed so he must lie. Comparative strangers, however intimate their souls might feel, could not bring financial matters into their relationships; her husband would murder her if he came to hear of it. Mr Sorrell could have no conception of that gentleman's ferocity. But the more she protested the more Mr Sorrell thrust his offer upon her, and at last, in the midst of a burst of tears, Mrs Lee-Egerton came to a pause. "There's the Tamworth-Egerton crucifix," she had said.

Mr Sorrell had never heard of the Tamworth-Egerton crucifix. It was a gold beaten cross of unknown antiquity. It had been in the hands of the family ever since the fourteenth century. It was considered to be of almost inestimable value. She had it actually upon the boat with her, for she had desired to impress certain choice members of American society by the sight of it now and then. If Mr Sorrell would lend her the money, or still better, would wire it to her son, she would at once give the cross into his keeping until she could repay him.

Mr Sorrell without more bargaining—for at the moment he did not want anything but this woman's gratitude—had routed out the Marconi operator from his supper, and had telegraphed by private code to his bankers instructing them to pay £250 to Mr Jack Lee-Egerton before noon on the morrow. Shortly afterwards in the public boudoir of the ship, Mrs Egerton had handed over to him the Egerton cross in its leather case, in return for an acknowledgment from him, that he held it against the sum of £250 that day advanced.

In the corridor of the train Mr Sorrell opened the leather case and looked at the battered, tarnished, light gold object. It was about the size of a dog biscuit and the thickness of a silver teaspoon. The cross was marked upon the flat surface with punched holes much like those on the surface of a dog biscuit itself. . . . The feeling that had been lurking in the mind of Mr Sorrell ever since, quitting the glamour of the ship, he had stepped upon the gangway at Southampton, put itself into the paralysing words: "Supposing I have been done."

After all, he did not really know anything about Mrs Lee-Egerton. The other things that she had told him might or might not be true. This object might just as well be a gilt fragment of a tin canister for all he knew.

He snapped the case to and determined to return it to the lady. If she were honest, she would pay him back the money in any case. If she was not the thing would not be worth keeping. . . . He swayed back into their compartment and sat down opposite her.

"I don't at all like this speed," she said. The train was shooting through round level stretches of heather. It seemed to sway now upon one set of wheels, now upon the other.

"That's all right," Mr Sorrell said. "Nothing ever happens in these days. I've travelled I don't know how many thousand miles in my life without coming across the shadow of an accident." And he extended the jewel-case towards her. "Look here," he said, "this thing's too valuable for me to have in my possession. You take it. After all, you're the best person to keep it."

In the unromantic atmosphere of the railway carriage Mrs Egerton appeared older. She was dressed all in black and her face was very white and seamed, with dark patches of shadow like finger-prints beneath her eyes.

"No, you must keep it," she said earnestly. "After all, it's a thing to have had in one's possession. Why, it was brought back from Palestine by Sir Stanley Egerton of Tamworth. Tamworth is quite close to here, and Sir Stanley, they say— that's the touching old legend—died on landing on English soil." The cross had been carried to Tamworth by a converted Greek slave, who was dressed only in a linen shift and knew only two words of English—Egerton and Tamworth. Of course, Tamworth had been out of the family many centuries now, but the cross never had. Never till this moment.

Mrs Egerton appeared to have grown older but she appeared also to have grown more earnest. She leaned forward, and taking the cross out of the case she put it into Mr Sorrel's hands.

"Look at the funny, queer old thing," she said. "And think of all it means, of loyalty and truth."

"Well, I suppose it does if you say so," Mr Sorrel said. "You mean the chap carried it about in his nightshirt? I wonder how *he* travelled? I suppose they had stage coaches then, didn't they?"

"Oh, good gracious, no!" Mrs Egerton answered. "He walked bare-foot, and the country was beset with robbers all the way from Sandwich to here."

"I don't know that I should like to do that," Mr Sorrell said. "Though I suppose it would take off some flesh! But you don't mean to say that they didn't have any kind of public conveyance?"

"Dear me, no!" the lady answered. "It was in the year of the battle of Bannockburn. Sir Stanley had set out for the Holy Land with twenty knights and more than a hundred men-at-arms. When he came back they were all dead and his only companion was this slave. . . . That's why," she went on, "I should like you to keep the cross, if only for a little time. Since it was in the hands of that slave it hasn't been out of the hands of an Egerton until now." But her son was the last of the family, and Mr Sorrell had saved him from a dishonour worse than death quite as certainly as that slave many times had saved his master.

Mrs Egerton went on:

"He lived for some time at Tamworth and there he died. He's said to have had weird gifts of prophecy and things. He prophesied steam-engines and people being able to speak to each other a hundred miles apart and their flying in the air like birds. That's recorded in the chronicle."

"You don't say!" Mr Sorrell said. And he took the cross out of the case by the heavy gold ring at its top. "I like those faithful characters of the Dark Ages. They didn't produce much else that was worth speaking of, but they did invent the trusty servant. Did you ever see the picture at Winchester? It is called 'the trusty Servant,' and it has a head like a deer and a half a dozen other assorted kinds of limbs. I'd forgotten about it now."

Mrs Egerton said:

"I don't think people have very much changed even nowadays." And leaning forward she spoke with a deep and rather sonorous earnestness. "They say that in all the ages the blessing of a mother upon the preserver of her child ——"

"Oh come!" Mr Sorrel said. And he felt himself grow pink even down into his socks.

"It hasn't," Mrs Egerton continued, "ever lost its power to console the unhappy. So that if ever you find yourself in a tight place . . ."

Mr Sorrell considered that that was scarcely likely to happen. They would have to bring down the country before they could bring down the house of Sorrell, Son & Nephew. Why, they . . .

Mrs Egerton suddenly clutched at her heart. Her eyes became full of panic, her mouth opened to scream. The smooth running of the train had changed into a fantastic, hard jabbing. The glass of the inner windows cracked with a sound like a shriek and fell, splintering over their knees. He was thrown forward onto Mrs Lee-Egerton and she back upon him. Then with a frightful jerk motion ceased. The glazed photographs of beauty-spots served by the line were descending towards his upturned forehead. The two opposite seats of the carriage were crushed one upon the other so that he screamed with the pain it caused his legs. The carriage turned right over; he was hanging head-downwards in a rush of steam.

3

T HE LADY BLANCHE D'ENGUERRAND DE COUCY OF STAPLETON
stood yawning on the watch-tower of Stapleton Castle. There
was no reason why she should have watched there—on the
highest of the three stone steps in the north-east corner the
ancient watchman, his horn slung from his neck, leant in an
attitude of boredom upon his rusty pike. It was his business
to signal to those in the keep below the approach of any traveller. He would blow four bass grunts for a knight at arms
with his company but five if any person in armour came with
an armed band whose cognizances were unknown to him.
For a merchant with pack-mules he would make one gruff
sound. His horn was of wood. If, apparently, the approaching
traveller was a knightly minstrel he would do his best to produce three high notes and a flourish.

For the last month he had been seeking to perfect himself
in the blowing of one very high, long and sustained note to
announce the approach of the Lady Dionissia de Egerton de

Tamville. She had lately been in the habit of riding over from the castle of Tamville to supper every other evening. This last call had of late been almost the only one that his aged lips had occasion to make. When it sounded it would cause some little commotion in the castle, the due states and ceremonies having to be observed. Thus in the quadrangle below he would see offal and egg-shells and hot water being thrown on to the heap of garbage that formed the centre of the courtyard. Women and pages and old men would hurry from side to side far down below. The Lady Dionissia would ride up with her attendant train of women, little boys, old men, a chaplain or so. Shortly afterwards the washing trumpet would blow and the commoner sort of people would be observed cleansing themselves in the courtyard. But at that time it was only two hours after noon and it wanted two hours more for supper-time.

The old watchman leant upon his pike; the Lady Blanche yawned. In another corner of the small, square enclosure formed by the breast-high battlements, and of sheet lead warmed by the sun underfoot, the Lady Blanche's ladies, Blanchemain and Amoureuse, whispered and tittered continually with the little golden-haired boy Jehan, her page and the cousin of her husband. The Lady Blanche could not imagine what they could find to talk about. As a Lady of the Queen-Mother she had never found the time hang heavy on her hands. If they had not anything else to do at the Court they could at least play cat's-cradle, and there had always been gossip. Except for the outlaws, the clubmen and robbers, who made riding out a dangerous pursuit, there was not probably an able-bodied layman within twenty miles of the neighbouring castles of Stapleton and Tamville. Her husband, Sir Guy, was tiresome and foolish when he was present. In espousing the cause of the late King—he was said by now to have been murdered in Berkeley Castle by means of a red-hot horn—in espousing the cause of the late King and his favourites as against the new Queen-Mother, the always foolish Sir Guy, who always did the wrong thing, had done it once again. The thought of it added to her nervous exasperation. This entirely foolish husband of hers had undoubtedly ruined her life. With the Queen Isabella she had always been a favourite. But her husband's insolence to Roger Mortimer, the Queen's leman, had cost him various fines and amercements amounting to more than two hundred pounds. This they could ill afford. By his silly joviality and easy manners the peasants had been encouraged to neglect their work upon the demesne lands. In his father's time they would have had at the end of the year seventy pounds from the sale of hay alone; even in bad years. Nowadays, it was much if they got forty in the best of seasons. And not only had his folly cost them two hundred pounds' worth of fines, but they were totally estranged from the Queen-Mother. She had returned from France with a small company of knights of Hainault and had utterly discomfited and put to death, not only the late King, but all his favourites.

And now Sir Guy, utterly without cause had got together all his fighting men and kinsmen and retainers, and had gone at his own cost to aid the new young King in his campaign against the King of Scots. This, indeed, was a crowning folly, for in this war Sir Guy had not been summoned to do any service at all. The war was in Scotland, and no knight had been called for by the King or by the Queen-Mother from farther south than Lincolnshire. It was an utterly foolish piece of braggadoccio. What Sir Guy had wanted to do had been to impress the Queen-Mother with the sense of his power and importance. But Isabella would see how Sir Guy was weaken-

ing himself and his cousin, Sir Egerton de Tamville. Even on
their own showing, these two foolish men had confessed that
the expedition would cost them at least two thousand pounds
apiece, and she had made her own inquiries of the Jew Goldenhand of Salisbury. Jews were forbidden to live or to lend
money in these parts at that time; but the town council of the
city had paid no attention to the writs that came down from
London for the expulsion of Goldenhand. They had baptised
him by force instead.

She had learned that the two knights had borrowed of him
at least eight thousand pounds, impignorating all their joint
and several rights over land in the lordships of Old Sarum and
Wiley. And where in the world should they find eight thousand pounds, even if they made fat plundering, going to and
from the war and in the war itself? Why, each man of the
four hundred that they must take must bring back, as the
Cantor Nicholas had informed her, the value of at least twenty
pounds in booty before they could make it good. And her husband and his cousin were not the type of men to bring back
money by way of booty. They were inspired by the modern
crazy notions of forbearance towards their foes if their foes
had fought well. These silly ideas had come from France.
Why, after the seige of Hardeville, when Sir Guy had taken
with his own hand the Sire Jehan D'Estocqueville, whose ransom might have been a thousand crowns, Sir Guy set the
Frenchman free. He had done it with great pomp and ceremony, approaching the French knight whom he had served
during dinner in the midst of two hundred people, and not
only bidding him go free but setting on his head the chaplet
of pearls that he had worn in his own hair. It was perfectly
true that Sir Guy had gained much praise for this absurd action and many amorous glances from the ladies, which had

[30]

been what he desired. But what lordships, demesnes or estates could stand this riotous drain, this foolish and sentimental ostentation, and what did it mean to her?

There she groaned and twisted her hands in aching solitude during how many months! Had they but husbanded their resources she might have ridden north with Sir Guy, and lain with the Queen, who was in the New Castle, just short of the Scottish border. And with twenty minutes of the Queen's ear, she would have done more good to Sir Guy than all he would ever get by the cracking of rusty iron on the heads of penniless Scottish knights. And, for all she knew, her husband had got himself into a new folly. Might it not be he who had roused the archers against the men of Sir John of Hainault, who were aiding the King in the Scotch war? These outrages were said by the juggler, who brought them the news, to have been committed by archers from Lincolnshire, who had fallen on Sir John of Hainault and his fellows as they went back at night from the King's lodgings to their own. But how could she tell that it was not their own Wiltshire archers, of whom Sir Guy and his cousin had taken many bands with them, in addition to the men-at-arms and the gentlemen armed cap-à-pie, and upon the greedy destriers that ate so much hay and fodder? It was part of the folly of Sir Guy and his cousin that they could not, like other knights, ride to the seat of war upon light hackneys, with their armour in carts behind them. They must go prancing England from north to south upon great wasteful chargers that they might very well have waited to buy until they came to the northerly parts. Of this folly and vainglory of men there was nowadays no end, and the Lady Blanche dug her fingernails into her palms and breathed a tense sound of exasperation and rage.

The old man with the horn blew a single high-stopped note.

"Oh yes, a woman upon the road from the Plain," she said impatiently. And she did not trouble to look over the battlements. "When will there come again knights riding or men with bears and jugglers with their little flutes and golden balls?"

She called petulantly to the old man who stood three steps high. "What woman is it upon the road?"

He answered huskily, wiping the rheum from his eyes with the back of his hand:

"Mistress, it is the nun Lugdwitha, upon her white mule."

"And what makes the nun Lugdwitha upon the road?"

"Mistress, I do not know," the watchman answered. "Maybe the Lady Blanchemain shall tell you."

"Why ask her," the Lady Blanche said. "I am tired of the sound of my own voice."

Being in private, for she could reach the leads of the watchtower by narrow stairs in the wall from her own chamber, the Lady Blanche was wearing only a tight-fitting dress of grey homespun wool that she had had for seven years. She was a woman of twenty-four, with a hard mouth, a high colour, a very erect back, and dark resentful eyes. The Lady Blanchemain, on the other hand, was quite fair. On account of the parsimony or poverty of her mistress and kinsman, she too was dressed in grey homespun wool, nevertheless from feudal respect she wore a large white coif and plaited sleeves of white and grey. The Lady Blanche liked her very well, since she was very tiny, for she had been born in the castle of Hardelot on the first day of the siege that lasted five months. Thus she had been very stunted at the outset of her growth, for, for most of that time, there had hardly been either spoon meat or mother's milk for her. Her father had died in a dungeon, her mother in a convent, and at the age of ten, according to the law, she had come to act as kinswoman and serving maid to her cousin, the Lady Blanche, upon her marriage to Sir Guy seven years before. And since she was very gay, insignificant, and contented, the Lady Blanche liked her well enough. She had, besides, a very nimble ear for gossip.

She looked, crinkling up her eyes, over the ramparts that reached almost to her nose.

"The Sœur Louise," she said, preferring for the moment to speak in French, "went into Sarum this morning to buy sugar and spices and eggs. She went along the valley with some merchants from Warminister. I think she will come back over the Plain, because it is a safer way along by the gallows that Sir Guy set up to be a warning to evil gentry."

"Ah, this convent!" the Lady Blanche said spitefully. "What surveillance is it that they keep up that they must needs buy eggs when to-morrow is Friday?"

"Why, all their hens have died," the Lady Blanchemain said. "A pestilence or a murrain struck them, and a mouldiness is fallen upon their corn wells, and their fowler was drowned on Monday, and their fishponds ran dry so that most of their fish is dead."

"That, then is a judgment upon them," the Lady Blanche said. "Blessed be He that has done it! They may know by their empty bellies what it is to grasp at the rights of the Lord that protects them." And, intent upon wounding the feelings of her other handmaid, the Lady Amoureuse, that was of a pious nature, the Lady Blanchemain opened her heart as to the grievances she had against the religious of both sexes who dwelt on either side of the castle, the convent being to the right and the priory to the left, though the priory was for the most part within the lands of Egerton de Tamville.

With that intent, the Lady Blanche went at extraordinary

[33]

length into grievances against the convent, priory, the lordship of Tamville, and the inhabitants of the little town of Wishford that was perhaps a quarter of a mile from the castle of Stapleton. It was a matter of extraordinary complication, and it was one of the Lady Blanche's chief grievances against her lord that he could not set his mind seriously to grasping what were his rights.

On the one hand, the lords of Stapleton Castle claimed by rights of the most ancient nature the service of the bullock teams of every peasant of the manors of Stapleton St Michael, Berwick St James, and Wishford le Virgin upon every third day of the week not being a holiday and the holidays being counted against the peasants.

The convent claimed by virtue of rights granted to them before the Conquest three-fifteenths of the labours of every ninth day. On the part of the lords of Stapleton it was argued that this right, because it was granted before the Conquest, had been abrogated by the grant of the land to Odo, Bishop of Bayeux, by William the First. The nuns set up the plea on account of the exceeding sanctity of their community, which had been established by the Blessed Edward Confessor; their rights had been specially preserved to them by the Conqueror. It had been represented on the parts of the lords of Stapleton that these three-fifteenths should be properly taken from the time of the peasants themselves and not from the time which the peasants owed their liege lords. But on the part of the nuns it was argued that they, being women, had no power to enforce obedience from the peasants. According to the spirit of the grant from the Confessor, it must be certainly intended that the three-fifteenths must be taken from the third day of the lord of the manor, since the lord of the manor had the means of arms to enforce his rights, whereas the nuns had not. It had been replied on the part of Sir Guy that since his grandfather had received the grant of the demesne his ancestors had hanged innumerable of the peasants, in the Christian and worthy endeavour to force them to give up their time to the service of the convent.

The nuns, despairing of enforcing their rights, had sold them to the priory of St Michael for the sum of nine hundred pounds. The priors, having occasion to send to Rome to appeal against the election of a prior forced upon them against their will by King Edward the Second of glorious and unhappy memory, had taken the opportunity to procure from the Pope a writ directing the lords of the manor of Stapleton to insure to the monks the due observance of the duties of the peasants of the manor. On the other hand, the inhabitants of the town of Wishford, owning as a community certain of the lands along the river Wiley, claimed as a right, which had been ceded to them by Sir Guy's grandfather, in return for certain monies amounting to three hundred and fourteen pounds and a cup of gold worth forty pounds, the pasturing of certain beasts upon the lands of the peasants of Stapleton, which lands the monks of the priory of St Michael claimed to hold in fee from the estate of Egerton de Tamville the cousin of Sir Guy de Coucy de Stapleton. The prior of St Michael's had threatened with excommunication, not only Sir Guy de Coucy de Stapleton, but also Sir Stanley de Egerton de Tamville, along with the inhabitants of the town of Wishford. And under the threat of this excommunication the jurats of the town of Wishford had withheld payment from Sir Guy of the rent of the knight's fields, a large stretch of land running up to Groley Woods, a rent amounting by the year to £47 3s. This was claimed, not only by Sir Guy, but by the prior of St Michael's, the chapter of the Cathedral of Salisbury and the Chancellor of the Queen-Mother Isabella.

"And my lord and husband," the Lady Blanche continued, having explained all these things now for the hundredth time to the Lady Amoureuse, "my lord and husband, having expended untold money in the prosecution of suits before the portman-mote, in the Sheriff's Court at Devizes, upon the sending of solicitors and learned clerks to the King when he was in France and to the Pope in Rome, is now minded out of a childish levity and weariness of the flesh to abandon all these rights, though he has spent upon the maintenance of them much more than his rights are worth."

The Lady Blanche paused, expecting some opposition from the Lady Amoureuse, whom she detested because she was as tall, as dark, and less high-coloured than herself. The Lady Blanche, to attain to the fashionable paleness, must daub her features with slaked lime, but Lady Amoureuse could grow as white as a sheet at the expense of one day's fasting and one night's vigil in prayer before the day of any ceremony when she might desire to appear at her most attractive in the eyes of men. The Lady Amoureuse, however, answered nothing, but kept her mournful gaze fixed upon the hills, and the Lady Blanche continued, speaking now in English instead of French.

"My ox of a husband, who can neither increase his family nor yet his gear, will neither go on with his suits, nor yet set his hand to the task of claiming his rights. If he had been a man in my father's day, he would have very lightly ended his quarrels. Upon the one hand he would have burned down the convent about the heads of the nuns, and upon the other he would have slit the throats of the priors and going with a strong many to the portman-hall of the citizens of Wishford, he would have taken from them their charters and have torn them into a thousand pieces, so that never more they could have been alleged against him."

The Lady Amoureuse, with her eyes upon the distant path, exclaimed in a deep, hollow, and mournful voice:

"I think some men of the same mind as you—some brigands or outlaws are pursuing the Sister Lugdwitha, so fast does she gallop upon her white mule."

At the same moment the watchman set his horn to his lips and blew a hesitating blast that was neither high nor low.

"And behold," the Lady Blanchemain said, "one comes trotting along the path in a white shift that appears neither man nor woman nor yet priest of Holy Church."

"What folly is this?" the Lady Blanche exclaimed. And to the watchman, "What rede you this pursuer to be that comes with such haste after the Sister Louise?"

The old watchman peered for a long time at the figure. "A beggar it will not be," he said, "for his robes are too clean. One it might be that had been condemned to do penance in a sheet. Nor yet 'tis no sheet he wears, and upon his head is bound a cloth for all the world such as is borne by the pagans that I have seen in the birthplace of our Saviour, and in his hand is a shining something that in the rays of the sun is like the weathercock upon a church steeple."

The Lady Amoureuse's eyes distended romantically. "Should it be," she said with her mournful and tragic tones, "the slave of the dead Sir Stanley whom we have so long awaited?"

With her quick dislike for the Lady Amoureuse, the Lady Blanche said sharply, "Pack of nonsense and legends! This is some beggar who is coming along with his clapdish in his hands."

The little page had stood all the while two steps behind the

Ladies Blanchemain and Amoureuse, in the proper attitude, one hand upon his hip, one hand behind his back, and his right leg drawn up so that the point of his long shoe rested upon the ground two inches from his left instep. A fly had alighted upon his nose, but he had not even stirred. Yet, at this moment he could not keep silence, his curiosity overcame him.

"Dear Lady," he said, and his tones were fluting, his face pink and white, and his curls long and golden, "what is even the truth about the slave of the dead Sir Stanley, for the pages say one thing and the old soldiers another, and the nuns another, and the fathers confessor another. So that by the one he is held to be a magician and by the other an angel, and this is a very marvellous matter and one worthy to be understood."

"Saucebox!" the Lady Blanche exclaimed haughtily but not so unkindly as she might have. "Our brachets and lap-dogs shall be daring next to ask questions." Then she turned again upon the Lady Amoureuse and continued: "Nonsense and these follies of chivalry will never be put out of your head. I tell you this slave is long since dead and his eyes picked out by ravens, and robbers have taken his cross. It is three months since he left the town of Sandwich, and though the news of his leaving has been with us sixty days, yet he is not here. Surely he is dead."

"But so sacred a relic is this cross," the Lady Amoureuse said, "that surely an angel will have walked beside him to render him invisible to evil men by day and to guide him by night."

"Then if he travelled by night and day he would have been here twice the sooner," the Lady Blanche retorted, "and he is not here at all." She looked upon the little page. "Saucebox," she said, "follow me into my bower. I will chastise and rebuke you, for all is not well with your bringing up." And she descended into the narrow stairway that went from the leads down through the thickness of the wall into her own chamber.

This bower of hers took up maybe one half of the watch tower of the castle and yet it was not so very large either. The walls were of bare stone, the small windows looked out on three sides into the blue air and the place, though it was then the heat of midsummer, was not so very hot, since the windows had no glass but only iron bars that had been painted red and white in chequers to make them look gay. In this room there was a bed, very large, with pillows of red velvet, curtains of blue and a coverlet of red fox-fur. At the foot was a great chest or hutch of oak, carved half-way across with figures representing cunningly the coronation of the Virgin in heaven. This carving was not yet finished, for since it took a long time, and the Lady Blanche had need of the hutch, the carver worked upon it when the chamber was unoccupied. Indeed, upon the stone floor were the shavings and chips that he had that day left behind him. Upon this hutch, at the foot of the bed, which was all there was to sit upon, the Lady Blanche seated herself and remained for a space grinning at the little page who stood blushing and silent before her. His doublet was of old brown fur caught in at the waist by a leather strap and reaching to about the middle of his hips. His stockings were of red wool, fitting very close and being at once stockings and trousers. His shoes were of old green leather, very long and pointed and falling in flaps about his ankles. He was fourteen years old, and having been seen by the Lady Blanche when she was upon a visit to her cousins, the De la Poers of Southampton, four years before, she had asked for and received him as her servant, though till that moment she had taken very small account of him. He had served at her table, he had learned to fight with her many other pages;

one clerk and another had taught him his letters and how to sail eastward to the Holy Land to aid in the perpetual task of recovering and retaining the Sepulchre of our Lord. But Sir Guy having taken off with him to Scotland all the pages who were of fourteen and a half years and upward, this little Jehan de la Coucy de la Poer had become a servant at her table and the sergeant of all the little boys that she had then in training.

He flushed and flushed again, and rubbed the instep of one leg upon the ankle of another, and at last his lady said, "Little Jehan, talk!"

He said nothing. His colour came and went.

"Little cousin," his lady continued, "talk, chatter! What is it that you find to whisper and to titter about with my ladies? You are at it all the day. Yet I do not see what there is to talk about in this place."

He was still silent, and large tears filled his eyes.

"Little Jehan, come hither," the lady said. "Tell me what lady it is that you love." And she took him by the hand and drew him towards her. She fingered the old shabby fur of his doublet, and the hairs came out upon her hands.

"This is the best clothing that you have?" she said; and then, "Tell me what lady it is that you prize above all others, and whose name you mutter beneath your breath when you turn over in bed in the deep night. Tell me, tell me!"

The little boy burst into tears.

"God is merciful," he said. "I love my mother and the Virgin."

"Oh, fie! Oh, fie!" she said, "to lie to your lady. Whom is it that you love?"

He continued to sob, and repeated, "My mother and the Virgin, and as God is my life none other."

"Oh, fie! Oh, fie!" the lady said. "This is very bad. For

either you lie to me, which is evil, or you have no lady that you love, which is far worse. For I suppose that now you have become the sergeant of the pages, you will desire shortly to be made a squire, and so to do great feats of arms and grow into a knight. And then you will send letters of challenge to fight other knights in the courts of France, of Navarre, of Spain, or even amongst the Saracens and the knights of Heathenesse, and how will you do all these things without the love of a lady to bear you up? Friend, it is time you bestirred yourself. Why is it that you are so badly clad?"

The little page answered nothing more, and she asked him again several times, "Why is it that you are so unfittingly dressed?"

Once more he burst into tears.

"It is because my little wages are not paid," he stuttered at last. "It is God's truth that I would be such a great and famous knight, but I do not know where I should find a lady to love except my mother and the Virgin."

"Why, go open the door of my closet," the Lady Blanche said, "that I may see my beloved birds."

Before the foot of the bed was a rough panelling of oaken boards shutting off a portion of the room, and the door of this, creaking upon its iron hinges, the page threw open. There came out an ancient and mouldy smell. Upon three perches there stood two hawks with their hoods over their eyes, and little plumes rising above them, and a lugubrious parrot that nonchalantly opened and shut one eye. Upon smaller pegs in the wall there were, moreover, falconer's gloves, jesses, straps with little brass bells sewn on to them, and farther along Sir Guy's tilting helmet, his winter surcoat of fur, and the splintered head of a large lance that Sir Guy had omitted to have repaired in the hurry of his departure for Scotland.

"Why, fetch me my parrot," the lady said. And whilst the page held out to that depressed green and blue animal a gilt staff towards which the parrot extended an enormous and threatening upper mandible, the lady felt in her bosom for the great key of the hutch. She had opened it, and from amongst a medley of silver vessels, plates, and silken clothes and furs, selected one of the many little bags of cloth embroidered with silk, and she had again closed the solid slab of the lid before the page had succeeded in coaxing the parrot on to his staff. The boy placed the bird upon the lady's knee, and it climbed slowly up her arm to settle on her shoulder, where from time to time with its long bill lugubriously but gently it nibbled at her ear.

"Now take this purse, my gentle page," the lady said, "and go when I have done with you to Master Simon the tailor. In the purse are six pounds. You shall buy with them clothes and a little steel cap and gauntlets and breastplates and such other things as are proper for the equipment of a page, and a little horse. And you shall let me see with what discreetness you lay out your money, and you shall tell the tailor and the armourer and the horse merchant that the lady, your mother, has sent you this money that you may be properly equipped because you have been promoted to the sergeantry of pages, and between that time you shall think upon a lady that you may love, and on Sunday you shall wear your new garments, and you shall come to me in them after the dinner is drawn, and I will send my ladies away and you shall tell me what you have devised." And the Lady Blanche raised her voice towards the little door that ran up the staircase in the wall:

"Ho, Blanchemain, ho, Amoureuse, come down and hear this tale of an awkward page!"

When the two ladies were come down, "Look upon this

awkward little page," she said, "who declares that there is no lady that he loves! And now his mother has sent him money to buy suitable apparel, he shall think upon a lady that he may love, so that her device may be embroidered upon the shoulder of his surcoat." And at the thought of a page who loved no lady, all the three women burst into loud laughter, until at last, crimson-faced, the boy blurted out:

"I am sure that in a week I shall not learn to love anybody but my mother and the Virgin."

He cast side-glances at the door for he desired strongly to run away from all this mockery. But the horn above was grunting out a series of harsh sounds.

"Mercy on me," the lady said, "is there an army afoot."

"The nuns of St Radigund," the Lady Amoureuse exclaimed, "with their confessors and the mass-priest and the almoner, with crosses at their head and candles burning, are marching out from the convent gate. And Jenkin the cripple is crying out from the tower foot that they are marching out to meet Sir Stanley's slave who is coming bearing the cross of St Joseph of Arimathea."

"Say you so?" the Lady Blanche exclaimed. And descending swiftly from the hutch she ran to the east window. It was so small that it shewed little of the valleyside, but there below her, their coifs waving like the wings of white birds in the breeze of their haste, a procession of nuns, two and two, filed along, priests going before them. A little further up the hillside a figure in a white shift stood still, astonished or afraid.

4

Mr Sorrell's blistered feet pained him very much. His legs ached from long walking; his head was dizzy with the heat of the sun, and he hated the voices of the larks that, with a monotonous and penetrating sound, drilled down all over the immense landscape. He seemed to have been walking for ages; he had no idea of where he was but it seemed perfectly natural that he should be there. Beside him there paced a large white mule with little silver bells on the tips of scarlet ear-caps.

He plodded on, mechanically and without will. There was a buzzing in his ears and his eyes were heavy.

He stumbled over a stone and a voice behind him said, "Gare!" A nun in a white head-dress was sitting sideways on the mule.

She had red cheeks, large teeth and a kind smile. The mule paced without any guidance. Slung around her were packages of coarse linen cloth tied with leather thongs and upon her arm was a large wicker basket filled with eggs. She spoke to Mr Sorrell and he muttered to himself:

"Some South French dialect."

He heard himself uttering the words "Egerton" and "Tamworth." The nun smiled energetically and said, "Yea, yea, yea!" She lifted her black draped arm towards the horizon of the ascending down. She said, "Là haut et puis descendre!"

Mr Sorrell found himself shaking his head in a muzzy fashion, and he uttered the words, "Serai-je en France?"

The nun shook her head. "Non, non," she answered. "Cestung paid bin Wiltshire, tousprès Sarum."

Mr Sorrell exclaimed, "Esperanto, by Jove!" And the nun exclaimed energetically, "Oi, oi, oi! Bonne esperantz, fidesle serviteur!"

Mr Sorrell's legs carried him perpetually and mechanically forward. "When I wake up," he said to himself, "I wonder if I shall remember all this. It's the flying dream, of course, and I'm short of clothing as usual, but I wish I could do the gliding step. We don't get along fast at this rate." And mechanically he attempted to pull what he considered to be his nightshirt further down over his shins. Then he perceived that he carried in his right hand a package swathed apparently in palm leaves. "That'll be the old cross," he said to himself. And still pacing onward he began to undo the stiff and cracked covering. The nun's eyes were large and eager. The thin golden object came out from amongst its brittle swathings.

"O bel! O gai!" the nun exclaimed. And suddenly she was down from her mule. She fell upon her knees close to his feet, and with avid fingers clutched the relic and pressed it to her lips, her eyes streaming with tears.

"I can't let it go out of my hands, you know," Mr Sorrell

said. "If I let go of it heaven only knows where it will vanish to! You never can tell in dreams."

The nun had burst into a great number of prayers in what Mr Sorrell recognised was Latin pronounced, he should say, in a Portuguese manner. And out of politeness Mr Sorrell remained still dangling the cross before the eyes of the religious, so that he felt as if he were holding out a watch to a little child who had asked the time in the streets. The beautiful mule had wandered to a little distance and was cropping the grass. From time to time it shook its head and the little bells jingled.

"By Jove!" Mr Sorrell said. "If anybody kodaked us now!" For there the three of them were in exceedingly bright weather —in weather so bright that all the little shadows were blue and sparkling—in an immense fold of the downs like a bowl with the blue arch of the sky inverted over them like another bowl, he himself in a single long white garment, the nun in a multiplicity of folds of coarse black, in a white head-dress spreading out on each side like a swan's wings, kneeling upon the soft turf, her hands upraised, her lips moving. . . .

"We should come out very well," Mr Sorrell said, "if the chap could get in the donkey and basket of eggs." His head paining him a little less, he lifted his eyes and took a glance across the valley. On the brow of the hill before him were a great number of sheep, all lying down in the noontide heat, and high against the skyline, very small, and draped in a cloak so that he resembled figures that Mr Sorrell had seen when surveying mines in Spain, a shepherd leant motionless upon the shaft of a great crook.

"These are the good old times!" Mr Sorrell said. "What set me dreaming of them? It's better than being chased by alligators when you can't run away. It's more tranquil, but it's

queer all the same. I wish the ants wouldn't run over my feet."
And with the sole of his left leg Mr Sorrell gently rubbed the
instep of his other foot. The nun rose slowly to her feet. She
pointed to the cross in his hand. "Vint de la Tierre Très-
saincte? Messire de Egerton a Tamville?"

"Why, certainly," Mr Sorrell said. "It was brought from
the Holy Land by Sir Stanley Egerton of Tamworth. Mrs
Lee-Egerton was telling me so only just—" Mr Sorrell stopped
and started violently. "Merciful God! What's that?" he said.
His eyes had wandered farther round the skyline, and where
their road mounted he perceived a solitary, broad-spreading
oak tree. From its great branches there descended three ropes,
and at the ends of them, their feet pointing straight to the
earth, their hands apparently clasped behind their backs, were
the bodies of three men, their heads cocked at one side with a
sort of jaunty defiance, whilst upon the crown of the highest
sat a large raven. The nun looked at them with a friendly and
cheerful smile. "Trèsmeschiants gents, voleurs attrapés par le
très noble Sire de Coucy avant son départ."

"So Mr Coucy left them when he went away?" Mr Sorrell
asked. "It's not the sort of thing a lady ought to have to take
the risk of looking at."

The nun shook her head to show that she did not understand, and then she walked up to the mule and clambered
slowly into the saddle. Having settled herself down comfortably, she made signs that Mr Sorrell should lift her basket
of eggs, and with slow footsteps they resumed their way, Mr
Sorrell carrying the cross by its large ring which he fitted on
to his little finger. They had hardly been gone ten yards before the nun gave a little scream.

"I thought you wouldn't get much nearer to those corpses
and still keep a brave face on it," Mr Sorrell said.

[47]

The nun once more got down from the mule, and having set the basket of eggs on the ground she ran swiftly with awkward movements back along the track they had taken, and Mr Sorrell perceived that she was bending down to pick up something, with her voluminous clothes disposed all round her.

"I'm hanged if she isn't picking up those palm leaves!" Mr Sorrell exclaimed. And when she returned to him with her hand stretched out holding with great care the thin, crackling objects he exclaimed, "Why, you can get half a dozen of them for a penny—fans, you know—almost anywhere. No, I don't want them," he continued. "I'll get a piece of brown paper and wrap the thing up the first place we come to."

The nun drew from her breast a little leather wallet closed by a leather thong into which, very carefully, she introduced the dried-up fragments. There sat upon her face an expression of supreme contentment. A sinister, earthy odour swept slowly down upon them from the large oak tree. The raven flapped slowly and heavily into the blue air.

"Oh, hang it!" Mr Sorrell exclaimed. "You aren't going any closer? I say, it's horrible and it's infectious, too. You don't know what you won't catch."

The nun was looking at him with a patient want of comprehension, and Mr Sorrell had the conviction that she did not smell anything at all.

"Il m'est impossible de la supporter!" he exclaimed. And closing his nostrils tightly with his fingers he ran up the hill at right angles to the course they had been pursuing.

And suddenly fear seized him. He exclaimed.

"This isn't a dream. This can't be a dream. It's all too clear. What the devil does it mean? Where am I? What country is this?" He looked down the hill. The white mule and the nun with her many packages were continuing their course, which led them almost immediately beneath the tree with its sinister decorations. The corpse which the raven had abandoned was veering slowly round and round. The others remained motionless.

"It must have been that thing that happened to the train!" Mr Sorrell exclaimed. "I'm delirious. I'm mad. I must have escaped from a lunatic asylum. That must be a sick-nurse—that was why she didn't mind the sight of dead bodies. But hang it all, they don't hang people from trees nowadays! Three chaps could not have gone and committed suicide at once."

He gripped his head with both his hands, the golden cross tapping upon his cheek, but his hands came away again in sudden astonishment. His whole head was enveloped in linen cloth. "That must have been the accident," he said. "My head is bandaged up. How could they have been so careless as to let me escape if I *was* in an asylum!"

The sun, great and glowing, was descending in the heavens, and, the heat being past, the sheep on the other hillsides were getting up to feed once more. The tinkle of their innumerable little bells swept down to his ears and mingled with the song of the larks. A couple of peewits rose from the hillside round the sky, uttering their cries that are like the last wails of despair. And with motionless wings an enormous bird sailed slowly over the lip of the down. Great, brown, and moving very slowly, it drifted down the valley. The shepherd on the other hill suddenly burst into loud cries and violently agitated his cloak. But with absolute indifference the great bird drifted on.

"An eagle!" Mr Sorrell exclaimed. "Good God! That must

[49]

have been an eagle! But there aren't any golden eagles any more except in Spain. I must be in Spain. My God! I must get to the bottom of this!" And suddenly bursting into a run he went across the hillside in pursuit of the nun, who had very nearly reached the rim of the valley.

5

In the ordinary course at such a moment Mr Sorrell would have cared little about views. He was very much out of breath and his feet hurt him a great deal; a strong wind coming over the hilltop fluttered the skirt of his single garment. For a minute he had to stop. He was upon the top of a high ridge; the aspect of an immense tract of country burst suddenly up at him. Though the sun still shone brightly, it was all blues and greys. In the distance the wine-purple of heather stretched out for miles. The view which lay behind him was simple and green. It was a closely grassed valley like the hollow of your hand, running downwards, the gallow-tree, little and plain at some distance below him, with the shadow cast by the climbing sun stretched flat on the turf behind it. Suddenly Mr Sorrell said "By Jove!" again. A long way beyond the descending lip of the valley, against the blue sky, a chalk-white object tapering to a point with, at its head, a glitter of gold, rose up exceedingly silent.

[51]

It affected Mr Sorrell as if he had been watched by something stealthy, and, as the vane veered round and lost the light of the sun he exclaimed: "Salisbury Spire!" He looked a little anxiously at the sun. It must be about four o'clock in the afternoon; he estimated that he was seven miles to the south-west of Salisbury and going south-west. He remembered distinctly that once he had motored from London to Bath by a road that went through Salisbury, but though he racked his brain he could not for the life of him remember the name of any single town or village through which he had passed.

He had travelled fast. He had thought it was rather fine. Leaving London at eleven and giving two hours for lunch at Salisbury itself, they had reached Bath at half-past four. That had given them an average of about thirty-three and a half miles an hour. They had run over a pig, but as they had not stopped to make any inquiries he could not tell what the name of the place was. There had been an awkward bridge off to the left and the main road was narrow with high hedges. It certainly was not, as he and his friends had said, the place to let pigs lie about on the high road.

And then, again, he remembered the railway accident. The last thing of which his eyes had been conscious had been the fact that the photograph of a beauty spot, together with the wall of the carriage and the luggage-rack, were descending immediately towards his forehead. The next thing was, that he was there in his night-shirt, seven miles from Salisbury. That the railway accident had taken place actually in Salisbury he was fairly certain. He had been trying to wriggle away from Mrs Lee-Egerton's maternal blessing, which she had administered to him sandwiched in between fragments of the tale of a Greek slave who had brought the Tamworth cross to Tamworth Castle, which was within a few miles of Salisbury. He remembered that the story of the slave had interested him very much—the barefooted traveller in a single garment of white linen, who, bearing a cross of gold, had travelled some hundreds of miles all alone through a country infested by robbers.

Decidedly, Mr Sorrell thought, he had escaped in delirium from the hospital to which he, along with the other victims of the disaster, must have been taken. The nun, who was a sick nurse, had been sent out to pursue him. He wondered whether he had better stop where he was until she sent someone to look after him, or whether it would be better to consult the shepherd, borrow a pair of trousers of him, and get up to London by the first train from Salisbury. He turned once more to regard the carcasses that were dangling from the oak tree.

"Of course, they don't hang people like that, even in these out-of-the-way places," he said to himself.

They had been having a pageant there. There were pageants in every corner of England. The thing was being a good deal overdone. And when he considered the tops of the other hills, he thought that they had been overdoing it a great deal too much. On the skyline of a very uplifted range upon his left hand he perceived the outline of no less than three gallows; and on his right, upon the summit of a dark and forbidding heather-clad hill, scalloped and ridged so that Mr Sorrell considered that it must be the remains of a Roman camp, there rose up desolately another gibbet. A heavy chain descended from its outstretched arm, and from the bottom hung a repulsive fragment decorated with rags.

"Someone will have to write to the papers about this," Mr Sorrell said.

They must have been searching for every blessed hill which had ever had a gallows in the good old times. Even in the

Dark Ages they could not have hanged as many people as that. It would have taken half the population.

Of its kind the thing had been well done. He had had a decidedly eerie sensation, as if the bat on his skull had knocked him clean through space into another generation. There really had not been anything whatever to show him that he was not in the thirteenth century. Except, perhaps, for the eggs. Eggs in a basket struck him as being modern. He did not believe they had eggs in the thirteenth century.

He did not know much about history. He thought eggs had been introduced into England by Sir Walter Raleigh, along with potatoes and brandy. He did remember—the fact had somehow impressed itself on his mind because it was philological, and he had always taken an interest in the study of languages, which was a sound commercial pursuit—he remembered distinctly having read somewhere that Chaucer or Caxton, taking a voyage from the coast of Kent to Suffolk, had landed in search of eggs. They had not been able to get them, because in Suffolk at that date eggs had been called *eyne*. In mediæval England there were as many different dialects as there were in South America. The word nearly resembled the modern German *Eier*, which signifies eggs. He had read this in two specimen pages from the encyclopædia published by him. He had reproduced them in facsimile for his prospectus.

A woodcut had illustrated his specimen page. It had the word *Harleian MS.* below it, to show the care with which the encyclopædia had been compiled, and it represented a mediæval gentleman with knock-knees and pointed shins, something representing a kilt and about forty yards of woollen stuff wound round his head. He was holding an anchor and jumping out of a boat about the size and shape of a piece of melon peel. He could have sunk it with one foot.

What were his people doing with the account of the travels of Mr Car K. Claflin, the intrepid explorer? He did not know how long he had been ill, but he started impulsively down the valley. He had got to get to the nearest railway station. He would have to take things in hand again. He stopped once more and with anxious eyes surveyed the immense view. He was looking for the trail of smoke of an approaching train. It was impossible that there should not be a line in all that expanse of country. He had never seen a really great view of England that had not at least one, two, or sometimes as many as three plumes of smoke ascending and flying across space. He saw none. He could not make out even a road running along the valley at his feet. He looked for the dust of an oncoming motor. There was none. Green grass ran down into the valley: in the bottom there were some high trees, dark and very full of foliage, like a ribbon along the stream. There were some thatched huts, so small that they resembled rabbit boxes. There were too, here and there, some small enclosures with little hedges round them. Mr Sorrell imagined that these must be Small Holdings. Hidden deep amongst some very tall elms he could see the shoulder of a square church tower. And then, coming round the angle of a spur of the downs, once more there was the nun progressing slowly very far below him upon the mule. Tiny and distinct, it appeared like a fragment of white chalk.

"Oh well, I'm going after her," Mr Sorrell said. She had seemed to know something about Mrs Lee-Egerton. She had certainly mentioned the family name, and the legend of the family slave who had travelled half England over with only the words "Egerton" and "Tamworth" in his vocabulary. No doubt Mrs Egerton had sat at his bedside whilst he had been in hospital, and had told the nun all about the cross. Probably he had held on to the cross like grim death when he had been insensible, and they had not liked to force it away from him. That was why it was still in his grasp. The palm leaf had been some patent hospital packing that they had put on to prevent the cross from being banged about.

He plodded on determinedly after the nun. But the grass was pierced here and there with tiny little, very sharp sprigs of broom, and Mr Sorrell had to tread with care. The mule on the other hand, as if it smelt its stable, was travelling faster and faster. It was fully a mile and a half ahead; and decidedly it was gaining upon him. And Mr Sorrell felt a desperate desire to overtake the nun. After all, she understood the position. She was, perhaps, the only person in the countryside who would understand the position. In the ordinary way he would have felt an extreme shyness about appearing before a lady in attire so exiguous. But if he met anybody else—even a man —he would have to explain, and that would make him feel very awkward. He had got the hang of the story by now; his head was perfectly clear, just as the wrappings round it were perfectly clearly hospital wrappings. But he did not want to have to explain to anybody that he had been practically a wandering lunatic. It would make him appear small and ig- nominious. He was actually one of the most up-to-date men of his day. No, decidedly, he would not mind meeting the nun. He wanted to meet her more than anyone else in the world. She was not much like a lady: she was more like the laundress of his chambers in the Temple. Probably she was a lower class nun. Besides, it was a sick-nurse's duty to look after her patients.

Mr Sorrell trotted onwards as swiftly as he could. He imagined that decidedly he must be losing weight; it was prob-

[56]

ably better than Turkish baths. The nun disappeared round another fold in the downs. From her swaying and uneven motions Mr Sorrell imagined that the mule must be actually galloping. And when, a little later, he came upon a broken egg, he felt positively sure of it. He trotted on.

Taking very little account of her eggs, the Sister Mary Lugdwitha of St John of Patmos galloped her astonished mule up to the locked and barred gate of the convent. That was built four-square of grey stone, a great pigeon-cote at one corner and a new chapel with a peaked roof at the other. The spire of the bell-tower was still in building with the scaffolding all round it. The surrounding wall was blank but upon two sides there were narrow slits, the loopholes for arrows. These had been quite newly made because there were so many evil men around of late.

The Sister Mary Lugdwitha rasped so violently the pin in its ring that the lay sister Mercy who kept the gate trembled. She thought it had been robbers.

The white mule stood with its heaving flanks amongst the garbage and the sunlight of the courtyard; the Sister Lugdwitha ran swiftly across the courtyard to the white thatched hut of the Mother Superior. Of these huts there were twenty-four. One of each was allotted to the Mother Superior, the Sub-Prioress who represented the Community of Nuns as against the Mother Superior. The Mother of Ways and Means represented the Community which was made up of the whole body of non-executive nuns and lay sisters who had all their goods and wealth in common. The Mother Superior managed her own finances. She managed them very well and not always to the benefit of the Community.

The twenty-four cells housed the eighty-four religious women who made up that jealous body. On the fourth side was the stone dovecot. It was as large as a church tower, and had built against its side a little stone box of about the size of a dog-kennel, in which there lived a pious and celebrated anchorite. He had no communication with the outer world save by means of an orifice about the size of a horse's mouth. Here there were, also built of stone, and against the wall, a large guest-chamber for the use of benighted travellers, apartments for the two confessors and the male almoners of the convent and for the fowler, the water fowler and the keeper of the fish stews, for four serfs who kept the mules, swine, beasts, and sheep of the convent. In the farther corner, was the large chapel itself, very splendid and highly painted inside. Across the centre of the courtyard there ran a high fence, separating the men from the quarters of the female religious. The gate of this was closed twenty minutes after the tolling of the bell at the conclusion of vespers. Thus benighted travellers who applied to the convent for hospitality after the closing of the gates must be waited upon by the mass priests or the almoners. When this occurred, these received for their services from the convent the sum of one halfpenny, whether or no the travellers next morning left any offering in the box that stood upon the altar of St Radigunda in the chapel. This fence and these laws were very much resented by the Community. They had been instituted about a year ago by the new Reverend Mother Mary Catherine of the Seven Doleurs, who had been brought from Bayonne, in France, and forced upon them by the Lord Bishop of Salisbury.

The nuns and sisters objected that this was not only harsh discipline, but bad husbandry. The nuns had been accustomed to take innocent delight in listening to the converse of the travellers, whilst at eventide they served and tended them. And the Mother Cellarer and Kitchen Account Sister declared that they could not possibly render their accounts reasonably, since the mass priest served out to the travellers ale, wine, and meat with a too lavish hand. It was none of his gear that he was giving away, and the travellers rewarded his vicarious hospitality with more cheerful and entertaining stories, the nuns hearing through the night only the echo of their stories and the choruses of their songs. The whole community murmured at the heavy burden that was cast upon them in the halfpennies paid to the priests for their services. If the Abbess would have this thing, it should be paid, they said, out of her own revenues, and not by the Community.

And they were saying even at that moment that the plague which had fallen upon the hens, so that they withered up and died, remaining mere trusses of dirty feathers—that this plague was a visitation upon the Mother Abbess, to whose revenues the poultry money contributed. They considered, also, that the running dry of the stew pond, so that they had no fish, and the breaking of his leg by the fowler so that they had neither wild duck, widgeon, teal, coot, nor moorhen to eat on fast days—these afflictions, too, should be considered as serious warnings to the Mother Abbess. But, since they fell upon the

Community and not upon her revenues, they feared that she would be too stiff-necked so to regard them.

But end the quarrel as it might, the Sister Lugdwitha, hurrying through the dirt of the courtyard, must make her way through the gate in the fence before she could reach the nuns' quarters and the cell of the Mother Abbess.

The Mother Abbess was a little, broad, brown woman with dangerous twinkling eyes; it was not by haughtiness but by good humour, imperious obstinacy, and never speaking at all except to promulgate her regulations, that she so strictly ruled the community. Her cell was formed by the bare walls of the hut painted blue, though in the right hand corner the Sister Mary Radigunda of St Veronica was standing painting in red, blues, and green the martyrdom of St Peter, who bore in his hand a key much greater than the gate of Rome itself. Rome was represented in the background with its name written above it in black letters. Upon a perch that protruded from the wall high up near the thatch of the roof, sat the Mother Abbess's favourite hawk, for the Mother Abbess was a lady of knightly habit of mind whose health demanded this exercise. Moreover, she was accustomed to sell at her own price to the community such plovers, bustards, wild pigeons, jackdaws as her hawks brought down upon the Plain. She was at the moment standing before a reading pulpit, whereon stood the almoner's book of accounts, and she was saying: "Set the price of the oil down to the community."

She spoke French-French with which the almoner was little familiar, for he heard and conversed mostly in the French of England. But so often had he heard the words, "set that down to the community," that he had no need to ask the Abbess to repeat them. He was a fat, dark man who loved peace, and wore a black gown with ragged white fur at its edges, and he sighed a little. "The cellaress will cry out at the cost of the oil for this lamp," he said. "There will be a great outcry. It will be better not to let the lamp be lit."

"Then the convent should lose its rights," the Abbess said.

"The lamp was never lit," the almoner said, "in the time of the late Abbess, and of the Abbess before her."

"Then that is greatly to our shame," she answered.

The Sister Radigunda, with her back to them painting at the fresco, thought that here once more the Reverend Mother showed that she was determined to ruin the Community. The lamp was one provided for in the deed of grant from the Blessed Confessor to the convent, which was set down there on Salisbury Plain mainly to be a comfort to travellers upon that great and desolate expanse. It should hang from a pole forty feet high, set upon the highest point of the convent chapel, and it should be watched, tended, and kept burning all night, to be a guide to such as were benighted upon the great Plain. Under the late comfortable Abbesses whom the sister sighed to remember, this practice had fallen into desuetude. It had two very serious disadvantages. Not only did it cost money for oil and watchers; it attracted many poor travellers who must be housed and fed.

But the new Abbess, coming from France, had straightway caused all the deeds and charters of the convent to be read out before her. Hearing that this pious practice had been abandoned she had for the first time spoken very harshly, as if the community consisted of fools and impious wretches. She had said that it was a great laches against charity, hospitality, and the love of God and His Mother, that this comfort to poor wayfarers should have been abandoned. Moreover, to show remissness in the very action for which the Community had been founded, on a day when lawsuits assailed them on every hand in times that were very evil—such a remissness was sufficient to jeopardise the very existence of the Community. Whereas, as the sister and all sane persons knew, the first duty of a Community was to itself and its purse. Even supposing that the bodies of travellers dead of exhaustion or cold on the heather, or drowned by night in the brooks of the Plain, even supposing these should be found, a mark or two slipped into the hand of the Bishop of Salisbury might persuade him very easily that these had been done to death by the wicked gentry in whom the Plain abounded. And by hanging up a lamp during such nights as those upon which the Chancellor would be visiting them, they could easily persuade him that a lamp did burn there always.

Nevertheless the Abbess had persisted in her own way. Now with a sigh the sister heard that the cost of the oil was to be set down to the Community.

The Sister Lugdwitha ran into the room very hot, speechless, and perspiring. Upon her black skirt was the yolk of a broken egg; her coif was disarranged so that there showed itself some of her tawny hair.

"Oh, Reverend Mother," she exclaimed, "the slave of Sir Stanley Egerton is coming with the Gold Cross from Antioch, which was fashioned out of the money of the usurers that our Lord drove out of the Temple!"

The Reverend Mother exclaimed, "Blessed be the Lord God and the saints in Heaven!" But she appeared otherwise unmoved.

"And, Reverend Mother," the sister gasped on, "as I rode along upon my way it came into my head to think—merciful God, how short my poor wind is!—it came into my head to think how worshipful, praiseworthy, and religious a thing it

would be to secure this Cross for the service and adornment
of our chapel of Radigunda."

"What a folly is this!" the Abbess said. "And how is it that
you have dared to gallop my own best mule?"

"But, Reverend Mother," the Sister Lugdwitha pleaded, "this
Cross is renowned throughout all Christendom, for it was fashioned by Joseph of Arimathea, who picked up secretly the
gold that had fallen from the tables of the money-changers
that our Lord upset. It works wonders, so that great crowds
shall come with offerings if we may but get it into our chapel."

"Reverend Sister," the Abbess said, "this Cross is none of
ours. And if our chapel should gain renown from it, it would
be a renown that by reason of outcries, lawsuits, and evil
rumours should ultimately ruin us. I will have none of this."

The Sister Radigunda dropped suddenly her palette and
brushes and she faced round upon the three of them. The
almoner was wiping his brow with the sleeve of his gown, for
the sight of the Sister Lugdwitha's heat made him perspire out
of sympathy.

"Then if the Mother Abbess will have none of this," the
Sister Radigunda said, whilst her eyes shone with a dark fury,
"the Community will debate upon it. For the chapel of St
Radigunda is our affair and not that of the Mother Abbess. To
consider of this most excellent project is our affair and not
hers. Come, almoner, come, sister, let us go swiftly from here
and call the others together."

The almoner rolled large eyes of appeal towards the
Abbess.

"Go, go!" she said. "Restrain them from follies if you can,
though I think you are not the man to do it."

Left alone, the Abbess blinked her eyes contentedly and
took the opportunity to tell her beads, for which task in her

busy life she had not often the time. She was contented that the Community should commit follies. With each folly the Community grew more weak and she more strong, and she was determined to turn these erring and wayward sheep into an efficient company for the services of God. All around her the convent began to buzz like a wasp's hive. It seemed not very long before she heard how they raised a pious hymn of glorification as they filed out through the convent gates.

Mr Sorrell, walking now somewhat gingerly on the warm turf and descending into the valley which lower down appeared much more full of trees, perceived a living being approaching him with singular speed. It resembled a crocodile. It was brown and earthy; it filled him at once with repulsion and with dislike for the fact that he was so scantily clothed.

It had the face of a very dirty man, scuttling towards him at a great speed and on all fours. Upon its knees and its elbows it had things like the clogs that women use when they are hanging out washing in wet weather; in one of its hands, which were disengaged because it used its elbows instead of feet, it held a large earthenware dish with a metal lid. It came quite close to him; it placed itself before him; it snapped the lid of the dish with loud sounds, and uttered words of which Mr Sorrell could not make head or tail. He imagined that this must be some kind of beggar, but he could not make out how it put its clothes on. Its clothes were made up of bundles

[66]

of rags, of wisps of dried grass, of straw bands; all these things seemed to be tied around its body with old cords. It filled Mr Sorrell with an indescribable loathing. It had always been one of his principles never to relieve beggars, and he had always considered that beggars ought to be reasonably clean. He did not object to a man looking like a clerk out of work standing offering matches for sale just off the kerb-stone in Regent Street. But this creature was grotesque, lamentable, mournful, and moving. It was like a disagreeably conceived picture executed with fantastic skill. It seemed to bring poverty much too close. He exclaimed:

"Go away. I've no change on me."

He walked round the creature and down the path. The beggar pursued him slowly on all fours, uttering mournful sounds and Mr Sorrell felt as if he were being followed by an objectionable and very dirty dog.

Coming round an angle of the Downs he saw a large, square, stone enclosure surrounding what he took to be a workhouse. It had what seemed to be an unfinished chapel in one corner. Behind this, erected on a great mound shaped like a pudding-basin rose up an enormous, grey, stone, very square, castle.

Mr Sorrell said to himself that he would not have thought they'd have been allowed to put the workhouse so near the castle.

And there was no park at all round it! It stood upon its green knoll with the walls set straight on the grass. It was quite square, with battlements all round the top at the height of about a hundred feet. In one corner was a tower; on its top the plainly discernible figure of a man and the heads of several women. . . .

This castle! It was very big, it was very perfect, it was

obviously inhabited. He ought to have known its name. There could not be very many edifices like it in England. It was nearly as big as Windsor.

In front of the workhouse was a great cross; then a number of hovels with untidy reed thatching. They were scattered here and there amongst trees that ran down to the stream. There was a grey stone bridge with what he took to be a toll-keeper's lodge in the middle. Yet it had pointed windows and a large gilt cross on the gable. And then there rose, at a distance of perhaps four miles along the valley the great towers of another castle.

That affected Mr Sorrell as if it had been something portentous. There were two great castles in one little valley. It must be a regular show district.

When he got back to town he might very well set Mr Pudden to look up less known castles. You could run excursions down to them, very likely. . . .

The beggar had scuttled from behind his back and was making for the buildings. . . . Mr Sorrell was confronted by a castle and a workhouse. He would have to knock at the door of one or the other. The castle probably contained automobiles. He certainly needed a car. No doubt if he told them who he was they would lend him one or run him up to town. But then his identity would be known. . . . In that state! It would cause him to be unmercifully chaffed for the rest of his life. None of his fellow publishers really liked him. He had better knock at the workhouse door.

That would cause delay. Didn't they take you into the casuals' wards and make you break stones?

He stood, rubbing his naked foot on his naked shin. He could not see how he was to get out of being a figure of fun for the rest of his life. He would not be able to take things with a high hand any more—knowing that fellows were laughing at him behind his back. . . . He cursed the authorities of Salisbury Hospital. They had let him escape whilst he must have been in delirium. He felt as if he were still in delirium.

The gate of the workhouse fell back. There came out a white figure, bearing on high a crucifix. . . . Several little boys in white, swinging brass censers with brass chains. . . . Workmen ran out of the adjoining ploughlands; some women in grey dresses. From the workhouse came a man in purple vestments; behind him two more in white surplices that shook in the breeze. . . . And after that there were nuns. . . . Great numbers of nuns, two and two. In black habits with coifs waving like the wings of swans. The sound of singing came to him; melodious and triumphant.

Mr Sorrell had thought that religious processions were forbidden by law. . . . When Roman Catholics had attempted to carry the Sacrament through the streets of Southwark some years before there had been a great public outcry.

He must be on the land of the Duke of Norfolk. The castle was one belonging to His Grace whom Mr Sorrell had once met at a dinner of the Publishers', Booksellers' and Newsvendors' Association last year.

The procession was coming directly towards him. They must be intending to march round the cross. They must be practising for a very large pageant.

Perhaps the whole of Wiltshire was engaged on it. They certainly could not have found a more picturesque spot. . . . His road towards either the workhouse or the castle was anyhow barred for the moment. Certainly he was not going to go through all that crowd. Men from the fields were coming up and as the end of the procession left the gate belated nuns ran after it by twos and threes. He had never expected to see nuns run.

They had not timed the matter very well. Oddly dressed figures were trickling hastily, by now, out of the castle-gate— an enormous pointed arch between two square towers.

The procession was making straight towards him, the con- founded beggar scuttling before it on hands and knees. . . . As if directing them to him! He wanted to turn back and run along the path by which he had descended the valley but he felt hopelessly tired. He could not bear to face the descent.

He said to himself:

"I have been on my feet ever since four this morning." . . . How the devil did he know that? It might be true. But how the devil could he know it?

There were just behind him some high mounds of gorse. He found a nearly circular hollow in one of the groups. When he knelt down he was there quite hidden. The spines of the gorse pricked him through his nightshirt but there was just a man's length of rabbit nibbled turf. He could not any longer see the procession and he lay down in some tranquillity. The sun poured its warm rays down into the motionless air. The place smelt of thyme; great bees buzzed sleepily just above his head. The sound of the singing died away. . . .

He was gently shaken. He did not know where he was. A dirty face was peering down on him; an old man in priest's robes was trying to remove from his finger the ring of the Egerton cross.

He scrambled to his feet. He exclaimed: "Something to put on," as the spines of gorse ran sharply into his back. "For goodness' sake!"

All round the little ring of bushes were nuns, priests, thuri- fers. Round them a ring of dirty people in dirty fancy dress.

. . . You'd have thought they would not have used such dull, greasy hodden cloth for a pageant in which nobility were interested.

The priest shook his head as if he did not understand Mr Sorrell. Once more he caught at the Cross.

Mr Sorrell exclaimed:

"It's extremely valuable. I can't let it out of my keeping."

He placed his hand with the cross behind his back. The old priest said: "Viang, mung fiss," and grasped his other wrist. Mr Sorrell ejaculated:

"I *couldn't*. . . . Before so many women."

The old priest forged gently ahead, pulling behind him Mr Sorrell. The spines under bare feet made resistance impracticable. And resistance would only render him the more ridiculous. They thought that that was his fancy costume. They had mistaken him for some one else who had not turned up.

Mr Sorrell would not have chosen to come walking in any such costume. The other chap must have queer tastes!

They were acting the legend of the Greek Slave. No doubt that was Tamworth Castle. Mrs Egerton had said it was not far. . . . What could they act more appropriately? A simple and touching story.

All the same he could not help feeling embarrassed. . . . He was surrounded by nuns. They called out with expressions of delight. He heard them cry "Glory! Glory!" and they threw up their hands ecstatically.

One after the other tried to take the cross from him. They seemed to be nearly all foreigners. He would not let it go. You never knew.

The other vestmented priest shouldered his way through the women—a bettle-browed, dark man. He took hold of the cross as if he expected no refusal.

"I'm not the man that's acting in this show," Mr Sorrell exclaimed and he pulled the cross roughly away. "This isn't an imitation."

The priest said some harsh words in a German dialect.

"Puisque je vous dise que je ne la rendrai pas!" Mr Sorrell said sharply.

The priest seemed to get the sense of that. He appeared to consider. Then he shrugged his burly shoulders. He addressed angry words to the nuns. They fell into ranks again. The procession was re-forming. The priest struck an angry blow at a knock-kneed old fellow who fell down into the bushes. He wore an unusual cape with an odd funnel that went down far below his twisted leather belt.

The nuns stretched out in a long double file; the old priest elevated his cross. The thurifers held their censers ready; the priest in vestments, motioned to Mr Sorrell to stand in front of him.

Mr Sorrell said:

"I don't really belong to this show."

The old priest stamped his foot. . . . And after all to follow in the procession would be the best way to get into the workhouse if not the castle. They seemed to be expecting someone in a night-shirt. He could apologise. Perhaps they would lend him the other fellow's clothes.

All these people seemed to be singularly intent on their acting. No doubt it was a strain, playing that sort of part. It was perhaps not to be wondered at that they would not listen to him.

Voices rose up in a choir. With the censers swinging and the fresh breeze blowing the smoke aside the whole body got into motion. A crowd ran along beside them.

8

A NUMBER OF PEOPLE WERE HURRYING FROM THE GATES OF the castle towards the building which he had taken to be a workhouse—old men with pikes and axes, two or three little boys with enormous swords which they bore over their shoulders. Four or five very old men carried crossbows.

Then there came running three ladies, one all in blue with a great head-dress like a steeple which raked high over her head and was tied round with gold cords. They glittered in the sun and from them depended a veil of white lawn that fluttered like a flag. She too shouldered a great sword.

She ran like a deer to get in front of the procession which was nearing the workhouse gates. The two other women were dressed in grey with sleeves of white lawn and coifs like those of the nuns. The lady with the sword took up position in the gateway of the workhouse. With high, harsh and angry words she called her incongruous array of old men and

boys around her so that the gateway was entirely filled up.
His own procession came to a halt.

"What the deuce is this?" Mr Sorrell asked of one of the
little thurifers in front of him. "What *is* the old story? Did
the lady of the castle. . . ."

The boy looked at Mr Sorrell stupidly and shook his head.

"Do *all* of you have to pretend not to understand English?"
Mr Sorrell had to shout.

For at this point there arose a great noise—threats from
the other party and consternation and anger from the nuns.
The priest was consulting with the foremost of them. He too
showed animation and bad temper. A very high voice called
out imperatively in French:

"Silence, hounds!"—It was the lady with the sword.

Mr Sorrell had let himself drop into the role of the dispas-
sionate spectator. No one appeared to notice his garments.
The pageant itself was really interesting. It might almost have
been real life.

There was one old chap with a double-jointed flail. It had
three spiked iron balls jangling about on chains at its end.
Another old man was painfully setting a rusty crossbow. He
put the point on the ground and pulled up the cord until it
settled into a notch. The lady with the sword was shouting
commands in a sort of French. She banged the flat of her
sword against the staggering members of her crowd. The
outer sleeves of her blue gown were so long they brushed the
ground except when she was waving them in the air. The bare
sword when it was not in use she carried over her shoulder.

After a long pause the priest and two nuns approached the
lady. Immediately her eyes blazed with wrath and indignation
and with both her hands she elevated her sword above her

head. The old men pushed forward their pikeheads, the little boys shook their swords as well as they could and cried:

"Ho! a Coucy d'Enguerrand!"

The bowmen pointed their crossbows; the lady seemed to cry that no one was to enter the convent. The priest uttered a number of inaudible words and one of the nuns said something very energetically, pointing to the priest. But there was no mistaking the lady when she said that she would split the priest in half.

Horror overtook the nuns and they screamed. The lady spoke in such a high voice and so distinctly that Mr Sorrell understood her very well, though it seemed to be odd that they were all such masters of French. He could only imagine that the Pageant Committee had hired French nuns for the performance. They were certainly quarrelling about the cross that he was carrying.

Mr Sorrell found himself moving continually a little nearer to that lady. After all he had a sort of proprietary interest in this legend. Finally he stood almost immediately behind the priest and the two nuns in a little open space from which the crowd had been driven by the bowmen.

He caught words here and there; his brain automatically filled much of the rest of the sense. The language seemed to resemble the Provençal he had heard when inspecting a supposed tin mine in the south of France. . . .

The haughty priest demanded that the nuns have the custody of the Cross of St Joseph until the return from the wars of Sir John Egerton of Tamworth. The lady insisted that if the Community once got possession of the cross they would never give it up. Her voice was high and hard. She cited instances. Such as how the monks of the Priory of Bridgewater went to Taunton and stole from the abbey there the relics of St Ostuarius which had been translated with only a feeble guard from Godstow. She mentioned also certain monks of near Cologne. They had broken into Cologne Cathedral and stolen from it a large number of relics of the Eleven Thousand Virgins. She had a memory stored with the misdeeds of various members of the monastic Orders and she cited grievances of her own against this very convent. These matters were too complicated for Mr Sorrell to follow but he immensely admired the lady's spirit and her flashing eyes. . . . If the nuns, she said, once got hold of that cross they would hide it away somewhere or build it into their altar and swear that it were sacrilege to take it thence by force.

The priests and nuns represented that even if they were not the proper guardians of the Cross, no more was this Lady Blanche de Coucy d'Enguerrand. The cross should be delivered into the hands of the Lady Dionissia de Egerton de Tamworth.

The Lady Blanche gave it to be understood that that was folly and frivolity. Was the Lady Dionissia even married to the Young Knight of Egerton of Tamworth? No, she was merely contracted by proxy and sent for inspection by the Lord of Tamworth. He had not so much as seen her. He had gone away on his Scottish wars before ever the Lady Dionissia coming from her home in the Northern Marches of Wales had ever reached that spot. It was therefore evident that the Lady Dionissia was not the proper custodian of the Cross. She—the Lady Blanche de Coucy d'Enguerrand—was and she alone. She was the cousin of that Knight and the next heiress to the fief of Egerton of Tamworth.

The priest on the other hand submitted that, failing the convent, the Lady Dionissia was the proper guardian. The contract of marriage had been duly made and during the period of inspection the lady enjoyed all the privileges of the Knight's wife. The Lady Blanche replied that it was true that the Lady Dionissia enjoyed the privileges and rights of the Knight's wife. But these only affected her bed, board, vestment and her rank and station. They gave her no title to property.

Mr Sorrell was amazed at the nicety with which these two people split hairs. It detracted from the merit of the pageant as a rendering of history. Life in the Middle Ages was a simple affair. He did not really suppose that they actually had any laws at all, whereas what they were carrying on now was rather more complicated than an average argument about mining rights in the Court of Chancery.

The Lady Blanche had been gazing hard at Mr Sorrell, who was looking at her admiringly over the priest's shoulder. Suddenly with both hands she raised her enormous sword. The nuns shrieked and ran away; even the priest, beetle-browed and militant, moved several paces to the right. And then, with an extraordinarily hard grip, she had Mr Sorrell by the wrist, dropping the sword on to the ground, where it jangled and vibrated.

"Come, thou!" she exclaimed, and Mr Sorrell felt a jerk on his shoulder such as pulled him past her and right in amongst her men with the pikes and the axes. He was surrounded by all these armed men, as if he were inside a British square at Tel-el-Kebir.

"Well now!" he exclaimed, "that's more like business."

The nuns surged around them, lifting their hands on high and crying out, their coifs waving. But the Lady Blanche called out to her men:

"Ho, fellows! March!"

Mr Sorrell had to move along with some expedition in order that his bare heels might avoid the points of their shoes.

Before they had gone a dozen yards the body of them all halted. They missed their natural leader. The Lady Blanche— Mr Sorrell saw her over an array of weapons that resembled a bedraggled hedge—the Lady Blanche was talking energetically to the Abbess, who had appeared beneath the gateway. She was telling the Abbess that thus she was foiled in her evil design. It was time that some of the great ones of the land thus handled the Churchmen who were growing too fat and haughty. She was minded to come in a very short time with some of her men and to burn the convent about the ears of the nuns. The Abbess blinked at her with mild and indulgent irony.

She said that it was none of her doing that the nuns had come to take the cross; the chapel was in the care of the community, and in nowise affected her revenue as Abbess.

The Lady Blanche shrugged her shoulders, and uttered a laugh of derision. She said that the Abbess was all one pack with the others.

The Abbess smiled again. She said that she would to God she might be the first to suffer amongst the religious of the Church. The Church grew fat by means of persecution, as was well seen in the case of the Blessed Martyr Thomas of Canterbury, whom the King having had killed, he was forced to do penance, and afterwards to forfeit to the Church a good part of his own lands.

The Lady Blanche laughed highly. They were not, she said, in those old, outlandish times, which were a hundred years ago, or more. Now they were differently inclined.

The Abbess said that that was very well, for no one had laid hands upon the Churchmen since that time. And if one once more should be slain, assuredly it would very much augment the faith of that realm of England in what was assuredly an age of unbelief.

The Lady Blanche retorted: Would the Abbess have them returned to the dark and gross superstitions of their fathers and grandfathers, when it was believed that by a stroke of the pen a Churchman could turn silver into gold, the blessings of heavy crops of wheat into black blight, or night into decay? Now that so many could write, these puffed-up pretensions had had the wind let out of them.

The Abbess raised her voice at last, because she intended to be heard on all sides:

"Go your ways off our grounds!" she said. "Madam, you are a foolish woman, and it was the best day that the convent has had that you and not my flock took the cross to itself. I had rather you had been the thief than we. But now go off this ground, which is holy, having known the tread and been the gift of the blessed Edward Confessor. Because you took the cross I have no ill-will against you. I have no time to bandy words with you, nor are a pair of women fit to discuss holy mysteries, though I dwell among them and more fit to discuss them than you. But this I tell you, that if you further profane this ground against the will of me who am Abbess, an action shall lie against you in the Bishop's court, and be referrable to the Court of Rome—such a lawsuit as shall cost you some of your land."

The Abbess retired into the little wicket chamber of the sister that kept the gates. She closed the door in the Lady Blanche's face, for it was her intention to have the last word.

The Lady Blanche breathed deeply in her chest with rage that she could not satisfy, and then she called to her the little page Jehan to pick up her great sword which still lay upon the ground. Fire flashed from her eyes, and her hands were clenched as she went towards her armed men, thinking of how she would be avenged upon this Churchwoman who had eluded her. She came right in among them, and, calling out to them to march, she walked herself by Mr Sorrell's side.

She looked at him with a keen, hard glance.

"You come from Cyprus," she said in French. And her words seemed to him the more intelligible because she must speak in a high voice to be heard over the clinking of old chain harness, the jangling of swords, and the brushing sounds of the buskins of her men as they marched over the turf.

"No, I come from New York," Mr Sorrell said as loud as he could.

"You come from Palestine," the lady exclaimed. Mr Sorrell conceded: "I've been a little all over the world. I have travelled a great deal."

"You were born in Jerusalem," the lady exclaimed.

"I was at the taking of Jerusalem. But I was born in Wimbledon," Mr Sorrell answered. "It's Wimbledon S.W. now, though when I was born it was right in the country."

"I do not understand you very well or hardly at all," the lady said, "But you come from Jerusalem and are a very holy man. Angels have guided you."

Mr Sorrell exclaimed:

"Couldn't we let up on the pageant just a minute? I should like to know about the trains."

The lady looked at him with the dull eyes of a person who cannot catch your words. She called to her the old man who had the flails with the cannon balls.

"Du,"—and now she seemed to speak some sort of South German dialect, "Thou wast in the Holy Land. Speak with this holy man if thou mayst."

The old man had lost an eye; his face was brown and clean though his jerkin was stained, weather-beaten and very ragged. He addressed Mr Sorrell in words that seemed all to flow by him.

"He seems," Mr Sorrell said to the Lady Blanche, "to be talking of Ragusa and Cyprus and Byzantium and Jaffa. What is *he* acting? A Crusader?" That wasn't so wet. He would have thought they would not have gone fooling up the Adriatic. They'd have sailed straight to St Jean d'Acre. . . . He imagined that he had caught the pageant authors out in a solecism.

"I know no Greek," the lady said and asked him if he could deny that he had been a slave of Mahound, or that he came from Sandwich all alone save for the angels who guided him.

Mr Sorrell was tired to the point of silliness. He had just got to give in. They were too persistent. And he answered: "Oui, je suis venu tout seul. À pied."

The lady said with satisfaction that without doubt he had been protected by angels and by a mother's gratitude, the roads being covered with robbers. She went on to say that the mother of the knight, his late master, had been living until a few months ago. The knight had sent several messengers home. From Palestine and whilst he had been returning. These had reported how the slave had watched over his master in gratitude for his rescue from slavery. . . . As that, in open battle he had saved his master's life when unhorsed; had extinguished the Greek fire that the Saracens had cast on the knight's helmet beneath the walls of Jaffa. When his master had been wounded by a poisoned arrow of the barbarous Ruthenians the faithful slave had sucked the poison from the wound; when the knight had slept in the desert the slave had watched over him and had driven away the venomous serpents and the fell tigers or had awakened him in time to confront his foes. All these reports had filled the knight's mother with such gratitude that unceasingly and from day's end to day's end she had sought the favour and protection of heaven for both slave and master.

It seemed to Mr Sorrell that he ran up against mother's gratitude all the time. It had been only the other day that Mrs Lee-Egerton had been thanking him for saving the last of the line of Egerton from prison. He said to the lady that he supposed that that wretched little moron would be the descendant of the old knight who went socking dragons round Cairo way.

"Therefore," the lady ignored his words, "because of the gratitude of this mother who was my mother's sister and because of the holiness that distinguishes your words and shines from all your presence, you shall be very honoured and feasted in my castle. Baths shall be made ready for you with new soap that has cost a king's ransom and great feasts so that your skin shall crack. All this is fitting for you have fasted long and travelled far.

"Well," Mr Sorrell said, "I sure have been in a few places. J'ai roulé ma bosse un peu partout."

It was the look of returning noncomprehension in the lady's eyes that really puzzled Mr Sorrell. The slang of that last French phrase had been so elementary and aged that *any* one ought to be able to understand, let alone a lady who could send out difficult old French in a cataract.

And, with a queer start, he found that he was not any longer thinking of these people as taking part in a pageant. They must, if they were, have been playing it for at least twenty years. Their lances were old and rusty, their pikes notched in the blade and greasy from long handling; their

[82]

clothes very much worn. . . . He could not get away from the feeling that they were just living their normal lives.

Supposing that the railway accident had really made him see something queer! Supposing that all these people were really . . . ghosts! He was modern enough to believe that in our day anything might happen. If he could not for the life of him say what he believed he certainly could not say that he disbelieved anything at all.

Queer things happened . . . that you would have called impossible in the day when he had been born in Wimbledon. How could a downright, really modern man like himself do anything else but keep an absolutely open mind? When he had been born people had laughed at the idea of flying as the dream of a visionary. Now you had the intrepid Mr Claflin who flew round the world as then people went to Brighton for the summer. . . . And there were new, odd religions. One evening at his club old General Lathrop had bored him to death by making him look at portfolio after portfolio of drawings. These, the General swore, had been executed by spirits in his own house at Reading. You could not prove that they hadn't.

You might be as busy as you liked but you could not help knocking against these things. He went to see his aunt, Lady Wells, occasionally on a Sunday. Her drawing-room was always full of the most estimable people. He had heard of the dead speaking, of the stone-blind being cured by Christian Science. . . . There was nobody dead with whom he in the least desired to communicate; he had never had any illness that he could not counteract with a pill or two at the proper moment. But he might come to suffer from nerves as the result of overwork. Then it would be a reasonable thing to put himself into the hands of healers claiming almost supernatural gifts. Why not?

Suddenly he asked the lady at his side what year that was. She looked at him with large eyes that were rather mysterious now that her temper had subsided.

"You have indeed travelled far, holy man," she said. "It is the year of Our Lord 1326."

He ran through in his mind the dates of the Kings of England. He could not get beyond "Henry III, 1216." He could not remember a single date between that and the battle of Agincourt. That was in 1415—four hundred years before Waterloo. Thus the battle of Bannockburn, which he knew happened in the reign of Edward II, must have taken place some time between 1216 and 1415.

But no modern man need bother about History. He would not mind betting that Spicer, of Spicer and Wells, would not be able to get as far as Henry III. Yet Spicer was one of the smartest men on the Stock Exchange.

The lady beside him was probably chock full of historical knowledge. Why shouldn't she be? Women had nothing in particular to do and could monkey with any sort of nonsense they liked. At the same time he did not care to confess himself ignorant—even of parlour tricks. She would probably look down on him, for she would not know much of his other splendid and varied attainments.

He asked her, in order to make conversation, why it was that whilst the youngest of her grown men appeared to be sixty, the eldest of her boys could not be more than fourteen.

Fury burned in the lady's eyes.

"Holy man," she answered, "can you really be so ignorant of what happens today? Do you not know that my husband is away at the Scottish wars?" . . . Did he not know that her husband would have taken with him all the able-bodied men? To fight in the battle of their Lord the King? So that in all the countryside, save for the robbers, there was no man so proper, so erect or so fearless as himself.

Mr Sorrell said he thought a husband should want to leave his wife better protected.

The lady's eyes hardened; her chest heaved swiftly and very high under her green dress.

"There you have the very truth of God," she said, speaking so fast that he had great difficulty in following her. "That is what the lords of this day are. There you have my lord and master gone away. A thousand or two of pounds he will squander and what will he bring back of booty? Not one penny's-worth. What honours? None at all, for he is embroiled with the Queen Mother past mending. Holy man, you do not know what a fool my husband is!"

And she poured forth a torrent of words in some story of how the Knight Enguerrand de Coucy and his cousin Egerton of Tamworth had set their archers to shoot arrows upon the knights of Sir John of Hainault who lay with the King at Newcastle.

"And by little good St Luke," the Lady concluded, slackening the speed of her words and gazing almost affectionately into Mr Sorrell's eyes, "can you wonder that some ladies are unfaithful to their lords as is the common complaint nowadays? Do our lords pay us the attention that wife should exact of husband?" . . . No, not at all. . . . In the last nine years my Lord of Enguerrand had not spent six weeks quiet at home. When he had not been prancing in Scotland he had been laying waste Flanders or tilting against Saracens in Spain.

And are not women of beauty made to be courted and treas-
ured? But Mr Sorrell would see that in all that countryside
there was not a personable man. So that she thought the best
of them was her little page, Jehan. He, Mr Sorrell could perceive, strutted gallantly enough, carrying the large sword. So
that it was a very tedious and disgusting life that they lead
who were the great ladies of the realm of England and for
herself she spent days in plotting revenge on that husband of
hers.

She looked fixedly into Mr Sorrell's eyes.

"Yes, I will take such a revenge—if only I can think of one—
as shall render my lord and master a laughing stock through
all the realms of chivalry."

Mr Sorrell exclaimed:

"But you oughtn't to think of such things. Men will be men
you know. And family quarrels only lead to everybody's being hurt and nobody gaining the value of a centime."

"Ah," the Lady Blanche said voluptuously, "if I can only
think how; I will have such a revenge. . . ."

"Oh, beautiful and dear lady," he pleaded. "Let me help you
with your business and you will feel better. And get up some
little fêtes with the ladies round if there are only ladies. . . .
Golf tournaments. . . . Tennis tournaments. . . . Any old
tournaments."

"God of mine." . . . The lady took a deep breath. Her eyes
sparkled. "Tournaments for women. . . . That is a very splendid idea. . . ."

"Little, innocent contests," Mr Sorrell said, ". . . to pass the
time gently away. . . ."

The lady said:

"Splendid . . . There shall some ladies yet . . ."

They passed at that moment under a great archway and

came into the courtyard which was all in shadow because of its high walls.

"Now I will take you to your bath," the lady said. "I hope you will clean yourself very well for, in order to do you honour I will have you eat out of the same plate as myself."

9

THE ARMED MEN ALL AROUND THEM HAD DISPERSED AT THE voice of the page Jehan, and the Lady Blanche was directing Mr Sorrell's steps towards the gate of the large keep. In the middle of the courtyard it frowned, a great mass of stone, towering high up above the surrounding walls.

Mr Sorrell said in English:

"Isn't it about time this pageant business came to an end? I am always anxious to oblige, but I've really got business on hand that makes me want to get up to town as quickly as possible."

The Lady Blanche shook her head, and then the two ladies attendant upon her came upon them. They were somewhat out of breath, for they had not been able to keep step with the armed men.

"Ladies," the Lady Blanche said, "it is very negligent of you not to have attended on me better; but take now this holy man to his bath, and attend upon him with all the diligence that you may. Such an excellent man as this is not often seen, and he has put into my head such an idea as, by God's grace, shall win us great honour, and redound for ever to the ridicule of our abominable men-folk."

Mr Sorrell had a vague idea that he ought to put his foot down and insist upon some sort of explanation. But his feet were the weakest part of him, and on the rough paving of the courtyard they betrayed him at every step. He was being gently coerced by people who were the most amiable in the world, but by people who did not pay the least attention to any of his desires or even to any of his words. The Lady Blanche had already, with her swift and determined gait, entered the arched door of the Inner Keep, the pendant cloth from her high steeple hat fluttering bravely behind her. The bowmen and pikemen had mostly disappeared into what appeared to be the stony hollows of the great walls. But all sorts of shaggy and tousled heads were peering at them out of crevices and crannies that formed the windows in the immense cliff of stone that shut them all in. A certain grimness, a certain ugliness rather astonished Mr Sorrell. He could not see why if people could afford to build a castle like this, they could not equally afford to beautify it. There were no rose bushes on the bare stone of the wall; there was no ampeloposis; there was not even any ivy. It was all straight up and down hard, grey stone, so that he had the feeling of being at the bottom of an immense well. Far up above them a flag of red and white chequers fluttered lazily against the blue sky.

The two ladies led him slowly forward; he was limping painfully, for his feet had become decidedly tender. He was being led up three stone steps into an immensely large, draughty, and bare hall. The roof was vaulted, and had wooden beams across it very high up. The walls were quite bare. On

[89]

the right-hand side, upon a sort of a platform ascending the wall and coming forward upon a square framework, was a broad and very long Turkey carpet.

"That's a daïs," Mr Sorrell said to himself. "I know what that is."

On each side of the daïs there protruded from the wall a lance, and from each lance depended a banner. The one was very faded and coloured light blue with stripes of pale yellow, the other was newer and with a pattern of red and white chequers. Against the right-hand side of the length of the hall some very long boards were laid, and beside them were upturned trestles and long wooden benches. In the left-hand further corner were a rusty plough, a number of spades, and perhaps twenty or thirty reaping hooks upon long staves. The windows along the outer side of the hall were without glass, arched and very tall, and barred with iron bars which had been painted red and white in chequers, like the banner to the right of the daïs. Near the door there was a great untidy heap of rushes nearly as tall as a man. This was being added to from the detritus of the rest of the stone floor by three old women with long wooden rakes. Through a window at the farther end of the hall, three other old women with pitchforks were shovelling new rushes from a cart that stood outside.

Mr Sorrell said pleasantly:

"Look at all those bones! I suppose this is your salle-à-manger."

He said this by way of a joke. He could not imagine that any people of distinction could, even for the sake of a pageant, sit down to eat in such a place. The flagstones were disgustingly dirty, and there must be a tremendous draught from all the unglazed windows.

But the Lady Amoureuse, catching only the one word

manger, hastened to assure him that very soon he should eat. The trumpet for washing hands would blow in a little half hour. The whiteness of this holy man's skin after so many days of travel evidenced that assuredly he had been under angelic protection—if, indeed, he had not actually been received up to heaven to rest himself after his journey from Palestine to Sandwich—or if, indeed, he was not actually an angel himself, who had been sent from heaven as a distinguished mark of favour to the very high and noble family of Egerton of Tamworth. She understood next that this very holy man positively desired clothes and linen. She had made out at least those words from the odd perversion of French French that he insisted on speaking. This was a singular desire. His single white garment, long and spotless in its purity, seemed to her to be exactly appropriate for one who came bearing the holy cross which St Joseph of Arimathea had fashioned from the gold of the money-changers in the temple. Why should he desire the ordinary and vile clothes of mankind? He had himself this garment of a whiteness so peculiar, of a smoothness so alluring, and of an unknown and possibly celestial fabric? But this holy man was persistently and even with agitation demanding clothes before he ate. She commanded, therefore, the Lady Blanchemain to go to their lady and mistress, and to put before her this singular demand.

The Lady Blanchemain grumbled ominously. She said that it was exactly like the Lady Amoureuse, with her pallid beauty, to insist upon being left alone with anybody of any distinction who chanced to be in her vicinity. But, with a haughty indifference, the Lady Amoureuse informed her that this was a command from a feudal superior to an inferior. She was forced to do her duty: the holy man desired clothes. And

reluctantly the little Lady Blanchemain ran over the dirty
floor of the hall to come to their mistress as soon as might be.

Holding his hand very gently, the Lady Amoureuse led
Mr Sorrell across the gloomy hall through a little door and
out into the warm sunshine of an inner court. Here in the walls
there were many doors, for it was in this courtyard that there
were the kitchens. A pile of the skins of cattle lay in one
corner of the yard, and all the ground was clammy and noi-
some with vestiges of the slaughter of beasts and of cookery.
The stench was almost intolerable to Mr Sorrell. The Lady
Amoureuse counteracted it by holding to her nose a small
bag of lawn filled with dry cloves, lavender, peppercorns, and
spices, which was hung round her waist by a silken cord. A
narrow causeway of white stones ran across this evil ground,
and in the farthest corner of the courtyard was a great wooden
vat standing high upon a platform. To this there ascended
wooden steps, and the Lady Amoureuse informed Mr Sorrell
that here was his bath. The agitation which ensued in the
holy man she was not at all able to understand. She told him
that it was a very efficient bath. The soap which would be
brought was of the very best that could be had of the best
soap-boiler in Coventry; the towels were soft and fine. The
warm water, she pointed out, ran along a wooden conduit
from an upper room of the castle, when it was heated and
poured in by scullions. Mr Sorrell halted resolutely some
yards from this large structure, whilst the Lady Amoureuse
called out for a page with towels and soap. The little Jehan
with his long curls came hastening. He stepped past them on
the causeway, the towels floating over his arm, the soap upon
a wooden platter. He approached the bath, and setting the
soap down upon the steps, he pulled out with all his force the
large peg at the bottom of the tub. A spout of water splashed

out and added to the unpleasant moisture of the sunlit court. The Lady Amoureuse explained to the holy man that this bath was always kept filled with clean water—firstly that it should be sweet, and secondly that the wood of it should not start in the heat of the sun. Such a bath as this was not known to be elsewhere in Christendom except at the Court of the French King. It was Sir Enguerrand de Coucy who had insisted on setting it up. And his lady took great pride in it, though she feigned she was utterly averse from all new and polite ideas, holding that knights and pages should bathe themselves in the old-fashioned manner in such streams, ponds, and rivers as the countryside afforded.

In the warm sunlight an ineffable bliss descended upon the Lady Amoureuse. It seemed to radiate from the holy man; it seemed to radiate from the gleaming and sacred emblem that he held depending from his finger. Here at last she who had lived for so long an insignificant life in this dull castle, subjected to the insults and jealous caprices of a mistress who hated her as well for her mind as for her looks—here at last there was come to her a holy man protected by angels and bearing a relic more sacred than all the feretories of Salisbury itself could show.

"And, O, holy man," she exclaimed, "if it is not permitted to me to show you such honour as should be accorded to great and gallant knights and to strangers of very high degree, blame not me but the lady who is my mistress. She sets her face against all that is new and polite and the fashion of the day." In all places now throughout Christendom, when a knight of highness had travelled far and came to a castle, he was very softly and ceremoniously entreated. Thus if she had her will, she should kneel at his feet and bathe them with warm water. She would anoint them with the most precious salves and ointments that the castle afforded. But so vigorous was their lady and mistress in her determination to set her face against all new and gentle usages that she must be gone, leaving him to anoint and tend himself, to stand behind the palisade which is beyond the bath, and to hand him his garments as he had need of them. "And this is the folly of our lady and mistress, who thinks that thus is a better discipline obtained. As if it were not manifest that that is the best usage and the most sure discipline which teaches us to be courteous and gentle in the proper fashion of our own day."

Having said this, the Lady Amoureuse went back along the causeway and picked her steps gently. At this moment, too, the Lady Blanchemain came out from the door in the corner of the courtyard, having behind her two pages each smaller than the little Jehan, and each bearing a quantity of wearing apparel. The Lady Amoureuse was able to marshal Lady Blanchemain and the pages upon the comparatively dry path that ran along the wall of the courtyard. Thus she had the added gratification of shepherding the little Lady Blanchemain away from her holy man, and of seeing the glances of vexation that the little fair woman threw at the palisade which finally hid them from view.

The little page Jehan had climbed the steps and was now in the great bath, and Mr Sorrell was relieved to observe that so large was that vat, that it entirely hid the page from view. It seemed to him possible, therefore, that he might be able to perform his ablutions without any embarrassments from these people, who seemed to him as shockingly lacking in any sense of decency as of sanitation. He mounted the steps and peered down into the bath. The little page with a hogshair brush was engaged in cleaning the wooden sides and bottom.

"I don't understand," Mr Sorrell addressed him, "why in the

world you take such a lot of trouble over washing yourself, when you keep the courtyard in such a disgustingly filthy state?"

The little page looked at him with large and serious blue eyes.

"Ick han ne Greek," he exclaimed gently.

"Oh, well," Mr Sorrell said, "I wasn't asking you to speak Greek. Though as it's part of the play that I'm supposed to be a Greek slave, I may be expected to speak it."

Mr Sorrell, indeed, had made up his mind that he was just going to speak ordinary English. It wasn't very much against his will that he was taking part in these absurd proceedings; he rather enjoyed it. It was like being taken behind the scenes of a theatre; but he did not see why in strict privacy he should not speak his natural tongue. The page, in spite of his pretending ignorance, must perfectly well understand.

He stepped over the side of the bath. The wooden breastwork formed by its sides came nearly as high as his chin, and upon looking round the stony walls of the castle he could see no window that commanded a view of him. On the other hand, when he looked downwards over the palisade he noticed that his head at least was in full view of the Ladies Amoureuse and Blanchemain and the two little pages.

"We are all ready," the Lady Blanchemain said in her barbarous French, "to hand you up your clothes."

"And very fine clothes they are," the Lady Amoureuse exclaimed. "Oh, holy man, they are the very habits that were worn by our glorious master, the Knight of Coucy, upon the occasion of the great supper after his jousting with Sir Walter de Marnay."

Mr Sorrell precipitately withdrew his head. The little page had climbed up on to the wooden side of the great tub. Here he sat astride, and lisped gently that if the pilgrim were ready he would call for the warm water to be sent down the chute. He had little serious and gentle airs, this page, and Mr Sorrell at once took a fancy to him.

"Oh well, nipper," he said, "if you clear out I'll be ready in a jiffy."

The little Jehan appeared to understand from his gesture what was required of him, nevertheless he remained astride of the wood.

"It is a good thing and a custom, and, as I have heard, very refreshing and sanitary," he said gravely, "to stand beneath the end of the wooden conduit. Then the slaves pour the water from within the conduit, and at first it is of the heat of one's flesh, and gradually they shall make it grow hotter and hotter, until it is very hot, and then again they let it grow quite cold." This was said to impart to the skin a beauty like that of the good knight Sir Paris of Troy, and to the courage such a force that you may easily overthrow three knights immediately afterwards. So it was said, but for himself he did not know if this were true. "For I am only a little page and have not the right to these knightly luxuries. I wash myself in the cold streams three times a day, by means of which I shall come to be a good and hardy knight."

Having uttered these words with extreme precision and gravity, the little boy cocked his other leg over the side of the bath and disappeared. His hand once more came over the side, holding the wooden platter upon which the soap reposed. Immediately afterwards, Mr Sorrell having thrown his nightshirt and his linen turban over the side of the bath, the little boy called out shrilly:

"Oh! let the water come."

It came, and falling deliciously tepid over Mr Sorrell's head and coursing down his limbs, it gave him really the first pleasant sensation of the day. Gradually it grew warmer until it was very hot, and then colder till it was very cold.

The water was agreeably scented with mint, and did away with the stench of the courtyard, and when he sat himself down it reached exactly to his chin. The platter with the soap upon it bobbed up against his face, and because the bath in which he sat was elevated so high, the sunshine poured down all over him. He sat luxuriously stretching himself and sighing. He sat still for quite a long time—he half dozed, and large flies buzzed all over him. Suddenly the voice of the Lady Amoureuse cried out:

"Oh, holy man, are you ill, have you fainted, for we do not hear the plash of the water?"

Mr Sorrell exclaimed that he was well.

"Because," the Lady Amoureuse continued, "knights have been known to faint and to drown in these large baths. Such was the miserable fate which overtook the miraculously gallant Sir Lois du Destrier Blanc in the Court of the French King only a twelvemonth was last June."

But the soap which he had taken into his hand now filled Mr Sorrell with a sudden panic. It was not like any soap he had ever touched before—or rather, it was exactly like a soap that he had once purchased when he was inspecting a mine for some Germans in Syria. He could not for the life of him understand how they came to have Syrian soap in the middle of Salisbury Plain. And then suddenly he exclaimed to himself:

"By Jove! I'm not only in the middle of Salisbury Plain, I'm in the middle of the Middle Ages!"

He put his hand up to feel his hair—there was not a vestige, there was not a trace of any wound, though there was certainly a scar that might have been two years old, just above

[97]

the middle of his left temple. And this scar had not been there of old.

It *was* that. Something must have happened. Something must have happened in the railway accident at Salisbury. He had got a knock—or perhaps it was only a mental shock—something mysterious, something that he could not understand. It had knocked him clean back through time—600 years, as a cricket-ball is struck by a bat. That seemed almost incredible. But there were the hard facts before him. He was not going to account for this, it was not any business of his to account for things.

And so essentially modern a man was Mr Sorrell, so excellently had he been schooled in worldly practicable things, that his mind immediately accepted the situation. He had not any doubt that one or other of the Christian Scientists, New Homœopathists or Psychics that he met at his aunt's could explain the matter in some seemingly nonsensical but probably quite true method. If the ghosts from the past could come into the present, why in the world should not ghosts of the future be able to go back into the past? That was all that it would amount to. He seemed, indeed, vaguely to remember that in the Scriptures there had been apparitions of prophets or even of Christ Himself, several hundred years before the births of the prophets or of the Saviour. This, of course, was a much smaller kind of thing. He did not regard himself as being as important even as a minor prophet. But if it could happen in the one case, why should not it happen in his own?

What he supposed to have happened was this: His soul had been shaken out of his body by the railway accident at Salisbury; it had gone wandering back through time until it chanced upon the body of the Greek slave, who had probably died upon Salisbury Plain 600 years before. Then his soul had

entered the Greek slave's body. It seemed ridiculous, but there
again he certainly was. He examined himself carefully, as far
as he could for the water. He could not find that he differed
from his ordinary self. But Mr Sorrell had never examined
himself minutely in a looking-glass. He was moderately familiar with his own face. One cannot help looking at one's face
at times. But he had not any mirror in which to inspect himself. The water had become too clouded with soap to afford
him a reflection.

Upon the whole he felt exactly the same. He was tired in
just the same portions of his limbs that usually felt tired; he
was hungry with his usual hunger.

Possibly, all this had something to do with the transmigra-
tion of souls. Perhaps his soul had formerly inhabited the body
of the Greek slave, and perhaps it had just gone back to it.
Something like that must have happened.

The only thing that appeared odd to Mr Sorrell was that
he had not himself the least feeling of oddity. He was just
there, just his normal self, ringed in by the wooden staves. He
was perfectly comfortable, and with no view save that of an
oval of blue sky above his head. Against it the banner on top
of the keep was just large enough to come into his view. It
flapped lazily its red and white chequers. He seemed himself
to be a sort of ghost but he could not discover that he felt
anything uncanny at all. Even the people around him did not
seem to see anything uncanny in him; on the contrary, they
welcomed him with rapture, and did him as well as their
barbarous means would let them.

The water was beginning to grow a little cold. Mr Sorrell
stood up and looked over the side of his bathtub for his little
page. The little Jehan was sitting on the steps that led up to
the tub, alternately meditating and telling his beads.

"Hallo, nipper!" Mr Sorrell exclaimed; "it's about time I got myself dressed."

The little Jehan understood from his gestures what he desired. He handed him the white towels, and once more removed the spiket so that the water gushed down into the courtyard.

"Now," Mr Sorrell said whilst he proceeded to dry himself, "pop along and fetch my clothes."

He had to repeat these words in French, for the boy did not understand him at all. Thus he made himself comprehensible, too, to the Ladies Blanchemain and Amoureuse.

"Ho, là!" the little Lady Blanchemain cried out from behind the palisade beneath him, "most holy pilgrim, here are your chausses."

She was handing up to him, at the full stretch of her arm and on tiptoe, a garment whose purpose he did not immediately understand. He took it, however, with all the modesty of which he was capable, so that he exhibited no more than his hand and the top of his head.

It fulfilled the functions at once of trousers and of stockings. It was all of one piece, one leg being of red woollen work and the other of white. The part which went about his waist was red and white chequers. It seemed to him to be a preposterous thing to put on, but having examined it and discovered that it was quite clean and apparently new, he slowly and with some difficulty inserted himself into the garment. It fitted as tight as the skin of an eel.

The Lady Amoureuse took from the hand of the page a white shirt, which in turn she passed up to him with an air of serious and reverent gravity. The shirt presented no very serious difficulties. It was of white, fine, and soft linen, and, having got into it, Mr Sorrell heaved a sigh of immense re-

lief. In a shirt and trousers of a sort he was sufficiently covered
to confront anybody in the world, though he would not much
have liked to walk in it about the streets round Covent Garden,
where most of his brother publishers do their business.

His feet had got wet. The bath was quite empty, but naturally a considerable amount of water remained upon the bottom boards. He approached with a great deal more confidence
the side of the bath. It gave on to the palisade. Looking down
upon the Lady Amoureuse, he told her that he wanted a pair
of shoes. These were handed up to him, two extraordinary
objects. Mr Sorrell could make nothing of them at all. There
was obviously a place for the feet to go into, but the toes were
prolonged in a sort of stiff leather tube for perhaps a foot and
a half. And at the end of each of these leather tubes was fixed
a small leather strap with buckles, resembling a dog's collar.
One of these objects was red in the foot part and white in the
tube, and the other white in the foot and red as far as the dog
collar.

The little page Jehan had climbed over the side of the bath,
and was standing beside him. With an air of reverent serious-
ness the little boy took one of the things from Mr Sorrell. He
knelt down upon the ground, and, lifting Mr Sorrell's foot
on to one of his little knees, he proceeded to put the shoe on
to it. The shoe was of soft and pliant leather, very beautifully
coloured red, and it fitted round Mr Sorrell's ankle by an
efficient strap and buckle. Very cautiously and tenderly the
little Jehan took the strap, which resembled a dog collar, and
buckled it round Mr Sorrell's knee. Thus the leather tubing
which had so puzzled him curved upwards and out from Mr
Sorrell's toes to his knee.

He approached the side of the bath with more confidence,
though the tubes bowing out in front of his shins made it

difficult for him. The Lady Amoureuse, tiptoeing, handed him up a garment all flaked in red and white, with a white fur edging. Mr Sorrell stood up in it. He must present a very splendid appearance. His jerkin was, on the upper half of the right breast, of vermilion velvet, on the lower half it was of white velvet. As to his left chest the upper half was white and the lower red.

"By Jove!" Mr Sorrell said, "I must look like a living chessboard!"

But a certain complacency came over his mind at the thought that he could wear such flaming splendours and yet not be a bit overdressed. He must present a really fine figure of a man. The little page now made it evident to him by signs that it would be appropriate to climb over the side of the bath. It was a task of some difficulty, and one only to be performed backwards because of his shoes. Nevertheless, Mr Sorrell did it with good humour.

He stood on the platform on which the bath rested; he carefully descended the steps, the little page leading him by the hand. On the lowest step but one Jehan placed a cushion of red velvet.

"My lord, the pilgrim," he said, "will be pleased to seat himself for his coifing and the care of his hands."

The Ladies Blanchemain and Amoureuse were approaching him side by side along the causeway, being followed by the two smaller pages carrying basins of silver, silver flasks, towels, combs, and various implements that he could not very well understand.

They surrounded him in a sort of busy swarm. First the little Jehan shaved him with dexterity; then, approaching him with a large silver comb, the Lady Blanchemain delicately combed out his hair, parting it down the centre and leaving a fringe over his forehead. Then one of the other little pages, with an air of serious reverence similar to the little Jehan's, slung round his waist a loose silver belt supporting a small dagger in a red velvet sheath. The other little page slung round his neck a long gold chain, which supported a pomander. The Lady Amoureuse approached him, having on the one hand one little boy with a basin and towels, and, on the other, the other page with silver flasks and little silver knives.

"I say," Mr Sorrell protested, for the Lady Amoureuse appeared to him to be of great beauty and obviously high social status, "this doesn't appear to be *your* work." But it appeared all to go by rote.

She knelt on the bottom step before him, and on each side stood one of the little pages. She placed his hands in the silver basin, not without exclaiming rapturously at their whiteness, their smallness considering he was a man, and the delicacy of their shape. She washed them very carefully with a white kind of soap; she poured over them waters that smelt of cummin and mint. And then, selecting the little silver knives, she carefully pared his nails and polished them till they shone like pink pebbles, her fingers holding his with an intense softness.

"And surely," the Lady Amoureuse exclaimed, "it is not such a hand that shall disgust our lady and mistress when it comes into her plate."

"I don't put my hands into other people's plates," Mr Sorrell exclaimed.

"And be very careful," the Lady Amoureuse continued, "that you do not pat upon the head the dogs that lie under the table before you have finished eating, for nothing can be more disgusting to a person of high stomach. This I tell you, for we have seen it done by many very excellent knights coming from Palestine, such as the Sieur Walter de Marney himself, for in other countries they have other customs, but this is our custom here."

And then, taking it from the little Jehan, she placed upon his head a small round cap of red velvet, edged with white fur. Round the cap was a chaplet of the largest pearls that Mr Sorrell had ever seen, and from within, round the hinder sides, there depended a half-circle of long golden curls.

"Oh, I say," Mr Sorrell exclaimed when he had it on, "nobody in the world shall ever make me wear a wig."

The Lady Blanchemain exclaimed with pleasure, but a tender and regretful dismay came over the Lady Amoureuse's features.

"This is the latest fashion of Paris," she said, "to wear the hair very long and curled. And our Lord Enguerrand de Coucy, being always inclined to gallantry and chivalry, wears himself this hair because he is slightly bald."

Mr Sorrell took the cap off and handed it to the little Jehan.

"Just take that hair out," he said, "there's a good nipper."

The Lady Blanchemain smiled. "It is our good lady and mistress that will be pleased with this. She is always against these new and foreign customs, and desires the simple old ways of her father before her. Those curls have been the occasion of much dissension between our lord and our lady."

The Lady Amoureuse took him gently by the hand and led him down the step. And the Lady Blanchemain approached him with her pink and white cheek extended towards him.

"What's the matter now?" Mr Sorrell said, and, little and small and gay, the Lady Blanchemain laughed aloud.

"Why, first you shall kiss me on the cheek as being the less in degree, and then the Lady Amoureuse, and this is the requital of our services for waiting on and attending you."

The Lady Amoureuse, however, would have him kiss her

upon the lips, and indeed she almost swooned in ecstasy at the embrace of this holy stranger, who appeared now like a prince in glory.

"Well, upon my soul," Mr Sorrell said, "these times aren't half as barbarous as I thought."

But then his gaze went over the squalor and filth of the courtyard.

"I can't understand," he said once more, "you are so polite and accomplished in yourselves. How can you put up with such dirt in your surroundings?"

The Lady Amoureuse regarded him with wide and apologetic eyes.

"Oh, holy man," she said, "it would be beyond human strength to imitate the spotless whiteness of the courts of heaven. There there is neither eating nor drinking. Consider that you are amongst the mortal inhabitants of this earth. Not even the palaces of the French King are cleaned more often than once a year, and there the greatest of politeness prevails, such as is not known in any other Court of Christendom."

Her eyes roved round over the courtyard, over heaps of straw and the rushes that had been thrown out from the great hall, over the skins of beasts, the offal, the mud, and the green slime. . . .

"Why," she said, "there is very little disorder here! I would have you see such a courtyard in time of siege. It is a very different sight, with all things thrown pell-mell."

"But the stench!" Mr Sorrell expostulated. "The want of any sanitary arrangements!"

"Oh, holy man," the Lady Amoureuse said, "for the stench it is very little, if anything at all, and you may easily counteract it by holding your pomander to your nose."

The Lady Blanchemain laughed again.

"In the name of the Seven Saints of the Brehon!" she exclaimed, "these things must lie somewhere."

"But what I'm contending," Mr Sorrell said, "is that they ought to lie where you can't see them."

"But if they have to be," the Lady Blanchemain said, "and if we know that they have to be, why should we not see them? There is nothing more disgusting in the sight of the hide of a beast than in the sight of its flesh smoking upon the board, and in this way our forefathers have lived healthy and lusty ever since William the Norman first built castles in this land."

"I suppose you can score that point," Mr Sorrell said. "There's no doubt that in the old days of 'Merrie England' we were much stronger and healthier, whereas we're a degenerate lot nowadays."

"That is very true," the little Jehan said bravely. "I have heard that in the old days there were knights who could fell an ox with a blow of their fist. There are very few that to-day could do that thing."

The sun in setting was sending great shafts of blood-red light over the tower of the keep and the upper walls of the eastern side of the castle, so that everything there appeared to be rosy and beautiful. A bell began to ring, and suddenly all of them fell upon their knees where they stood.

"They certainly do seem to be the most extraordinary set of people," Mr Sorrell said, as he followed their example out of a desire not to seem conspicuous. "You never know what they'll be doing next."

A little time afterwards a number of high, clear calls came from the horn at the head of the tower.

"That will be the Lady Dionissia approaching. In a few minutes the trumpet for washing hands will blow."

"There doesn't," Mr Sorrell observed, "seem to be any end to all this washing."

PART TWO

I

Mr Sorrell had kept the golden cross attached to his little finger by the ring that was on top of it. He could not attach any particular supernatural value to its possession; but he had a very definite feeling that as long as he kept hold of it he was a personage of importance, and, since it fitted on to his finger really very well, he did not intend even to put it in his pocket. For the matter of that, he could not discover any pocket in the close-fitting garment that he wore. He could only suppose that the gentleman who usually went about in these clothes was attended upon by pages, who carried such trifles as his pocket-handkerchief, or whatever it was that he carried instead of these necessaries. It seemed to him besides that this was the proper thing to do, even if he were merely acting in a pageant.

On the other hand, it was certainly his line if the things that he saw going on about him were what you might call authentic. Mr Sorrell disliked putting it to himself that he was back in the Middle Ages. It sounded ridiculous. He was fully prepared to take things exactly as he found them, and to accept the idea that he was back in the fourteenth century if there was no other way out of it, but he was quite determined to leave no stone unturned in the effort to detect any flaw in the proceedings of these people. On the face of it they had appeared perfectly convincing, but he might be able to trip them up in some anachronism. At dinner they might be supplied with artificial lemonade sent down by some caterer from London. Or they might be given New Zealand mutton. He was pretty certain that he would be able to detect the flavour of either of these things. Or he might discover one of the supers smoking a surreptitious pipe behind a battlement; or, since the castle contained such a very high tower as the central watch-tower of the keep, it was possible that there might even be a lift.

At Braby Castle, in Suffolk, where he had once spent a week-end, the Isaac Goldsteins, when they had been making their restorations, had included one of these modern facilities in their architect's design.

He had paused half-way up the interminable, narrow, winding, and very dark staircase up which the little page Jehan was conducting him. He was to have an interview with the Lady Blanche d'Enguerrand de Coucy before the dinner-bell rang. Mr Sorrell wished indeed that he had come upon some traces of a lift. He was leaning against a stone beside the opening of a very narrow window in a very broad wall. He held in his hand the shoe portions of his leg-gear, for he had found it utterly impossible, with those obtrusions before him, to climb the exceedingly narrow triangular steps that wound away up into a very profound darkness. He could not do it, and he was relieved to be informed by the little Jehan that the great lords and knights of that day invariably climbed stairs in what Mr Sorrell would have called their stockinged feet.

The little Jehan indeed informed him that Father Bavo thundered unceasingly from his pulpit in Salisbury against this monstrous fashion of nobles. They were daily becoming more idle, more dissolute, and more extravagant.

The landing upon which Mr Sorrell stayed to recover his breath was dimly lit by its window. It was, however, no more than a slit in the wall, and the whole staircase had a damp, musty, and sepulchral odour which reminded Mr Sorrell of the Twopenny Tube at the time of its opening. The diffused and feeble ray of light fell upon the pleasant form of the little Jehan, who with his candid blue eyes, his golden curls, and his little ragged, furred doublet, stood seriously at attention and gazed at him. Mr Sorrell felt a real liking for this little lad, and asked him pleasantly where he went to school.

He found that when he talked French very slowly and distinctly the little boy understood him. And the little boy had such a fluting and grave voice that he himself had little difficulty in understanding his answers. Jehan answered that the Manage fields were about a bowshot to the west of the castle, and the elder pages did their dismounted exercises with sword and lance in the great hall after the boards were cleared. Mr Sorrell said he did not mean that; he meant the sort of school where you went to learn the three R's and geography and things.

"Ah! sir," the little page said, "we do not have schools for such things, though, without doubt, they are many and excellent in the land from which your pilgrimship comes. But I have been taught by Brother Squerry, so that I can write my name fairly, and can read a passage in the Book of Hours, if

I know beforehand what that passage is. This much I have learned, in order to have benefit of clergy in case I should fall into any crime."

Mr Sorrell laughed so loudly that the sounds echoed up and down the darkness of the stairway.

"You commit a crime!" he said. "Why, I don't believe you'd whip a cat."

"Ah! sir," the page said, "I don't know why I should desire to whip a cat, nor do I know that it would be a crime to do it. But it is my desire to be a great and gallant knight, such as have been written of in the Chronicles and in Holy Writ. A great knight, being a man of hot blood, will sometimes commit crimes against the law, or, by taking arms for one King when another deposes him, he is discovered to be guilty of treason. And this was seen very clearly in the case of our late King, that was put away and murdered with a horn in Berkeley Castle this very year. Many knights and great lords that were of the late King's party have been put to death very cruelly—though without doubt they deserved it—by the Queen Mother of the present King, who is a little boy not much older than I, but much more worshipful. And for those poor dead knights and lords, it would have been very well if they could have pleaded benefit of clergy."

Mr Sorrell laughed again.

"I suppose," he said, "your mother and father know their business best, but it seems a droll way to bring up a child to have such ideas."

"These matters," the little Jehan said gravely, "are above my head. It is for me to do what my parents command and to make no bones about it."

"Why, so it is, sonny," Mr Sorrell said; "but I should think a year or two upon the modern side of a good public school without any classical tomfoolery would be a great deal better for you."

In spite of the dampness and the chill, Mr Sorrell became intolerably warm. He brushed against the rough stones of the wall; he stumbled and hurt his feet against the hard stairs. After an immensely long time, they came into a room which Mr Sorrell, whilst once more he paused to take breath, considered must be a servant's bedroom. There was a large chest at the bottom of the bed, and across the bed itself a great covering of the red fur of foxes.

"This," the little Jehan said, "is my lady's bower."

"Now is it?" Mr Sorrell asked. "I always thought a bower was a summer-house. I suppose your Lady Blanche is going in for an open-air cure, because there's no glass in the windows. The air must be very good up here."

"I do not fully understand what you say," the little Jehan said; "but this is my lady's bower."

"Well, you said that before," Mr Sorrell answered, "and I was only uttering my observations."

When they came to the tiny little stairway that ascended from the room, Mr Sorrell exclaimed:

"I do wish your architect had made some allowance for persons of my figure."

But the little page did not hear him.

.   .   .   .   .   .

The Lady Blanche was leaning out of the battlements, watching the approach of the Lady Dionissia and her train that, very far below, wound slowly along beside the River Wiley.

"It is natural," she grumbled to herself with an air of vexation, "that to-night she comes with more armed men than usual."

She counted carefully, and could perceive the Lady Dionissia in yellow and green, two ladies in scarlet that attended upon her, all these three being upon white horses. And there were two priests and thirteen men-at-arms, as well as five pages that ran beside the horses. This gave the Lady Dionissia eighteen armed retainers as against the Lady Blanche's thirty; but, on the other hand, the Lady Dionissia had ten very able-bodied Welsh pikemen among her men-at-arms. These ten alone, once they were inside, would be sufficient to take the whole castle from the Lady Blanche's retainers, so weakened were these by dysentery and summer coughs. The Lady Dionissia had this good fortune, because these ten Welshmen had been part of the guard that had come down with her in her bridal tour from the Welsh Marches. Without doubt, had her contracted husband Egerton of Tamworth not already set out for the Scotch wars, he would have taken the Lady Dionissia's men to fight under his banner. But as it was, the Lady Dionissia had come a full three weeks too late, having been impeded by the great floods of the River Severn. So that she had never even seen her husband to whom she had been married by proxy already three months. She had in exchange what was at the moment more valuable, these ten able-bodied fighting-men, who were reported to be extraordinarily ferocious and devoted to their mistress.

The Lady Blanche had in her mind a problem of how to retain in her own keeping alike the holy cross of St Joseph of Arimathea and the holy and mysterious personage who had brought it to her. Her first impulse had been to close the castle gates against the Lady Dionissia, and to repel even with arms any attempt that she and her men might make to enter.

But she had to consider the ferocity of her Welsh men-at-arms. They were said to be able to run up precipices, sticking to them like flies. She had, besides, to consider the probable return from the war of her husband and of Egerton of Tamworth. Her husband and his cousin loved each other with the deep love of boon companions. If upon their return they should find their respective castles warring the one upon the other, she would certainly have to face her husband's anger. For that she cared very little, but it had to be further considered that Egerton of Tamworth would probably desire to espouse the quarrel of his wife, the Lady Dionissia.

Her own husband, who was exceedingly hot-headed, would probably take up her own quarrel, if only because he too would desire to retain possession of the golden cross, if not of the holy man. There would thus arise a private war between the two castles. And this would be a very costly and extravagant affair, lasting perhaps for a couple of years. During them, since they would not be able to get any crops in, both combatants would have to have continual recourse to the Jew Goldenhand of Salisbury. Force, therefore, was almost out of the question, though she would dearly have loved to use force, which was more in her character than any kind of guile.

That it should ever occur to her not to attempt to obtain possession of this relic, which was plainly not her own but the property of her cousin of Tamworth, was out of the question. In the hardier old times of which she had heard her grandfather and father speak, and to which she felt herself to belong—in those times she would calmly have killed the bearer of the cross, and have hidden the cross itself in the stones of the wall of her bower for two or three years. But nowadays that sort of thing was growing too troublesome, if not too dangerous, for it would signify endless lawsuits, the expense of which she dreaded almost more than anything in the world. But

[115]

if she could get possession of the cross, she certainly meant to do it.

In the first place, it was of gold, so that it was desirable; in the second place, it was miraculous, so that to possess it would make her very much looked up to throughout the whole of England, or, for the matter of that, throughout the whole of Christendom: and to render herself notorious along economical lines was the chief desire of this lady's life.

With great eagerness, hearing the sound of voices behind her, she turned upon Mr Sorrell. He was putting on his shoes, and the little page Jehan was explaining to him that although getting upstairs was impossible in these garments, descending was perfectly easy. She sent the little page immediately downstairs to wait for them in her bower, and at once she tackled Mr Sorrell.

"It is about this cross," she said. "It is a very valuable and holy cross."

Mr Sorrell replied that he believed that it was both these things, and very ancient to boot.

"Has it not occurred to you," the lady asked, "to think that you might be very easily killed, and the cross stolen from you by robbers?"

"Why, my lady," Mr Sorrell said, "I suppose you have not any robbers knocking about in the castle, and I am quite determined to send it by registered post to Mrs Lee-Egerton as soon as we have done dinner. I suppose there is a post office somewhere near the castle?"

The Lady Blanche said that she did not know what sort of thing a *bureau de poste* was, but she thought that, after having witnessed the way the nuns had attempted to take the cross, the pilgrim would be an exceedingly foolish man to let it out of his possession at all.

"Well, there's something in that," Mr Sorrell said; "but how in the world do you send letters and parcels if you haven't got a post office?"

"My friend," the lady said, "we send letters by trusted messengers if they are of importance, or if they are about trifling matters we send them by means of the chapmen that travel hither and thither selling merchandise. So that if you desire to send the cross to any destination you had better give it to me, and I will send it by a messenger that I can trust better than myself."

"Why, my lady," Mr Sorrell said, "I think I won't send it at all. I'll keep it till I get up to town, and give it to Mrs Egerton myself."

"Then you had better," the Lady Blanche said, "give it into my keeping. I will have one of the stones from the wall of my bower taken out, and I will have a little cavity made behind. I will lay the cross in there, and I will have the stone put back again, and it shall all be done up fair with mortar, so that no one shall know in what place it is."

"Oh, I don't think you need take so much trouble," Mr Sorrell said; "I suppose I shall be moving on this evening."

"This evening!" the Lady Blanche exclaimed highly; "would you adventure yourself with that thing of great price into the mists and perils of the night that is all darkness, and where many robbers abound?"

"Dear lady," Mr Sorrell exclaimed humorously, "I have been very well protected so far, it seems, and I do not know what I have done that this protection should now cease."

"Oh, holy man," the Lady Blanche exclaimed, and her voice had in it a great deal more of reverence, "there must be no talk of your leaving this place. For here you shall stay for a long time, for many months and years. And you shall be treated like a prince, or like the Pope himself if he should come among us."

"But my dear lady," Mr Sorrell argued, "I couldn't possibly stop here more than a day. Let alone that I want to give this up to its owner, hasn't it occurred to you that I've got work to do."

"But oh, holy man," the Lady Blanche said, "if you have angelic work to do, if you desire to spread enlightenment and knowledge, and to do such things as befit the holy, where could you do it better than here? This is a very evil place, and one where many stiff-necked and ignorant people much need teaching how to behave themselves in this world?"

The Lady Blanche was making in her mind a rapid calculation as to what was the value of the golden cross, whether as money or as a social asset.

"Oh, holy man," she exclaimed, "if you will stay here you shall have a bower tricked out like the bower of the King of France. And assuredly, here you shall fare much better than you should with my cousin's half-wife. Never at dinner shall there be fewer courses than four, each course of fourteen dishes; and never at supper less than three courses, each of nine dishes; and the least of your drinks shall be mead and nearly always the best wine from Romney and Bordeaux. You shall have such garments as my lord wears, and four horses to ride abroad on; and you shall have hawks from Norway and of everything the best, such as my cousin's half-wife could not possibly afford. And has she in her castle a bath, such as to-day you have tasted the merits of?"

"It's a most excellent bath," Mr Sorrell said, "and I don't in the least doubt your splendid hospitality, but I can't possibly stay here. It's out of the question."

"Then if you cannot yourself stay," the Lady Blanche said,

"leave at least your cross here in safe keeping, for it must be obvious to you that I, who am the Lord of Egerton's cousin and not his foolish and frivolous half-wife, am the proper keeper of the sacred emblem."

"I'm really not going, you know," Mr Sorrell said with the most bland obstinacy in the world, "to give the cross up to anybody but Mrs Egerton. I'm perfectly able to take care of it myself, and I'm just going to keep it hanging from my finger until the proper time comes."

"Then you are not afraid," the Lady Blanche said, "that I shall slay you and keep the cross for myself?"

Mr Sorrell answered amiably that people didn't do that sort of thing nowadays. "Besides," and he smiled as at a hidden witticism, "the protection that I spoke of will operate just as freely now as it has hitherto."

She recognised the appropriateness of this contention. There seemed to remain nothing for it but an appeal to the reasonableness of her cousin's half-wife, and from her she anticipated very little reasonableness at all. The Lady Dionissia was young, of great levity, and of the most headstrong obstinacy, so that hitherto she had accepted none of the Lady Blanche's suggestions, though the Lady Blanche, as the cousin of her husband by proxy, stood surely in the position of a feudal overlord to a ward. And neglecting to talk any longer to Mr Sorrell, the Lady Blanche remained plunged in a fit of abstraction.

On his part Mr Sorrell had new food for reflection. The dark earnestness of the Lady Blanche seemed to him to remove at once all idea that she was playing a part; no actress could possibly have kept it up so well. And although she had submitted him to nothing but a personal gentleness, he could not help thinking that his cross, if not his person, was in very exceptional peril.

And suddenly he felt himself rather alone and rather lonely in this immense place. It spread its grim walls far below and far around him, filled with unfamiliar men, speaking an unfamiliar tongue, the servants of this woman with the ferocious eyes and the hard voice. Mr Sorrell was a man so modern that he could not get it into him to feel any sense of physical danger: he felt rather as he had felt on several occasions, when in rather questionable company, that he might be about to become the victim of some exceedingly skilful pocket-picking. But he did not see how, if he kept the ring carefully all the time upon his finger, they were going to get the cross out of his possession without offering him physical violence.

And to his moment of vague fear there succeeded a sort of elated amusement. After all, if they wanted to get the cross, they could not possibly get it off his finger without his consent during the day time, and at night he was quite capable of putting a chest of drawers or something of the sort in front of his bedroom door.

A great many sounds of trumpets came from the castle below to proclaim that supper was about to be set on the boards. The sun was just down below the hills, for at that harvest time of the year, when all men and women were wont to be in the fields helping to get in the oat crop and the last of the hay, supper, which was usually at four, was not partaken of till after sunset.

It was not really dark, but blue shadows had fallen all over the long valley of the Wiley, mists were arising amongst the heavy foliage of the trees. The castle of Tamworth, farther down the valley, showed enormous and purple, as if it blocked up all the passage way, and the houses of the little town of

Wishford, which was beyond the bridge, being visible from that high place, showed their white mud sides all pink in the light reflected from the sky. From the top of the Portmanmote Hall, the gilded effigy of the Dragon of Wiley turned slowly in the capricious air of the evening, sending forth now a stream of light, and again being obscured. The cavalcade of the Lady Dionissia had reached the foot of the green knoll, and her trumpeter blew a turn of notes to demand admission to the castle of Coucy.

"So that you are determined," the Lady Blanche said at last, "neither to stay here, nor to leave here the cross that you have brought?"

"My lady," Mr Sorrell answered, "this demands a great deal of attention. If this really is England of the year 1327, it is quite obvious that I can't behave exactly as if it were 600 years later. But upon the whole, the lines of my action must be pretty well the same. If I cannot put the cross into the hands of Mrs. Lee-Egerton, I certainly ought to keep it until I can put into the hands of some Egerton of Tamworth."

"But you will not give it to the Lady Dionissia?" the Lady Blanche said eagerly.

"I think," Mr Sorrell answered, "that I probably shall not until all parties together are agreed as to whom I should confide it to."

He considered once more, and then he continued:

"Of course, it's a nuisance to have to carry this thing about with me, and I shouldn't in the least object to getting rid of it. For there's nothing in the world I hate so much as family quarrels; what we've all got to do is to kiss and make friends, and toss up, heads or tails."

He paused, and again he spoke quickly:

"Now, there's the very idea," he said; "why don't you toss

up about it, you and the other lady, as to who shall have its custody until the gentlemen of Tamworth Castle come back?"

The Lady Blanche looked at him with wide and serious eyes.

"I do not very well understand you," she said. "What is it you would have me do?"

"Oh, you take a penny," Mr Sorrell said, "a 10-centime piece, or a 5-franc one."

"I don't know what any of these things are," the Lady Blanche said.

"Oh, hang it all!" Mr Sorrell exclaimed; "then play a game of cards."

"I do not know what that game is," the Lady Blanche said.

"Well, what *do* you know?" Mr Sorrell asked. "You must have a precious dull time of it in the evenings. Don't you play bridge, or chess? Oh, hang it all! what's an old-fashioned game? Well, now, what is it, cribbage, my old aunt plays? or draughts. Don't you know *le jeu de dames*?"

"Assuredly I know the *jeu de dames*," the Lady Blanche said; "but what would you have me do?"

"Oh, why," Mr Sorrell said, "play the best out of five games, and the winner to have the custody of the cross."

"That I never would do," the Lady Blanche exclaimed; "for my cousin's half-wife is a much better player than I, and assuredly she would win!"

"Well," Mr Sorrell said, "you must think of something of the sort for yourself—something that you are fairly equal in, and let the winner be the winner in a proper and sportsmanlike manner."

The Lady Blanche's eyes became full of a smouldering fire, she broadened her broad chest, and erected her fierce head.

"Now indeed I see that you are a very holy man," she said, "and if you will kiss me, you may kiss me."

"But," Mr Sorrell exclaimed, "is that a proper thing to do? What about your husband?"

"In the first place," she answered, "it is a very proper thing to do, for it is the custom of this country, though I have heard it is not so in other lands, not even in the country of France. But it is obvious that a reward for favours should be paid, and this is a reward of a trifling kind for favours very great. And it is also obvious that upon making an acquaintance which is likely to become a dear friendship, some seal should be set upon the bond. But of these things I will let my old jongleur sing to you of an evening, so that you may become acquainted with the knightly customs of our country of England. And for my husband, he is away at the wars. If he were here, I do not think it is he that would grumble if you courteously saluted his wife; and if he did, you might very rightly put on your steel cap and take your sword and go at him, as he at you. For it would be a great discourtesy of him. But since he is not here, and I have not been kissed by a proper man these three months—or since the Knight of Steeple Langford rode by on his way to Barnstaple—I am not minded at all to consider my husband in the matter."

And suddenly she cast herself into Mr Sorrell's arms, and began to kiss him hotly on the lips.

"Holy man," she whispered, "I do this that you may not have a mistaken view of my character. All day long you have seen me acting in a high, haughty, and militant fashion, and you will have heard that I have frequent dissensions with my husband, and that with ferocious determination I must set my peasants to do their work. But all these things are necessities forced upon me by the hard nature of my life, and actually I am such a tender woman and as well fitted for the gentle sports of love as ever was the Countess Helen, for whom great battles were fought in past times. Nay, I am as patient as Grisel of the Balance, who had in truth not more need for patience than myself."

Mr Sorrell felt himself in an exceedingly awkward and somewhat ridiculous situation. He had a feeling that he had his arms round an exceedingly savage tiger, whom, on the one hand, he might enrage if he were not warm enough. On the other hand, he might enrage her still further by going too far, and he wished to heaven he could come across some man who could give him a hint or two as to how to behave upon such occasions, which, as far as he could see, appeared likely to crop up every ten minutes or so.

The Lady Blanche exclaimed:

"Press me close to you, and say that you do not believe I am a sharp-toothed wolf."

She was very warm and smelt of musk, and Mr Sorrell half sighed, and exclaimed:

"Oh, well ——!"

And after a minute he asked, as if the time for tender confidences had approached:

"Now, tell me really, really the truth. Is this a pageant, or is it the year of grace 1327?"

"As surely as that lark sings in the sky," the Lady Blanche answered, "so surely it is that year and no other."

High in the air above them a lark was sending down high thrills of song, its little breast illuminated by the light of the upper air.

"Well, *that* is not an anachronism," Mr Sorrell said resignedly; "and anyhow, I suppose I must believe that you aren't kidding me. For the life of me, I don't know what is an anachronism in these days, and what isn't. You may have cannon or you mayn't, and you may have eau de Cologne, and you mayn't. I'd no idea I was so ignorant; but I am, and it puts me into your hands—I'm entirely in your hands."

She disengaged herself slowly and regretfully from his arms, and she gazed at him with a level and devouring glance.

"Oh, pilgrim," she said, "yes, you are entirely in my hands; and of this you may be very certain, that I shall never let you go till you or I are dead. It is all very well to put it to the test of a game. But, if I win the game, I will keep you and the cross, and no one shall gainsay me; and, if I lose it, I will keep you and it by force or by fraud. I have some stores of gold unknown of by my husband or any man, for that is fit and proper in these idle and extravagant days. Your captivity shall be a very sweet one, since you shall be more splendid than all the men around. But by this you shall know that never with your cross shall you leave this place till you or I be dead."

Mr Sorrell said: "I can't go in for that sort of game, you know. If this is really the fourteenth century, I daresay I could put you up to some uses for your money that could pretty well do anything for you. I believe I could make you Empress of the World."

And suddenly at the prospect he became enthusiastic.

"Why, good Lord," he said, "if it's the fourteenth century I can do anything. Just think of the things I can invent! Why, we can begin right bang off with aeroplanes. There's no need to go through any intermediary stages. How would you like to go flying through the air, my lady? I've done it, and there's no reason why you shouldn't. Why, we can terrorise every city in the world. We could burn Paris down in a night. They couldn't do anything—anything at all."

The Lady Blanche looked at him, with her broad nostrils

quivering and her eyes alight with the contagion of enthusiasm.

"That is how I would have men speak to me," she said; "that is how I would have my lovers speak to me. And if you will make me Empress of the World, surely you shall be my Emperor."

Mr Sorrell exclaimed: "You've really got to remember you've got a husband. I've always found—all history shows it, too—that if you've got a big thing on hand you've got to behave respectably. You've got to make large masses of men obey you, and you can't ensure obedience if you have scandals. It simply can't be done."

"As for my husband," the Lady Blanche exclaimed, "we will kill him in the night. I will make him sleep heavily with very much wine, and you shall stab him while he sleeps. That was done by the Lady of Mormand. And you will make me an Empress! You will make me an Empress! You are a very great magician. I knew it the moment I set eyes on you."

"Oh, I'm a very great magician," Mr Sorrell said; "but you aren't going to get me into that sort of game. It can't pay! You've got to behave respectably if you go in for a deal with me. It's always been my first business principle."

The trumpet blew three times to show that the meats of the first course were coming from the kitchen, and the Lady Blanche gave Mr Sorrell her hand, that he might lead her down the staircase. In the thick darkness she kissed him three times, exclaiming:

"My magician! my magician!" and several other things that seriously discomposed Mr Sorrell.

It left him in a very angry and discomposed frame of mind. His brain was commencing to boil with plans for exploiting the fourteenth century. There were so many things to do that he did not know where to begin to think about it, and he did not want to have any red herrings drawn across a trail that, he felt confident, would lead him to an unheard-of glory. He would have a fleet of airships hovering over the Channel within three months' time, and he did not see who in the world was going to stand against him.

2

THE LADY DIONISSIA DE EGERTON DE TAMWORTH WAS THE
eleventh daughter of Henry de Mabuse, Earl of Morant. The
earls of Morant had been great and independent noblemen in
the days of Henry III, but the accession of the third Edward
found them somewhat impoverished, owing to a succession of
heavy fines which had been incurred by the Lady Dionissia's
father. The Earl had been of the Queen Isabella's party before
her flight from the Court of Edward II to France. Thus no
sooner had the Queen been gone than the Earl had been fined
no less than a sum of six thousand pounds at the instance of the
De Spensers. This fine had converted him into a strong supporter of Edward II. So that, upon the return of the Queen
with a small handful of men from Hainault, the Earl, dreading
further fines from the King, and regarding the Queen's exploit as foolish and foolhardy—the Earl had hastened with all
his men into the south to oppose her coming.

He failed to find the Queen. But when she had succeeded

in deposing and murdering her husband, she fined the Earl another seven thousand pounds. These successive fines, which would have amounted to about one hundred and eighty-two thousand pounds in the currency of Mr Sorrell's date, were not sufficient entirely to ruin the Earl, but they made him unreasonably anxious to marry off his daughters, of whom he had thirteen. He desired to marry them off, not only in order to avoid the expense of maintaining them, but in order to contract alliances with noble families so that he might once more become the head of a powerful faction in the country and get his fingers round the national purse-strings.

The matches which he made were mostly in the West of England and along the Welsh border where his own lands lay. And amongst the families of the West of England few were more powerful than that of the Egertons of Tamworth, of Creswell, and of Bedington—three castles each of prime strength. It is true that the marriage which he made for his daughter Dionissia was with Sir Stanley Egerton, a younger son. But Sir John, the elder, was away in Palestine, and was reported to be so ill with poisons and wounds that he could hardly come home. And, indeed, the Lady Dionissia, attended by her ten savage Welsh men-at-arms, had not been set out three days upon her journey to Tamworth before the news reached the Earl that the Crusader had died at Sandwich. In the ordinary course, the Earl would have been too proud to let his daughter make a marriage of the sort that was known as de Changellerie, and prevailed much amongst the knights of the West of England and the Welsh Marches.

But the younger Knight of Tamworth was accounted for his deeds of arms so very famous throughout chivalry, and appeared so certain in those modern and degenerate days to become one of the most powerful knights in England, that the

Earl, after protracted bargaining, had consented to the proposition. The young knight had done extraordinarily well in tournaments, having sent his cartels to the Courts, not only of Spain, but of France and the Roman Emperor. In his conflicts he had been uniformly successful, and he had gained great renown by fighting in Spain against the heathens. The Earl of Morant being of the old school, which included the Lady Blanche, regarded these exploits with a certain amount of contempt, as being on the one hand modern, and on the other hand rather unprofitable trickery. They did not pay and they cost a great deal of money, bringing in very little more than fame and no land worth speaking of. The Earl of Morant's idea was to get hold of land by force, to occupy it, and to sit down over many miles of territory until the King, for the time being, was in sufficiently low water to ratify the conquest. This, of course, was the frame of mind of a nobleman whose family had for long been established on the Welsh or Scotch borders. It was already, as the Earl recognised, a little antiquated for the Marches. It had become antiquated as soon as Edward I had seized all Wales. There was not any land within a hundred miles of the Earl that had not been granted, upon the conferring of the Princedom of Wales on the late king, to English knights whose land it was altogether too difficult a matter to appropriate.

Thus, although the Earl was an old-fashioned man, he realised that the days of forays and raids were over in his part of the country. It was difficult for him to move with the times, since he had never been able, try as he would, to master the elementary details of modern tournaments and single combats, but he was quite determined to choose as his sons-in-law men who were as entirely up-to-date as it was possible to find. Pure Norman in his blood, the Earl had a great deal of shrewdness. Indeed, the first of his family to come to England had been an excellent lawyer, who had arrived when things were settling down after the Conquest, and had gained his advancement very much more as an administrator than by means of his sword. Thus the Earl recognised that even a marriage de Changellerie with so eminent and modern a personage as the younger Knight of Egerton would be very well worth having. According to that Western custom, which prevailed perhaps more in Scotland than in England, a wife was married for one year, during which she enjoyed all the privileges of the married state. At the end of that time, if in her mind and body she satisfied the necessities of her husband, the marriage became permanent—or if she bore him a child. If it was not so she returned to her guardians with her honour untouched, except in so far as it was affected by failure in the undertaking. And with her there came back from one-half to two-thirds of her dowry, this being a matter of bargaining. The Earl felt, however, fairly sure that this transaction would turn out very well. His daughter was perfectly healthy, and so, he had ascertained, was the Knight of Tamworth. So that he had very little doubt that a child would result from the union. The parties' predilections or aversions to or from one another would have very little to do with the matter. As to his daughter's dowry, which was one thousand pounds in gold and some parcels of land, which the Earl happened to have in Gloucestershire—in that respect too he felt fairly confident, for he would find means to delay paying it over until the marriage was finally ratified.

The Lady Dionissia, who thus set out, was at that time nineteen years of age. She was tall, large-limbed, and of an exceeding and most unusual fairness. Her features were oval and aquiline, but she had at the same time so abstracted and reflective an expression that all the harshness of their aquilinity seemed to be tempered and done away with. It was always very difficult to get at what she thought, for she spoke extremely little, being immersed in frequent and very long daydreams, which would fall upon her in the midst of the gayest of companies. Her ten sisters regarded her as being slightly mad; for, when it came to action, her actions were of singular abruptness, and of some inscrutability as to what caused them. And since she was of extreme physical strength, though she was the youngest but two of them, she was allowed to go her own way.

Their castle, which was about twenty miles towards Wales from the city of Chester, was remote and solitary, but it contained so large a number of squires, retaining knights, men-at-arms, and other dependants, that they sat down usually 300 to table, with one man or page to wait upon every three of them. And jongleurs and minstrel knights and ballad-singers in great numbers travelled that way, for the Earl was notedly liberal in his rewards, and the daughters were reputed beautiful and kind, so that the castle had of late years been nicknamed "The Maidens' Hold." It was accounted fashionable to pass that way, and there spend a night or two.

Thus the Lady Dionissia was as well acquainted with the gossip of the day and with the high feats of chivalry as was any lady of Salisbury or the other metropolitan cities where the tournaments were then held. And her mind had roamed over great expanses of the world. She heard them described with their strange trees, flowers that devoured wanderers, apes, dragons, parrots, and porcupines that discharged their quills like arrows and sands of the desert so heated that their fire melted at noon-time the armour of men and horses—yet she could not in her mind picture them as otherwise than resembling the dark blue distances that she had seen from the tops of her craggy Welsh mountains, with their deep ravines, their swiftly descending streams, and their endless rain-clouds. Travelling southwards, she had come by way of Upton over the Severn and to Worcester, and so by way of Devizes down over the great Plain.

She had seen walled towns and great abbeys and minsters, and she had become acquainted with strange tongues. Norman-French was her own language, for she was of Norman blood on both sides, and of English she had very little, for upon the Welsh border the poor spoke Red Welsh alone, and that was a language not easy to learn, and not worth the learning. Still, in English she could make herself understood, and could understand most things, English being the language of daily matters, such as the washing of linen or the slaughtering of beasts.

Arriving at Tamworth, she had found herself in command of a castle a little larger than her father's, spreading abroad over a fertile champaign country, with the low hills of the bare Plain all around it. This delighted her eye and pleased her sense of command, so that she had no impatience because her husband by proxy was away at the wars. It pleased her, indeed, to be able to settle down before he should arrive there. The Lady Blanche she had found very much inclined to rule within the domains of Tamworth, but the Lady Dionissia, without contradicting her cousin when she was present, exactly countermanded each of her orders as soon as she rode away. For the sake of safety, when they heard that Hugh of FitzGreville, the outlaw, was anywhere within twenty miles of them overnight with his band that infested the Plain, they slept in each other's castles together for two or three nights on end. This they did for greater safety, so as to join their bands of ancient armed men. For, although it was unusual, it was not at all an unheard-of thing that outlaws should take a kernelled castle in the night-time, sacking the place, and carrying off to hold for ransom such women as seemed worth the trouble. Whereas, joined together in one strong place, the two ladies would be very well able to hold it against Hugh of FitzGreville, whose band did not number very much more than forty men, roughly armed—for the most part with clubs.

It was their custom to set forth a little before sundown with all their men and all the furnishings of the castle, which were no great matter, and could be carried upon mules. The unoccupied castle would be left quite empty, except for ploughs and such implements as could be of little value to the outlaw, whilst the castle itself would be too strong and too stony for Hugh to do it much damage. Besides, why should he desire to damage it, which would be a strenuous and very difficult enterprise, at which he could gain nothing at all?

Thus they passed some agreeable days together, playing draughts and walking in the gardens after supper, and going a-hawking or shooting with bows, and listening to stories during the day-time. It could not be said that the Lady Blanche did anything more than heartily dislike the Lady Dionissia, or that the Lady Dionissia did anything more than good-naturedly ignore the Lady Blanche, whom she regarded as a disagreeable person. But, on the other hand, their attendant ladies met and mingled and laughed and were good sisters, and their young pages strove in a very friendly manner with each other at running races, jousting at the ring, or casting quoits. So that there was generally laughter to be heard and little tittering over small secrets, and in that way much pleasure in the air, though it would have been better had there been also able-bodied men of good birth and gentle courtesy.

The peasants of their respective domains grumbled a little

when their ladies were absent, for thus they lost their natural protectors. But it had to be remembered that these peasants were so extremely poor that they had nothing whatever for the outlaws to take away except now and then a beast or a sheep for food, or a daughter for their recreation, or a son that they would train up to be an outlaw. And, as all the world knows, it is the will of God that a peasant should lose an occasional beast, sheep, daughter, or son, though at such times as the lord of the domain was at home and had with him a strong force, he would frequently revenge the wrongs of his subjects. Thus before the Knights of Egerton and de Coucy had gone away to Scotland, they had made a drive of all the outlaws that they could catch in the Plain, Egerton hanging eighteen, and de Coucy twenty-five, whose bodies might still be seen decorating gallows and oak trees all round the hills of the valley. And this was to be held as a very high and knightly kindness shown by these lords to their dependants.

．　．　．　．　．　．　．

There were at the high table on the daïs at supper six ladies —the Lady Blanche and her two attendants, and the Lady Dionissia and her two, who were named Amarylle and Cunigunde. These ladies who had come with the Lady Dionissia were of very high English families from the neighbourhood of Chester, the one being called of Rolls, and the other of Birken, both being descended from great English earls that were before the Conquest. Of men there were Mr Sorrell, who sat beside the Lady Blanche; the Dean of Salisbury, who ate out of the same plate as the Lady Dionissia, and was a fat man of about perhaps forty. He had come to Tamworth to get some hawking and for change of air, he having been ill of a surfeit. This was his general custom when he found that he was growing overbearing to the chapter. For he was normally

a man of a good-natured and chuckling disposition, beloved
by such of his inferior clergy as were submissive in habit; yet
at times, fits of anger would visit him, and there would arise
great quarrels or troubles among his officers.

At such seasons it had become his habit to go for diversion
rather to the Castle of Tamworth, where they made him welcome, than to his own country house which was above
Winterbourne Gunner, on the windy plain. The Dean loved
a good hawk and a good hound, and had many of these. He
would make presents of these to kings and to such people as
could be of service to the Deanery of Salisbury. These hounds
and hawks he would have set in motion before him upon wide
expanses of open country, so that he could see them well. But
the Dean himself had never been seen either to ride hawking
or to the chase. He did not enjoin this abstention upon his inferior clergy, but he considered that it made his office more
dignified if he were not seen to do these things; though occasionally when they were alone he would force his chaplain to
ride a race with him.

His chaplain, a very bald, lean old man, had been one of the
Regulars, a Canon of the Order of St Dominic. But having
made a pilgrimage to the Holy Land in the fiftieth year of his
age, and having borne a double-headed mace and chain mail
in a fight against the Saracens, this Father Giraldus had lost all
taste for the confined life of a priory. So, at the intervention
of the Dean, who loved him for the good and holy stories of
travel, miracle, and feats of arms that he could tell, he had
been absolved of his Monastic Vows and had become the chaplain to the Dean. This Father Giraldus sat between the Ladies
Amarylle and Amoureuse to the right. The Ladies Blanchemain and Cunigunde, who were upon the left, had no man
to them at all. They grumbled that the Lady Blanche might

just as well have set the holy pilgrim on their side of her so that they might have some share in the conversation, instead of between herself and the Lady Dionissia, who had the Dean for her own comfort. There were thus but three men, two of whom were priests, against six ladies, all of them young, lively, handsome, and clean. They were served by the four eldest pages, who stood on the other side of the table and carved before them. Two of these were the Lady Blanche's, and one the Lady Dionissia's. He was called Gilleblois, and he was very dark and mischievous. The fourth page was the Dean's, a red-headed boy of sixteen, who was soon to be made a squire of the Chapter's Military Knights, and would in turn become one of the knights whom the Chapter kept to do service when the king demanded it. In twenty minutes he had become exceedingly enamoured of the Lady Amoureuse, she being seven years his senior, and he carved for her all the best bits of the meats, so that the Lady Amarylle protested laughingly from time to time.

The little Jehan carved very carefully, kneeling upon one knee and putting only the first two fingers and the thumb of his left hand upon the meat that he carved. But his fellow page of the Lady Blanche's was too little to kneel, and the other two pages had not been bred in this custom, so that they could not do it, though the Lady Dionissia and the Dean chided them majestically from time to time, and held up to their admiration the little Jehan, who was indeed the perfection of pages. There was thus a great deal of laughter at the table, for all these people had different habits, the Churchmen being Churchmen, the pilgrim being from Constantinople, three of the ladies from Wales, and three from the southwest of England.

Being upon the Lady Blanche's right hand, Mr Sorrell had

his own right, from which the cross dangled, towards the Lady Dionissia. The Dean and his chaplain upon their entry both lightly kissed this sacred emblem but no mention was made of it at all, whilst they ate.

The first course consisted of fourteen dishes, the dishes themselves being mostly turned wood, though one was of gold and two of silver. The golden dish held a gilt structure of pastry, shaped like a castle. From this the Dean, Mr Sorrell and the two ladies were first plenteously served, having only two plates of silver between the four of them. But such a taste as distinguished the fragments of meat, and force-meat balls that came out of this gilt erection, Mr Sorrell could never have imagined. Encouraged by the Lady Blanche—and, indeed, he was so hungry as to need little encouragement—Mr Sorrell took with his fingers a piece of dark-looking meat. It was sweet, it was salt, it tasted overpoweringly of nutmegs and of cinnamon, and it was of the consistency of soft jelly.

Mr Sorrell exclaimed: "Oh, my God!" and drank quickly from a cup of silver. But even the wine was spiced with cloves. He ate a piece of very coarse bread, and then he hesitated. The Lady Blanche was so occupied with observing how much meat was served out at the lower tables, and how much metheglin poured into the leather cups—for she was of opinion that there was a mighty waste in the cellar, the kitchens, and the pantries—she was so much occupied with indignantly observing these things, that she did not perceive that Mr Sorrell of the first course ate little or nothing at all. But then she gently chided him. Mr Sorrell replied that he was used to something much simpler, something old-fashioned like a sirloin of beef or a loin chop, something really old English. The Lady Blanche said that, of course, as an Anchorite or a holy man, Mr Sorrell must have fared very simply. But his travels were at an end, and he might very well pay more attention to the pleasures of the table. The first dish of the first course was, she said, very excellent, being compounded of the tongues of rabbits, hedgehogs, deer, geese, and wild boars, together with the breasts of partridges and the livers of pheasants. It contained, moreover, force-meat balls made of honey, cinnamon, and flour boiled in wine, and the sauce was made likewise of honey, nutmegs, cloves, garlic, and mint. All these things had been stewed together so that there could not be found anywhere a dish more savoury.

But Mr Sorrell still said that as a foreigner and a new man he desired something less costly and more simple. Thus, for the next dish the Lady Blanche must be content to share with him a panade of herring boiled in white wine whey and covered with a sweet sauce compounded out of cherries. This appeared to the Lady Blanche to be unreasonably homely and tasteless fare, so that she regretted almost having shared her platter with the holy man. Mr Sorrell, on the other hand, could not get his mouth to receive more than one taste of what, since he did not know its contents, he regarded as a mixture of strawberry jam and oysters. But he was very hungry indeed. Of the first course he managed to eat some of the breast of a bird which had been pickled in fermented honey, and was laid over with a paste of almonds and cheese. And he regarded with envy the hinds of the lowest part of the low table, who were gnawing half-cooked flesh from great bones. He indicated this to the Lady Blanche. She said:

"Holy man, in the days of our great-grandfathers and our great-grandmothers, when life was very active and forays and strifes abounded, it was very well for men to eat such dull food. For their minds were very full of other things. But in these degenerate days, when all life is dullness, we must have our foods highly spiced and seasoned according to the precepts and the science of cookery."

The pages carried away the plates and emptied them into a great tub with two handles which served for the broken meat of the poor waiting outside the castle gates. This was done to the sound of trumpets. Whilst the second course was being brought, a man came in with a bear that danced in the sort of horseshoe formed by the two tables along the wall and the small table on the daïs. This man had with him, a girl, who danced upon her hands with her feet in the air, and shouted answers in this posture to the exclamations that were shouted to her from the tables. The talk at the high table was, for a time, mostly of journeying to the Holy Land, and of the places that one passed on the way, and of the perils from the pirate ships of the Saracens, whom with difficulty the ships of the Emperor of Byzantium chased off from galleys bearing pilgrims. This conversation was mostly monopolised by the chaplain of the Dean. Bald, lean, and old, and with fiery eyes, this Brother Ording had the voice of Stentor. He could make himself heard above all the din of the hall, and he told them of many strange things that happened in the Adriatic, and of what churches in the town had pictures and of which were kept in a slovenly way, and of the sloth of the Greek monks and of the miraculous islands of Greece and the strange things that happened there. Thus near Corfu there was a small island whose inhabitants were protected by St Nicocias. So efficient was the miraculous protection of this saint, who decreed that no stolen thing could be taken from the island, that once when pirates landed there and slew a sheep and devoured it, contrary to the habits of pirates, they vomited forth all that they had eaten. This was known to all men of these parts. And the Brother Ording appealed to the pilgrim for confirmation of these things. But in the din of all these people—for with the servers and the occupants of the lower table there must have been ninety of them, of whom by far the larger part were below the great pewter salt-cellars—with all this din of knives, teeth, crying out for more wine, more ale, and more metheglin, Mr Sorrell was unable either to hear or to make himself heard. Mr Sorrell mentioned this to the Lady Blanche. She spoke at once to a man who stood below the table armed with a long stick like a hop pole. Immediately he ran down the tables striking with his stick here and there at hands and heads, upsetting drinking vessels and sending platters of meat skimming on to the rushes. Then their contents were devoured by the many and large dogs that lay beneath all the tables.

The deep silence was now broken only by the deep grunts of the bear, the panting of the girl who danced on her hands, the low shrill sounds of the bearward's pipe, and the light crackle of the torches of pinewood that, stuck into iron rings on the stone walls, were beginning to be lit, for it was growing dusk. The Dean, who was leaning back in the chair with his hands clasped across his stomach, was amiably remonstrating with the Lady Dionissia for riding so large, fierce, young, and half-trained a destrier. He had remonstrated for a long time. This beast might not only be of danger to the valuable life of the lady herself; it might very seriously put in jeopardy the limbs of those who rode with her, as well as the lives of the beasts they rode on. This destrier was being trained for the use of the Knight Egerton her husband, so that it would attack his enemies like a fury with teeth and with hoofs. But it was but a half-trained thing. How could they tell that it might not one day mistake her friends for her enemies and, getting out of hold, worry them in the terrible manner that stallions have? Such animals, he said, were fit only for male control. This beast was as large as an elephant and as cruel and treacherous as a tiger, having slain in its stall already two men. And the Dean appealed to Mr Sorrell as to whether fierce horses were fit to be ridden by gentle women.

The Lady Dionissia turned her deep and bewildered glance upon Mr Sorrell. For the first time he really saw her curiously fair features, and the run of her limbs beneath her dress, which was of scarlet velvet with white sleeves laced with silver cord. The forehead cloth of white lawn, which beneath her steeple hat of red velvet and gold descended over her forehead, was edged also with silver wire. That, being heavy, had held the forehead cloth down, so that hitherto it had hidden her face from his sight. She looked at him for a long time, and he could not find any words in which to reply to the Dean. For the effort to be comprehensible to these people was tiring to him, and he always felt a difficulty in speaking foreign languages when he was at all fatigued. Suddenly the Lady Dionissia spoke in a very deep and abstracted voice, as if she was coming up out of a dream:

"Why, I am as good as any man," she said, "and I do not know what fear is."

"That is very well," the Dean replied; "but there are things that are the province of men, and things that are the province of women."

"Assuredly," the Lady Blanche exclaimed, "you shall not ride my cousin's charger, lest, running away and being impaled upon a post or stave, it should be imperilled in its life or even killed."

The Lady Dionissia continued to gaze into Mr Sorrell's eyes. Mr Sorrell was trying to think how he should say that of course there were limits, but for his part he had always thought that in the hunting-field a woman with a perfect seat was a better rider than the best of men. He himself was pretty keen over the hurdles, but in the mid-Shropshire, which was a pretty stiffish country, there had been a Mrs Nicholls who could give him a lead all the time. And in his travels he had ridden pretty well any kind of horse you could find, no matter how tough a customer it was.

But whilst these thoughts went through his mind, Mr Sorrell continued gazing back at the Lady Dionissia as if the sight of her had struck him with a disease of muteness.

The four pages were walking up between the tables with towels, basins, and ewers, so that the suppers at the high table might wash their hands between the courses. The servers behind them were marching with their dishes held on high over their heads; the two trumpeters at the door had their horns to their lips all ready to blow as soon as the dishes were set upon the table. And suddenly from amongst the poor who were waiting for the broken meat outside, there rose a shrill clamour like many shrieks of surprise and joy. There ran into the hall a brown-grey object, filthy and hideous, leaping up in the rushes so that it resembled the bear itself, and having upon its elbows and its knees two pairs of clogs such as women wear out of doors in wet weather.

Mr Sorrell exclaimed:

"Good God, the beggar!" and the beggar, rushing between the bear and the dancing girl, threw himself under the high table and began to kiss Mr Sorrell's feet. This filled Mr Sorrell with disgust and repulsion. But from the lower part of the hall they began to cry out that the beggar had been miraculously cured, because he had been the first to welcome the holy cross to that place. The Dean stood up in his place, and so did the chaplain, who in a stentorian voice ejaculated:

"*Te Deum laudamus!*"

And then, whilst everyone stood still in confusion, the pages in their places, the servers in theirs, and all men held their breaths or chatted to their neighbours, a man in a clerk's dress of black with furred edges, and with an ink-horn slung from his chest, rushed into the disordered hall, almost unnoticed, and fell on his knees before the Dean.

"Hugh of FitzGreville," the Lady Dionissia exclaimed deeply, "is laying siege to my Castle of Tamworth."

In a very misty half light, caused by a small moon shining down through vapours arising from the River Wiley, the
black shapes of men to the number of thirty or forty were
moving in front of the black walls of the Castle of Tamworth.
They were carrying bundles of faggot wood and parcels of
thatch, which they had torn from the roof a hunt that was
not very far distant. They were piling these in front of the
great gate of the castle. Others were hauling up from beside
the pale stream the huge trunk of an elm tree. It had been
blown down a fortnight before in the high wind, and now,
lopped of its top branches, lay there awaiting a convenient
season for carting.

They worked for the most part in silence, for these outlaws were very barbarous men who had hardly any words to
utter at all. They were armed with clubs, though two or three
had bows, and Hugh of FitzGreville himself had a double-
handed sword, a cap of steel, and two daggers. With the fag-

gots and thatch they intended to make a fire before the great gate so as to weaken it, and with the trunk of a tree they were going to make a battering-ram, supporting it two and two on either side with ropes of ox-hide. They worked industriously and with haste, and when they had dragged the tree trunk so that its butt end was within a few feet of the gate, they set fire to the mass of combustibles that there lay heaped up. It smouldered and sent out a great deal of smoke. And then, so that they might have more light to work by, Hugh of Fitz-Greville commanded them to set light to the hut from which they had already torn half the thatch.

All these scoundrels tugged and sweated at the ox-hide ropes that went beneath the battering-ram; the alarming flames crept towards the dark heaven, and a sickly flickering light fell upon the malefactors' forms and faces. They had little discipline and no unity, all these fellows, so that at one time twenty-five upon the one side of the tree trunk would be lifting, whilst the other twenty-five would be letting go of their ropes.

Having hidden himself for the last ten days, Hugh of Fitz-Greville had used the time at once to make himself acquainted with the habits of the castle people, and to make them think that he was far away and upon other errands. Indeed, he had sent a treacherous packman down to the castle that afternoon to say that he lay well away to the east, even as far as Andover. Thus, as he had hoped, the Lady Dionissia had been beguiled into security, and she had ridden over to Stapleford with all her men, leaving the castle almost uninhabited, but with most of its furniture, which must have been worth nearly £150, and with what was still more desirable, a certain quantity of arms. These included even, it was said, one of those new and devilish inventions which spits forth stones and fire and fills the beholders with fear. Thus, lying up during the evening in the heather, Hugh of FitzGreville, a man of forty, with a very black beard, gnarled fingers, and a huge sword, who had been outlawed for many outrages, from the taking of the King's deer to the murder of several people, male and female, and religious as well as laymen, Hugh of FitzGreville perceived with satisfaction the Lady Dionissia riding towards Stapleford with all her armed men. Near nightfall he heard from one of his men, the son of a peasant of Stapleford, that to that castle there was come the holy pilgrim that for so long all the countryside had awaited, bearing with him a golden cross that worked astounding miracles. And this all the more determined Hugh of FitzGreville to make his attack upon Tamworth Castle that very night. For he expected that the destination of the pilgrim and the cross was Tamworth itself; and he very much desired to have arms for his men. The season for violences was passing over. With the end of the summer, the knights and their retainers would be back in Wiltshire, and he himself would have to go into his winter quarters in the little town of Imber, which was inaccessible to mounted knights once the winter rains began to fall.

He desired arms, for he wished to sack Harnham, the southern suburb of Salisbury, where all the Jews dwelt, and where there was in consequence very much money. There were arms in the Castle of Tamworth—not many, but sufficient, and there were not anywhere else any that he knew of or could lay hands upon. But if on the morrow the cross came to Tamworth Castle, his chance would be gone. For it was very well known that this cross shed a miraculous protection over all such as possessed it. Thus with the dusk Hugh of FitzGreville slipped with his men down the hillside towards the stream.

It had chanced that there was walking there the Clerk

Nicholas. Him the Dean of Salisbury had left at Tamworth to watch over such books as he had brought with him, and more particularly an edition of Ovid's *Metamorphoses*, which were the Dean's favourite reading. This Clerk Nicholas, walking in a shady grove, had perceived how Hugh of FitzGreville and his men had come down to the gates of the castle, and what they had set about doing. Thus, after watching them for a time, being himself unseen, and uncertain whether they were friends or foes, he had set off, running at great speed, as if the devil and all his imps were after him, towards the Dean in the Castle at Stapleford. But not knowing this, the outlaws set about their work with great determination, though with much clumsiness.

Hugh of FitzGreville was cursing lustily all the while, and thwacking them over the shoulders with a great stick. At last he called for silence, and commanded that they should all stand there with the hide-ropes slack in their hands whilst he counted four, and upon the word four they should all lift together. They must batter down this great gate. There was no other way into the castle; the walls were too high and the windows too narrow. He made three attempts at counting four, each of them ending in failure. But at the fourth attempt they got the tree trunk lifted up and stood trembling at their knees with its great weight. He commanded them to swing it against the gate. But when they had swung it they tottered so that it fell again to the ground a little farther away than before it had been. Cursing, sweating, and screaming, their leader forced them to another attempt, and again they had it poised and trembling in the air.

There was already fear abroad amongst all these men. This attack upon a great castle was a larger and more dangerous enterprise than any to which they had been used. And descending into the valleys was a thing they always dreaded. They were men who wrought violences upon the open Plain; here in the darkness and the mists they felt themselves shut in. Nor, indeed, did they very well know the ways of escape, for it was unfamiliar country. Thus the trembling of their hands beneath the great weight of the tree trunk was a symbol of an awful fear that beset them, and the angry agitation of their leader made them all the more dogged and cowed. But they swung the tree trunk back, and with an enormous thud it fell against the great gate; the lock split, the bolts split, the gate itself, dividing into two parts, flew right back. Suddenly they felt—and they screamed aloud—that the devil was amongst them.

The men on the right-hand side only heard the hoofs—the men on the left saw, enveloped in the clouds of smoke from the burning hovel, an immense white horse, that fell in amongst them. Upon its back was a terrible man all in red and white, waving a steel mace above his head and calling out in an unknown tongue. Those who saw horse and rider let go their oxhide ropes so that the released tree trunk fell across the legs of the other half. Twelve of them were pinned down and lay screaming.

The horse reared on high and seemed itself to scream in continuous bursts of sound like the high laughter of fiends. The firelight was reflected in its eyes which appeared to pour forth streams of flame. The black wall of the castle came into sight, dun-coloured in the light of the flames, and vanished when the wind beat the flames low. It rose in front of them like a great cliff, and the uncharted night surrounded them on all other sides. The horse reared. It struck out with its right foot and with its left; its enormous jaws closed with a panic-bearing sound.

[149]

FitzGreville struck with his two-handed sword a desperate blow at the man on the horse. The sword fell upon the iron handle of the mace that the man carried and its blade shivered like brittle glass. When the fragments fell over its back and crupper, the horse squealed as if with a wicked rage. And even whilst the outlaw, with a gesture of despair, dropped his ruined hilt to the ground, the horse was upon him. The first blow with its right foot smashed his head like a nut, so that he was at once dead. Then upon the prostrate body it executed its rage, stamping with its feet, tearing with its enormous teeth, until there remained only the pulp of the human being. Then the horse stood still and trembled in all its limbs; it raised its nostrils towards the open gate and snuffed in the air. All the robbers had fled, only those who were pinned down by the tree trunk lay still and groaned. The stallion, with its head erect, trotted in through the dark gateway, its rider powerless or unwilling to prevent it.

.   .   .   .   .   .

A short two minutes later there came riding into the circle of light the Dean, his shouting chaplain who brandished a morgenstern, his page upon a black horse and four more pages who were the eldest of the Ladies Blanche and Dionissia, together with the five Welsh men-at-arms who had clung to their stirrups and ran uttering wild shrieks. It appeared in the light of the dancing flames that a miracle of God had been worked. There lay three men dead by huge blows, and one crushed out of all semblance of a man. Beneath the tree trunk, in an orderly row, the twelve others were pinned to the earth and screaming. It was as if Providence had neatly arranged this device that in a seemly manner there might be several captives of whom to make an example to all evil-doers. The old men-at-arms, who had followed them on foot, came dropping in by twos and threes; many awakened peasants appeared far off, slinking in the outer ring of the firelight, and asking what all this could be but a madness of their lords, or a miracle of God. Some thought the one and some the other.

And suddenly, staggering from under the archway, faltering here and there, they perceived a knight in a garment of red and white chequers, who bore in his left hand a mace, and from whose right depended an ornament all flashing gold.

Many great cries went up; there was such a babble and such a confusion of voices, that no man knew very well what he said or what was said to him. But all were agreed that the bearer of the Cross of St Joseph and the cross itself had wrought this miracle for the protection of the noble House of Egerton of Tamworth. All men ran about seeking what vestige of fray they might find, and at a little distance there was discovered a man with his shoulder broken in, who had been crawling down to the river to drink. The great gates of the castle they observed to be thrown asunder as if miraculously, to permit of the entry of the Messenger of God. Nothing else in the castle was disturbed—nay, not so much as the books of the Dean of Salisbury. And the great white destrier in its stall with its favourite mare was quietly munching beans, the stable cat seated upon its whethers. Thus upon that memorable night two miracles were wrought by the Cross of St Joseph. The cripple was made to walk, and the most formidable band of outlaws was broken for ever. Its leader was slain and mutilated beyond recognition. So then here indeed the finger of God had been made visible. Four others of them were killed outright, ten were taken ready to be hanged; and the rest, leaderless and broken men, were dispersed all over the Plain. Most of them never again met together.

WITH THE GLORY OF TWO MIRACLES TO HIS CREDIT MR SOR-
rell was borne once more into the lights of the great hall of
Stapleford Castle, seated on high, on a litter supported by the
shoulders of four Welshmen. All the countryside was abroad,
torches here and there gleamed on the black wall of night and
a great crowd of people, who by their position or their rights
were deemed fit to have ingress into the great hall, were already there, whilst huddled round the central doorway was
a crowd of peasants and their wives. Mr Sorrell could not have
given you a coherent account of the proceedings.

At the moment, he was sober enough, though he was ready
to admit he had drunk too much wine at supper. He excused
himself by the fact that he had not in the least known how
strong the liquor was. He had eaten so many sweet things
and so many salt things, that an unheard-of thirst had possessed him. No doubt in the ordinary way he would have
wanted to ride with the expedition. He would have done it for

the fun of seeing what happened. But without the wine he would probably not have insisted upon riding the white stallion or on taking with him an iron mace.

He was conscious of having behaved boastfully and of having been enormously elated. There had been a great deal of hurry; he had been hoisted up on to the great horse before the castle door. Other men had ridden beside him. They had gone down to the river and along it. He had laughed and cried out with excitement. The pace of the great horse had been extraordinarily easy; it had trotted with a level, heavy action. He had ridden most things, from mules in Spain to camels in Egypt and some sort of ox on the Thibet frontier. And the pace of the great horse had seemed to him absurd; he had wanted to go faster. He had kicked it with his heels; he had hauled upon the bridle; he had called out.

At last he had struck its sides with the iron mace. Immediately it had become another creature, bounding with the elasticity of a steel spring, snorting and screaming. It had taken its own head, and he had found himself galloping through the night with immense bounds. He was far in advance of all the other men, going on farther and farther towards the glare of a large fire that was all he could see in the darkness. It had grown larger; it had become a conflagration; he had seen many men; he had heard their cries; he had noticed that a man with a black beard and a convulsed face had struck at him with a great sword. He had struck in return with his mace, meeting nothing. He had had too much to do to keep on the back of the horse, which swayed like a small boat in a very choppy sea, pitching now on one end, now on the other. For all he was a good rider, at last he had to hang on to the mane and the saddle.

Then the horse had stood still; it had neighed; it had trotted in under the dark arch into the darkness of the castle. It had come to a standstill by what was obviously a closed stable with a rough thatch that came down almost to Mr Sorrell's knee. And here, breathing hard and slightly pawing the ground, it had been answered from within by gentle whinnyings. For the first time fear had come to Mr Sorrell. It went quickly through his mind that if he did not let the horse in it would kick its way into the stable. On the other hand, if he descended, might not the terrible beast, not knowing him for his master, tear him, as Mr Sorrell had seen it tear the outlaws? With fear possessing him all over, Mr Sorrell had slipped down from the horse, caught its bridle near the jaw, and, tremblingly, had found the latch of the stable. It was part of the odd jumble of fear, elation, and the natural tendency of his nature to do things in a ship-shape way that he unstrapped the unfamiliar saddle-belt, and took off the head stall and bit before he let the horse go into the black darkness of the stable. He could not for the world have told why he did this. It was hardly the desire for tidiness, since he dropped the saddle and the bridle immediately on the ground. But the great horse trotted quietly into its stall; Mr Sorrell slammed the door to, and, leaning one hand against the lintel, he became violently ill.

This sobered him. But it left him very dizzy and faint, and, like a man in a dream, he stumbled amongst heaps of offal and the handles of ploughs, which are weary and troublesome things, towards the light of the castle gate. Here, among torches, glare, and the shouts of men, he seemed to be seized upon by friendly savages. He was hoisted shoulder-high on to a litter covered with cushions. The little Jehan was immediately busy about his feet. He had, he discovered, been riding in boots of jointed steel, and almost immediately the little Jehan had these off, and was putting on the now familiar red and white shoes. He sat on high supported by the shoulders of four shaggy-haired, black little devils of mountaineers. He could not make himself heard; he could not ask any questions. It just seemed odd, and he just supposed that the gentlemen of those days went about with pages carrying their slippers behind them, because their iron riding shoes might be calculated to blister their feet.

There was an extraordinary amount of chatter and babble in the hall of Stapleford Castle when they reached it. There were nuns, priests, old men-at-arms, men in costumes that he could not account for, a man who might be a mayor in a red garment with a chain round his neck, though he was treated as if he were of no account at all. On the daïs there still sat the ladies, as if they had only just finished their supper, their nefs of silver and gold standing solitary on the white cloth before them. He was conscious of the Lady Dionissia gazing at him with a fixed and bemused glance. The Lady Blanche, with triumph upon her face, held out her arms towards him, and the four other ladies rose up and called out. Still bearing him on high, the mountaineers kicked and shoved their way through the crowd till he was come right up to the daïs. Everyone else stood upon their feet and shouted and called out; only the Lady Dionissia sat still and gazed at him in silence. And he was conscious that he must present a splendid enough figure, all in red and white velvet, if indeed it had not become dirtied by what he had done that night.

They began almost immediately some sort of religious service in the body of the hall. They appeared to be returning thanks. The ugly but now cured cripple figured prominently in the middle of a body of kneeling religious people. But it was all very confused, for not everybody took part, and pages or servers moved about clearing the boards and removing the trestles of the lower tables to set them along the wall. Then the little pages came to take away the nefs from the daïs. The Lady Blanche had one, the Lady Dionissia a second, and the Dean one more. But as for the chaplain and the ladies-in-waiting, their knives, cups, and napkins were simply wrapped up in cloths. The nef of the Lady Blanche was formed of a huge shell, in shape like a snail, that had come undoubtedly from the East. It had feet of silver, and there were attached to it sails and rigging, and a crew of tiny men of silver also. It contained as table furniture the Lady Blanche's knife of gold, her small golden drinking-cup, her napkin ring of tortoise-shell, her napkin, and the beads which she used at table when she was piously inclined. All these things were carefully wiped before her face by the little page Jehan upon pieces of soft leather. Then the Lady Blanche fetched from her bosom the large key of the hutch in her bower, and, giving this to the page, she bade him very attentively to stow away the nef in her hutch, and to bring her the key again. This was the first time she had showed so much trust in the little page. Similarly, the Lady Dionissia and the Dean had their vessels cleaned by their pages, and stowed away in their nefs. The Lady Dionissia's nef was of silver-gilt, in the shape of a man-at-arms who bore a large chest of booty upon his back. This figure stood upon a silver-gilt plate. From this the lady was accustomed to eat at table. The Dean's nef was in the shape of a chasse or feretory. It was of gold, with a peaked roof, and it had small carved saints and angels at each of its four corners, whilst on the peak of

[156]

the roof was an image of St George trampling upon a dragon, and holding it transfixed between his pointed shoes with a long spear. Round its stave the golden beast twisted its neck, sending upwards flames of gold. And no sooner were the nefs off the table, than all who were on the daïs rose up and filed out of the hall, completely ignoring, as if with haughty indifference, the religious ceremonies that were there taking place. This a little disconcerted Mr Sorrell. He would gladly have taken the opportunity of returning some thanks to some deity for his having come safely through rather considerable perils.

He followed the white head-dress of the Lady Dionissia through miles of stone corridors. The little Jehan walked before them carrying a torch, whose flame smoked redly, and filled the air with a fat, resinous, and stifling vapour. They went along narrow passages, up narrow stairs, and round long galleries. Mr Sorrell tried to say to the Lady Blanche that he could not understand how they estimated their expenditure. It seemed to him to be very badly managed. Thus, on the one hand, the lady had a nef—a mere implement for containing table things—which must have cost £300 or £400. Would it not, he asked, have been more reasonable to keep her things in an ordinary plate-basket, and to have the passages lit by candles, or, at the very least, by night-lights? Everything that they did seemed to be unbalanced, so that at the one point they had a most unreasonable luxury, and, on the other, a great deal of discomfort. There did not seem to be a pane of glass in the whole castle, and yet he had upon his head a chaplet of large pearls, which must have been worth at least £3000 or £4000. The lady said that this chaplet had been brought from the Holy Land by her husband's grandfather after the Crusade of Richard I, when knights were more practical and less given to romantic notions. It was a chaplet nearly as fine that her husband had put upon the head of Sir Guy de Hardelot after he had taken him prisoner, because, forsooth, he had fought very well. Whereas it must be obvious to any person of sense that if an opponent has given you a great deal of trouble you should make him pay heavily for it. But for the other things Mr Sorrell said, she did not at all understand them.

Mr Sorrell said:

"If you're going into partnership with me, you'll have to get to understand this sort of principle." She must have her expenditure level and sufficient all round. It was no good being ostentatious in one place and niggardly in another. That was the sound business principle.

"I do not at all understand you," the Lady Blanche said. "What can I know of the high principles of magic?"

"Oh, it's perfectly simple," Mr Sorrell said, and he cast about in his mind for some illustration that would make her understand the absolute necessity of mastering this elementary business principle.

In the upper part of the castle the corridors were wider, more high and more gloomy. The shadows of extravagant and protruding sleeves, veils and head-dresses jutted and waved over rough walls of stone upon the one side, and untreated wood upon the other. They walked very slowly, the little page going ahead with the smoking torch held on high.

"It's like this," Mr Sorrell said. "Supposing you want to publish a book. You have to consider two things: the get-up of the book, and the amount you spend in advertisement." It was no good getting up a book handsomely unless you could spend a good sum on publicity. You might have the very best etching for illustrations, and you could have it printed in what's called golden type with red lettering on the title page, the half-title, and you might have it printed on the very best hand-made paper at God knows how much a pound. But if you didn't spend a high sum on advertising, you would not sell twenty-five.

"I do not understand any of those terms of magic," the Lady Blanche said, "though I listen with all my ears."

"I'll try to talk about your sort of life," Mr Sorrell said. "Don't you understand that time is the most valuable thing in the world? Well then, just consider how much time your servants must lose in doing the work of the castle, just because these passages are not lit. You could do with half the number of servants if you organised properly."

"Ah, dear friend," the lady said, "then the other half would starve and become bandits. And oh, holy man, if these passages and corridors were lit at night, surely it would be very easy for my servants and serfs to come to me where I lie in the upper part of the castle, and to cut my throat and do other outrages. So I should lose my costly gear, and there would be an end of me. No, very assuredly I will keep all my passages quite dark, and the law of the castle what it is, that any serf who is found in them after sundown shall have his ears cut off and his nostrils slit as a suspected thief."

Mr Sorrell had been meaning to say that when they came to build his airships, he was not going to have the propellers made of silver-gilt set with carbuncles, or the wings of embroidered silk, whilst the dynamos were scamped for want of money. And he was not going to have his gun-carriages carved in fantastic shapes and gilded whilst the barrels were made of cheap pig-iron.

But before he could recover himself sufficiently to be coherent, they had entered a room which almost exactly resembled the bower of the Lady Blanche. Here too there was a bed covered with skins of the grey wolf, and at the foot of the bed was another large hutch, and this was all the furniture save that in a corner of the room there lay a large leather portmanteau. Except that it had no brass lock or fittings, this so exactly resembled Mr Sorrell's own largest piece of travelling gear that he had a momentary impulse to say to the Lady Blanche:

"Now I've caught you! I bet that thing has got some chap's ordinary clothes in it!" But, racking his mind, he once more discovered that he did not in the least know what would be an anachronism and what would not. And for the moment this cost him a bitter mortification.

The Ladies Blanche and Dionissia sat themselves at either end of the hutch, the four other ladies perched on the sides of the bed. The Dean sat himself between the Ladies Blanche and Dionissia; the Bishop's chaplain pulled out from the wall the leathern portmanteau and sat himself down upon it. The little Jehan entered the closet, which was made of planks walling off one end of the room, and fetched from it a torch, which he lit and stuck in an iron ring in the wall. The ring was so high that he must stand on tiptoe to get it there. Then he went outside the door and stuck his own torch in yet another ring.

All their eyes were fixed upon Mr Sorrell.

"Oh, hang it all," Mr Sorrell said, "do you expect me to make a speech?"

The Dean yawned suddenly.

"It is very late in the night," he answered, "yet it would be well if the most weighty matters could be now debated and set to rest."

"Why," Mr Sorrell said, "I'm very tired, and I don't feel as if I had anything to say whatever."

[160]

Ladies Whose Bright Eyes

The Lady Dionissia was gazing at him with her lips slightly parted. It distracted Mr Sorrell more than he could say. The dazzling whiteness of her skin made the Lady Blanche's weather-beaten and coloured beauty appear dusky and negligible, so that for a short moment Mr Sorrell wished that he had not so precipitately entered into a business partnership with the Lady Blanche.

The Lady Blanche started suddenly with vexation.

"By the eyes of Christ," she said, "I had forgotten that I had meant to have the Abbess here, so that she might hear of her utter downfall, and be properly chastened."

And immediately in high tones she bade the little page run to bid the Mother Abbess, who was in the Great Hall, to hasten before her. The Lady Dionissia said in deep, and startling tones:

"Lie down upon the Dean's bed, holy man, and rest your limbs." And before Mr Sorrell could recover from the emotions which her voice caused in him, with exclamations of delight the four youngest ladies had seized Mr Sorrell and had conducted him to the bed. They laid him down and, screaming with laughter and tittering, they kissed him upon both cheeks before they left him alone. He could not bring himself to remain in a recumbent posture, but he was glad enough to sit down on something soft, so, leaning against the pillows, he crossed his legs as well as he could beneath him and sat up.

"So! It is even in that way," the Dean's chaplain exclaimed in his huge voice, "that the heathen peoples of the East sit upon their cushions. I have seen them do it in Bethlehem."

"I learnt the trick in Syria," Mr Sorrell said cheerfully. "It's quite comfortable when you've got used to it, though these hoops on my legs are rather in the way."

And suddenly the Lady Dionissia exclaimed again:

"Let us pull the hutch from the bed and sit round the other way so that we may all face the holy man."

This proposal appeared to fill the Lady Blanche with a deep anger. She had never heard of hutches being sat upon in that fashion. The Dean smiled with indulgent surprise. He too had never heard of such a thing, but it appeared to him to be reasonable to act exceptionally in exceptional circumstances.

"When the stream is full," he said, "we cannot go by the ford." And he chuckled amiably, regarding the Lady Dionissia as a madcap, but exceedingly attractive child. The Lady Blanche was protesting that such a thing should never be done in her castle. But with her large hand the Lady Dionissia beckoned to her two ladies to help her, and bending down powerfully, she lifted the one end of the hutch without effort, whilst it took all that the other two girls could do to scrape the feet of the hutch along the floor.

"Now let us sit down," the Lady Dionissia said gravely.

The Dean sat himself beside her, facing Mr Sorrell with his hands clasped upon his stomach, and his eyes blinking, whilst he shook gently with contained laughter.

"Surely," he said, "with these varieties, I shall be cured of my jaundices and distempers. And since to-morrow is blood-letting day, I think on the day after to-morrow I might well get me back to my chapter, though I have never before been cured under three weeks. Yet so it is as Ovid says: *Lætet Sanguis*. A constant occupation of the mind makes the blood limpid and not thick and heavy."

The Lady Blanche stood behind them, her eyes flashing appeal to Mr Sorrell, to strike with lightning both those people who defied her.

"Never shall I sit upon a hutch," she exclaimed, "with my back where my face should be, and since this is my castle,

I will call immediately four men to set you all in irons and in dungeons for disobeying my orders, which is a feudal laches."

The Lady Dionissia paid no heed at all to her cousin's speech, but gazed at Mr Sorrell, who gazed back at her. The Dean turned his chubby and comfortable head over his furred shoulder, and blinked at the enraged lady.

"Ah, dear dame," he said, "you have so great a knowledge of the law, that I am astonished in your haste you should so slip up and trip. As Tatianus has it: 'in the passion of the head, wise tongues speak folly.' For I have paid the Lady Dionissia for this my room, and the Lady Dionissia has done that suit and service of one shilling to you for it. Thus you have no more right of ingress or command here than has the King into our Chapter House of Salisbury, once we have done him proper suit and service."

"Ah, Dean," the Lady Blanche said—and the prospect of a legal argument with a man mollified her very quickly for the moment, "yet custom and the law have it, that if in a tenant-right, the tenant should do anything sacrilegious, outrageous, blasphemous, or against the Will of God and the duty to his Over Lord, the Over Lord has the right to enter upon the holding, and to take the person of the wrong-doer and to enact justice upon him."

"Ah, dear lady," the Dean said, "and is it sacrilege, outrage or blasphemy to move a hutch and to sit reversed upon it?"

"Ah, Dean," the lady said, "is it not wilfully to molest and to despoil the gear of an Over Lord, thus to drag a hutch over a rough floor, so that its legs and the feet upon which it stands may be chafed, strained, and parted from the body of the piece?"

"So it might well be, our dear lady," the Dean said; "but this hutch is my hutch which I bear about with me on the

[163]

back of a mule, and is no hutch of yours at all, for I believe you have two or at the most three hutches in all your castle, and yours that was in this room I have lent to my chaplain that he might store in it certain charters and cartilleries, that upon this journey we are meditating to devise to tenants of the Chapter of Salisbury: so it is all well," he added, "and come you and sit upon my hutch." And leaning back he caught her by the hand.

"Ah, Dean," the lady said, and she surveyed with kindly friendship his twinkling eyes, since a man of any sort was a pleasant object for her to survey. "It is you that have found the solution to our quarrel, not my cousin's half-wife, who has the obstinacy and unreasonableness of a white devil." And leaning back so that his arm encircled her waist, the Dean comfortably and courteously set her upon the hutch. Nevertheless, she sat with her back to Mr Sorrell, looking at him over her shoulder. And then the Abbess came in, followed by the little Jehan.

"Ah, Abbess," the Lady Blanche said, on a high note of ironical laughter, "we have asked you here that you may listen to the judgment of the Holy Man in the matter of this cross, that you desire sacrilegiously to steal and convey away, after the sacrilegious and blasphemous manner of all the priesthood."

"Ah, dear lady!" the Dean expostulated.

"Oh you," the Lady Blanche said, "you do not belong to the monastic orders, you are no more than a clerk, and clerks are sometimes honest people."

The Abbess made a slight reverence to the Dean, who slewed round upon the hutch, and nodded to her over his shoulder.

"Father Dean," the Abbess said, "if you will, I would have you come to-morrow morning to my little nunnery, to judge in friendly way between my community and me. For you are a man, very learned in the law, descended from those first Normans who were always barrators and cunning men at haggling."

"Why, Mother," the Dean said in his husky, pleasant voice, "it is not for me to judge between you and your community. That is a task for my Lord the Bishop's Chancellor."

"Ah, Dean," the Abbess said, "that I very well know. But very well I know that if this should come before Sir Chancellor, then would result an eternity of lawsuits—so I would have you give judgment on this matter in a friendly manner, I making you some small presents as my humble means afford."

The Dean waggled his comfortable thumbs that were crossed upon his comfortable stomach.

"Even what is the cause that you would have me consider?" he asked.

"Ah, Dean," the Abbess said, "I trust it is one that has no precedent in Christendom, for what will you say to a convent that rushes pellmell with all the nuns and its prioress at its head and its almoner and its sacrist and its mass-priest and its little thurifers, all of them rushing out to do robbery upon a highway, against the will and consent of their abbess, whose province it is to take order for them?"

"Why, what is all this folly?" said the Lady Blanche.

"I have had put," the Abbess answered composedly, "the sacrist and the thurifer and the sub-prioress and the cellaress all in irons, but the prioress and the higher priests I have deemed fitter to spare, since their position is of prominence in the community. But if you will give me your opinion upon it, I will abide by it, as a judgment between them and me. For myself, I think the community did very wrong in thus acting against my desires, and I think that they should pay me some heavy fine to benefit not my private good, or to be left to my heirs, but to go into the coffers of all the Abbesses that shall ever succeed me."

The Lady Blanche had been gasping with indignation. "It was not for this that I sent for you," she said, "but to hear what the holy pilgrim has judged and decided concerning the cross of St Joseph, that he brought all the way from Bethlehem."

"I might say," the Abbess continued in her calm and level tones, "that what may be decided concerning this cross is in no way an affair of mine. But since you have called upon me, as being very assuredly moral supervisor of these parts, and as far as the Priory of St Stephen's bounds, I take it as being very courteous in you, and shall be glad to hear this history."

The Lady Blanche was convulsed with rage.

"Abominable Prelatess!" she exclaimed. "Is it you that are set in command over the morals and orders of this district?"

The Abbess looked at her with straight and twinkling glance.

"Very assuredly it is," she said, "and so it is according to all the precedents. For the Bishop of Salisbury is away at the war, and so is the Chancellor of the diocese, and the knights of Stapleford and of Tamworth have gone. The Prior of St Stephen's is but a minor prior, whereas I, though a very poor one, am a full Abbess. So I am above everyone else in this district, as being like a Baron of Parliament and able to wield direct authority."

The Lady Blanche exclaimed, "By the eyes of Christ! . . ." but her utterance was choked within her.

"And that this is according to all precedent," the Abbess continued almost jocularly, "I will prove to you by many instances. Thus, the Abbot of St Edmunds, being desirous to go to the aid of King Richard I in his French wars, it was answered to him that since the Bishop of Ely and the Bishop

of Norwich, and most or nearly all the knights of Suffolk and
Norfolk were away, the Abbot must stay in his monastery of
St Edmund's, since there was none other but he to keep order
in those two counties. And, indeed, for what else are convents
and monasteries? Do you think they are for the support of lazy
nuns and idle priests? Not so. They are here to keep order
in the world beneath, to pray to heaven that things may be
well above, and by goodly example to win to God the un-
godly, the lecherous, the blasphemous, and the idle."

"Mercy of God!" the Lady Blanche said. "These are the
very newest fashions that you bring with you from France."

"Far be it from me," the Abbess said, "to cast aspersions on
the holy women who have preceded me. They were so lost
in prayers and visions of heaven and in fasting and vigils, that
the things of this earth were sealed up for them. But being less
holy, I deem it my duty to be the more vigilant."

The Lady Blanche dug her nails into her palms so that the
pain might cause to die down within her her enormous anger.
"We shall see how it will fare betwixt you and me," she said.
And then she turned upon Mr Sorrell. "Holy man!" she exclaimed, "tell us in three words what you have decided to do
with this cross."

"Oh, for goodness' sake," Mr Sorrell said with a start, "tell
them yourself. I'm not up to talking French before such a lot
of people."

The Lady Blanche looked round upon her assembly. "The
holy man," she exclaimed, "has decided to leave it between me
and my cousin's wife by proxy, to settle which of us shall
have the custody of this cross until the return of the knights
our husbands from the war!"

"Ah, but how will you settle it?" the Dean asked. "That is
a very difficult question, for I think that neither the Lady

Dionissia nor yourself, our dear lady, are of such a kind as to surrender this sacred and desirable emblem without a struggle."

A malicious and haughty fire came into the eyes of the Lady Blanche, and she stared hard at the Lady Dionissia.

"Why, these are the days of chivalry," she exclaimed, "when all things are settled by single combat and by spear and shield. Thus now I will challenge my cousin's wife to fight this thing out with me, and the winner of us shall have the cross; or if she will not accept this my challenge, she shall be accounted what is called, I think, a recreant, and so the cross and the man who brought it shall remain in my keeping."

Mr Sorrell exclaimed, "Oh, I say!" and from all the other people came many exclamations, whilst from most of the ladies came a shrill sound of laughter.

The Dean looked at Lady Dionissia, whom he regarded with the fondness of a guardian for his protégée.

"This is a mere counsel of madness," he said; "such things have never been heard of, and the lords of chivalry are the men only. For what a thing it would be if ladies should go endangering their sweet limbs in the hard knocks of fearful war."

The Lady Dionissia said nothing at all, but sat fair and drooping as if she were in a dream. The Abbess stood with her hands on high, as if she were turned to a stone in an attitude of horror.

"Oh, you couldn't come to fighting!" Mr Sorrell exclaimed, looking at the Lady Dionissia. "Why can't you toss for the thing, as I suggested in the beginning."

The Lady Blanchemain said gaily to the Ladies Amarylle and Cunigunde, "Why, if our mistresses fight as knights, we must be squires, and have a goodly mêlée."

"Ay, that must we!" the Lady Cunigunde laughed, and

these young things raised their hands on high as if thy were striking with swords—and then they tickled each other under the arm and screamed with laughter so that they fell off the bed. The Lady Amoureuse was tenderly stroking Mr Sorrell's hand—and the Dean smiled.

"This is all very nice nonsense," he said, "but the hour is very late. I am going to bed, for, as the Duke Virgil of Mantua says: '*Suadentque cadentia sidera somnum.*' The falling stars persuade us to sleep."

And suddenly the Lady Dionissia spoke in her deep and dreamy voice:

"Why, this is a very good proposal," she said, "and I am heartily in accord with it. I have not had until now much love of my cousin Blanche, but now I love her as if she were my own sister. I have often been minded to put upon me the harness of knights and to travel into deserts seeking dragons and adventures. And now this thing is come to my own door. Very heartily I will be a partaker in this high enterprise."

The Dean looked at her with outraged perplexity.

"My child—" he was beginning.

But his chaplain, arising from the portmanteau, gaunt and fanatical, approached them with enormous and hungry eyes. It was his private conviction that all women were fiends sent for the temptation and misleading of humanity, and that any two or six of them should be soundly cuffed, thwacked with swords, or struck black and blue with the heads of lances, seemed to him very desirable, and a thing for which to praise God. And his stentorian voice filled the room.

"Let them go at it," he exclaimed. "Let them fight; why should they not fight? It is very common among Saracens that women put on caps of steel and betake themselves to the lists.

And shall Christian women be behindhand with heathens? No, let it not be said that Christian women are wanting in valour, for is it not recorded of the first Christian woman that ever was that she lingered last by the cross, thus showing that she feared not the Roman soldiery, and came first to the grave where the stone was rolled away?"

"Many ladies have put on armour and fought," the Lady Dionissia continued. "Thus was Arabella of the Red Hand, who went to seek her lover, a good knight that was cast into the prisons of the King of Bohemia, and there was Eunice of the Lions, who slew seven of these beasts in the sands of Africa. And there was Thecla of the Blue Mountain, who fought with Sir Bors of Troy for the life of her husband, and overcame him."

She arose from the hutch and went suddenly close up to the Lady Blanche.

"Cousin," she said, "let us go apart into a private place and discuss at more length how this shall be done, whether in the lists or in the open field; whether we two alone, or whether with our ladies as squires."

The Lady Blanche, on her part, was not ill-pleased, for she very much desired to do this thing at once, in order to mar her cousin's beauty with sword-strokes, and to render her husband ridiculous by the reports of an excess so outrageous. Nevertheless, in places she was a little disappointed; she disliked to have pleased the Lady Dionissia by any means at all, and she had some vain hopes that the Lady Dionissia, by refusing the combat, would give her a colourable claim to the custody of the cross. For he who is ready to take a thing by the sword is obviously a fitter guardian than he who fears. Nevertheless, their way was barred by the Lady Abbess.

"Impious females!" she exclaimed. "Have my ears lived

long enough to hear such speeches? Ay, they have lived long enough. But never whilst I myself do live shall such a thing take place in a country where I have any say. Will you defile the bodies that God has given you by sweating under heavy armour? Will you harden hands that God has made soft upon the iron hilts of swords? No, by my faith you shall not, whilst I have a voice to upraise against these things."

"By the eyes of Christ!" the Lady Blanche said, "this woman talks!"

"Aye," the Abbess continued, "are not these things lamentable enough, and is not this a lamentable house? Into it is come a pilgrim bearing a holy symbol, and lo! what is fallen upon him? Here was a man that, simply clad, endured the hot burning sun at noonday, and the dews and frosts at night. Simple, pious, and bearing those hardships that conduce to sanctity, he travelled through the wilderness, and by the protection of the dear angels escaped many and fell perils. Now, being come into this accursed house, he lies upon a luxurious bed, tricked out with silks and velvets and pearls and silver and gold. Gorged with food and heavy with wine, he is hung over by immoral damsels and kissed and stroked, so that it is an abomination of desolation. How is holiness fallen, how is piety come down!"

"Say you so?" the Lady Blanche exclaimed indifferently. "Insolent prelatess that have found a tongue at last!—for I have not heard you speak so many words in all the year together that you have molested this soil. Get you gone out of this room, and go yelp to the sheep in the darkness."

And setting her hand upon the Abbess' black shoulder, she pushed her without more words out of the doorway, and followed with the Lady Dionissia. Mr Sorrell had sprung off the bed and approached the Dean.

"I say," he exclaimed, "have I been behaving in an improper way?"

The Churchman looked at him, at once friendly, astonished, and humorous.

"Man of sanctity," he exclaimed, "if, as seems true, you have been nourished with the bread of dear angels, assuredly our finenesses here are very little things by comparison. Or if, on the other hand, you have endured perils and hardships, it is very fitting that now you should rest and take your ease, and I have not observed that you have in any way transgressed against the rules of decorum that are such and such in one country, and such and such in another. For my Lady Abbess I would have you take little notice of her. She is a woman of great piety and shrewd common sense, as she has given evidence by coming to me rather than to the Chancellor or my Lord Bishop. Yet she has not been long enough in harness to learn that in the Church, as in the life of everyday, first we fare hard and then by hard faring we earn the results of toil. And so day leads on to day. But before very long she will have learnt that lesson, and will no longer speak words so fanatical and foolish."

At this point the comfortable Dean yawned very loud, and very long.

"Man of sanctity," he said, "the hour has approached for sleeping. You have brought to us a very holy relic, and we have seen pleasant things of the high spirits of young damsels and great ladies, but there is a time to sleep. To-morrow we shall discourse with these things with heads much more clear."

The Ladies Blanchemain, Amarylle, and Cunigunde had drunk in the words of the comfortable Dean with evidences of the highest satisfaction. They surrounded him, and made him say that the Abbess of St Radigund's was a horrid old woman, who had shamefully miscalled them. And he bustled them out of the room, his amiable countenance relaxed into happy smiles. Last of all went Mr Sorrell and the Lady Amoureuse, being followed by the little page Jehan, who took the torch from the ring outside the door and led them to their respective apartments.

PART THREE

THE YOUNG KNIGHT OF EGERTON WAS SEATED IN HIS BATH, therefore there was a fire in the room. It was nevertheless July, and his leman, a young girl whom he had purchased of her mother, a peasant's widow of Derby, was oppressed by the heat. She had taken off her coif, her upper dress and skirt, and, her neck and arms bare and white, she was blowing the brands in the great stone fireplace. Her hair, which was usually confined by her coif, had fallen into disorder, and a strand hung down on her bare shoulders. This afforded the young Knight of Egerton a great deal of curious entertainment.

"Now, I have never seen a woman's hair before," he repeated. "Do thou not fasten it up."

The young girl flushed so that it went down over her neck, but mutely and sulkily she took her hands down from her head. The hair continued slowly to uncoil itself, and the young knight, with an air of malice, hummed between his teeth a tune of three notes. He began to upbraid the girl because she showed no signs of being about to become a mother, but kneeling on the hearth, her hands on the ground before her and with distended cheeks, she continued to blow the fire.

"It is my fault then?" the young knight grumbled. "Say it is my fault if you will. I am a very unfortunate man. I have eaten salmagundi and the powdered bone of unicorn, and ginger and costly spices. I am a very unfortunate man!"

Gertrude, the leman, took no notice of his complaints. A flame had started beneath the black crock on the fire and, sitting back, her hands folded in her lap, she gazed at the bevies of little sparks that began to run here and there over the sooty surface of the crock. She was hoping that her next purchaser would prove younger, richer, and more generous, so that she might have finer dresses than any other woman in the camp.

She had three dresses, two pairs of gloves, a necklace of peridots that the young knight had taken from a dead woman's body in Scotland; she possessed even a dried orange in a pomander of silver, which was a rarity possessed by no other woman lying then at Newcastle. Yet, though she had run about naked till she was fourteen, which was the year before, and only half clothed till the day she was taken to the young knight; though she slept now in sheets of silk beneath furs that were sack from the Castle of Kirking across the border, and she had before then only lain in the straw with the pig; though before then she had never had but cuffs and kicks from a man so that her body had been all grey with dirt and blue with bruises, whereas now it was all white and washed with soap, and from the young knight she had had nothing but clumsy caresses, even when her sulky air made him curse with rage; though she had been a very beggar and was now apparelled and fed better than any middling knight's wife, yet she looked sulkily at the fire.

She desired to have velvet gloves set with stones of price; she desired a hawk from Norway; a white horse of her own with trappings of silver; a monkey, two collars of pearls, five pounds of sugar a week, a ring of silver, three rings of gold, and quite a young lover who would beat her, or else she desired to be such a rich, free courtesan of a fabulous great city as the other women talked of having seen. By some of these she had been told that she was worthy of a younger and more sprightly companion than the young knight who was turned of thirty-five, had already grey hairs in his brown head, and was stiff and clumsy with rheumatism.

The young Knight of Egerton had been called by that name for so long, his elder brother neglecting to die, that he was now long past the middle age of knights of his day, who died mostly old men at forty-two. He was rather a small man with brownish features, very large in the bone, with knitted joints, a foxy and good-humoured expression, and brown hair, which he wore long in the French fashion, and which his leman curled when he went banqueting.

He was subject to great changes of humour. At the one moment he would swear great oaths as to what he would do with the spoils of the palace and the wives of Mahound, promising to dress Gertrude, his leman, in pearls from head to foot, and to give her three hundred women slaves, each one a princess, as well as one of the stones of the birthplace of the Redeemer when he had taken and sacked Palestine. For this was his high and devout intent, now that he was come to be the true knight of Egerton and had the real disposal of all the goods, gear and land of Egerton of Tamworth, and all its villeinies and dependencies.

[179]

At other times he would sit for hours in his bath with Gertrude pouring hot water on him, or over his wine at the board of the public room of the inn where all the knights that lodged there dined. After his thirteenth cup he would throw his arms round Gertrude, who sat at his side, and would burst into tears before all the people there, declaring that he was an old and a ruined man. And, with his head upon her shoulder, whilst before them the courteous and fat hostess commiserated him, he would declare that Goldenhand, the Jew, and the other Jews of Harnham-by-Sarum would have all his substance; that he would never ride plundering again along the Loire; that he would never see Palestine, the land of his Redeemer, but that he and Gertrude, from whom he would never part, would be cast out to lie in the straw like rotten and decayed horses that have done their work.

Most bitterly of all he would weep when, with his fifteenth cup of French wine, there would come to him the thought that he would never have children by the Lady Dionissia, his wife, so that he would lose all her dowry and a forfeit as well. And lugubriously, whilst Gertrude, supporting him, looked straight ahead and said nothing, the young knight would describe his doubts to the kindly hostess.

The hostess, broad and comfortable, in her brown worsted gown, with an enormous white coif, larger than any nun's, would sigh: "Ah, gentle knight!" many times, for she too had no children by her husband. And the knight, being carried to bed by his two little squires and two men-at-arms, the hostess would chide Gertrude for her heartlessness. She would bid her support the knight's head carefully that it might not come to cruel knocks against the stone of the winding stairway. She would bid Gertrude in all ways strive to remove the doubts of the knight and so to comfort him, and she would bid her remember that the knight had raised her from the straw.

This, however, would in no way placate the leman, who desired velvet gloves, a hawk from Norway, and a white horse of her own, with velvet and silver trappings. And for long after the young knight was by turns groaning and snoring between the silk sheets, she would remain brooding out of the window, returning the jests of street boys below, calling back ribald answers to the ribald proposals of men-at-arms, or yawning when the Wiltshire archers of the two Knights of Egerton and Coucy would come tumultuously down the streets, driving before them the Flemings of Sir John of Hainault, with whom they carried on a perpetual feud.

And what Gertrude revolved always in her mind was whether the young knight was really rich or whether he was poor. She never had the means of being certain. On the one hand, he would vow the most desirable vows as to what he would do in Palestine, and she heard him often described as the most famous, gentle knight of all chivalry. But then, during all the time they had been in the town of the New Castle, from all the six forays and rides that he had been upon, he had brought back no spoils, except the necklace of peridots that he had given her and the sheets of silk and the furs that covered their bed. It was very little to her that he might be the most famous, gentle knight of chivalry. Other knights, not so famous, would have given her the velvet gloves, the falcon from Norway, and the sugar that she desired to crunch beneath her sharp white teeth. When he had given her her first dress, coif, and stockings of fine silk at Derby, she had cast her arms round his neck, and had kissed him as if he had been a doll that she passionately desired. But it had not gone on as it had begun, and she was filled with doubts that to be the mirror of chivalry might mean that he would never give her a silver mirror in which her ugly little face, her pretty teeth, and her white body might be reflected.

And it seemed to her ridiculous that he should sit in his bath whilst she poured hot water over him from time to time. The young king had gone on a foray into Scotland. Who knew whether this time, at last, they might not bring back some plunder worth the name? Yet here the young knight sat in a long, wooden tub. He had round his neck his mantle of devise that he wore at State ceremonies, of chequers of red velvet and white. It spread from his neck and covered in the oblong tub, whilst his face, hot and perspiring, looked from the top of it as if out of an inverted funnel. He had explained to her that the hot vapour gave him ease from the pains in his limbs, and that in this way they sat in the castles of France before the fire, whilst the dependants stood round and the minstrels chanted romances and lays. Nay, more, he had said that, along a river called the Loire in France, there were places where hot water gushed out of the earth, and here were sheds erected, and ladies and knights sat in them to bathe all day, and practised the gentle rites of love and had their healths and pleasures. There was thus a long lay of a gentle lady called Biangobin and a knight called Lois, and of how they met at such a bath to fool a jealous husband. But this seemed to her a fabulous, foolish, and disagreeable story; for how could water ever come out of the earth but cold?

Whilst she sat, looking at the fire, she was aware that the young knight was telling his beads beneath the cloak; there was a little clicking; the folds of red and white chequers moved slightly and with regularity, and from his lips there came little whispers of sound. His piety was the thing about him that pleased her most, for she was deeply religious and went to Mass every morning at five. The gilding and the scarlets and greens with which the church there was painted pleased to the bottom of her heart her being that was avid of colour, and she was determined that when she was a courtesan her bower should be painted all scarlet and crimson and green, with the ceiling gilded like a church.

In the room in which she had to live in this hostel, the walls were all of bare stone. The young knight was exceedingly jealous of her and was accustomed to lock her in there for days at a time so that she knew every stone and every patch of damp. There was a long green mark in shape like a cluster of circles beneath the window, where the rain entered; there was a large dull purple stain beneath one of the grey beams of the ceiling. Nearly all the walls were greenish with damp. One of the corbels that supported this great beam was carved like a leering devil with high cheek-bones, and one like a placid queen, her head erect and crowned, with a cloth that flowed back over her hair. The bed was of walnut wood gone black and very huge, so that it would hold four persons; the hutch at its foot was of a rough oak gone grey. The lock on the painted oaken door was as huge as a cuirass, and bright red with rust. In the door itself was a trap-hatch through which her food was passed to her by the hostess when she was locked in. At these times she was allowed a brachet for her company, but when the young knight was there he would not suffer this dog to be near them, for it disturbed him with its affection.

The young knight continued to tell his beads; Gertrude continued to gaze at the fire. By intermittent and vicious spurts in the wood she knew that it must be raining, but she did not turn her head to look out of the window. A young page entered, dressed all in black velvet, with a strap of red and

[183]

white leather about his waist and a little badge of red and white chequers upon his shoulder. He was the elder brother of Little Jehan and had long golden hair, but his face was ugly. He bore in his hands a shoulder-plate of shining steel with fluted ampicas, and he grinned maliciously when he saw Gertrude's disordered hair. With a sulky mutiny she caught her cloth which lay on the hutch and tied it over her head and beneath her chin.

The young knight continued his prayer, though his eyes were upon the piece of armour. At last he said:

"Hum!" and then gradually he scowled.

The young page meanwhile reported that the body of the Knight of Coucy's Wiltshire archers who were in advance of the army were returned almost starved, having been wandering for three days in the bottomless valleys of the Tyne.

"Well, that is the old tale," the young knight said. "Turn the harness askew! What booty have they brought?" All the while his keen little eyes scrutinised the shining steel. Sir John of Hainault, being come from Flanders, had brought with him a harness that was of the latest fashion of the King of France's knights. This had the round bolt that protected the shoulder-joint, not spiked like a unicorn's horn, but beaten flat like the petals of a dog-rose, and inlaid with gold. And the young knight, taking advantage of his holiday, had bidden his armourer exactly to imitate this new fashion of rondelet. But his scowl deepened, for he saw before him rondelets that were an inch broader than Sir John's and very clumsily inlaid.

To his inattentive ears the young page said that he had heard that the Knight of Coucy's men had brought back nothing but some of the iron plates upon which the Scots baked their bread, and a quantity of the new-flayed skins of beasts that they had found in a deserted camp of the Scots.

[184]

"That is the old story," the young knight said, and then he exclaimed again: "I am a most unfortunate man!"

He stretched his naked arm, with its huge and bony elbow, through the opening of his cloak, and pointed at the armour.

"Mark that!" he said. "I did bid Gorhelm son, the armourer, to make me that rondelet, such as those Sir John of Hainault wears. Now mark, I bring Gorhelm son with me because Gorhelm the old is too obstinate to make armour after the new fashions. Now it appears that Gorhelm son is too stupid. For that rondelet is no more like those of Sir John of Hainault than an egg is like an onion."

Gertrude said nothing. The page continued to turn the armour, now that way, now this, before his lord's eyes.

"Mercy of God!" the young knight exclaimed suddenly in a high bellow; "there are spots of rain upon the steel. Ay de mi! You have carried my armour through the rain, and it is not greased."

He leant back in his bath exclaiming:

"Mercy of God! Mercy of God!" many times, whilst his mouth fell open with amazement.

"Ah, gentle knight," the page was beginning to explain, when with a marvellous spring—it was reported that many times in full armour the young knight had sprung right over his war-horse—he was out of the bath. His mantle, blazing red and white and clasped at the neck with a buckle of gleaming beaten gold weighing three ounces, whirled out all round him; the water dripped from his wet and hairy limbs that, white beneath the scarlet and all knotted and distorted, fell like the sails of a windmill about the page's ears.

The page dodged that way and this; he held up the armour to defend himself from the painful blows, and upon it the knight's horny hands fell with metallic and hollow sounds, whilst he bellowed with fury. The page yelped like a small cur at each blow. And then from the street, rhythmic and mingled with cries, came the light, measured tread of the returning soldiery. Evading the body of the page, which the young knight, who now had the boy by the throat, was whirling around the room, Gertrude, the leman, went to look out at the window.

In greens, in browns, in greys, all woollen and wet, the Wiltshire archers were tramping home through the rain. They raised their hands, and cried out to familiar faces at the windows of the street. One bent beneath the weight of a table strapped to his back; another was burdened with a bundle of hides like a harness; yet another bore a sackful of meat and bones. Yet, upon the whole, they had very little booty, and they marched rhythmically, at each step there coming a little clittering sound like hail from all the arrows shaken in the quivers behind their shoulders, and from the strings that flapped against the mighty bows that were slung across their backs. From them all there came up a warm odour of wet woollens and of humanity. They had been for three weeks incessantly upon the search for an enemy that constantly evaded them, amongst the stony bottoms of stream-filled valleys, and amongst the stinging mists of the heathery uplands.

From the room there came a mighty splash. The knight had thrown the boy into the wooden bath; the water gushed out on to the dirty stone floor; the shoulder-piece rolled into the corner. The young knight held the page in the bath, pressing him down with a bony foot and a leg scarred with the chafing of steel armour. His cloak flying round and round as with fury he waved his bare arms, he addressed the back of Gertrude, who was leaning from the window. His misfortunes poured out from his mouth in loud and grating howls.

Did ever, he asked her, any man have such misfortunes? Was ever any knight so served by dolts?

The boy was sobbing in the water; the knight, still pressing him down, began to howl an immensely long story of how Gorhelm the old, his armourer, whom he had left behind in Wiltshire, had flatly refused to imitate a cannon called a saker, one of which the young knight had bought, along with twenty hundred-weight of soft iron, from the ironfounders in the weald of Sussex. Gorhelm the old was to have forged this iron in the shape of the other saker—so that the young knight would have four when he went sieging to strong castles. But would Gorhelm the old do this work? No. He said he was a smith, a swordmaker, an inlayer of harness; with iron logs he would have no truck. He had been beaten, but this had only made him the more obstinate. He would have nothing to do with any new fashions which were all toys and folly! Then Gorhelm the younger was an incapable fool; this page was ill-trained! And, by the five wounds of the Redeemer, his ear listening to the sounds in the street told him that his archers were marching back in the rain—with their bows out of the cases and the covers off their quivers!

"In the rain!" the knight called out. "Merciful God, in the rain! There will not be feather on arrow or bowstring that will not be frayed and perished! And these are my men!"

Gertrude turned slowly from the window.

"Ah, gentle knight," she said sulkily, "it has not rained more than three minutes. It would take them longer to cover their bows and to cap their quivers than they will need for reaching shelter."

The knight's mouth fell open with rage and despair.

"By the bones of the Virgins of Cologne!" he called out, "is it thus a courteous leman speaks to her paramour? Merciful God, do you too side with this idle, dissolute, and neglect-ful rabble? I will sell you to Mahound and the Anthropophagi! I will throw you into chains in the town gaol. Merciful Saviour, I will tie you down upon the bed and beat your naked flesh with rods until you bleed from shoulder to thigh. All this I will do because you have no heart nor bowels of com-passion."

Gertrude raised her shoulders slowly to a level with her ears; she let them as slowly fall, and then turned her back on him.

The unfortunate knight's arms fell desolately to his sides, and he remained lost in dismal thoughts. He imagined he must be bewitched, and he thought it would be well to consult a wizard or a priest. For, try as he would, deserve it as she might, he could not raise his hand against this insulting atomy. And yet he was the young Knight of Egerton who had been famed for having in but ten years seven of the most famous lemans in Christendom. There had been Isabelle de Joie, with hair like corn; Constance de Verigonde, with teeth like pearls; Bearea la Belle, with breasts like mother-of-pearl; Bice de Car-nas, with arms like alabaster; and Jeune la Ciboriée, whose breath was sweeter than the odour of pinks. And there had been Margaret of Wyvern. . . .

All these famous and beautiful women had wept, sighed, groaned or coaxed according to their natures when he had only frowned. Why, if it had come into his head he would have beaten them in his cups for the amusement of hearing them howl! But this wretched, ugly, mean little girl controlled him as she did the brachet dog. She had a face like a rat, limbs as thin as stalks of corn, the insatiable hunger of a leech. Yet she—she kept him there. For he knew that long since, packing his arms upon waggons and setting his men to march afoot, he would have gone back home to Tamworth—but for the fact that the Lady Dionissia awaited him. He could not tell that the Lady Dionissia would not send Gertrude packing, sell her to some strange man, at the thought of which his bowels turned over, or slay her with a dagger as the Queen Eleanor had done to Rosamond of Clifford. Yes, assuredly, but for this mean girl he would have gone to the south again. Then, equally assuredly, he must be bewitched. Bewitched! She must be Garanigonione, the leech of the desert that Holy Writ and the Lays tell us of! Her filthy old mother had appeared to be a witch!

He had loved her with jewels, fed her with sugar; he had borne her device on a shoulder knot at the Queen Mother's table, which was beyond reasonable decency. He had composed in her honour five rondels and three virelais, which his jongleur had sung to her during the day before the hearth in the guest-room of this inn, and which he himself had recited to her in the dusk of the night when his pains prevented his sleep. During the day she had shown no sense of the honour; at night she had turned over in bed, yawned, and fallen asleep at once. Perhaps that was because the young knight could compose poems only in French, for he spoke English indifferently, whilst Gertrude understood only the language of the Midlands. . . .

So the young knight meditated, his foot pressing down the wet page in the bath, whilst outside the archers went by, and Gertrude watched them from the window.

His own incomprehensible condition engrossed him so much that he did not come out of it even when the sound of iron armour came knocking along the staircase wall into the very door of the room. A huge figure, all black and rusted mail, with the high cheek bones of an enormous red face peering good-humouredly from the visor, creaked stiffly across the floor. The young knight turned his head despondently, and muttered:

"Hum!"

And, tranquilly peering out of his black helmet, the Knight of Coucy and Stapleford said nothing at all. At last the young knight came out of his reverie.

"Why the devil!" he exclaimed, "do you come here in these greasy potlids?"

His jovial and sagacious eyes upon the young knight's face, the Knight of Coucy set one mailed hand heavily upon the other, and with a gesture of weary satisfaction he pulled off one gauntlet and cast it rattling upon the hutch at the foot of the bed. His armour was very old, and had seen much service; it was coated deep with a mixture of grease and soot to keep it from the mist of the weather. When they went against the Scots they were thus homely clad, for there was no eye to see them and only too little glory to be got. Therefore the Knight of Coucy wore a very old helmet, sorely dinted at the top, much like a sooty crock with an iron flap that he had pushed up the better to see. Clenching and unclenching his huge fists that were covered with hair of a bluish black, he said:

"My hands are as stiff and cold as a skeleton's. I thought it was never coming to the time when I should get these things off."

The young knight vented another "Hum!" of less ill-humour, and like a threatening spectre of iron the large knight moved himself towards the fireplace and stretched out his large cold hands.

"If you have pickled your Henry enough," he said, "lend him me to take off these things." My Jeannot has a broken arm. My Peter has a crushed leg. Griselda is gadding God

[190]

knows where. I have not one to undress me in my chamber. So I came here."

"Mercy of God!" the young knight said, startled into a sudden hospitality, and removing his foot from the page, he bent down, and catching at the wet velvet of the boy's throat he threw him out into the middle of the floor. "Dirty little bastard, who have wetted my armour and art thyself wet, hurry to take off the gentle knight's potlids!"

And with a shivering, hurried obedience, the miserable page, his long hair hanging about his shoulders like rats' tails, ran to kneel down about the great black limbs of the knight before the fire. And Gertrude, coming slowly from the window, stretched out gingerly her white hands to the greasy straps and buckles round the knight's neck.

"Ha! saucy one!" the knight exclaimed. "Here is condescension!" and with his hairy fingers he touched her bare neck and shoulders. Her tiny and delicate hands slapped at his immense paws, and, when she had loosened his helmet so that he could take it off, she went to the bed and slipped herself into her dress, which was all of one piece, long and trailing in the skirts, so that she might appear taller, and of blue cloth, the sleeves, lined with yellow silk, falling to the dirty floor.

"There have never been so many broken arms and crushed legs amongst my villeins," the knight said. "We have been stumbling amongst wet rocks all these three weeks."

"Well, you are back," the young knight said. He stretched his arms wide apart with an easy gesture. "My pains are much better."

"That too is well!" the Knight of Coucy commented; "but there is plaguey trouble coming. Three times today the Lord Mortimer has been in my rooms with messages from the Queen Mother."

"Let her rave!" the young knight said. "Gentle knight, the Queen Mother is a very evil bitch. I have dined at her table but three times whilst you have been gone, and the nearest I have sat to her has been six away."

"Then there will be new fines asked you!" the Knight of Coucy said slowly. He had got his helmet off, his huge red face appearing above his iron shoulders whilst, holding his helmet patiently on his chest, he waited for the page to peel off his black thigh pieces beneath which was a suit of brown leather, marked here and there with grease.

The young knight had set himself down on the edge of his bath.

"Let the fines come!" he said. "I shall get me away to the Holy Land with Gertrude. I have a plan for assaulting the Holy Sepulchre."

"Well, it is Gertrude here and Gertrude there," the large knight said sagaciously. "You had much better see to it that your wife gives her a kennel in the yard and stay at home."

"See to it that *your* wife gives Griselda a dovecote!" the young knight gibed back. "If my wife proves to be like the Lady Blanche, she shall go packing back to Wales."

"That shall be as the cat jumps," the Knight of Coucy answered.

"Mercy of God!" the young knight said suddenly. "You have been afforded no wine. What a household is mine!"

"I was thinking as much," the Knight of Coucy answered.

Gertrude, whilst she pulled tight the laces of her dress behind her hips, was moving towards the door.

"Ho, leman! Wench! Worst of loiterers!" the young knight said. "Hasten! Run! Fall down the stairs and bring wine for the gentle Knight of Coucy! What a household is mine!"

Gertrude, who had a friendly feeling for the Knight of

Coucy because he was gross, jovial, and tickled her as often as he saw her, had been already intent on fetching him wine. For that, indeed, she had put on her dress to go below the stairs, since it would have troubled her little if he had seen her stark naked. But now she turned her head disdainfully over her shoulder and looked at the young knight.

"It is for servers, not ladies, to bring wine," she said. "I will bid the servers bring it and, when they have brought it, I will pour it out!"

The young knight exclaimed: "Mercy of God!"

The Knight of Coucy grinned broadly.

"I must get me to a witch doctor," the young knight exclaimed. "It is certain that I am bewitched, or I should take your sword, and with a turn of the wrist take off that thatch-sparrow's head. But, before God, I will be unbewitched with fumigations, and prayers, and sorceries, and then I will have that weeping mouse dropped into a fire on the city wall as a warning to all witches."

"That would be a very good thing to do," the Knight of Coucy said ironically. The infatuation of the famous young Knight of Egerton was a byword of the host in Newcastle, and many said that it was a black shame to the order of knighthood that a knight's neck should be so beneath a peasant girl's heel. These said that one day they would beat her with rods, naked, round the market-place of Newcastle and home again, to teach her manners. But many knights who made poetry held that it was very touching, and worthy of virelais or a romaunt that a knight should so love his leman, for they talked of King Cophetua and his beggar maid. As for the Knight of Coucy, he thought that it benefited his boon companion to be plagued, since it ridded him of the fits of mad temper he was used to have. Besides, Gertrude was small and like a child, and it pleased him to tickle her.

"But alas!" the young knight said, "if I have her burned I should have her no more."

The Knight of Coucy smiled sardonically.

"What can be done for a prisoner," he said, "who loves the chains that kill him?"

The Knight of Coucy was now all brown leather, immense and slightly corpulent. He looked down at the page who was gathering up the black strands of the harness from the wet floor.

"Thou, Henry," he said. "Can'st thou write? I forget. But write it down, or have it written, these words of mine before I forget them." And he repeated his last speech, counting the rhythm with his fingers on his leather chest.

"I will compose a canzone with these words for a burden and have them sung to Griselda," he said.

A PLEASANT PEACE REIGNED IN THEIR ROOM. GERTRUDE HAD
returned, bringing herself the wine, because she liked the
Knight of Coucy, and had sufficiently asserted her dignity by
the speech of refusal. The Knight of Coucy drank a huge
draft from the leathern flagon, tilting his head back. Except
upon occasions of ceremony, he disdained to drink from a
goblet or a jack, for he said that with such inferior vessels a
man could not drink himself out of breath. Then, panting and
in a deep satisfaction, he held the leather vessel before his
chest and slowly stroked his stomach. His cousin sat on the
edge of the bath and swung his naked legs.

These two knights loved each other well, and were less
resolute when they were parted, for the Knight of Egerton
could be counted on for a rash, sudden, and desperate resolution when a pinch of affairs needed it, whilst the Knight of
Coucy had a heavy peasant cunning that had served them well
when there had been time to think. So in armies and courts

they were by-named Castor and Pollux, and they were accounted the two strongest knights in the world. The Knight
of Coucy had pulled against a plough-ox at the end of a rope
and had stopped it dead, the Knight of Egerton had killed the
same ox with one blow of his fist; and it was these two knights
together who had held the lists at Bucesvalles against fourteen
picked knights and fourteen knights of Spain and High Ger-
many, running their courses through three hot days until there
were no more spears left to tilt with. This was a very famous
deed of theirs, and is recorded by four chroniclers.

The Knight of Coucy drank once more from the flagon,
and once more panted comfortably for breath; then he said
slowly:

"When I went to my chamber to find Griselda, who is
gadding it about the town, I saw there a hind from Wiltshire.
Says I, 'You are none of my men, but I know your face,' and
the fellow falls on his knees and holds me out a letter which
he says is from the Abbess of St Radigund."

"May she drown!" the young knight said. "She is the most
thorny woman that ever I met."

"What shall be in this letter?" the Knight of Coucy said.

"Please God," the young knight answered, "it be to say that
my wife Dionissia has gone with another man."

"Then you would lose her," the Knight of Coucy said.

"But her dowry would fall to me as forfeit. But I am a very
unfortunate man. It will be to say that your wife, Blanche, or
my wife, Dionissia, or both together, have done some sacrilege
for which we must pay a fine. It is a plaguey world where a
man may be fined for the sacrilege of a wife he has never
seen!"

"No, it is about miracles," the Knight of Coucy said. "I have
asked this hind, and he said it was about miracles."

"Miracles!" the young knight wondered. "Shall one write letters about miracles! Miracles will keep, and letters are nasty things to have to do with."

"So much I gathered—that it was about a miracle worker," the heavy knight continued. "It is a very stupid hind, and has not read the inside of the letter. And when I kicked him to have more news he could only blubber and curl about my knees."

"I do not like letters," the young knight said. "Let us not read this letter. Letters bring always evil tidings. I have observed that. If a woman would kiss you she does not write it in a letter; she waves her handkerchief from the top of her tower as you ride by. But if she will have money of you, or her wrongs righted, or tell you that your wife has cuckolded you, or that your house is burnt down—then she will put it in a letter."

"Well, we must read this letter," the Knight of Coucy said impassively. He waded in his leather suit to the door and called down the stairs:

"Ho, Henry! Ho, page! Ho, server! A hind waits in my chamber with a letter. Ho! A hind with a letter, convey him here."

He returned to the fire.

"Why must we be plagued?" the Knight of Egerton grumbled. "Mark me, no good will come of this!"

"If there is ill news," the Knight of Coucy said, "the sooner we have it the sooner we may plan to avert the disaster. If there is good, then it is well to know it soon."

And again he shouted to the door and called:

"Ho! a hind with a letter from Wiltshire. Ho, Henry, Ho! Hostess! someone to convey hind and letter here."

He called the words very loudly, for fear the first time no

[197]

one should have heard him. But his words, which at first had reverberated down the staircase, became as it were corked up and dull in their flight. Several persons were mounting.

And first there came, in a cloak of parrot-green velvet, with an undervest of leaf-green and fleshings of that colour, a round cap of green with three ostrich feathers, painted green and set in a brooch of gold—there came in Roger Lord Mortimer. He had a reddish, square, and curly beard, golden hair depended from his little cap; his eyes were very narrow, and he swung himself from left to right as he walked, having upon his left wrist a leathern glove painted green and with many tassels, pieces of glass, and beads of gold. Upon this glove sat the Queen's hawk, with its cap and plume of green velvet with stitchings of gold.

Roger Mortimer was not yet come to the extreme height of his ascendancy over the Queen-Mother, though it was known to be very dangerous to stand up against him, and the young king was entirely his toy. He entered the room with a little inclination of his back, saying:

"God save you, gentle knights and leman! The Queen is upon the stair."

"The Queen is welcome," the Knight of Coucy said. He held the flagon to his lips and once more drank to get it done before the Queen should be in the room. Sitting upon the side of the bath, the Young Knight continued to swing his bare legs whilst he uttered a "God save you!" beneath his breath. There was much rustling from the stairs; then, all in purple and gold, the Queen-Mother came in with the little King, as if he were in the folds of a curtain, half hidden in her immense sleeve. The Queen was a fat matron, with a cunning, determined face. Her eyes were small, brown, and keen. Her dress was of purple velvet, all of one piece, and sewn with thick gold thread that glinted in the seams. About her waist she had a rope of amber beads that was twisted before her and fell in two ropes to her feet. The King was all in scarlet, a boy of fourteen. Upon his yellow hair was a small circlet of gold; round his knees were two garters of solid gold links; the ends, passing through the buckles, fell down to the tops of his shoes that were very long and gilded. He gave his hand to Gertrude the leman to kiss, and the Queen-Mother kissed her courteously upon the cheek. But these were the only salutations. All the persons in that room gazed into each other's eyes warily and in silence, the Lord Roger in his green, swaying upon his feet in a nervous nonchalance.

"Ah, gentle knights," the Queen-Mother said, "I have a great grief against you twain."

"I have a great grief against you, gentle Queen," the Knight of Coucy said.

"A grief too, I have," the Young Knight said.

"Then have we three griefs in one room," Roger Mortimer minced. "And that is good, for Holy Writ tells us that all good things are three."

The Queen erected her head more haughtily.

"Speak your griefs," she said.

"Nay, by God, speak you yours first," the Knight of Coucy answered. He had turned round and stood back upon his heels, his considerable protuberance, all of yellow leather, stained with black grease, bowing out towards the Queen-Mother.

The Young Knight stood up suddenly beside the bath, on whose edge he sat.

"If there is to be long speaking," he said, "I will get me into the closet and put on my clothes!"

"No, do not do it," the Queen-Mother said. "I will have you hear me. You shall not escape into the cupboard. I will see your face, so I may know when this knight lies. For I know that though there are two of you you will leave the talking to the Knight of Coucy."

"Well, I am too cold without my clothes," the Young Knight answered. "Gentle Queen, if you would see me you may, and that is all there is to it." And, going to the door of the whitewashed closet, he fetched out a pair of full hose, of which the one leg was white and the other blue, a shirt of fine lawn, another shirt of steel mail which he hung ostentatiously on the side of the bath after he had rubbed it almost under Roger Mortimer's nose, and a doublet of blue with white fur.

Roger Mortimer bent down and fingered the shirt of mail.

"Well, gentle knight," he said, with a sort of sneering jest, "we shall not put a knife through that."

"Neither you, nor Sir John of Hainault could," the young man sneered cheerfully back. "I doubt I am strong enough myself. It is mail of the Saracens that will turn the edge of a scimitar; yet, as you feel, it is so light you would say it would float like the Virgin's web, and I wear it for my comfort."

"Sir John of Hainault is an honourable knight," Roger Mortimer said darkly. "He will do no stabbing in the back."

The Young Knight whistled between his teeth.

"Ah, gentle Earl, I was not miscalling the Knight of Hainault," he uttered dryly. He held before him his blue and white hose, being about to step into them. For only answer, the Lord Mortimer delicately ran the point of his white forefinger round his throat.

"Ah, if it comes to beheading," the Young Knight said, "Roger Mortimer, thy throat is as thin as mine. And remember that the wise woman of Torrington has prophesied thou shouldst be short by a head when the day came."

Roger Mortimer swallowed with rage. The Young Knight had on his hose, and coolly he stripped off his long mantle. His bare body was all marked with scars and blisters. He put his finger in a livid weal above his left breast.

"That scar, gentle Queen," he said, "I had at Bannockburn. You remember Bannockburn?"

At Bannockburn the Young Knight had been the last but one off the field, the Knight of Coucy having been the last.

"We fought into the light of the morn, gentle Queen," he said, "when King had fled, and Queen had fled, and little people like Mortimer and such were fled. So we fought on, and when our horses were dead we fought afoot. A year we lay in a Scots prison."

"Take care ye lie not ten in an English one," the Queen said highly.

The Young Knight had his head in his shirt of lawn. When it came forth, and he was clothed:

"Gentle Queen," he said, "ere we lay there ten days Roger Mortimer would have our heads!"

"That is true," Roger Mortimer answered.

"Ah, gentle Queen," the Knight of Coucy said, "what is this talk of beheading, and why should we to prison?" His voice was heavy, and he bent his brows deeply upon the Queen.

"For that you are traitors and cowards, knight," the Queen said, "and have put disorder in our army, and shamed the King and us before all our people."

The Knight of Coucy drew himself up with a minatory gravity.

"Gentle Queen," he said heavily, "you are the first that has called me coward in my life. No other would have lived after that word."

"Knight," the Queen answered, "in this you are a coward,

that you will never meet with the Scots, and so there is murmuring in the country that I and the Lord Mortimer are sold to the Scots King. But I think it is you that are sold to David le Bruce."

"Gentle Queen, you lie," the Heavy Knight said.

"It is what is told to me," the Queen answered. "And who can doubt that you have spread disorder in our forces? Two months ago your Wiltshire archers set about the knights of Sir John of Hainault. At night they fell upon them in the streets. Many they slew. Others they pursued to their houses. And there has been no peace between your men and the Flemings since that day."

"I have hamstrung twenty of my archers," the Knight of Coucy said heavily. "It is the Flemings that have laid on first every day since then. And it is all the English army now that fights your Flemish friends."

"But it was you who set your archers to this fray," the Queen said.

"Not so, Queen, and well you know it," the Knight answered. "It was the Flemings set them to it. I saw with my own eyes—and you saw from your balcony—how the Flemings carried horns, and they set spear heads into the horns and cried out, 'Berkeley!' And well you know what a horn and a spear head did at Berkeley Castle. Who knoweth better, save Lord Mortimer?"

For it was at Berkeley Castle, by means of a red-hot spear, run through the orifice of a horn and so introduced into his body, that Edward II, the husband of this Queen, was by her orders and Roger Mortimer's done to death.

The Queen-Mother shrugged her shoulders with contempt.

"Yet it was you and your cousin who stirred up the archers to their fray against the Flemings," she said.

[202]

"It was the Flemings themselves," the Knight repeated doggedly. "Whether the King, your husband, was good or bad for this nation, is not for me to say, who had nothing but good at his hands. But these Flemings—it is their boast that it was by their aid the King was cast down. They boast it in all the taverns. And they cry aloud that it is they who rule England now."

"It was you who stirred up the archers to fray against the Flemings," the Queen repeated. "I have a letter from your wife in Wiltshire praying me to pardon you for this deed and to be favourable to her."

The Young Knight had got himself into his coat.

"Merciful God!" he said, "the Lady Blanche again! Is there nothing we can do but this fool will be in it? A thousand miles away, and she will still poke her fingers in. She has longer arms than the giant Hobokolus, who picked apples in Wales when he stood in Ireland."

The Knight of Coucy strode heavily towards his armour, which lay still upon the hutch at the foot of the bed. He caught at the hilt of his sword and shook it out of the scabbard, so that all the harness fell on to the stone floor with a threatening and echoing clang. The Lord Roger Mortimer shrank back against the wall; the young King hurriedly stood out before his mother.

"Will you kill us!" the Queen cried out, and she felt behind her back for the hasp of the door. The Knight of Coucy set the point of his sword on the floor. His chin he leaned upon the hilt that was like an iron cross. He fought still with those great, long swords, though it was the fashion then to have them lighter and easier to wield; but he was a very strong man.

"Gentle Queen," he said, "I desire no more than that you

[203]

should see my strongest argument, for I am a man of little skill with words."

Swaying gently as the sword bent like a great spring, he grinned with his cunning peasant's face at the Queen.

"Would you make war upon us?" the Queen said hotly.

"May God forbid it!" the Knight of Coucy answered. "May God forbid that I should make war upon my King. But what would you have, gentle Queen? If I am put to it with imprisonment and the losing of my head, it is certain that I will do what I may to save my neck."

"What would you be—aye, you and your cousin—against all our many," the Queen said contemptuously.

"Ah, do not be too certain of your many," the Knight said. "It is certain that the great strength of the army if ever we had found the Scots would have lain in the archers. And our archers and the Lincolnshire bowmen are all you have. Nor have you even all the knighthood with you, as well you know, if it is a matter of Flemings against Englishmen. And that is all the quarrel that there is between us."

"Is it the Knight of Coucy who upholds the peasants' vile bow?" Lord Mortimer swung himself away from the wall to sneer. "The peasants' vile bow against the knight's spear and mace."

The Knight of Coucy bent his brows upon Mortimer.

"Is it the Lord Mortimer who talks of things of arms?" he asked. "He knows of them very little if he knows not that, in wars as in policies, arms have their day. So the day of the bow has come, the spear being left to be the arm of knight against knight in the tournaments that are so gentle and joyous. So, if you press me, Sir Mortimer, I will rely upon my bowmen and the bowmen of Lincolnshire against your knights and the

Flemings. And well you know that there will be with us not a few knights."

The Lord Mortimer said:

"Before God, that I should hear a knight uphold the bow! These are indeed degenerate days."

The little King said suddenly:

"Will you make war upon me! Ah, gentle knight, this is sad hearing."

"Nay, surely I will not make war upon thee," the Knight answered. "It is a far way from 'can' to 'will.'"

"You are a very traitor, Knight of Coucy," the Queen said. "I have it in your wife's hand against you. And you have other letters come from Wiltshire; I heard it as you called down the stairway. What new treacheries are you preparing in the south?"

The Young Knight, all in white and blue, said with a jocular irresponsibility:

"Nay, if the letter would but come you might keep it for yourself. I do not like letters, and would sell this for a groat."

The Knight of Coucy looked for a moment at his cousin and then at the Queen.

"That is very true," he said, "and welcome you are to the letter, for I cannot read it, nor my cousin."

"I do not believe we shall have this letter," the Queen said. "You will edge it away by some trick. You are the cunningest man that ever I saw, gentle knight."

"Well, I am a cunning man," the Knight said complacently, "so you would do better to have me upon your side than against you."

"You are as bitter a foe as ever I had," the Queen said.

"Gentle Queen," the Knight answered, "for a clever woman you are a very foolish one. And it is your cleverness that

makes you foolish. You know very well what make of a
woman my wife is—how she will never let me be; how she will
always be putting her nose in and crying out so that for peace
and comfort I am nine months of the year driven out of my
home. My wife was a lady of your body, and very well you
know her. Knowing her, you should know that she knows
nothing of my mind, for she has never listened to words that
came from my mouth. She has embroiled me with priests, with
peasants, with nuns, and with burgesses, so that that house is
a hornet's nest for outcries and complaints. It may well be
that she has heard that I set the archers upon the Flemings!
Your flatterers and favourites have been buzzing that story
abroad till it would be a deaf person that should not have
heard it. So my wife will poke her nose in where I should be
safe away from her. But if you will be such a fool as to believe your flatterers and favourites and my wife as against me—
well, your folly will skip it till it skips into a war between us.
That I swear is the truth of the matter, and you are not the
woman that can look me in the face and say I lie."

The Queen looked at him for a long time, but said nothing.
At last she brought out:

"Nevertheless, your archers did set upon the Hainaulters."

"And I have hamstrung twenty of them, and my cousin
twenty more. Forty good men that will never march again! I
wish I had them now."

"But you did not do it till after I commanded it," the Queen
said.

The Knight roared out suddenly:

"A lie! It was done before your messenger reached me.
Your messenger was Lord Mortimer, and well you know that
he would not put his nose out of the door—and you would not
let him—till twelve hours after all the fighting in the streets

was over. Whether you made that story or he is all one—it is a foul lie. You live among lies, and should know it. I am tired of you: I am tired of this place. To-morrow I and my men will get me gone from this place to the south. You may fight the Scots how you will without me."

And casting his sword contemptuously on to the pile of his black armour, he turned his back upon the Queen. Then slowly he winked at Gertrude the leman, who was beside the fireplace, for he was a much more patient man than to have lost his temper so early.

The Queen cast a look of concern at Roger Mortimer. This was what she had the most to fear. For it was agreed between them that if they were to carry on this war against the Scots they must do it with the archers, light horsemen, and the more agile of the knights. And they must carry on the war against the Scots; for there could be no doubt that the country of England cried out that the Scots must be chastised, so that already there was dissatisfaction with the Queen and her party. Liars had said that the Lord Mortimer had been paid by David le Bruce to let their troops be worsted. So that she cried out to the Knight's leathern back:

"Nay, you shall not go."

The Knight crossed his arms and did not speak.

"It is against the law that you should go," the Queen said. "You are here by the King's summons."

Gazing at the fireplace, the Knight addressed nobody, but spoke as if with himself:

"Hear how this Queen lies!" he said. "No summonses were issued to knights south of the Trent, and none called me for a war in Scotland. I am here at my own cost and will."

Again the Queen glanced with perturbation at Roger Mortimer. Though she had forgotten it, it was true what the Knight of Coucy said.

"Ah, gentle knight," the little King said, "if you are here without my summons you are a very good servant to me."

The Knight slowly shrugged his huge shoulders, and at that moment the leman Griselda came into the room with the wallet that held the letter from Wiltshire. She was tall and blonde, and her bones were well covered. She wore green and gold, and her coif of white linen was very large and folded like a napkin.

Having been kissed by the Queen out of courtesy, and having kissed the little King's hand, Griselda, who had come hurrying as soon as she had heard that the Queen was there, went with the letter to her paramour. The Knight kept his arms crossed.

"I will not take it," he said. "Give it to my cousin."

The Young Knight put his arms behind his back.

"I do not like letters," he said; "I will not take it. Give it to the Queen."

The Queen took the letter as if it had been something dangerous. Having been persuaded that it would be kept from her, she could only believe that it was some new trap when it was so surrendered. She looked at the wallet, turned it this way and that, and then handed it to the leman.

"Read you this letter," she said, "and tell us what it says."

"Ah, gentle Queen," the leman said, "letters I have none."

The Queen looked round the room.

"Who of us can read?" she asked.

And there was a silence until the little King said:

"I think I am the only one of us that can."

"Then take you it and read it, gentle son of mine!" the Queen said. The Lord Mortimer sprang to disembarrass her of the wallet; to take from it the sealed scroll of the letter; to break the seal, unroll the many sheets of vellum, and to hand them half kneeling to the King.

The Young Knight shot a glance of question at the Knight of Coucy. But the Knight had his back to them all, and the Young Knight turned to the window and called out to a man in the street, bidding him saddle a horse as soon as the shower was past, since his pains had left him and he was minded to supple his limbs by riding.

The little King read with puzzled brows, and his lips moving slowly. It was not easy for him to read anything but Mass writing.

"Do you find anything of treason?" the Queen asked.

The little King shook his head impatiently, for what he read engrossed him.

"Nothing of treason," he said; "but a very strange story." And he continued to read on, raising his small brows.

The Queen looked down upon the letter over his head. The Lord Mortimer edged nearer and nearer to gaze over his shoulder at the incomprehensible marks upon the vellum. The young King frowned.

"Now this I do not understand," he exclaimed suddenly, and he smote his little thigh. "How that thing should be a disgrace to these two knights!"

The Knight of Coucy asked suddenly:

"Nenni?"

And the Queen said:

[210]

"What things?"

"Even," the King began, as if he were talking to very stupid people, "that the ladies of these two knights should fight a tournament and a mêlée the one against the other."

"Merciful God!" the Young Knight exclaimed. He looked amazed, puzzled, and then suddenly joyous.

"Cousin," he said, "if thy wife kill mine, or mine thine, what a grace would God be showing us! If mine were dead, I should have her dower intact; if thine died, you would have joy of your fireside."

"And you would take your leman safe into Wiltshire," the Lord Mortimer laughed at him.

The Young Knight looked him coolly between the eyes.

"I will take my leman into Wiltshire," he said, "if all the wives of all the devils in hell await me there. And Roger Mortimer may be at the head of them."

The Knight of Coucy had come round upon his heel.

"Gentle King," he said, "of your mercy read us this letter."

The King had finished his private perusal, and he looked up at his mother for encouragement.

"Read! read!" she said. "I warrant there is treason in it."

"No treason," the King said; "but a very strange story!"

He arranged the sheets, coughed in his throat, and addressed his eyes to the page:

" 'From the Abbess of the poor convent of St Radigund by Stapleton-by-Salisbury, to the Knights of Coucy and of Egerton, greeting in God!' "

The young King stuttered a little.

"Who is this Abbess?" the Queen asked of Roger Mortimer. He shrugged his shoulders.

"What know I?" he said. "I think she is from France."

" 'Know,' " the young King read again, " 'that a very great

disgrace awaits ye at the hands of your intemperate wives. It behoves ye at once to leave all other things and to hasten back here.' "

"Ha!" the Queen exclaimed, "here is the treason that I knew I should smell out. These knights have had this letter written to them as an excuse to hurry away from our army. This plot is very plain!"

The Knight of Coucy bent his brows upon the Queen and cleared his throat, but the young King stamped his foot.

"Queen-Mother, be silent," he said. "If I am to read this letter I will have peace," for he was proud of his reading. Nevertheless, he had never before so spoken to his mother, and she glanced at Roger Mortimer.

"I think we will not have this letter," she said. "It is like to be all a parcel of lies."

"But I will read the letter," the King said angrily. "We are the King; we do not leave off what we have begun." And the Lord Mortimer almost invisibly shook his head at the Queen.

" '. . . hasten back here,' " the King began once more to read. " 'For of a truth,' " he continued, whilst the Queen snorted, " 'here all things are at a very evil pass, and there is no more any order in this countryside. It began with the coming of the Greek slave of the old Knight of Egerton of Tamworth, and since then there has been no more peace in this world.' "

"Ha!" the Young Knight interjected; "that slave of my brother is come, then. We had awaited him for a month before I left. It was a very faithful servant."

The King frowned, and once more let his fluting voice sound out.

" 'If this slave, who is called the Sieur Guilhelm Sorrell, were not come with a very holy miracle, I should write that he is the son of the devil. But in truth I know not what to think. Know then that, upon his coming, he wrought several miracles among the halt and the maimed. Our hens of this convent, too, he has restored to health in a singular fashion. And, with his own hand alone, by the aid of spirits in shining armour—as has been testified—he slew and put to flight one hundred robbers, taking many prisoners and laying a log across their legs to hold them down, ten in one row.' "

"Nenni! that was a good stroke," the Knight of Coucy exclaimed.

" 'And since then his miracles have never ceased,' " the King read on. He stopped and looked at the Knight.

"Now what is in all this to make a cry about?" he asked. "I see nothing, nor in this that follows:

" 'The sacred relic which this pilgrim or slave bears is the cross which St Joseph of Arimathea fashioned out of the gold of the money-changers whom our Lord did scourge in the Temple of Jerusalem, and though this is a very sacred thing, yet it has what must, in my blindness, appear an evil property. For no sooner do the eyes of beholders fall upon it than they are filled with desire for its possession. My own nuns became mad at the sight of it, so that they sought to take it by force. And when I prevented them they cried out upon me. And they continue to cry out, so that there is no more any peace in this convent. Work that should be done is neglected; the gardens are no more cultivated; the fruit upon the trees goes unpicked; the very prayers are hurried and gabbled through, so that the sisters may come together at the hour of blood-letting and cry out against me, their Abbess and shepherd, for that I did prevent their taking this cross into my keeping. All this is very strange.' "

Again the King looked at the faces of his hearers.

"Now this I do not find strange at all," he said. "If a sacred relic came, what more natural than it should work miracles, and if it be of gold, what more natural than to desire to possess it? I think that this Abbess was very foolish to prevent the nuns from taking it. I should desire to take it myself."

"Yet it is *my* cross!" the Young Knight said.

"Someone's it must be," the King said, "that is evident." And he read on:

"'Thus things are in a very evil pass. But worse is to be told: worse things, almost unimaginable; for no sooner does this slave come to the castle here than a great wrangling breaks out between the wife of you, gentle Knight of Coucy, and the wife of you, Young Knight, as to who shall possess this cross. The Lady Blanche says she will have it, being the cousinly blood of the Young Knight. The Lady Dionissia says she will have it, being his wife. The Lady Blanche says that the Lady Dionissia is no more than the wife for the time of you, gentle Knight of Egerton.'"

"Well, that is a very nice point," the Young Knight said. "Who won it? If it was my wife whom I have never seen, I dread for my life. For anyone who can beat my cousin Blanche will throw me over a windmill."

"And your leman too?" the Lord Mortimer said.

"Nay, that she shall not," Gertrude exclaimed suddenly from the bed on which she was sitting. "I will not go into this Wiltshire."

"Aye, you shall," the Young Knight said. "I will bind you hand and foot, and throw you over a pack-horse."

"Now this is a very hot passion of a knight for his leman," the Lord Mortimer said; "there shall be many ballads made of this ride into Wiltshire."

"'Oh, the shame! oh, the disgrace!'" the King continued to

read out the Abbess's words. " 'I have seen these two ladies at it. Almost they did tear each other's coifs in their straining desire to possess this cross. And—I shudder to write the words —now they will fight a tournament and a mêlée, they and all their ladies, for it.'

"There is something fanatical about this Abbess," the King broke off to comment. "Why should ladies not fight a tournament? I will have some of my own do it before me. But here this Abbess goes on:

" 'What more filthy, what more foul could be thought upon than that ladies should put upon them the armour of men, defacing the bodies that God has given them with sweat, maiming, and other iniquities. For their bodies. . . .' "

The King blushed.

"This sentence I will not read aloud," he said, "but I will pass on to:

" 'Therefore, good and gentle knights, hasten home and stay this great disaster and shame. They will fight this damnable tournament upon the 27th of September.' "

The Knight of Coucy said:

"Hum!"

" 'Much trouble, too, is caused by worshippers who come to adore this slave and this relic,' " the King read on. " 'They camp them down before the castle in great hordes so that the grass whereon we pasture our geese is defiled and trodden down. To this slave or pilgrim they bring many offerings of great value. I have heard that in one week he has had as many as £94 in money alone. They follow him in great crowds wherever he goes.

" 'In short, I do not know what to think. For the image is holy and the man protected by Heaven. Yet I have heard from a person I believe, that is in the castle, that there is not one

woman there that has not lain with him at night. That perhaps is not a great thing. So at least I am told to consider by
the excellent and erudite Dean of Salisbury. But I think, none
the less, that it is not a very becoming thing that maidens,
meeting each other in the dark on their way to caress and
fondle this pilgrim, should fall one upon another. And all
these women are packed into the castle of Stapleton, living
there together to be near this slave and to prepare for this
damnable enterprise of the tournament. This, too, should be
of import to the Young Knight, that the Lady Dionissia follows this slave about as if she were his shadow. They hold
hands all day long, and gaze into the eyes of one another. And
this pilgrim has been heard to ask whether such a marriage as
that of the Lady Dionissia's might not, by the grace of the
Holy Father, be done away with if she lose her dowry.' "

"Please God, it might!" the Young Knight said. "I will
help it all I can with my prayers if I may have the dowry. For
this would be a miracle of wonder beyond all the cross."

"Well then, may it so turn out," the King said. He glanced
down at the letter again. " 'Touching the Lady Blanche,' " he
read ——

The Knight of Coucy exclaimed: "Ha!" and the Lord Mortimer grinned.

—" 'I cannot discover that she has done deeds of sin with
this slave. Maybe she waits till he shall tire of the other lady.
I cannot read her heart. She occupies herself much with the
little page Jehan, having him in her bower and buying him
fine clothes. Aye, he hath a hawk of his own. But I think he is
too young and simple to do deeds of love, and the servants
say he declares himself to love only his mother and the Virgin.
So of that I will say no more.

" 'Thus much have I reported to you, gentle knights, for

it is my duty, being Abbess and the highest religious person now in these parts, and I think we have only half done our duty when we have stopped at uttering prayers. But though I have the will to stop this infamous disorder of a tournament, I have no power. Hasten, then, hasten upon your swift horses and come—purge this country of its disorders. Your friend in God.' "

The King ceased reading and looked over the letter. His hearers were all silent, and he exclaimed:

"I think this is a very masterful Abbess. I am glad she sits near no castle of mine."

"Ah, gentle knight," the Queen said darkly and insultingly to the Knight of Coucy, "did I not say that this was a treasonable letter? This is all the lies that you have had written to you to have a colourable excuse to be gone."

The young King looked up at his mother with candid eyes.

"Ah, gentle Queen," he said, "I do not think that that is so. It is too great a story to have invented, nor do I think the Knight of Coucy is the man to invent these things. I think his motto is like mine: Keep troth! And he will keep it. But yet I do not see that this letter should call these knights away, for of them we have great need."

The Knight of Coucy looked at the little King with pleasant eyes. During the reading of the letter he had not spoken, save when the question of his wife's honour had been broached. But being appeased on that point—for he knew that had the Abbess had any grounds she would have known of them, being a very skilful spy—being appeased on this point, he had sunk into listening silence again.

"Gentle Queen," he said, "I think the King, being English, shoots nearer the mark. You are a French woman, and the French are always over clever, so that they miss the truth because it lies too near them. Now, if you will hear me speak I will deliver my thoughts as far as they have gone."

"Speak on," the little King said.

"Now, I will not hear them," the Queen called out. "Come away, my son. Stay you, Lord Mortimer, and hear this fellow!"

"Nay, I will not get me gone," the little King maintained. "I will stay with the Lord Mortimer."

The Queen clenched her fists with rage: she wavered for a moment, and then brushed through the door, taking leave of nobody.

"Ah, gentle King," the Large Knight said, "hear, then, all that I will speak truly." He cleared his throat and breathed deep. "To the King, your father, I was a true servant; but he we have heard is dead. Upon the news of his death, my cousin and I and many knights that you know of, came together and consulted as to our duty. And so we made it out that our duty was towards you. Had the King lived we would have fought for him, for we are men made for fighting and for little else. But your mother was too quick with us, and had him down and dead before we could rise, as you know. So he was dead, and it was perhaps as well. As for this talk of wrangling with the Hainaulters, that is folly. But it was natural that my men should fall upon them. For it was they who landed with your mother from France and did the King to death. That might have been well. But now they give themselves great airs of how they rule this our country of England: they are loud about it in the market-place and in all the inns. This my men will not stand. I did not will them to set upon the Flemings: I have honourably punished them when it was to be done. But my men and I are as of one family, after the old fashion of things. I cannot keep them from the Flemings; they will always be about their ears, so that our marches are hindered and our strategies come to nothing. And, since my men are as of my family, I will not punish them any more. So I must needs get me gone, if you will not send away the Flemings."

"And if that be declared a treason?" the Lord Mortimer asked.

"In the first place it is no treason," the Knight answered, "for my cousin and I came here of our free will and without summons, since by law and custom no knight south of the Trent can be summoned to serve in a Scots war; but, if you will call it a treason, then we will quarrel upon it. I am a man for fighting, and so are many of my friends. To me it is little odds against whom I fight, and I had rather fight you than many others."

"But that would be to fight against me!" the King said.

"Not so, little King," the Knight answered, "for I think it would be all one to you whether we or the Lord Mortimer counselled you, and I think it would be better for your realm if we did."

"This is monstrous free talking," the Lord Mortimer brought out. His mouth grinned, and he was white about the nostrils.

"It is well that it has come to free talking," the Knight answered, "for it was time!"

He paused, and continued after a moment:

"I will speak my thoughts roughly, and do you consider them at leisure. It is evident to me that no good can come of this Scots' quarrel whilst the Flemings are of the army. If you will send them home, this I will do. With the Flemings we can do nothing, and they are of no avail against the Scots. They are heavy armed men upon great horses, and time out of mind it has been proved that what is needed against the Scots are bowmen. If you will send them home we shall be the stronger;

for as it is, whilst we wait for their heavy horses to stumble amongst the rocks, the Scots break camp and are away, so that we never come at them. In this way great discredit has come, as the gentle Queen said, upon her and the Lord Mortimer. But it is because of the Flemings. I do not say that without them we can do much, but we can do more."

"I think you have the right of it," the King said. "I have often observed that whilst we waited for Sir John of Hainault the Scots got them gone."

"Sir John of Hainault," the Knight of Coucy continued, "is a great knight and a famous captain. I have never known a better. But for this enterprise he is a hindrance. I am not at one with you when you say that there is nothing in the Abbess's letter to call us back. I think this tournament of women is a disaster, and if I may catch my wife sword in hand, so I will lay my sword upon her that she will not again be as froward for many years, or never again at all. But it is six weeks to the day for that tournament. Now this I will do. Let us leave the Flemings, and for ten days let us ride straight into Scotland, burning and harrying. Let us ride ten days back by another road, burning and harrying still. If the Scots will meet us, so much the better. I do not think that they will; then shame will fall upon them because they have let their land be harried. If you will, you may leave the Flemings for the protection of the Queen and of this city of the New Castle. It is all one to me, so they ride not with us. But in three weeks' time I will be back here, and next day I will ride to Louth, so that in another three weeks I may come to Stapleton."

The Knight of Egerton exclaimed:

"Oh! oh!"

"I think this is a very gentle offer," the King said.

"Then devise upon it with the gentle Queen, and to-morrow

by day I will come and devise more," the Knight of Coucy said.

"I do not like this freedom of the tongue," the Lord Mortimer said.

"Ah, gentle lord," the Knight answered, "let me tell you this in your ear. All lessons of honourable chivalry teach us this: It is good to fight; it is good to lay on the hard blows of gentle prowess. But it is bad to have bad blood against a gentle knight. Fighting is the day's work, as revelry is the work of the night. If so you will observe the rules, you may yet die well. But I think you will yet die by the headsman, as the wise woman has foretold. So God keep you."

The little King was gone down the stairway, having made his greetings modestly; but before the Lord Mortimer had made his exit the Knight of Coucy had sat himself heavily upon the hutch. He breathed with a heavy satisfaction, and, pulling his fair leman to him, he sat her upon his knee and squeezed her waist. Of this leman he was very fond. She had been the wife of a goldsmith of Viay, and after the sack of that town he had bought her of a bowman, who had, with others, plundered her house, and was leading her through the streets naked, and with her hands tied. And since that time he had seldom been without her company upon his campaigns. In the winter she lived very virtuously in the city of Salisbury, where many of the clergy came to eat at her table, for she was too stately and proud to consort with the wives of the citizens of that town.

"Ma mie!" the Knight said. He tweaked her chin, which was like a peach for fair softness, and he smiled as if at a foolish thought. "Almost I have it in me to say that I will so maim my wife that through all this winter you shall live in my castle of Stapleton whilst my wife lies abed. So the Knight of Egerton would do for his Gertrude."

"In God's name, castle me no castle," the leman said. "I am much better when the winter howls in my little fair house in a cosy city, and I have windows of buttered paper and lie warm."

"Aye, so thou does," the Large Knight said; and she kissed him on the lips, for she liked him very well.

"Ah, gentle knight," the Young Knight said, "that is your resolution upon this letter?"

"That is my resolution," the Knight of Coucy said over his leman's shoulder. "In six weeks, upon the day of the tournament, we will ride into their lists to challenge, and, if my wife will ride against me, I will throw her very ill. And if she will not, I will so belabour her with heavy blows as she flies that she will not again rise from her bed in many days. And this, I think, is her due. For whilst she made life unendurable for me at home, she was acting like most wives. But now that she has written a fool's letter to this Queen, meddling with my affairs abroad—for she will always be with her nose in things—now that she has taken a man's part she must ensue a man's burden. For this is intolerable and past bearing. Or so I think, and this is my plan. If you have a better you shall tell me it."

The Young Knight looked at Gertrude, but upon her sulky face there was no inspiration.

"Ah, gentle knight," the Young Knight answered, "it is a very good plan, and I see none better. But I would it had been a plan that had kept us away a year or more. For you have perceived from this Abbess's letter that my wife has an amourette for this slave, and would break our marriage. Heartily I wish it were done; but this will take some time, for there must be messages to Rome on their part about it. And I cannot, within the rules of chivalry, sit in my castle with my wife in my castle and her paramour in my castle and all. I must of duty kill the one or the other, or both."

"That is even so," the Large Knight said gravely.

"Yet I bear them no ill will," the Young Knight continued to muse. "I am a very unfortunate man. For if I slay my wife her dowry passes back to her father. And if I slay the slave, I remove that which should make my wife desire not to be my wife. And yet again, I cannot, by all the rules, go wandering houseless through the winter months. That would be an unheard-of thing!"

"That truly you cannot do," the Knight of Coucy agreed. He lifted his leman from his knee and gathered up most of his armour upon his right arm. His left he set round Griselda's waist.

"Well, we will go eat and do gentler things," he said. "If you can think upon a better plan I shall be very glad. But I see none better. I pray you send Henry the page after me with the rest of my armour." And he padded from the room in his stockinged feet.

The Young Knight sat mournfully himself down upon the hutch, and called Gertrude to sit upon his knee.

"Why will you not be to me as Griselda is to her paramour?" he asked mournfully. "You see how I cudgel my brains for you." And he kissed her for a long time. She withdrew her cheek patiently when he was finished.

"Did you not observe that Griselda had a new green dress?" she said. "It trailed behind her for a bow's length. This is the newest fashion of Paris. Even the Queen has not such a dress. Give me one like it, and I shall know that you are a mighty lord."

The Young Knight groaned deeply.

[223]

"Get the sempstresses here and the clothiers to-night," he said.

Gertrude looked him in the eyes.

"And it shall be of grass-green velvet? And upon the sleeves shall be points of gold? And the train shall drag out behind me a bow length and a half? And it shall be so heavy with stuff that I can scarce walk? And I may have a folded hennin so broad that I cannot come in at the door?"

He said, "Yes! Yes!"

Then she threw her arms about his neck and kissed him on the lips with all the ardour of her young body.

PART FOUR

I

M̲ʀ Sᴏʀʀᴇʟʟ ᴡᴀꜱ ʀɪᴅɪɴɢ ɪɴᴛᴏ ᴛʜᴇ ɴᴀʀʀᴏᴡ ꜱᴛʀᴇᴇᴛꜱ ᴏꜰ Sᴀʟɪꜱ-
bury. The houses appeared to him to be indescribably squalid,
and the roads filthy. Before him ran a great rabble crying out
and casting up dirty caps, and behind him was the Lady Dionissia. She was upon her white horse, in her green dress, and
she had with her four of her Welsh men-at-arms. They had
round caps of steel, jerkins of russet leather, and short spears
whose heads divided into hooks with which they could pull
horsemen from their saddles. In all this tumult Mr Sorrell
could hardly keep his head, for though he had been in Wiltshire nearly two months, this was the first time that he had
entered this city.

The houses were all very low; they were all built of mud,
and they were all raggedly thatched, house-leeks growing
from many roofs, and on others great tufts of flags. The houses
were set down at all angles to the road. Sometimes it was very
narrow, so that they could hardly pass with all their rabble,

and the geese fled shrieking at their approach. Sometimes it was so broad that, as if it had been a village green, the great pigs would continue to wallow undisturbed in the pools of mud.

But it was the noise of the crowding alone that troubled Mr Sorrell. Her Welsh men-at-arms could beat old women out of the road of the Lady Dionissia's horse, giving great, brutal blows with their spear-staves upon heads, faces, and breasts, and it in no way aroused feelings of indignation in Mr Sorrell. He had become so much a native of the place and time that nothing any longer much astonished or disturbed him. Besides, he was so immensely engrossed in his own thoughts that he observed no more than as if he had been hurrying through the streets of an Oriental bazaar upon some important mission.

He observed only noise, dirt, nauseous smells, and great crowds of importunate and ugly people. They were nearly all in ragged clothes of a grey homespun. Some had capes, some hoods with long tails like funnels; most of the men had leather belts; most of the women went bare-legged, and were very dirty; most of the children were naked, or nearly naked, and nearly all of them had wolfish eyes, and were crooked, distorted, or bore upon their faces pockmarks of a hideous kind. To Mr Sorrell they appeared to be all very disagreeable and negligible animals—grey, colourless, hungry, and clamorous. From time to time they would pass a friar in his long brown robe. With brawny bare legs, girdle of white rope, and shaven crown, he would stand and gaze nonchalantly at the passing crowd, crossing himself suddenly when he perceived the sacred relic of St Joseph that Mr Sorrell wore now round his neck.

And as they came more towards the centre of the town, having wound through innumerable alleys and lanes, the

shadow of the immense cathedral began to fall upon them.
Here there were one or two houses of stone, and below such
as were still of mud there were huge cellars, with great steps
going down to them, so that you could perceive bales of
cloth set out to attract customers, men weaving at looms, or
great joints of meat hanging upon hooks. Over these cellars
there were suspended signs—gilded suns, boys painted green
and brown, swans all white or unicorns all white, but with
collars and horns gilded. From these cellars there would
emerge stout men in green jerkins or red surcoats furred with
white lambswool. Upon their heads they wore head-dresses
of four or five yards of cloth, folded together and falling
down over their ears upon the one side. Their thumbs they
would stick into their belts of leather, and from the cellar
steps behind them, upon a level with their calves, would appear the broad white hoods and the wondering eyes of their
wives.

They passed under a narrow gateway, and came into an
open space with small houses, mostly of stone, and some of
two storeys, dotted under the protection of the enormous
cathedral, like little vessels in the convoy of a great galleon
here and there in the shadow. The spire towered up into the
serene blue of the sky; round the top, like an untidy cluster
of mistletoe, there was a scaffolding, with upon it the tiny
figures of men at work. And around and below the spire the
great white nave of the cathedral rose up clear-chiselled, and
decorated with the figures of saints as if it had been an immense
jewel casket.

At the door of the cathedral the Lady Dionissia abandoned
Mr Sorrell, leaving him in charge of an old man in a black,
furred garment, who was going to lead him to the place where
the Dean was. She herself was going back into the town to

[229]

purchase a preparation of the juice of fir trees which was said to be sovereign for hardening and strengthening the hands of warriors, and she went away between the little houses, her men-at-arms around her, one of them leading Mr Sorrell's horse.

Mr Sorrell followed his guide into a bright, gaudy place that was the interior of the cathedral. The immense pillars were painted a strong blue, and the little pillars running up them were bright scarlet; the high windows through which the sun fell were all in violent, crude and sparkling colours, and these colours, thrown down, splashed a prismatic spray all over the floor. This was of bright yellow tiles.

Mr Sorrell exclaimed:

"My God!"

For although his head was full of his mission to the Dean, to the exclusion of all other thoughts, nevertheless he had so confidently conceived of a cathedral as all grey, solemn, and ancient, that he could not but be overcome. Here was such newness—here was such a brilliant profusion of colours, that even the vastness of the building seemed to be lost. Far up in the choir was a great glare of gold utensils, and there many candles burnt, flickering and twinkling in the draughts from unfinished windows, and it was only when he noticed how small the men around him seemed that he understood how great was the building, whose roof, so far above his head, was all of grass-green, picked out with the bright golden images of angels, of serene queens, and of grinning fiends. The men all around him were talking at the tops of their voices, so as to be heard the one above the other. An old peasant in a black hood was screaming into the ear of a townsman in a green cape, that if he sold corn for less than a penny a quarter, ruin would fall upon his roof; the townsman shouted back that his neighbour Jenkyn had bought corn for three-farthings from Will of the Dyke. A man with roses in his hair, his hood thrown back, and a musical instrument of yellow wood with a black neck slung at his left side, was telling the news from Devizes and the west to a dozen men and women of the better sort. A horse-merchant, with a great whip, was extolling the merits of his mare called Joan. This animal had carried three fat persons from Swindon to Salisbury in an afternoon. Her price could not be less than twenty-two shillings. Two journeymen butchers, seated on the ground with their backs against a pillar and their long flesh-knives falling from their belts, were drinking from a black leathern flagon turn by turn, and talking at the tops of their voices about the bad women of Fallow. And with the constant coming and going of the people, and the clapping of the great doors, all this place was like a sea of sounds that echoed, eddied, and trembled beneath the coloured distances of the lofty roof.

Pushing his way through the crowd in the aisle, where it was mostly small hucksters who had brought little baskets and frails of cherries or of eggs to sell, the old guide held Mr Sorrell by the stuff of his sleeve and pulled him along.

In the wall of a lofty side-chapel, that was painted all blue with gilt stars, the old man opened a little door, and they came out into the sudden peace of cloisters. Here walls were frescoed in gold and red, with scenes from the life of Our Lady. Before each of the pillars of the long corridors there stood a monk or a chaplain reading in a book. Sometimes there were two, holding their heads together and whispering. One monk was painting the music in a psaltery. The sunlight poured down to the bright grass of the one side; the great tower of the cathedral went away up into space. A peacock with its bright hues paced slowly over the grass, its tail spreading far behind and its crowned head erect. Upon a long bench in the farther wall there sat many of the chapter clergy. They leant their heads together and whispered and laughed, for that day was blood-letting day, and they were permitted to take their ease. One of them was feeding a number of pigeons with peas that he dropped one by one to the ground, laughing with pleasure to see how the pretty blue creatures crowded one upon the other, and telling his neighbour that this should be a lesson to them against the sin of gluttony.

Beyond another little door Mr Sorrell and his guide came into a sunlit garden. Here there were paved walks of stone, plots of grass, and little low fences of trelliswork along which there grew a great profusion of red and white striped roses. A white deer that had about its neck a collar of gold came trotting towards them, and it was followed by a brown monkey that sprang on to the gown of Mr Sorrell's guide and felt in his pockets for food. In the middle of this garden there stood a fair house all of squared stones. It was of three storeys, and had five high gables. In the large stone hall of the ground floor five boys were playing ball. These were the Dean's pages, and upstairs in a little room sat the Dean, to whom his lean chaplain was reading a book of the travels of Dares and Dictys.

"Ha!" the Dean exclaimed, and pleasure showed itself upon his face, "you are come to tell me more prophecies! I had rather hear you than many books." For this Dean was a man with an insatiable taste for hearing tales, and, above all, prophecies. Mr Sorrell reflected for a moment.

"Holy man of God," he said—for he had already so far learnt his manners—"I am come to buy very valuable advice. I will have your advice first, and then I will pay for it by telling you what I know." The Dean looked serious for a moment, then he smiled all over his broad and comfortable face, and sent away the chaplain and the old man who had brought Mr Sorrell there. Mr Sorrell sat down on a wooden chest, and looked round the room whilst he collected his words, for he wished to be very precise.

The room contained several chests with great locks of iron, some shelves upon which were a few books bound in velum, a great reading pulpit, the chair with the back to it upon which the Dean sat, and a little three-legged stool which had lately served the chaplain. The windows were square and of transparent talc, for the Dean was a very wealthy man and could afford himself such luxuries. These windows let through a soft and golden light in the summer, and in the winter they served marvellously to keep out the draughts. So it was said of a pleasant and kind woman in that country, that she was as warm as the Dean of Salisbury's bower.

For the first time since he had been in those parts, Mr Sorrell felt that he was about to conduct a sane and ordinary business interview. The Dean smiled upon him indulgently, his hands folded upon his comfortable stomach, and, making no more words about it, he said:

"I desire to marry the Lady Dionissia."

The Dean surveyed him for a moment or two of silence.

"I do not understand why you should desire to marry her. Besides, she is married already."

"But you understand," Mr Sorrell said, "that I desire to do things respectably."

The Dean looked at him rather blankly.

"I do not understand that word," he said. "I have never heard it."

"Why, it means," Mr Sorrell answered—and he racked his

brain for a French word with which to make his meaning clear—"it means decently, in order . . ."

The Dean threw his head back and laughed.

"That you can hardly do, for it is neither decent nor in order to desire to marry a lady who is already married."

"I desire to do it," Mr Sorrell said, "with the sanction of the Church."

"That, of course," the Dean said seriously, "is another matter."

He was silent for some moments, and then he said:

"Can you not be persuaded to abandon this endeavour? For I am sure you may enjoy, if you have not enjoyed already, all the little delights of love."

Mr Sorrell attempted an "Oh!" of scandalised protest, but the Dean waved it aside with one fat hand.

"For consider," he said, "what troubles this shall bring upon the head of you and of this gentle lady. What outcries will there not be; what journeyings backwards and forwards to Rome; what rages of fathers and husbands and cousins! I am sure the Lady Dionissia is not of one mind with you."

"The Lady Dionissia thinks as I desire her to think," Mr Sorrell said. "Hitherto she has not given much thought to such things; but she listens to my desires, and I desire that this should be arranged decently and in order."

The Dean looked at him with an air of pleasant mystification.

"This is a very strange matter," he said, "but I cannot find that it is discreditable in you to desire to have the blessing of the Church upon your union. Nevertheless, it is strange and unnatural."

"Such, nevertheless, is my desire," Mr Sorrell said obstinately. And then, his troubles overcoming him, he began

[234]

to speak with an eloquence that he had never really known before.

"Sir," he said, "this desire is so strong in me that I am a changed man. I no longer know myself. At night I cannot sleep for thinking of it, and by day I can give no attention to matters which should occupy my thoughts. I find myself sighing and groaning when I walk alone in the fields."

"I think you do not walk very often alone in the fields," the Dean said pleasantly.

"In short," Mr Sorrell continued, "my nights are unbearable, and my days are like my nights, so that if I cannot find relief I think I shall lose my reason."

Leaning back in his chair, the Dean continued to smile pleasantly and amiably.

"Well, I have heard the tales of many lovers, and they are all much alike—all tales of sighing and groaning and sleepless nights, and walking alone in fields, and complaining and calling upon death to end their pains."

"But I have never called upon death," Mr Sorrell said. "I desire to have life and peace."

"That is the most godly thing I have heard you say," the Dean commented, "for most lovers desire self-murder, which is a mortal sin against the laws of the Church. But this is a very whimsical and comical affair, for most lovers complain and call upon death because their ladies are ungentle, do not give ear to their suits, spurn their lovers, or are shut up in strong castles by fathers, mothers, or cruel and ungentle husbands. But you sigh and groan because of obstacles that you yourself have set up to the crowning of your desires. Now tell me this. You have had, since you have been here, many amourettes with ladies who were not married, but I have not heard that for these you desired the sanction of the Church."

"Oh, my God," Mr Sorrell said, in tones which exhibited both shame and horror, "how can you mention these things in the same breath with my passion for this lady, who is like a thing holy and set apart? Since I have known her well . . ."

"Yes, yes," the Dean interrupted, "I have heard of such feelings, but I have never known them fall so suddenly upon any sinful man."

"It has been like a thunderbolt," Mr Sorrell said, "like an avalanche."

"I do not know what an avalanche is," the Dean answered, "but indeed it has been very sudden. And I might congratulate you upon your return to a greater chastity of life were it not that I foresee, arising from that sudden change, a great many troubles for this gentle lady whom I regard as my ward. That you were preparing for some such step I was well assured; but I thought it would rather have been that, getting yourselves into disguises and laying hands upon such money as you may take, you would have gone away together to other lands."

"That, too, we had thought of," Mr Sorrell said; "but you will admit that it is much more satisfactory to put matters upon a proper footing. The responsibility would have been too great. How could I take her bright and splendid life into my hands, when for all I know at any moment I may disappear back to where I came from?"

"But supposing that marriage is broken, and you yourself married to her," the Dean asked, "what would the marriage profit her if you should disappear, as you say, to the place from which you came?"

Mr Sorrell passed his hands over his eyes. He was perplexed and worried. "Of course, it is not very much to offer her," he said, "but she would at least have the benefit of a name and a position."

The Dean shrugged his shoulders very slightly.

"Oh, I know," Mr Sorrell said, "it is miserably little to offer, but what can I do? As a gentleman I know I ought to go away, to take myself out of her life. But I have not the strength of mind; besides, where could I go to?"

The Dean appeared no longer to be listening to him. At last he said slowly:

"And how do the offerings of the faithful and the grateful come in?"

"In the last two weeks," Mr Sorrell said, "there have been brought to me innumerable pigs, sheep, eggs, cheeses, firkins of butter, and yards of cloth for the poorer sort of people, and from the better class, in the last fortnight, forty-seven pounds in gold and silver."

The Dean leant slightly forward.

"And the disposition of this gold and silver, and these beasts and food?" he asked.

Mr Sorrell considered for a moment; having been prompted by Dionissia, he knew his ground very well. And this was business.

"Man of God," he said slowly, and with unconcern, "as for the beasts, and the meat, these I have given to the Lady Blanche. And it has been decreed that if in the end the custody of the cross falls to the Lady Blanche, then these sheep and other beasts shall be considered to be hers, and the Lady Dionissia shall pay the Lady Blanche for the food and lodging of herself and men. For they are all now, for greater safety, and better to practise feats of arms, living in the castle of Stapleford."

The Dean nodded his head slowly.

"So much I knew," he said; "but if the cross falls to the Lady Dionissia?"

"Then," Mr Sorrell answered, "such beasts and food as the Lady Blanche has had shall be considered as the Lady Dionissia's payment for her food and lodging."

"That seems to be a very reasonable arrangement," the Dean said. "But still, it appears to me that the Church is left out in the matter of geese and cheeses."

"No, no," Mr Sorrell answered, "that too has been thought of. For I am aware that such miracles are in a sense Church matters, and that if I had not the sanction of the Church these things could not take place, for I might be turned away and discredited. So that already, as you know, we have made separate offerings of food and cloth to the chapter; and now such things come in so fast that the pigsties, the sheep-pens, the larders, the cellars, and the butteries of Stapleford Castle are all overflowing. And for the sustenance of the people of the castle one-fourth of these provisions is more than sufficient, so that three-fourths of them we will very willingly give to the chapter."

"That is well for the chapter," the Dean said. "But how is it as to the gold and silver?"

"For that," Mr Sorrell said, "in these six weeks I have had given me ninety pounds. In the first four weeks it was forty-three, in the last two, as I have told you, it was forty-seven. The forty-three pounds are in a bag which is carried by one of the Lady Dionissia's retainers. It is now in the city of Salisbury, and will presently be brought here as an offering to the Church."

The Dean leant still further forward.

"To the Church?" he asked.

"Man of God," Mr Sorrell said, "I am a stranger here, and it is with difficulty and only in a stilted manner that I speak the language. But I considered that the Church and the most eminent pillar of the Church are one and the same. So that when I said that these forty-three pounds would be given to the Church, I meant they would be given to yourself."

The Dean nodded slowly.

"And for the future?" he asked.

"For the future," Mr Sorrell said, "we had determined to give in that proportion to the Church—that is to say, of every ninety pounds, forty-three."

"It would be better," the Dean said warily, "if the proportion were forty-seven to the Church, and forty-three to yourselves."

Mr Sorrell seemed to himself once more to be a publisher negotiating percentages with a bookseller.

"That, too, might be possible," he said, "if your Holiness could bring about the dissolution of the Lady Dionissia's marriage before the return of her husband from the war."

The Dean considered for a time.

"That, I think, will be very difficult," he said, "for at the most the gentle knights will be three months at the war, and the hearing of your cause at Rome will take a long time, even though I report most favourably upon it. And it is a fit and proper thing that the Church should have the major part. This will be a very difficult matter to argue."

"It is not for me," Mr Sorrell said, "to dispute what is said by one so learned in the law of the Church, but I think, just because your Holiness *is* so learned, it should be a comparatively easy affair. For permit me to observe that it is more easy to dissolve a marriage that has already taken place, than it is to break the validity of a precontract of marriage. In short, if the Lady Dionissia should be now only precontracted to marry, instead of actually married to the Knight of Egerton of Tamworth, it would be much more difficult."

The Dean gazed pleasantly at Mr Sorrell.

"I perceive," he said, "that you have not come here without being prompted by the Lady Dionissia as to what it is that you should say."

"It is not my habit," Mr Sorrell answered, "to go to market without learning all that I can about the merchandise that I desire to buy, or how the sale should be conducted."

"That, too, is very prudent," the Dean said. He remained silent, and appeared to be pondering deeply for some little time, and then he brought out the words:

"You are aware of all that you desire to commit yourself to? There is, for instance, the Lady Blanche."

"Why," Mr Sorrell answered, "it is true that there is the Lady Blanche. But she is a very unaccountable lady; it is so difficult to foresee what she will do that it is almost a waste of thought to attempt to prophesy. For that we must wait and see. But I hasten to assure your Holiness that my relations with the Lady Blanche have been of the most respectable kind. It is true that I have promised to enter into a commercial alliance with her—and I wish I had not—but nothing more than a few kisses have passed between us."

"I am glad to hear that," the Dean said; "but that is very unlike the Lady Blanche. What do you imagine that she is aiming at?"

"I have it from the Lady Amoureuse," Mr Sorrell said, "that the Lady Blanche considers my attachment to her cousin's wife as a mere passing whim. She says that it is only a temporary clouding of my intellect. Her contempt for the Lady Dionissia is so extreme, that she imagines that very soon I shall tire of that lady, and in the meantime she is very busily engaged in teaching the page Jehan what sort of a thing is love.

In short, she refuses to believe that my attachment to the Lady Dionissia is a matter of any moment at all."

"That," the Dean said, "is so exactly like the overwhelming pride of the Lady Blanche, that I daresay you are in the right of it."

He reflected again for a moment, and then he said:

"Besides that, there is the lady's husband. How will you meet him?"

"If you will contrive it that the marriage, which is no marriage, shall be dissolved before his return, I trust," Mr Sorrell said, "that I may never meet him. But if this cannot be done, we trust that the surrendering to him of the Lady Dionissia's dowry may content him; or, if this will not content him, there will be nothing for it but for me to meet him as one man meets the other. But I should think that the surrender of the dowry should be sufficient to content him, for, since he has never seen the Lady Dionissia, he cannot be suspected of any violent attachment to her. And if he enjoys the possession of the dowry, and is in a position to marry another lady with another dowry, surely he should be very well contented."

The Dean asked then:

"And if you marry the Lady Dionissia, how will you support her? In what castle will you live, and how will you feed the necessary retainers?"

Again Mr Sorrell passed his hand down his face.

"A little time ago," he said, "that would have seemed the most easy question in the world to answer. And, indeed, it should seem so still. You would say that it should be the easiest thing in the world for me—for a modern man with all my knowledge—to occupy very soon a commanding position in these barbarous, ignorant, and superstitious times. I confess that I see more difficulties than I expected. But my time and thoughts have been so taken up by other things that I have hardly given the subject any real attention. When I come to do so I have no doubt that it will be easy enough."

"I understand almost none of the words you have uttered," the Dean said. And, indeed, Mr Sorrell, finding English-French at all times a little confusing, had dropped into the language which had been most familiar to him in the Paris of his day.

"I understand almost none of the words you have uttered," the Dean repeated, "but I think I understand your sense. Or if I do not understand your sense, you must be more mad than any man I have yet met. I think it is very plain that you mean that you are a great magician, and that, by means of your magic powers, you intend to acquire vast sovereignty either in this or in some other land. Against that I have nothing to say. I should not dare to arrogate to myself the title of a practitioner in the black arts, for whenever I have attempted myself to put them into practice I have been uniformly unsuccessful. I have never succeeded in raising the smallest of fiends, imps, devils, succubi, or so much as the spirit of a fair and kind lady. Nevertheless, I have somewhat studied these matters, and this much I know—that powers are of two kinds, black and white. If white, they are of heaven, and the wonders that they perform are called miracles. If black, they are of the fiend, and they are black magic. I have never had the impertinence to ask you of which sort are your powers. But I would like to point out to you that if they are of heaven, celibacy is an absolute necessity for their holy practitioner."

"I don't see what this has got to do with me," Mr Sorrell said.

"But you desire to marry the Lady Dionissia. Then if your gifts are from heaven, they will immediately lose all their potency."

"I am going to marry Lady Dionissia," Mr Sorrell said grimly. "I am going to marry her in spite of all the devils in hell, or with their assistance." He paused and added slowly: "And I am not going to lose any of my powers at all."

The Dean uttered a prolonged "Oh!" for he took this utterance to be a declaration that Mr Sorrell was indeed a very powerful magician. His admiration for Mr Sorrell became enormous. The Dean had for long doubted in his mind whether this man, appearing, as he had done, so unaccountably in their midst, and performing as he had done such singular miracles—as to whether this man, who appeared one time a miracle of ignorance and another wise beyond mortal knowledge, were an emissary of heaven or, indeed, the most terrible of necromancers. Now he had it from his own lips that he was this last. And immediately the Dean's respect became enormous.

For miracles performed by saints, relics, or by other holy agencies, he had a proper respect; but they were things with which he was familiar, so that such powers appeared to him comparatively pale and ineffective. Innumerable ones had been performed by innumerable saints. There was no doubt of that; but real black magic was altogether another matter—a thing to be craved beyond anything in the world. By its aid you might become Pope, lengthen your life out to immortality, transmute iron into gold, or revel for ever in unholy joys.

"It becomes, therefore, all the more mysterious to me," he said, after he had thought for some time, "that you should desire to attain your ends by ways so circuitous. Why do you not, by means of your arts, slay her husband, and, at a distance, take possession of his castle, his lands, and his wife, and terrify his retainers and the surrounding countryside into submission?"

Mr Sorrell could only utter, "Ah, my dear sir!" with so

[243]

much horror that the Dean shrugged his shoulders coldly, and said:

"This seems to me to afford you horror; nevertheless, I cannot see that you desire to do anything else in the long run than to possess yourself of the gentle knight's wife, and, if not of his lands, castles, and retainers, at least of those of someone else now possessing them."

"But can your Holiness not perceive the difference?" Mr Sorrell asked. "I will admit that, supposing myself to be successful in my schemes, something very like what you propose will have taken place. I shall secure control over a vast amount of territory—but it will be by proper commercial methods. I certainly should not think of soiling my hands with the blood of any lady's husband."

Again the Dean slowly shrugged his shoulders.

"Once more," he said, "I can only say that I do not understand you. The ends you propose to yourself appear exactly to coincide with those I have supposed you to have. Whether you kill the lady's husband, or whether by magic you strike him with a palsy or otherwise render him impotent, seems all one to me. You will have his wife, his gear, and his lands."

Mr Sorrell vented a heavy sigh of puzzled exasperation. He realised that it would be impossible for him to make this singular clergyman understand the difference between their respective views. Nevertheless, he felt a strong desire to vindicate his ideas of what was sound commercial morality as he understood it. He managed to get out:

"Can your Holiness not see that it is the means and not the ends that have to be justified?"

But the same look of incredulous non-comprehension remained in the Dean's eyes, and at last, in order to change the subject, Mr Sorrell asked:

[244]

"You would very much aid me if you would tell me what, in your language, is 'saltpetre.' "

"I have never heard the word," the Dean said. "Is it a moral scruple?"

"No, it is a mineral," Mr Sorrell answered. "It should be sold by apothecaries, but I have no means of making myself understood. That is one of my chief difficulties—either these people do not understand me, or it is obvious that they do not possess the material that I require."

"I will certainly assist you in any way I can," the Dean said, and, his mind running upon magic, he added: "I could give you, for instance, the skulls of three murderers, of whom one killed his mother; or a vessel filled with the blood of a new-born child who was killed when the moon was at the full—at least, this was said to be what the phial contained. But since I used it in some attempts of my own, and those attempts in no way succeeded, I am under the impression that I must have been deceived by the person who procured it for me."

"I am afraid that these things would be of little use to me," Mr Sorrell answered; "but my gratitude to you would be great if you could procure for me the substance I have mentioned."

"I would certainly do all that I can," the Dean said, "but I doubt whether our poor city of Salisbury will afford the substance that you desire. It must evidently be one of the constituents of a brew of great magic potency. So that I hardly think that you will find it in any of the inferior cities of this land, where magic is practised with but little success. In London, where the King so incomprehensibly places his Court—for why should he do it when the much larger, fairer, and more opulent city of Salisbury would afford him a far more comfortable retreat?—In London, I think, you will scarcely find it, though you might in Dover, or in Sandwich, which are fair cities to which come many tall ships."

"But saltpetre," Mr Sorrell said, "isn't anything rare, or any new discovery. I have an idea that they used to find it under dung-heaps; but, although I have had many dung-heaps turned over, I have been unable to discover any of this substance."

"Without doubt," the Dean said, "this substance will be to be found beneath the dung-heaps of Byzantium, or of the Eastern countries from which you come. For there are many strange beasts, and doubtless they are to be found in the stables and byres. But our poor common cows, oxen, bulls, and swine cannot produce this inestimable commodity."

The Dean's face, which had been by turns rendered keen in bargaining, ironical, apprehensive at the thought of his inter-locutor's possibly destructive powers of magic—for it had lately been in his head that Mr Sorrell might have it in him to blast by fire and lightning not only the Dean himself, but the cathedral, the cathedral clergy, and all the city of Salisbury—his round face, which had hitherto expressed several passions, none of them very pleasant, became suddenly sunny and alto-gether benevolent. He had perceived in the doorway behind Mr Sorrell the form of the Lady Dionissia, carrying a small leathern pouch that depended weightily from her right hand. She was dressed all in green, with white cords to her sleeves, and little tassels of gold on her silken gloves. Her head-dress of white linen was curiously folded, so that it stood up high over her head, and came down low beside her ears and over her white forehead. She was a little flushed with riding, and her very fair, large, and honest face expressed at once curiosity to know what had befallen between the two men, and a smiling belief in the benevolence of the Dean.

She came, with her long green sleeves trailing behind her, over to the Dean's chair, and knelt down to kiss his hand.

Mr Sorrell's eyes followed her with such admiration, such devotion, and such longing, that the Dean felt himself slightly affronted. Jovial, comfortable, and easy, it was not possible for him to avoid these slight pangs of jealousy. And this jealousy had given a tinge of coldness to all his colloquy with Mr Sorrell. He had been ready, as it were, to do anything he could to help the Lady Dionissia; but it was impossible for him not to feel piqued at the object upon whom she had elected to bestow her affections.

At her coming, he became at once brilliant and jovial. Leaning back in his chair, he held his hand beneath the comfortable pouch of gold as if he expected her at once to permit him to relieve her of this burden. It gave him another pang of jealousy to think that her blue eyes beneath their dark brown brows were immediately bent upon Mr Sorrell for guidance. But immediately afterwards he was consoled to feel upon his hand the full weight of the little bag which she had relinquished to him. He weighed it meditatively for a few moments, and then, with a smiling benignity, he assumed the expression of the distinguished Churchman that he was, and laying his hand gently upon her head-dress, he let his lips move for a moment whilst he conferred on her his blessing, and then he said aloud:

"All that you desire of me I will do—your paramour has driven a very hard bargain with me, but I will do it. And now, with no more words, I will call in Nicolas, my chaplain, that he may take down some of the prophecies of this gentle pilgrim, who is no more a pilgrim. For I think that there are few things more edifying for the soul, or more useful to one's fortunes, than to listen to prophecies if they be not procured by unlawful means."

The Lady Dionissia had risen from her knees, and standing between the two men, looked down upon the ground with her absent and deep gaze. One of her hands went up to her cheek, and her body all in green swaying a little to one side, she looked at last into Mr Sorrell's eyes.

"There will be very great joy," she said in her deep and sonorous tones.

2

THEY RODE OUT BY THE GREEN PARK-ROAD BESIDE THE RIVER OF Wiley that runs from Warminster to Salisbury. They passed Bemerton with its tiny church, and Wilton embowered in tall trees. On their right hand the Plain stretched up the hills, but they kept to the valley. Along the stream here and there were clumps of high elm-trees, though many of these had been blown down in the great gale of six weeks before, and they lay across the water like bridges with earth and grass attached to their broad roots. Many moorhens, teal, grebe, and coot swam in the silver waters, and grey herons stood like sentinels or like philosophers who meditated, as they rode by. Once, a stag which had come down to drink at the water ran swiftly over the grass on the other side of the stream; a dappled brown, it lifted its slender legs very high and laid its crown of antlers low along its back. They passed now a shrine, now an image of the Virgin, and now a cross set up to commemorate the murder of some poor traveller by robbers. The merciless sun shone in a blue heaven, the valley was very broad and green, and beside them walked the Welsh mountaineers. With their spears resting upon their shoulders and their caps of steel, they stepped with long strides, and from time to time they sang the long and melancholy songs with which their Welsh mothers had lulled them to sleep. The Lady Dionissia was all in green, and the wind played in the folds of her linen head-dress. She controlled her white stallion by means of two silken threads, for she was training him to be very obedient. Nevertheless his reins, which were of the breadth of a man's hand and of white leather sewn with gold, lay upon his neck ready for her to take hold of. For at times when he passed other horses he would be seized with fits of ungovernable fury.

Mr Sorrell was dressed all in red, but he had a hood of black cloth. The long toes of his shoes went downwards far below his stirrups. And the horse he rode was dark brown with a back so broad that it resembled many cushions.

The evening sun was down behind the great mass of the Castle of Stapleford before ever they were within sound of the cocks of Wishford town. Enormous, with its one square tower and its many turrets with the conical roofs, this castle seemed to fill up the whole valley, casting a large tract of land into shadow. It appeared all black, and from behind and above it the sun hurled immense shafts of light through the air. They had ridden silently, for the Lady Dionissia was filled with joy, and Mr Sorrell had many things that filled his mind.

Presently they came to a little square field that was all green grass between black woods. Here, as was their custom, they descended from their horses. These the mountaineers led away beyond the corner of the thick woods that on three sides enclosed the little field. The two walked over the grass, for the field sloped upwards. It had in it several little mounds and hillocks. When they were nearly into the wood the Lady Dionissia sat down upon one of these little mounds. She drew her skirts about her feet, and the ragged brambles from the wood caught at them, whilst Mr Sorrell walked up and down before her. His face was full of melancholy, and his shoulders bowed in dejection. From where they were the walls of the little town of Wishford were visible to them, and the grey bridge which spanned the stream. A wild cat called from the woods a shrill and tearing cry, and silently a huge white owl floated over their heads and skimmed low down over the mists that were beginning to rise from the grass.

"It seems to get farther and farther," Mr Sorrell said suddenly. The Lady Dionissia did not speak, but she looked up into his face with a great and confiding love.

"Farther and farther!" Mr Sorrell repeated; "it goes back; it disappears. Do you know what is happening to me? I am becoming one of you. I can't get back into what was my past—into what is your future. I can't get back into it."

"Surely that is very well," the Lady Dionissia said slowly. Her voice had very deep chords; it was one of those sounds which give an idea that they express the thoughts of a very honest and simple heart, like the baying of a mastiff.

"I don't want to get back into my past," Mr Sorrell said. "I wonder now that I could ever have lived it. It appears little and grey and cold and unimportant. I don't know what could have kept me going then, for there was no you in all the world."

The Lady Dionissia looked at him with a deepening love, but she said nothing. The owl, turning at the bottom of the field, floated slowly back, ghostlike amidst the mists along the dark shadows of the woodside, searching for such small mice and frogs as the evening called to their avocations in the grasses.

"I don't want to get back to it," Mr Sorrell said, "but I can't even get back to that frame of mind. I used to be what we called a good business man. Now I don't care. I don't care for anything but walking in the fields and talking to you."

"Surely that, too, is well," the Lady Dionissia repeated.

"Surely it is pleasant," Mr Sorrell said, "but I cannot see that it is well, and pleasantness is not the whole of life."

"Is it not?" the Lady Dionissia asked wonderingly.

"No, surely not," Mr Sorrell answered. "Are there not such things as duties, ambitions, and responsibilities?"

"I do not know what these things are," she answered. "In the spring the moles come out of the woods and the little birds sing, and we walk in the gardens and take what pleasure we can. And then comes the winter, and shuts us up in our castles so that it is not so pleasant; but with jongleurs and ballad-singers we pass the time as well as we may. And what is there to do?"

"Ah, it is just that that is so fatal," Mr Sorrell said agitatedly. "It is just that that I am slipping into. You dress me up in these scarlet clothes, and I take a pleasure in it; you ride a-hawking, and it seems to me the whole end of life when your tassel strikes down a heron or a daw. But I ought to be up and doing. I ought to be—I ought to have been master of the world by now."

"And how would it help you?" the Lady Dionissia asked. "You are my master and my lord. You are bright and glorious —what more should you ask?"

"Oh, no, I am nothing," Mr Sorrell answered in a deep dejection. "I am entirely useless, and there is nothing I can do well. Even that prophesying for the Dean was nothing. I am so ignorant. Of history I am ignorant—I hardly know the names of kings, and nothing of what they did . . ."

"Oh, peace," the Lady Dionissia said; "my mind still trembles at the wonders you unfolded. What could be more miraculous than the flying of men through the air, or their rushing faster than the flight of swallows beneath the ground?"

"All that is nothing," Mr Sorrell said. "Do you not understand how it only proves my ignorance, and how useless I have been? I ought to know how to do all these things. But I know nothing. Don't you understand, I have been so in the habit of having all these things done for me that I am useless as the grub in the honeycomb that the bees feed. It is no use my saying that I can do nothing because I have not the materials—that is an idle excuse. We might fit out ships to go to the end of the world to get rubber; but even if we did that I do not know where rubber comes from, nor if I knew should I know from what tree rubber is procured. Nor, if I had the rubber, should I know what to do with it. And it is a condemnation of a whole civilisation. There was not, of the men I knew, one who knew any of these things. There was not one of them who knew that a beefsteak comes from an ox. Or if he had known that it did, and if he had possessed an ox, he would not have been able to kill that ox. Or if he had been able to kill the ox, he would not have known how to cut the steak or to cook it or to make a fire or to light it when it was made. I do not believe that a single man that I knew would have been able to black his own boots."

"I don't know why boots should be black," the Lady Dionissia said. "I myself have never seen any black boots, and it would be a very ugly colour."

"Yet I here stand useless," Mr Sorrell said with deep bitterness. "I know nothing of my own arts. I said I was going to set out to conquer the world, yet I should not even know how to form a limited company. And of your arts I know nothing —I cannot fight, I cannot tilt at the ring, I cannot shoot with the bow, my muscles are too slack to let me take part in any manly exercise. Of the laws of the chase I know nothing. I cannot tell the roedeer from the fallow; if I can tell a daw from a dove it is all that I can do, and I cannot tell a cushat from a turtle, except when you are there to point out the difference. And I am the man that is going to take you from your life of splendour with nothing but my arm to rely upon. My arm is no stronger than a reed in a thatch, and my brain is more useless than an empty pot with the wind whistling in it."

"It is not grateful to God," the Lady Dionissia said, "so to speak, when God has given you such powers, and if I did not love you I should think it evil of you to speak in this way. For you have healed many hundreds of the sick; and you have ridded this whole countryside of robbers, and even miraculously you have cured the hens and chickens of the Convent of St Radigund."

"Oh, heaven!" Mr Sorrell said, "what is all this? It was not I that put down the robbers, it was their superstitious fears. It was not I that cured these cripples and the sick. There was no miracle about it; it is what we used to call natural suggestion. Haven't you heard of Lourdes? I tell you all these people were not really ill. It was what they believed. They thought they were ill, and the sight of the cross cured them."

The Lady Dionissia rose from her hillock where she had been sitting with her chin upon her hands and her elbows upon her knees, raptly listening to him. In the gathering dusk she came very close to him, her face near to his, and her eyes gazing into his eyes. Her voice was more deep than ever when she spoke.

"Almost you make me enraged with you," she said, "almost you make me desire to shun you. For what you have spoken is a very damnable blasphemy. Here have the dear God and the blessed angels of God and God's Mother been pouring down, through your agency, great blessings upon poor and miserable persons. Joy and solace and peace and comfort have been given in abundance in place of agony and anguish and cares and solicitudes. And these splendid and comfortable miracles of God and of the blessed angels of God and of the Mother of God, you, a poor sinful man—for every man, no matter how glorious he be, is poor and sinful before the face of Almighty God that sent His Son to be our comforter—you poor sinful man, who are privileged to be the agent of these most gentle and splendid doings, you cry out upon your fate, and refuse to put your trust in God for what in the future shall happen to you and me. I am a woman, and should be the more timorous part of us two who stand here. Oh, take courage, take courage! For what God has done, God again will do, so you deny Him not."

Her voice had grown deeper and deeper, and she seemed to wave a little back into the shadows of the evening, as if in her anger she were denying herself to him. A great wave of passion came over him, and he stretched out his arms.

"Oh! have pity! Oh! have pity and do not deny yourself to me," he said. "Remember what strange things all these are. Though I have many times tried to explain myself to you, I have never been able to explain, so strange it all is."

She came closer to him, and set her two hands upon his shoulders.

"Ah, what is all this of explaining and explaining that you will always desire to be doing," she said almost despairingly. "Many hours of unhappiness it has caused me. Do I ask from whence you came? No, no! All I ask is that you should take me whither you go. When I first set eyes upon you I knew that I loved you, and what more is there to ask or to say? You are like no other man that I have seen, nor do I believe that ever there was before a man so gentle and so good, so true or with such great gifts. I think there was never such another man since Christ was, and that it is a miracle of the little angels of God that you should love me who am nothing, or very little. And each night when I go to sleep I am afraid of the waking; so precious a thing is this love that I dread to find it a dream. But I wake, and I find it is no dream, so that I have all that I ask."

He put his hands upon her shoulders; his arms were outside hers, and in the gleaming twilight they stood gazing into each other's eyes. From a thicket close at hand there came out the shadowy forms of a vixen with her three cubs. A little moon had got up and was sending feeble gleams on to the grass that was all grey with dew. The vixen and her cubs played together, running round in circles. From the wood there came the sweet scents of damp verdure and of wild lavender. A bat fluttered close round their heads, its wings making a faint buzzing sound, and every now and again came the long call of the restless peewits on the Plains far away.

"Yes, I see nothing else," he said.

And she answered passionately:

"And what else would you see? Is it that we are merchants who must have goods stored up in our houses where we shall live for the rest of our lives? No, surely I think we are better than that. For there are in the world great plains and wide rivers and woods of a month's journey in extent. And there are castles and cities, and there are kings and emperors and high adventures. If you would take me to live in such a merchant's house, surely I would not do it."

"But would you have us go about the world and not know upon the day where at night we shall lay our heads?" he asked.

"Aye, surely," she answered, "for what better or gentler life could you ask?"

"But how should we gain our bread?" Mr Sorrell asked.

"Gentle friend," she answered, "is it a new thing that a great knight, putting upon himself the garb of a minstrel, and accompanied by a page or two and a few men of arms to give him sufficient state and respect, should journey through the world and sing of the high things of love, or of great adventures in arms? So he goes from castle to castle, and great is his welcome. And so shall you not do? For you have more wonderful things to tell of than any knight ever yet had. And so we should travel through the world, and you shall heal many sick persons. And a king shall give you a castle here, and an emperor shall give you broad lands there. For it should be a very niggardly king or a very miserly emperor that should not do so much. And so we should travel through the great forests and along the broad streams and over the endless plains. And our lives shall be very pleasant and restful, and you shall not ever be sad."

"But this is all a fable," Mr Sorrell said. His voice had fallen low; his resolution was fading away within him. It was as if in that dusk, and before his desire for her and for peace, he were sinking into deep waters and into darkness. He bent his arms a little and she hers, so that they came closer and closer together.

"No, no," she said, "these are no fables. This is the world as we live in it beneath the starlight and beneath the sun. In the summer the little birds will sing and it will be joyful, and in the winter we shall get us into the great castles. Many knights have done so; many knights shall do this again. It is you that by thinking on things that are beyond the power of man betake yourself into lands all fables, and not worth an old wife's song that is feeble and cracked in an aged throat."

With insensible pressure they drew each other closer and closer. The sinking moon went down behind the hills. There remained of her visible only a face that seemed silver in the growing starlight, and the great white hood curiously folded that stood out above her head like an aureole. The world had gone; it was all darkness, all shadows. It seemed extraordinary to Mr Sorrell that there should be so close to him this woman, with the warm face rendered pale by light of the stars, with the earnest and shadowy eyes and the curiously folded hood all white. It seemed to him odd, it seemed to him unthinkable; and yet he felt upon his face the breath from her lips. The breath from her lips was sweet like the breath of cows that have come out of the clover fields. It was inexplicable that she should be there and he; it was inexplicable that his will should be surrendering before hers. For he felt that he was surrendering, as if he were sinking down between the myriads of stars into unknown spaces.

Their knees trembled so that they sank down on to the wet short grass. Their arms were about each other, and in his she was a heavy weight.

"Before you came," she said, "there was nothing in the whole world. Surely the little birds did not sing; surely the sun did not shine."

"There was no sweetness in the world before I came here to you," he answered, and he did not know with whose voice he spoke, or from what world his thoughts came. "The light

[258]

of the moon was a pale thing, and the voice of the little larks said nothing in my ears."

"All my life I have waited for you," she answered.

"I have come down to you through centuries," came from his lips; "all the men of my past are like a few phantoms. It is as if they walked upon shrivelled leaves in an autumn wood. There is only you in all the world."

"In all the world there is only you," she repeated.

With a great rustling there came from the wood a wild sow, but they did not hear it. It looked to right and left with its tiny and fierce eyes. Perceiving no motion, it adventured itself into the little field and went down towards the river. The mists rose up to join with other mists that descended from the skies. The light of the stars was hidden, and in the great stillness the slight gurgling sound of the river among the reeds made itself heard. A heron flying overhead croaked three times. It was answered from a distance by its mate. Because it was already August the last of the nightingales had flown away.

Lying upon his back and looking into the darkness, Mr Sorrell was aware of sounds and glimpses of sights. It was as if very dimly he saw about him the shadows of white walls. A drilling sound went on. Above him the shapes of white-dressed women, as indistinct as, in the twilight, are the shadows of poplars, seemed to advance and to recede, now from this side, now from that. It was as if they bent over him and whispered solicitously. But it was as if he could neither see them nor hear what it was that they whispered. There stole into his nostrils a penetrating perfume. An immense dread swept down on him, the dumb agony of a nightmare. He seemed to be unable to move; his hands were stretched down at his sides as if he were a corpse laid out for burial. Agony was in his heart, on his lips that would not speak, in his throat whose muscles would not act. The perfume overwhelmed him, suffocating, warm, sweet in the throat, sinister and filling him with a mad foreboding. It was the odour of chloroform.

He screamed out loud; great beads of sweat burst out on his forehead. He stretched out his hand like a madman and clutched at her dress.

"Are you there?" he asked. She answered:

"I am here," and he lifted his face towards hers which was slightly cold with dew and the night.

"It is so well with me," she whispered; but Mr Sorrell was full of fears.

3

The Lady Blanche d'Enguerrand de Coucy de Stapleford was awaiting the signal to arm herself against the combat. In a new man's suit of brown leather she appeared less tall than when she was dressed as a woman; but in revenge, her broad shoulders and her flat chest, that was always heaving with emotions of rage, of hot joy or of cold indignation, seemed to be broader by far. And her hips were very broad too, so that she gave the impression of having a massive and heavy trunk, long arms, and rather short legs. Her face was flushed and her eyes very bright; she sat upon a stool and talked of what she would do.

It was in a large pavilion of linen and silk, red and white in great bands, that stood at one end of the lists. From outside, and all around, came the clamour of an intolerable crowd of people that had come together from all over the south parts to see these famous joustings. The lists had been set up in a broad field along the river Wiley about half-way between the castles

of Stapleford and of Tamworth. Many that had come to see
these adventures had slept the night before on the grass beneath the stars; many more had slept in the courtyards of
one or other of the castles, in the stables, or, if they had been
able to scrape the permission, in the empty rooms, the cellars,
or beneath the gate-ways. And this great crowd of people
had very much delayed the preparations, so that it was already
noon, though they should have begun at eight o'clock in the
morning. At each end of the lists was a string of people coming and going as if they had been ants revictualling an ant-
heap; round the lists themselves the populace spread out over
the grass in a huge swarm. Men and women who had brought
provender for sale cried out incessantly that here you might
have hot pies, ale, furmety, black puddings, metheglin, roasted
apples, and the flesh of swine. They spoke English of the
South, English of the West, English of the Midlands, French
of London, French of Salisbury, and there were several jugglers and players of pipes and tabors of the lower orders who
cried out shrilly for pence in the French of France, saying:
"*Par pitié! des sols, des deniers!*"

Horsemen rode about amongst all this many, and there were
a number of shepherds from the Plain, gazing about them
stupidly in their long cloaks of blue woollen. They leant upon
the shafts of huge crooks, at whose heads there hung leathern
bottles filled with mead, and at the foot of each crook was
an iron trowel. With this they could dig up fragments of turf
which they hurled to immense distances, using their long
staves. Thus they could protect their lambs from foxes or
themselves from robbers, who gave them a wide berth because
they were mostly very poor men and very formidable.

The lists themselves shone green and white and red and white,
the pavilions at each end being of these colours, and each as

large as a merchant's house of Salisbury. The bearings of
Coucy were of red and white chequers, those of Egerton were
green and white, the families being allied. Thus, beneath the
sun the pavilion of the Lady Blanche showed her colours, and
the Lady Dionissia had green and white, but across the roof
ran a zigzag of yellow because she was the daughter of the
Earl of Morant. The lists themselves were very strongly built,
though fair cloths of linen and silk hid their strengths with
their straight lines of red and white and of green and white.
Along each side of this railed-in space there had been made,
with strong banks of timber, a rampart going the whole length
of the lists upon each side. This had been the labour of thirteen hinds for three days to set it up. But their labours were
hidden by the labours of twenty women, who for a week had
sewn the red and white and the green and white chequers of
the cloths that covered these erections down to the green
grass. Upon the right-hand side the chequers were red, and
upon the left they were of green. Down the centre of the
lists, there ran such another balustrade covered with just such
cloths, the red and white and green and white meeting about
half-way, or just where the tilters should encounter each other
if their horses ran justly. About the middle of each side of the
lists was a wooden erection for such spectators as were of
gentle blood. These had over them canopies of green boughs
to shield their occupants from the sun, and these canopies
were supported upon little posts of which each alternate one
was gilded, and others being painted red and white and green
and white as the case might be. The passages formed by the
balustrade in the centre led on the right-hand side to an opening in the tent of the Lady Dionissia, and on the left to one
in that of the Lady Blanche. Each opening was large enough
to let through an armed knight upon his destrier. And every-

one who perceived this array of white and green and red was agreed that these lists were very properly laid out and in the due fashion of chivalry. Part of the crowd considered that it was strange that ladies should thus run against each other with shields, with sharp spears, with axes, swords, and the little daggers that give the stroke known as the *coup de grâce*. But, for the most part, the common people considered that the doings of their betters were no affair of theirs, and they took pleasure in the occasion that thus joyously called them together. Thus, though some lewd fellows sang ribald ballads that they had prepared, they found few listeners, whilst many men and women stood round the French ballad-singers who told them of the ladies Isegonde and Belforest, who had put upon themselves the armour of knights, journeying over the world in search of their paramours that languished in the dungeons of the Soldan.

Not many knights had come to see this fray, for nearly all those of that countryside were away upon one war or adventure or another. But there were many ladies who were with great gaiety eating their dinners in the castle of Stapleford or of Tamworth as the case might be. And there was one old knight, too stiff with age to manage any more fighting. His name was the Sieur de Ygorac de Fordingbridge, and it had been agreed that he should be the judge of this combat, for he had seen many such, and was well versed in their laws.

He was a little man in a blue surcoat, wearing round his neck the collar of the Knights of St Stephen of Portugal. He had thin white hair, he was past fifty, his blue eyes twinkled always, and before he spoke he generally uttered a "Ho! ho!" that was like a laugh. All these ladies that sat at board in one castle or the other agreed that this tournament was a fine and a gentle thing. They ate delicately from silver plates, their head-dresses waved in long lines, about half being of the shape of steeples and the other half broad like the wings of swans. Some of them wished that it had come into their head before that to engage in such a tournament; some declared that such tournaments they would have next year; and a few said that they had not the courage, but wished that God had given it them. Many agreed that it was shameful that their lords left them as if they were widowed through all the summer months, journeying off one way or another as soon as the ice were melted and the snow gone from the ground. But many others said that so it was the nature of men to do, and even so they must abide it. Then they began to talk of the differences between man and woman, how that one would have this and the other that, and how they could console themselves for the absence of their lords. There were many gentle and joyous things said there, so that some laughed, some blushed, and some held down their heads with the cloths fluttering behind them.

·   ·   ·   ·   ·   ·   ·

Sitting upon a stool in her tent, the Lady Blanche discoursed of what she would do to the Lady Dionissia. She said:

"Spears are little use. What can you do with a spear? It strikes upon a shield, and if it strikes true, it shivers into pieces. And if it strikes not so true, it glances away, so that you lose your little mark on the judge's tally. Or you aim at the helmet of the one riding against you. If you strike the mark, in one case out of ten your spear point may go in at the visor and carry away helmet and all. Or if you strike the helmet and your spear glances off, you have gained your little mark in the judge's score, but it is not so good a mark as if you break your spear upon the shield of the one that rides against you. Now this is what I will do in the matter of spears, for those come first."

The Lady Blanche looked round at the faces of those who heard her. These were the Ladies Amoureuse and Blanche-main, the little page Jehan, and Gorhelm, the old, her armourer. The Ladies Blanchemain and Amoureuse were, like the Lady Blanche, in men's clothes of buff leather that fitted like eel-skins to their bodies. Over this the armour was to go, for they were to fight in the mêlée with the ladies of the Lady Dio-nissia, all fighting together after their two mistresses had fought with axes. The little Lady Blanchemain had tears in her eyes, and trembled continuously. She did not love this adventure at all, because she was so little, having been born whilst her father's castle was closely besieged, so that her mother at that time had had little or no milk to give her.

The Lady Amoureuse also regarded this adventure with little favour. It was true that she was taller and more deft than the Lady Cunigunde, with whom it would be her lot to fight. She could run like a lapwing; she was five foot six in height, her back was straight, she rode a horse well, for she was long in the leg, and she could throw a light spear to a distance of twenty-five yards. The little Lady Blanchemain was squat in the body and knock-kneed, and the Lady Amoureuse regarded her with contempt as she whined and grizzled in her suit of yellow leather. But the Lady Amoureuse regarded her mistress with such hatred that she did not wish her to win in this con-test, so that she was setting about it with little joy. Indeed, with such passion did she adore the bearer of the cross of St Joseph, that for his sake she wished that the Lady Dionissia might win that day and that she herself might die. Yet she did not wish to die by the sword or dagger of the Lady Cuni-gunde; she desired rather to pine away as ladies do who love hopelessly. So ladies do in ballads and lays, lying in great beds with many knights and others round them, all together sighing out, groaning and lamenting of the great power of tyrannical love. She did not desire to help her mistress, whose pride and jeering had become unbearable to her, neither did she desire to die in this mêlée, or to have her limbs broken or her head split, for so she would not die beautifully in her bed. And all this appeared to her a foolish and a disagreeable plan.

The Lady Blanche set her hard, green eyes first upon her, then upon the little Jehan, who held upright her red and white shield with its point upon the ground. The shield was so tall that it came almost up to the little boy's chin, and nearly hid the black velvet in which he was dressed. The Lady Amoureuse returned the Lady Blanche's glance with a mocking and obstinate smile, such as made her whole being revolt within her. She wished for whips to lay across this lady's back till she screamed out for mercy. The little page Jehan looked back at her with candid blue eyes, and listened to hear her plan. The armourer, who carried a turnscrew, blew his nose in a corner of his greasy hood. He was a man very begrimed with the smoke of his furnaces; his face was a dull brown, his eyes were bloodshot, the lids being rimmed with coal-dust, and even in his pale white hair there were gouts of soot. He wore a long black apron of leather that covered his whole body, and was burnt here and there where coals had fallen upon it. He looked obstinately at the ground, and paid no attention to what was said there. It was his business to screw up the nuts and bolts of the armour that these ladies saw fit to put on, for the little Jehan was not strong enough.

"Now in the matter of spears, which come first, this is what I will do," the Lady Blanche said. "For the first two courses I will break my spear upon that lady's shield if she can remain in her saddle. But this last I doubt, for though she is heavier than I am, yet I am stronger and more determined.

Then at the third course I shall aim my spear point at her helmet, so that the point, going in at the visor, may haply enter this lady's eye and pierce through her head. This I very much hope, for I desire to be rid of such vermin."

Again the Lady Blanche paused and looked round the pavilion. No one answered her. The sun shining down made it very hot there, so that they all perspired. The armour that these three ladies were to wear was disposed round the tent upon wooden horses. Over the shining steel were laid their surcoats of red and white silk. And, through the opening at the back of the tent, they could perceive how two hinds led up and down the destrier that the Lady Blanche was to ride. This was a very great beast and savage, being not so very well trained. Its body, neck, and chest were covered by steel harness, but this again was covered by silken cloth of red and white. Through the holes of this covering its eyes looked out savage and inflamed. The harness was very heavy, nevertheless it so bounded and shook its head that it was difficult for the two hinds to keep upon their feet. By rights it should have been squires, or at least men-at-arms, that led this beast; but the Lady Blanche had no squires; her pages were too little and her men-at-arms not strong enough to hold him.

"Now, for the second course," the Lady Blanche said, "this is what I shall do. The second course is with axes. For the first stroke I shall strike this lady upon the left shoulder so that her shield shall drop to the ground. And the second stroke shall be very weighty upon her right shoulder, so that her axe likewise she shall drop. And the third stroke shall fall, weightiest of all, upon her head, so that she shall fall to the ground. Then, descending from my horse, I shall spring over the barrier as the law provides, and whilst she lies upon the ground I shall seek with my dagger for the joint in her harness. And so she will die then. But I hope I shall have killed her before with my good lance, though that is more difficult. Then for the mêlée, we being three against two, I think the Lady Dionissia's ladies must yield themselves up without blow struck, and so they must serve me till I choose that they may marry and I shall take toll of their dowries. And this shall be to the eternal disgrace of the Lady Dionissia, and much it shall redound to my glory."

Nobody spoke, till at last the little page Jehan said seriously:

"Ah! dear lady, this, I think, is a very good plan, but I do not know or I fear me that your horse Roland will not stand very still when it comes to axes. This is what I fear. And, but that I must hold up your shield, I would kneel down and humbly pray you that you have great care when you come to this passage with the axes. For ah! dear lady, your good horse Roland will run very well when there is tilting to do, but stand he will not, as I very much fear."

"In this I am agreed with the little Jehan," the Lady Amoureuse said disdainfully, "for you have not so practised your horse as the Lady Dionissia has done in the manège. All day long she has ridden him abroad, so that he will stop, curvet, or turn suddenly round at the mere sound of her voice, she using no reins, so that it is a pleasure to see, and I think few knights of Christendie have such another horse."

"Oh-well-away!" the little Lady Blanchemain wailed suddenly in a high note, like the voice of a pig that is in the butcher's hands, "Ah! dear lady, what shall we do if you are cast down at this passage of the axes? For how shall we two stand against the Lady Dionissia's three, who are all savage and well armed?"

A sudden rage convulsed all the features of the Lady Blanche. Her eyes grew enormous, and glowed as if she did

[269]

not believe what her ears heard, and it was as if the lamentation of the Lady Blanchemain were the lash of a whip falling upon her skin. For a moment she sat still upon her stool, the red patches upon her cheeks becoming a brilliant scarlet. Then, suddenly, she sprang up and ran towards the little Lady Blanchemain, for even in her rage she was afraid to strike the Lady Amoureuse.

"What is this I hear!" she screamed out. "Is it I that shall fall at the passage of the axes?"

With her long yellow arms, she smote savage blows upon the face of the weeping Lady Blanchemain. The Lady Blanchemain turned to run, but the Lady Blanche caught her by the two shoulders. She shook her backwards and forwards, so that at one moment her head seemed to strike her back and her chin immediately afterwards thumped upon her chest. The little Lady Blanchemain screamed, so that it was like a streak of flame.

"Mercy of God!" the Lady Blanche brought out between her teeth, and she set her knee in the Lady Blanchemain's back. Then she hissed with the expiration of the breath from her lungs, and the little Lady Blanchemain fell, expelled by a great strength, across the tent and against one of the horses of armour. All this iron fell to the ground with a great noise.

The little Jehan stretched out his hand over the shield and touched timidly the Lady Blanche's wrist.

"Ah! gentle lady," he said gravely, "I think it is not wise in you to maim your side before you come to the mêlée. For if you have not the Lady Blanchemain, then the Lady Dionissia's many will be as three are to two."

"Little fool," the Lady Blanche breathed heavily, "there will be no mêlée. Mercy of God! shall I not have slain this insolent and unworthy woman before ever we come to the mêlée?

This, I tell you, I will do, and none has ever withstood me. I tell you I will so slay this lady that her face shall be deflowered, and none shall ever call her fair again if they remember her, her face I will so cut and mangle with my little dagger. And the cross I will take to myself, and there shall be great joy through all this countryside where I am beloved and that woman is hated. Is it that white milk creature that shall triumph over me? I tell you never; but she shall die unshriven, and her miserable ghost be wracked for ever in hell. She is a liar and a cozener, a cheat and a false whisperer, a foul slut and evil in her life, envious and hating all that is good. Well does she think with her milk-white and pink to lord it over me. But her hour is come, and the little devils in hell are throwing coals upon the fires that are reserved for her. Neither do I pity her, for she is hardly a Christian—almost a brute beast, and it was a very evil day for her when she set herself up against me, she an upstart from strange wild places, a nothing come from desert lands and seeking to make herself of importance here in Christian territories."

"Ah! dear lady," the little page Jehan said, "I am very glad that you are of such a high courage for this adventure."

She straightened her back and made her shoulders appear very broad.

"Little fool," she said to him with a kindly scorn, "would you have me ape the tricks of grooms and fellows that run with horses? No, surely I was made for higher things than that. It is well for the Lady Dionissia and such low creatures to go riding about over the countryside, for they have need of such practice. But I am of a better blood, and my horse shall obey me because, of instinct, it knows its master."

"That may well be, ah! gentle lady," the little Jehan said; "and your horse is very large and strong. God keep the issue!"

A faint sound of distant trumpets came through the noise of the multitude without that all that time had buzzed in their ears like the voice of a sea surrounding them. The little Lady Blanchemain still sobbed where she had fallen amongst the armour; the Lady Amoureuse looked at the ground with her nostrils distended in contempt.

"I think that will be the signal for arming," the little Jehan said. "Yes, I hear it again, and yet a third time."

And he repeated: "God keep the issue, and uphold the right," whilst he crossed himself behind the large shield.

"Well, I am content to rely upon my good arm," the Lady Blanche said. "It was the Lady Dionissia, not I, that spent the whole of last night whining over her sword in her little chapel. ⌐ne, put on my arms."

4

The old and gentle knight, Ygorac de Fordingbridge, was sitting with the ladies at dinner in the castle of Tamworth. So when he thought that they had sufficiently devised of love and of the nature of men, he rang a little bell that stood before him upon the tablecloth.

"Now, why do you ring that little bell, ah, gentle knight?" Mr Sorrell asked. He had had himself set beside the old knight so that he might learn by asking many questions all the nature of chivalry in such ceremonies as that day should go forward.

The old knight said: "Ho! ho!" in a little sound like a laugh. And he smiled at Mr Sorrell with eyes that twinkled, but that were of a blue gone very pale with age. "By my faith, gentle stranger, I ring my bell that silence may fall." And because there was still much talking and tittering in the hall he rang his little bell again. Then indeed there was a silence. The ladies did not chatter or laugh; the pages all stood still as they carved before them; the servers who were bringing in dishes stood still where they were when the sound of the bell reached them. Then the little old knight said to the two pages that carved before him:

"Go, fetch me the circlet of gold and the small sword of State."

Then he looked at Mr Sorrell and laughed.

"The circlet," he said, "is the token of authority in matters of chivalry that has been given me by several kings, of England as well as of France and Aragon, because in my day I did certain feats of arms that were deemed noteworthy; and the sword is to perform one of the functions of the most noble arm."

Little joyous whispers passed among the ladies all down the table, and most of them cast friendly glances at Mr Sorrell, and kept their eyes upon him as well as they could for their hennins, coifs, and hoods. Then the circlet was brought, and the old knight set it upon his thin white hair. The sword, which was not very long, in a sheath of shagreen and tortoise-shell, was laid upon the table before him amongst the nefs of gold, of silver, and of parcel gilt. The old knight looked at Mr Sorrell.

"Gentle stranger," he said, "I will have you go round the table and stand among the pages."

"What is this that I must do?" Mr Sorrell said. The old knight repeated that he should go round the table and stand among the pages. This Mr Sorrell did, brushing gently the backs and the hoods of all these ladies, until he stood just before the old knight in between the pages who had been carving. Then the old knight clapped his hands, and outside a trumpet blew.

After a little while there came in a great number of people who had been dining in the castle of Stapleford—that is to say, all such as had been ready to lose part of their dinners in order to witness this thing. Amongst them were the Dean of Salisbury and the chaplain, and several of the chapter-priests, the almoner and the mass-priest of the Abbey of St Radigund, and a great many ladies and others who were unknown to Mr Sorrell. For, if the truth must be known, those who had come to Stapleford Castle were the larger in number; the Lady Blanche was not loved in that countryside, but her cooks were renowned throughout all the south. Whereas of the Lady Dionissia little was known, for she was only two months or a little more in that country. That was why the Dean and all the religious men had eaten at Stapleford. Nevertheless, they were come over to Tamworth in order that, as far as they might, they should give countenance and honour to Mr Sorrell, for he had mightily made presents in gold and in kind, not only to the cathedral in Salisbury, but to many churches and hospitals of the neighbourhood. But the old knight had determined to do honour to the Lady Dionissia, who was his kinswoman, and so, being king of those ceremonies, he had eaten at her board. And, in truth, since he had been daily in converse with this lady whilst they were regulating how the ceremonies should be carried out, she had got Sir Ygorac very much upon the soft side, and could make him do all that she asked, he being a widower and childless.

When all the new-comers were in the hall and standing decently still, the knight rang his little bell again. Then the silence was breathless, and all those motionless people gazed upon Mr Sorrell. The old knight too looked at him seriously.

"Gentle stranger," he said, "is it true, as I hear, that you passed last night from sundown to cockcrow in vigil and prayer and abstinence in a little chapel, containing amongst other things the good arms of a gentle knight?"

"Why, it is true," Mr Sorrell said. And, indeed, it was true that that night he had knelt for many hours beside the Lady Dionissia in her dark and cold chapel, whilst she prayed over her arms as if she were indeed a young knight. For she said that she had more need of it than many others. Mr Sorrell's knees were still stiff with kneeling for so long upon the stones of the chapel, though he had been very glad to do it, and it had seemed to him that the Lady Dionissia was very right in what she did.

"And is it true," the old knight asked, "that after this vigil you did not break your fast till noon was gone by?"

"Why, it is true," Mr Sorrell said, "that I did not eat until just now, and I think we did not sit down till after noon. But I did not notice that I was fasting, for there have been so many things to do."

"Nevertheless, you have abstained," the old knight said. "And is it true that, as I have heard you say this morning, you are determined to live according to the rules of high and honourable chivalry such as I have explained them to you—to draw your sword only in high quarrels, not to oppress the poor, but to succour them and all good knights and gentle ladies such as may be in distress? And will you give freely of your goods to the Church, as I hear you have done in times past?"

"Why, all this as I have told you," Mr Sorrell answered, "I shall try to do to the best of my ability; but I should wish to know why you ask me these questions?"

The old knight smiled gently and faintly.

"And will you," he asked, "if the occasion serves, give all that you are possessed of, whether of money or of goods, whether of life or of endeavour, to the joyous and noble emprise of redeeming the sepulchre of our Lord Christ from the hands of all pagans and Saracens whatsoever?"

"Why, indeed," Mr Sorrell said, "I would do it very gladly if the occasion offered."

"And will you pray for me who speak to you, that my life may pass in honour, my death be duly shriven, and my hereafter blessed in the path of the saints?"

"Why, truly, that I will do for you and for the souls of all Christians whether they are alive or dead," Mr Sorrell answered, for so the Lady Dionissia had taught him to answer this request.

"Then if you will do all this," the old man said, "and if you have done as I have been told you have done, I think you will be, if God help you, a very proper man and one fitted to enter into an honourable order. And I would have you now instantly to kneel down and pray truly. Kneel you down!"

And with his hand he indicated the rushes where Mr Sorrell should kneel, but a little page brought him a cushion of black velvet.

Then the old knight clasped his hands and held them above the sword that lay amongst the nefs. His lips moved, and from time to time he crossed himself. And when he did so all the rest that were there, whether they were sitting or standing, crossed themselves too, so that nothing was heard but the whisper of prayers and the slight rustle of all their hands as they moved together.

Then in a similar silence the old knight drew his sword from the scabbard. He stood up upon his feet and, being a little man, he leaned right across the table to touch Mr Sorrell upon his left shoulder with the point of the sword. Then very quickly came a page and buckled a spur of gold upon Mr

Sorrell's right heel, and another, taking the scabbard of the sword off the table, belted it round his waist where he knelt.

"Now you may rise up, Sir Guilhelm," the old knight said, "for the rest of your name it is not easy to pronounce. But I will call you of Winterburne of St Martin, after the name of the little castle that now I give you, along with this sword, if you will vow honourably to do such suit and service as is due to our Lord the King for it."

And immediately there began a great outcry of pleasure and acclamation amongst all who were in that hall. Then most people said that it was a very worthy and honourable thing for that knight to have done, and that it gave honour to all of that countryside in showing hospitality after a chivalrous fashion to a gentle stranger.

Mr Sorrell rose to his feet and, with a dazed face, he leaned over the table and asked the laughing knight:

"What is this that has happened to me?"

The knight laughed joyously back in his face.

"Ah, gentle knight," he said, "it is that you become Sir Guilhelm de Winterburne de St Martin, with a little castle that is hardly more than a stone house with battlements, fifty villeins, a number of hides of land, and such other things as go with them. That is all I have to give you. I wish it had been more, but I am not a very rich knight."

"But I have done nothing to deserve all this. If I had known of this before, I would not have taken this honour for which I am unfitted. I have none of the arts of chivalry, and I shall look like a fool parading as my betters. I am grateful to you, but you should not have done this thing."

The old knight still smiled gently.

"Ah, gentle knight," he said, "it is done and it cannot be undone, so these things you must take. As to who is fitted and

[278]

who unfitted for honours, it is not for you to say. This power has been placed in my hands by three kings—of England, of France, and of Aragon. Neither is it for you to say whether you will take this honour or no, any more than it would be for you to say whether you should be degraded from a high position or no. The one or the other you must suffer, as it pleases those set in authority above you, who promote now one and now put down another. And this is a very good lesson to learn."

"But I have done nothing to deserve this," Mr Sorrell protested again.

"Ah, gentle knight," Sir Ygorac answered, "I am of another opinion. For alone and without aid you ridded this country-side of a weighty pack of robbers by whom we were all oppressed. And the accolade of knighthood is fittingly conferred upon one who has done this, whether by the aid of the little angels of God, or by his own arm alone."

"But I did nothing," Mr Sorrell said.

"Friend," the old knight answered, "that I do not believe, for it is all part of a modesty in you of which my kinswoman Dionissia has told me. And it was to avoid protestations from you that I have carried out this project behind your back. For you are fit, and I protest that you are fit, who am a Commander of the Order of St Steven of Portugal and Aragon, and have weight in such matters. That the little angels of God aided you in that combat I can well believe, for such things are frequently known. But that you did nothing I cannot well believe. Or if it is so, then God surely so aided you that it was a mark that He desired to point you out as being specially fitted for the order of knighthood. And it is presumptuous, and not truly humble in you to protest against this."

"Ah, gentle knight," Mr Sorrell said, "still I cannot think

that I am indeed deserving of this honour, and I will prefer to imagine that it was the Lady Dionissia who begged it of you. She is not easily denied, and I can understand that you would not desire your kinswoman to be allied with one below the degree of a knight."

The smile died away from Sir Ygorac's face, and his friendly eyes became cold and hard.

"Gentle knight," he said, "that is the most discourteous speech that ever yet was made to me, and I think if I were a younger man you would not have made it, for surely I should have killed you. By my faith, I am sorry now that I have made you a knight, for such discourtesy is likely to do honour to no order."

"Alas! gentle knight," Mr Sorrell said, "what words have I uttered to so enrage you, for I do not know what they are?"

"Death of my life!" Sir Ygorac answered, "is it not foul to say that I have conferred upon a man a sacred order of chivalry at the request of a kinswoman? Could anything more foul be said to me? No, I think not, by my faith, and by little good Saint Hugh of Lincoln!"

A great many persons had listened to this conclave. They broke in with many voices, some commending the new Knight of Winterburne of St Martin's because modesty was a very proper thing, some blaming him and recommending that he ask very humbly his pardon of Sir Ygorac. Some said the old knight was too hasty, and a few were ready to believe that the old knight had indeed favoured the new one, only because he was the paramour of his kinswoman. So there was a great clamour, but at last the Dean's chaplain shouted in his stentorian voice, quelling all the others, that silence should be made because the Dean desired to speak.

Then the Dean set himself to reconcile these two. He said

that in the first place the knighthood was a very proper one. For knighthoods were conferred for great feats of arms, even men-at-arms having been made knights when they held the field being one or two against twenty or forty, more particularly if they had stood it out against knights. And in his overcoming the robbers the new Knight of Winterburne of St Martin had observed this too. For they were not all low men and hinds that he had overcome, but on the contrary they were led by a knight, though a bad one, and an outlaw. So the knighthood was very fittingly conferred.

Then, to Sir Ygorac he said: that it was known that the new Knight of Winterburne was of a modesty that was almost a squeamishness. Nay, at times it approached near even to blasphemy, as when he denied that he had gifts that other men knew to be of heavenly origin. But he would have Sir Ygorac to observe how abashedly the new knight stood before him, how his knees knocked together, and how tears might be observed to be starting in his eyes, and how ready he was to make apology and all due amends.

"Yes, indeed, gentle Knight," the Knight of Winterburne said, as soon as he could make his voice heard for the applause that the Dean's speech had caused to arise, "I will make any such amends as may be enjoined upon me. And I would ask you to remember how that I am only a stranger in these lands, and that I was so overwhelmed by the greatness of the fortune that has befallen me, that I may well be pardoned if my tongue in this great amazement slipt into discourtesy where I meant none. And this I swear by my faith that from now on I will be a very proud man. For I will take such pride—and I do it now—in this order of knighthood that has been given me by you—I will be so proud that perhaps many will find cause for complaint in me. So now observe that I look round upon this assembly with a haughty gaze, for I think that there is no one present who is so fine or so gentle a knight as I."

At this speech there was much laughter, for amongst them all there was no knight but Sir Ygorac, all the rest being ladies or priests or friars. Then the Knight Ygorac laughed too, and said that it was very well said, and that his anger was over. And he commanded the new knight to take for his arms such a cross as the one he had brought from the Holy Land.

"And," said he, "gentle knight, when you have kissed all these ladies, then we will go to the tournament, and now I command the trumpets to sound for arming."

Outside then the trumpets sounded, and the new Knight of Winterburne of St Martin kissed all those ladies upon both cheeks, beginning with the highest of them and going down to the humblest, and they were very glad of it, and kissed him joyously in return.

"Now by my faith," he said at the last, "I begin to feel that I am indeed a knight, and I think that this is the pleasantest place that ever I was in."

Then the old knight put round the new one's neck his own collar of the Order of St Steven, and so they went out towards the lists, Sir Ygorac walking first because he was the king of those ceremonies, and having upon his right hand the new knight.

So they sat down beneath the canopies of green boughs, some on the one side some on the other; and when they were all seated there came out of the pavilion that was green and white a man-at-arms who blew a shrill trumpet. There followed him another that was dressed as a herald in a square tabard. It had quartered upon it the arms of the Knights of St Steven, these being a golden portcullis upon a green field, along with the arms of the Knight Ygorac, which showed a leopard passing across a field of red. This herald had been lent to the Lady Dionissia by the Knight of Fordingbridge, for she had none of her own. Then, when the trumpet had blown three times, all the heads beneath the canopies being properly turned towards him, and a silence having fallen upon the crowd of common people who pushed and struggled and leant over the fair cloth of the balustrades along the lists, the herald read out in a clear voice the challenge of the Lady Dionissia. This was to all the world to run against her there in those lists three courses with the spear, three with the axe, and so afterwards a mêlée of three against three. And so the herald, having delivered himself of these words, walked in a stately manner down the lists, having in his hand a gauntlet of bright steel. When he was come before the place where the Knight of Fordingbridge sat with the new knight upon his right hand, after he had made reverence to the Knight Ygorac he cast his gauntlet on to the grass.

"By my faith," the Knight Ygorac grumbled beneath his teeth, "this fellow will never learn his trade. Look, that glove has fallen upon its palm. It should have fallen upon its back, with its fingers apart, to show that it was ready to encounter the grasp of whoever would take it up."

"Ah, gentle knight," the new knight asked, "is this, then, a bad omen?"

"I do not know that it is an omen," the old knight answered; "but it is a piece of very clumsy throwing, and I have had that fellow training him to be a herald for two years now. But I think no College of Heralds will ever take him into their body."

"Ah, gentle knight," the new knight asked, "tell me now truly, why did that herald challenge for the Lady Dionissia against all the world? For surely she is only to fight against the Lady Blanche?"

"That is the proper form of it," the old knight said; "for a good knight, when he is in armour of steel, must be ready and willing to fight with all the world."

"But if others should come against her?" the new knight asked.

"Ah, gentle knight," Sir Ygorac answered, "of that there is very little likelihood. For there is not, that I know of, another knight in all of this territory. But if another knight should come she must meet him, or claim that she is a woman, which I do not think she would easily do, and I should be sorry if she did it. But now let us be silent, for the trumpeter comes from the other tent."

From the pavilion of red and white came out the little Jehan. He carried before him in the one hand the great shield of the Lady Blanche, and in the other a long thin trumpet of fine silver. He was all in black velvet, having upon his shoulder a little badge of red and white, and upon his fair head a circlet of large pearls. So he put the trumpet to his lips and blew a not very strong blast. Then there came out from the pavilion behind him such another herald as before. Again silence was established by the trumpet sound—for all the people there had been crying out that this little page was properly accoutred and duly solemn, so that it was a fair sight to see. Then this herald said in a clear voice how he came on the part of the Lady Blanche d'Enguerrand de Coucy. And upon that shield which the page supported were emblazoned her signs and tokens, so that all men might know who she was. And she was ready to meet with the Lady Dionissia of Morant of Ecclesford upon those terms of spears, axes, and mêlées. So he asked permission of the king and ruler of that tournament to come forward and pick up the glove of the Lady Dionissia de Morant of Ecclesford. Then the old knight cried out as loudly as he could:

"Herald, by my faith you have spoken very well. Come forward and pick up the glove."

"Ah, gentle knight," the new knight asked, "why does this herald style her the Lady de Morant de Ecclesford?"

The old knight said:

"Hush, hush, now there must be silence. This is solemn."

The herald was walking in a stately manner along the grass

of the lists. He stood squarely before the old knight and made three reverences. Then bending his left knee and stretching his right stiffly behind him he bent to take up the gauntlet. Then he stood up once more; made new reverences to the ruler of that tournament, and so walked away under a great shower of cheering, for, the glove being picked up, it was permitted to people again to talk.

"Now that fellow," the old knight said, "did much better. For you will perceive that he bent very proudly and only one knee, so that it was evident that he showed no fear before this glove. This was very well done, and I take joy in having trained this fellow."

The old knight leaned back upon his bench, and folding his hands leisurely before him:

"This is a very pretty and gentle sight," he said; and he looked to the right and to the left upon the silks and linens of the bright cloths, upon the pavilions that rustled in the wind and shone in the sun, and upon all those people who pushed and jostled and pressed and were pressed upon the barriers. Suddenly he said:

"Why, she styles herself de Morant de Ecclesford, because she is the daughter of the Earl of those places, and because she protests that she is not the lady of the young Knight of Egerton. She alleges that in this marriage there were forms and ceremonies omitted. So the Dean of Salisbury has sent to plead before our Father who is in Rome. And this I should think you would know better than any other."

"Well I knew it," the new knight said; "nevertheless, hearing it, and before all these people, it sounds strange."

"It is by way of making a proclamation of it," the old knight said, and he looked at the new knight with a friendly and ironical smile. "The sooner these things are done, the sooner they are established in the minds of people. So now this is done, and the Lady Dionissia is without castle or home, being cast adrift and errant upon the face of the earth."

"Ah, gentle knight," the new knight said, but his voice trembled, "what is all this, and what are these riddles?"

"Ah, gentle knight," Sir Ygorac laughed finely, "this lady having proclaimed that she is not the wife of the young Knight of Egerton, has plainly also proclaimed that she had no right either of ingress, egress, or regress in his castle of Tamworth. So she, with her ten good men-at-arms and her two ladies that wait upon her, must go wandering from castle to castle seeking hospitality. And I think that the first castle she shall come to after these joys and tournament of to-day are over will be the little castle of Winterburne of St Martin. This is only a little castle of no more than a stone house with battlements. Yet it is the one that lies nearest after the labours and travels of this day are over. So I will ask you to give hospitality to my kinswoman, her men-at-arms and her ladies, in that your little castle of Winterburne of St Martin. And I think it would be a very discourteous knight that would refuse my kinswoman this boon."

"What is all this?" the new knight asked. "I am lost in amazement and joy. I do not know what words to find. There is all that I asked, and more. For now I have a castle to my name and a knighthood and a home, I do not know what to say or how I shall prove my gratitude."

"Why then you had better lose no more words," Sir Ygorac laughed; "and, indeed, I perceive that the trumpets are about to blow, and it is a grave discourtesy to speak after that sound has been heard until the course is run."

"I am very afraid," the new knight said: "I do not know how to keep my seat between joy and fear."

[287]

"Now by my faith," Sir Ygorac said, "gentle knight, those are not good words. You should say, 'God keep the issue,' and believe that He will, for all these things He sees from where He sits amongst the pavilions of heaven. This it is your duty to believe as a good knight and a Christian one."

And immediately a trumpet blew. Then all eyes were turned upon the two pavilions, first to the one, then to the other, and so back again. But all the people were silent because the trumpet had blown. So the curtains were drawn back before each tent, and there came out two figures all in steel upon great chargers that were covered with gay housings of silk. The one upon the left had the long lance already in rest and hooked upon the steel gueridon that protruded from the right breast of the armour through the gay surcoat of red and white silk. Before this body of steel was the great shield in red and white chequers, so that it was covered from chin to thigh, and the helmet, which had ears like wings, shone as brightly as a mirror, and reflected the blue of the sky. The helmet peeped over the great shield, leaning forward so that its visor appeared to leer grotesquely and with an enigmatic threat, and the great horse danced rhythmically up and down, gently swaying the rider from side to side.

Many people frowned slightly, because generally it was held as being a breach of manners to ride out of the pavilion with the lance in rest, since it showed too great an eagerness, though it was not forbidden by any rule, and some knights would do it.

The Lady Dionissia, on the other hand, sat upon a horse that was so still it might have been of marble. Her shield hung from its longer strap by her side, so that it covered her axe which was strung on her saddle bow. Her saddle was very deep and high, and the butt of her spear rested upon the broad

[288]

steel shoe that covered her foot in the stirrup, its point of polished steel being many feet above her head. Her visor too was up so that her face showed, and she appeared like one abstracted and dreaming. She sat leaning far back in her saddle, and the only motion of her horse was that it perpetually lowered its head as if it had been bowing. Upon her helmet she had a little circlet of gold worked into points to show that she was an earl's daughter, and it was observed and commented upon that the surcoat which covered loosely her body armour, the cloth which covered her horse to the ground, and her shield too were tricked out, not with the chequers of Egerton, but with the yellow and white zigzag of Morant de Ecclesford. Then the first trumpet blew, for Sir Ygorac had raised his hands. The horse of the Lady Blanche bounded with all its feet in the air. It was a very fierce beast, and it neighed so that the sound was like a scream and a laugh. The Lady Dionissia put down her visor and covered herself with her shield, so that her helmet too appeared grim and ironic. The whole of this visor was pierced with holes, so that its wearer looked out as through a veil of lace. This was a new fashion then, and it was afterwards abandoned, since, though no spear head could enter in the little holes though it were ever so sharp, yet the perforations themselves were held so to weaken the visor that it might easily give way before the side-way stroke of an axe, a handpike, or even a slung stone.

At the second trumpet she lowered her spear slowly, setting it to rest in the gueridon beneath her right armpit. Now her horse was swaying a little from side to side. The third trumpet came. Then both those great horses, who had more hostility even than their riders, bounded forward, the first bound being of two yards or two yards and a half. And so swiftly they ran that, though their hind hoofs were not shod, they cast great turfs of grass high into the air, and the forefeet made deep marks in the turf, for these had iron shoes, with which these beasts fought in battle. Then they came together. The new Knight of Winterburne closed his eyes, for this was a bitter moment for him. There came a sharp and splintering sound like the scream of glass that is harshly broken. And then a great outcry, and "Ho! ho's!" from deep throats of men. Then the new knight opened his eyes and saw that the Lady Dionissia sat back upon her horse, which was a little more than a yard beyond the half-way of the barrier.

Its forelegs were protruded very far in front and it had sunk back; its haunches beneath the armour and the cloth nearly touched the ground, so suddenly had it obeyed its rider's command to halt. In her hand the broken spear-shaft protruded upwards. The head lay full three yards behind the horse and very near the cloth of the barrier. The great outcry from hundreds of throats continued, and then the new knight perceived that far down the lists, so that she nearly touched the curtains of the other pavilion, the rider in red and white chequers had brought her horse to a halt, and held high above her head the butt of a broken spear. Then a trumpet blew to show that that course was ended by the coming to a standstill of the Lady Blanche.

"By my faith," Sir Ygorac said, "that course was very well run. I had never thought that ladies could so do it, and very seldom it is that you shall see two spears broken at once. I think I have not seen it more than twenty times."

The riders had turned their horses and were going slowly back to their pavilions.

"That is a horse that I would desire to have," the old knight said when the yellow and white went by them, its rider holding now the broken spear above her head to show that she claimed that course.

"No, no," the old knight said, though he spoke to himself, "that course I cannot give you, for both lances were broken."

And then he called aloud:

"Ho! let the tallies be brought."

From each pavilion came its herald bearing solemnly in his hand a stave with a handle, the one being painted red and the other yellow. These staves they handed up to the old knight, who laid them upon the table that was before him, the two heralds standing side by side below. Upon this table, too, there lay a sharp little knife that was shaped somewhat like a sickle. This knife Sir Ygorac took into his right hand, and with his left he held the tally upon the table.

"Look you, gentle knight," he said, whilst his eyes remained intent upon the yellow stick that he was cutting, "this course shows you that it is evil to have much hatred in your heart, whether you ride in tournaments or where you will. For you will perceive that this Lady Blanche, being so full of eagerness, omitted to check her horse until it was far beyond the half-way of the barriers, and this is a discourtesy. For you should check your horse very soon, as the other lady did."

All the while he continued slowly cutting a little white notch in the yellow wood of the tally. Then he took the red tally and began to cut at that. He hummed between his teeth a little tune.

"Ah! gentle knight," the new knight said, "I wonder that you can be so calm, for assuredly you love your kinswoman, and I think here she is in very great peril of life and limb."

"Hum!" the old knight said, and he continued to whittle away at his stick with his weak and deliberate fingers. "That would be the fortunes of war. I have seen too many taken up

[291]

with the blood flowing from their mouths and nostrils. It is God, as I have told you, that keeps this issue, and these ladies are very well matched." By this time he had made a notch in the red tally, and then again he took the yellow one and began to cut it.

"Then if I may not tell you of my fears," the new knight said, "let me talk of my gratitude."

"Ah! gentle knight," Sir Ygorac said, "talk of it if you will, but only a very little."

"Sir," the new knight said, "you have made me a very happy man, so that I think that if this accursed folly of a tournament were over I should be the happiest man of this earth. For, whereas yesterday all the world seemed full of doubts to me, to-day everything seems plain and easy. For it is one thing to set out upon adventures from a house or a castle which is your own and to which you may return, and it is another to go wandering about the world when you have no habitation and almost no name. Now I sit in this place and am of this place, and I can look other men in the eyes and think I am as good as they or better or a little worse as the case may be. So that in very truth I may say that you have made a whole man of me."

The old knight surveyed carefully the notches that he had made in the tallies, feeling them with his fingers to assure himself that they were cleanly cut and straight. Then with slow gesture he gave them down to the two heralds who, patient in their gold and green and yellow and red, stood below him. Then with slow steps they walked round the lists, holding before them those staves so that all the people could plainly see. Then a great acclamation went up from all the throats, for it was observed that the Lady Dionissia had two notches to her score and the Lady Blanche but one.

"Why," Sir Ygorac said, "for the quality of your joy I am

in no way to answer, but only you yourself and the circumstances in which God placed you. As for my merit in conferring upon you that accolade it is nothing, for you have done a deed that deserved it. As for the gift of the little castle, I take shame to myself that it is so little. And surely very great would my shame be if I had not given you at least so much. For an open-handed giving is the mark by which you may know a true knight, and that is why certain orders of bannerets take for their device an open hand. And a very shameful thing for this countryside it would have been if no one had been found thus to requite you. But for one thing you may thank me, in that I gave you my collar which hangs round your neck. For that to me is very precious, since it was given me by a king when I was a very young boy in the Spanish lands. I gave you this as a token that our late quarrel was over, for at such times it is fitting that precious gifts should be exchanged. And if you will take time to think of it, I will presently ask a boon of you."

And with that Sir Ygorac waved his hand, so that the trumpets might blow and his companion be unable immediately to answer him. At the second course the Lady Dionissia, as was plain to be seen, aimed her spear at the Lady Blanche's thigh, where the shield did not cover it. This was a very difficult stroke, and one which, when it succeeded, usually unhorsed the opposing rider. But the horse of the Lady Blanche did not run steadily, so that the Lady Dionissia's spear, glancing off the armour of the thigh, thrust itself deeply into the crupper of the Lady Blanche's high saddle. The Lady Blanche's spear, upon the other hand, struck the Lady Dionissia's shield high up in the left-hand corner where the yellow bend of the blazoning began. It glanced off, but not so soon as to let it be said that she had not scored her stroke. And between the en-

tering of her spear into the saddle and the stroke upon her
shield, the Lady Dionissia was almost thrown back over her
horse's thighs. All people there heard her high cry to her
horse in the stillness after the clash of metal. The horse fell
back on its haunches as it checked dead. But the Lady
Blanche's horse forged ahead, though this time she did not
forget altogether to check it. The spear, being fixed deep in
the saddle, was twisted round as the horse went by and torn
nearly from the Lady Dionissia's grasp. Indeed, it was taken
right behind her back, so that her arm was stretched right over
her horse's hind-quarters. Then they saw her lean forward
in her saddle and, with a great wrench, she had the spear away,
so that she was saved from this disgrace. Nevertheless, her
helmet with its circlet of gold and its enigmatic grin bowed
with humiliation forward over her shield, and she did not hold
her lance above her head to show that she claimed that course.
Then the supporters of both riders, when the trumpets had
blown, cheered hotly against each other, for it was held that
both had done very well, the yellow and white having shown
great strength. Yet it must be conceded that the Lady Blanche
had scored her point, though with a less ambition.

When it was a little silent, Sir Ygorac cried to the herald for
the red stave. The new Knight of Winterburne wished to
assure Sir Ygorac that he was ready to grant him any boon
that he could ask beneath the sun. But having seen the Lady
Dionissia nearly cast out of her saddle, his heart had leapt
suddenly in his side, his throat felt weak, and in a sort of confusion he could not for some minutes think of any word
either in English-French or in French-French. Sir Ygorac
looked at him with his fine and friendly smile.

"Ah, gentle knight," he said, "I think if you may you will
grant me this boon, and it is this: You have a great skill in the

curing of all diseases; many people you have cured, from the cripple that ran on all fours, to the hens of the Abbess of St Radigund. Now certain grievous maladies beset me. My eyes they are dim, my teeth they shake in my jaws, my hair grows thin, and I cannot well ride my horse. My hands are very weak, compared with what once they were, nor does my mouth take any longer much joy in the savour of meats and the goodly fruits of the earth. Now, gentle knight, if so be you can, of your gentleness, let me lay my fingers upon the cross that depends from your throat, and let all these grievous and creeping ills, or some of them, be taken away from me."

"Ah, gentle knight"—the new knight was beginning his speech, and at first he was minded to say that he had no power to cure. Then he bethought himself, and desired to say instead that such ills as the knight had catalogued were the creeping ones that old age draws behind it, and that for these there is no cure known under the sun or the stars. But this, again, he did not say, for he was thinking that now he was a knight and sat in that place, and must say only such things as were fitting. And seeking to remember how the Lady Dionissia would have spoken, he delivered himself of the words:

"Ah, gentle knight, we are in the hands of God and His little angels. Of how much I may cure or of how little, that I cannot tell you, but I think that surely the cure under God lies more in you than in me. For your faith will make you whole, or more, or less, according as it is great or little. This I believe to be the truth of the very truth. And in this way only, and in no other that I know of, do I think that you could find the fountain of youth. But for the cross, surely take it into your hand and feel what it is like."

"You have spoken very gently and courteously," the old knight said. He stretched out his trembling hand, and for a long time fingered the cross of gold where it hung beneath the new knight's throat.

Then the herald of the Lady Blanche brought the red stave and laid it upon the table before Sir Ygorac. So the old knight left fingering the cross, and took into his hand the little knife like a sickle, and the red talley-stick. He pressed the blade of the knife into the wood, and, with one stroke this way and one stroke that, the little chip of a full notch fell out and showed a white incision. So he handed down the tally-stick to the herald. And this man, with slow steps, walked round the lists. There rose up a joyous outcry. The Lady Blanche had scored two notches to the Lady Dionissia's two. Beneath this clamour the old knight clasped his hands and raised his eyes to the canopy of green boughs through which here and there appeared the blue of heaven and the dancing light of the sun.

"Ah, gentle knight," he said, "did you perceive how I notched that tally? Before this it caused me many little cuts. And behold, you hear my voice is fuller. The sun is more bright, the grass is greener, and I perceive now many waving coifs where before was only a white confusion. Of a surety, under God, you have worked a miracle in me. For though it is only a little thing to cut chips out of a stick, or to speak more loudly, or more plainly to see, yet it is with such little things that the joys of life are made up. So this is a great joy to me, and a most heavy return for the little castle I have given you. I think that yesterday I would have given all that I possess except such clothes as would be sufficient to make me decent only to have as much as this. For the grass is green, the sky blue, and I hear a hundred little sounds of voices and winds that before I did not hear. And this much is to the great glory of God."

In the third course the horses ran so swiftly together that

it was difficult to see how the spears were held, and the sound of the onset at their meeting was very little. But when they were come to a standstill, it was perceived that the Lady Dionissia's spear was shivered, but upon the point of the Lady Blanche's spear there hung and shone in the sun the little gold circlet that had been upon the Lady Dionissia's helmet.

"By my faith," Sir Ygorac said, "that was a great stroke! Seldom I have seen a better, for there are few things more difficult than this, to pick a circlet or a feather from a helmet, if it was so intended."

Then he called to him the herald of the Lady Blanche, and when the man stood below him:

"Now, herald," he said, "upon life and truth, did your rider declare before setting out upon this course that it was her intention to ravish that circlet from that helmet. For if that was her declared intention she should score three notches, but if it was no more than good fortune, no more she scores than one."

"Upon my faith," the herald said, "my rider said nothing of this beforehand, but declared that her intention was to bear in her opponent's visor and so to pierce through the eyes and skull."

"Well, I am sorry to hear it," Sir Ygorac said, "for it appeared to me a joyous and skilful feat, and I wish it had been. Go now and fetch the tallies."

The Lady Blanche had now scored three notches and the Lady Dionissia three. So when this score was made known there was great outcry and contentment. The riders got down from their horses and went into their pavilions to rest themselves and to gain their breath for the combat of axes. And all the people arose from their seats or pressed away from the barriers to stretch their legs by walking over the green grass.

PART FIVE

I

WHEN THE NEW KNIGHT OF WINTERBURNE CAME DOWN from his seat and the people perceived him, they began running together in ones and twos. Soon there were about him a great many and he must walk slowly. Some cried to him for cure of their sickness, some desired alms, some largesse; some wished him to hear that they prayed for the success of his gentle friend, the Lady Dionissia. Others declared that she had not been fairly judged and that the last course should have been judged to her. Thus there was great noise and Mr Sorrell could neither hear nor speak.

There were, too, indescribable odours. Some sort of leech with a steeple-crowned hat and a robe covered with spangles and the signs of the zodiac stood in a booth of branches behind black jacks and bottles. An alembic bubbled over a fire of bones. The man, to call attention to himself held a brass mortar inverted. Inside it he vibrated his iron pestle. It made a continual drilling of metallic sound.

Always more people came running towards Mr Sorrell. He could no longer see over their heads and their stinking bodies made a wall round him. He moved onwards slowly and they receded before him, closing in behind. He had never felt so alone. And always, through the stinking effluvia of their bodies and the chorus of their voices came the drilling sound of the mortar and the piercing odours from the alembic and its fire. . . . Insupportable! There was a mist before his eyes.

Chloroform. . . . And a telephone bell!

Was it then possible that the ages superimposed themselves the one over the other? That they co-existed? Why not? . . . Once in Aleppo. . . . Or was it Caïffa? . . . Yes, probably Caïffa. . . . It did not matter which. . . . He had been talking to a rabbi in his hole in a wall. To improve the Hebrew he had learned in Jerusalem. The hole had been some sacred place hollowed out in the city wall. They had been talking about the establishment of a national home for the fellow's compatriots: the return of the tribes that had been lost for two thousand years. In face of the scrolls and lamps and brasswork, in the stuffy, odorous dimness suddenly he had felt himself as if bound hand and foot. He could hear from outside the click of the horses' bits and the low voice of his Arab orderly talking to the driver of a mobile searchlight whose car had broken down not five yards away. And it was as if a curtain had been between him and them. If he had been able to stretch out a hand he would have been able to draw the curtain. But for a long time he had been unable to move. He had been back two thousand years; speaking a language two thousand years old; listening to, sharing even, aspirations that too had been two thousand years old amidst the perfumes of herbs the secret of which had been as long forgotten, in the interstice of a wall that had crumbled equally long. And with troops in khaki and screw-guns on mules passing in an endless stream. . . .

Why shouldn't ages co-exist? But they co-existed. The half minute last past was now as dead as any half minute of a thousand years ago. As dead; but no more dead: as irrevocable, but no more irrevocable. Then why not as immortal?

Yes, they co-existed. It was perhaps only the human perception that could not appreciate co-existing scenes. Though you can of course. You can look at thin mist and see the mist or you can equally look through the mist and see the sun. . . .

It was like that. . . . In the insupportable odour of chloroform, to the ceaseless, maddening drilling of the telephone bell he could see the pockmarked features of a fat, one-eyed man with a fur necklet and a hat of enormous dimensions made of folds of cloth. The mayor of Wiley. . . . But across his face was the simulacrum of a paper nailed to a white shiny wall with drawing pins. . . . A paper with printed vertical and horizontal parallels—and an inked, ruddled line that rose and descended on the parallels. . . . The mayor of Wiley—and a temperature chart. His own temperature chart, the inked line descending impressively low. . . .

Above his head were little fleecy clouds superimposed on a translucent and shining blue. . . . It became suddenly as if he saw them through an iridescent film of glass. . . . Tears in blue eyes that looked down on him! What did you know about that? . . . The Chronicles of Froissart? Of Shropshire? Of Wiltshire? A coif, white across the forehead? Nurse Dionissia, you read too much. A blond, broad face. . . . A little worn. . . . Bending over him against the sky. . . . No, against a shining ceiling. . . . "We'll get him back."

Dionissia's face: but worn with anxiety. She should get out into the open air. She read too much. Presumably Froissart.

[303]

. . . But was Froissart going in 1326? . . . By God his Chronicles began in 1325 . . . 1325 to 1400. He could remember the dates on the back of an edition of the "Chronicles" that he had published. In gilt!

A voice said: "Guéris moi par pitié, tressainct!" but across it, as across the Mayor's face the temperature chart had shewn went the sound of a dark, thin-lipped woman's voice: "We'll get him back now . . . In a month . . . Five weeks. . . ."

In the name of Hell! . . . One age could superimpose itself upon another. But one human consciousness could not appreciate two superimposed currents of time . . . The Lady Dionissia was awaiting him in her tent. In the year 1326 . . . He struggled violently with the crowd that hemmed him in . . . They were making incantations to get him back . . . Those others . . . A cold, complacent, dark-lipped woman to the infernal drilling of the telephone . . . Not back: forwards . . . Hundreds of years . . . He would never go back . . . Forwards . . . Six hundred and twelve years . . . Never, never, never . . . Where are you shoving? . . . No: 602!

A peasant of the Plain, long crook and all, had been pushed up against him. He snatched the lean fellow's great staff . . . They should see if they would get him back . . . Those who were immediately before him pushed back . . . He was snorting like a stallion; he had brought the staff down on heads and shoulders . . . He would go free in spite of a million serfs . . . Nevertheless they were cheering him. . . .

There was still greater outcry.They made a little way for him and he pushed on. He laid about him as strongly as he was able. Still they cheered him, for those whom he did not strike thought he had done well and those upon whom his blows fell considered that they were deserved.

At last he came near her pavilion. Her Welsh mountaineers,

[304]

some catching at throats, rushing in, others striking with their pike-staves had very soon cleared the way.

With her fair and candid face framed in bright steel that was inlaid with little scrolls of gold she answered him seriously:

"Why, I do not think, gentle friend, that you need have much fear for me. For I am much the stronger of the two, and, if my cousin's strength be increased by hot rage and hatred, I think that should she strike such a blow as I found inconvenient that should rouse such an anger in me as should increase my own strength. For I have not yet struck as hard as I could have done. You will have perceived that I aimed at her thigh in the second course—a too difficult stroke. Yet I was willing she should have that course though nearly it brought me to disaster . . . But I think you need have little fear, for my horse is good, my armour very strong, so that I think that at the worst I may come off with but a few bruises, unless God judge otherwise."

At this moment the trumpet blew for her to get upon her horse, and she must go, so that the new knight had found nothing to say of all that he had desired to utter.

The people who had beset him were beginning to run away, to get the best places at the barriers of the lists. The new knight stayed until they were all gone, so that he might walk unhindered over the grass. Now it chanced that while he so waited he looked up the valley towards the castle of Stapleford. Then he saw a great number of people, some on horse with a line of spears, and many on foot, whilst at their head was a knight upon a great horse and in dark armour. They were so far away, however, that the new knight could not see any cognizances or arms. He thought to himself that if these people did not hurry they would not see much of the jousting, and so he went back to his seat.

As soon as he was seated the trumpet blew. Then the horses came towards each other, both riders having their shields before them, and shining axes with double heads held on high. The first stroke red and white struck, but the Lady Dionissia caught it upon her extended shield, and in turn she struck a blow that fell upon the helmet of the Lady Blanche, but the axe glanced off and came down on the red and white shield, so that it was bent a little. The next blows each of them caught very well upon their shields, so that no damage was done. But all this while the great and powerful horse of the Lady Blanche was screaming out and squealing with rage, for it hated above all things to be made to stand still when another stallion was near, and once it swerved when the Lady Blanche was striking, so that her blow fell short of the Lady Dionissia, and dropped with a hollow sound into the barrier that was between them, cutting deep in the wood of it and tearing open the fair covering cloths. And this was considered a disgrace to her and to her horse. Then they rode back to their pavilions when six strokes had been struck by each, to deliver up their shields to the herald. For the next battle of six strokes they must fight without shields, according to the rule. So they should have walked to the centre of the lists, and there have stood until three trumpets blew, their axes hanging all the time to their saddle-bows.

But suddenly it was observed that the horse of the Lady Blanche was bounding down the lists, each bound being one of many yards. A great shout went up from all the people, for this was outside the laws of true tourneying, so that they were not called upon to keep silence, nor yet could they have done so had the laws been never so strong. So the great horse continued on its way until it was come almost level with where the other walked stately and slow. Then, enormous, it

rose upon its hind legs and struck forward with its forehoofs
that were shod with iron. But this blow fell short, and it
descended so that its belly struck upon the barrier. Then the
barrier fell to the ground, and the great horse sprang forward
through the tangle of cloths and of wood. It rushed upon the
other, seeking to bite with its huge teeth, but the armour and
the covering cloths impeded this. Then all the people there
heard how the Lady Dionissia within her helmet cried out:
"Draw off! draw off!" But though they saw the Lady Blanche
pulling at her reins and driving in her spurs so that blood
showed upon the covering cloths and they were all torn, none
could say whether the Lady Blanche was seeking to draw off
her horse, or whether she was urging it on, hoping that with
the terrible blows of its feet it might mount upon the other
and so slay her cousin. Then, to the amazement of all there,
the Lady Dionissia raised her visor, and all heard her cry out:

"Will you not draw off? Or I will not hold in my beast."

All the people there said afterwards that they had never
seen the like for horror to the combat of these horses, so they
laboured, cried out shrill cries, and moved terribly their enormous limbs, whilst their riders swayed backwards and forwards in their saddles. Then all heard how the Lady Dionissia
cried out:

"Up, Coppin!"

The Lady Blanche's horse was then upon its hind legs, bal-
ancing to strike with one foot. But the Lady Dionissia's Coppin rose, mountainous, and as it had been well trained for this
adventure it struck with both its feet at once, and at the same
time by use of its hind legs it bounded forward. Thus, all its
body being off the ground and springing through the air, its
forefeet struck the neck of the other horse beneath and at the
base, where the breast armour begins. The Lady Blanche's

horse was then upon its hind legs, so over it fell, backwards, a tower of iron, and when it fell it lay upon its rider's thigh, so that she was crushed down upon the cloths and the ruins of the barrier.

Being down, on account of its heavy armour the horse could not rise, but lay kicking in the air its enormous and hairy legs. Amidst many cries there came running four of the Lady Dionissia's men-at-arms. They dragged the horse to its feet, but sideways first, so that it should not tread upon its rider. So they led the horse away, and there the Lady Blanche lay still amongst the ruins of the barrier. Her surcoat had been torn away, and all the steel of her armour showed, her hands being spread abroad. One of them still grasped the battle-axe, and the visor of her helmet directed a shining and malicious grin to the bright skies. Then when silence was called, the old knight said clearly to the Lady Dionissia, where she sat still upon her horse:

"Now you may get down and, setting your foot upon that rider's chest, you may claim the victory if she do not rise before."

"That will I do," the Lady Dionissia said.

So she came down from her horse as nimbly as she might for the weight of her armour. She walked across to where the other lay, and, lifting her foot which was cased all in steel, she set it upon the other's chest.

"Thus do I claim the victory of the day," she said; "and if there be no other to come against me, so it is mine. And if this lady's ladies will not meet with me and mine in the mêlée, I claim that they should be my ladies to serve me as I will. For this is my right and due."

Then there came four men-at-arms with the litter covered with green boughs, and so they bore the Lady Blanche off that field. Then the heralds went to ask those ladies if they would fight in that mêlée, and after a while the trumpets spoke again, and then the herald of the Lady Blanche said from his end of the lists:

"No, these ladies will not fight. They say that three to two is too many, and so they yield themselves."

"Then the day is mine," the Lady Dionissia said, "if there come no other to fight against me."

.   .   .   .   .   .

The New Knight of Winterburne of St Martin thought he had never seen anything so fair as she was standing upon the crushed barrier. For she was very bright in her yellow and white surcoat, and the blue of the sky was mirrored on her helmet and on her shining arms that were covered with steel.

"Now thanks be to God that this day is over," he said to the old knight beside him. "But what is that?"

Amongst the crowd on the farther barrier there had grown up a great array of light spears and pikes. Many bowmen were there with their bows pointing upwards from behind their shoulders. And in the middle of them all rode a knight in darkish armour, with a long spear, who held before him a great shield chequered in red and white.

"Mercy of God!" said the new Knight of Winterburne, "I think that is the Knight of Coucy of Enguerrand of Stapleford."

"Why, those are his cognizances," Sir Ygorac said. "Let us see what he will do."

The Knight of Coucy sat still upon his horse, his visor was up, and with his large face and cunning eyes he surveyed that scene. It seemed as if he smiled, but that might have been the shadow of his helmet.

"Mercy of God!" the new Knight of Winterburne said, "what will he do?"

"Why, that we shall see," Sir Ygorac answered. "That is why I wait."

Then suddenly from the red and white pavilion there came out a herald bearing upon his tabard the chequers of the Knight of Coucy quartered with the arms of the heralds of the King of England, which are three leopards. Behind him there walked out two trumpeters bearing short trumpets from which there fluttered two square banners, chequered also in red and white.

"Why, this is to do things better," Sir Ygorac said.

"Ah, gentle knight," the Knight of Winterburne asked, "he has with him a great army of men well armed. Do you think he will now set about us?"

"No, I do not think that he will," Sir Ygorac answered. "Let us hear what his herald has to say."

The trumpeters having blown, the herald stood forward and said in a clear voice:

"Lo, my masters, this is the will of the famous and gentle Knight of Coucy of Enguerrand of Stapleford. Now he will run three courses with light spears against this rider who has properly and under all eyes vanquished the lady of this knight, and the prize of these three courses shall be £100 in gold, and this the gentle knight will pay if he is overthrown, together with a great chaplet of pearls which shall be the prize of the overthrow of the Lady Blanche. But if the gentle knight be vouchsafed by God the victory of this field, they shall cry quits. And if either rider shall be cast from his horse, the victory shall be to the other, and no more courses ridden. So speaks the gentle and most famous knight by my voice. With this addition, that if this lady will claim that she is a woman and so yield her up, the Knight of Coucy and the rest will claim of her what amends he afterwards will."

The Lady Dionissia had stood motionless during this speech. And first she had gone red and then white, waves of colour pursuing themselves over her face. And for a long time afterwards she stood gazing down at the green grass where it was trampled by hoof-marks as if she neither saw nor heard all the noises and movements that there went on. For many women cried out that their husbands had come back from the wars, some thanking God and some the reverse. And children cried out to fathers, and friends to friends amongst the bowmen and men-at-arms that stood there behind the Knight of Coucy. So at last the Lady Dionissia motioned with her hand that her trumpeter should sound. Then she spoke in a clear voice:

"So God give me grace, and for the honour of my womanhood," she said, "upon these terms I will meet with this gentle knight."

At this there was a greater outcry than any there had been that day, for all the bowmen and the men-at-arms cried out too, and it was very joyous. The new knight said:

"Mercy of God!"

But Sir Ygorac, looking round upon him, answered his former questions.

"No," he said, "now I am very certain that this gentle knight will not lay hands upon you and that lady. Or if he did he must meet with me, and I will bring my many to the rescue. But he is a very good knight, and will observe the laws of chivalry. For it would be a foul discourtesy to lay hands upon the person or the friends of one with whom you have ridden in jousts. And this, I think, is why this lady has elected to meet him, and why she reflected for so long before coming to that decision."

Then the new knight could no longer bear himself. He rose from his seat and ran so swiftly to the pavilion of the Lady Dionissia, that no one would come before him. He found her there with her two ladies, who were in caps of steel and other light harness, for they had expected that they must take part in a mêlée. The Lady Dionissia had her helmet off, for she was very hot.

"Now by my faith, gentle friend," she said, "I am very much afraid."

"Oh, even now," the new knight cried out, "even now claim that you are a woman."

"No, no," she answered; "and it is not of this jousting that I am afraid. For I think this knight will run very negligently, and I will bear myself as well as I may, and try a difficult trick that I may unhorse him if he do not await it."

The new knight said:

"No, no; it is too dangerous."

"Ah, gentle friend," she answered, "it is not this of which I am afraid, and I think that even if I am cast from my horse I shall not die of it, for I am a strong woman. But that which I fear is the coming of the young Knight of Egerton. For, as I hear, he should have come with all his many, and they are three hundred or more, whereas I have but half a score of men-at-arms. He should have come with the Knight of Coucy and have ridden against my cousin Blanche and me, but this morning, as I hear, he was gone from his lodgings where they lay last night at Salisbury. And this is why the Knight of Coucy came so late; for he waited that this cousin might come, but at last set out alone. Now at any moment this Young Knight may come, and I am very much afraid, for with my ten we could not well fight against his three hundred, so there is much for you to do whilst I ride these three courses."

"I will not have you ride them," the new knight said.

"Now, that must be," she answered; "but, gentle friend, lose no more time, and listen to what I have to say. And first, you must see that these ladies get themselves into their women's clothes, and all their belongings from the castle of Tamworth must be got into their hutches and on to the backs of my pack-horses that I brought with me from the Welsh borders. And so it must be done with all my gear, too, and with yours. And my men-at-arms, four of them must have a litter ready in case I fall. And you must have your horse ready and saddled, and you must send to the ladies of the Lady Blanche that they must get them ready to come along with me, for now they are my servants, and I will have their bodies or a proper forfeit. And some meats and bread we must have too, and some hides to make the beds to-night. Or if they have not these things ready by the time I have run my courses we will do without them, so much I am afraid of this Knight of Egerton."

And at that moment the trumpet blew for her to get to horse, and she set her helmet upon her head, and the Lady Cunigunde buckled it for her.

Her horse having been brought in from outside, she mounted it, making use of a stool, and, having set down her visor, she took her shield and her spear, and, having her battle-axe at her saddle-bow, she rode out when the curtains were drawn.

She was quite calm, for her pulses beat hardly at all more quickly. Through the little bright interstices of her visor she could see far away down the lists the immense figure of the Knight of Coucy, holding his lance as if it had been no more than a twig, all in black armour both for himself and his horse —such armour as he had used in his battle against the Scots. And if she had been very intent on scoring her notches, he would have seemed to her a very formidable figure. But what she desired most was only to get these courses over, and to go away from the danger of the Knight of Egerton. Whether the Knight of Egerton would bear a great grudge against her and her friend she did not well know, but she thought that it was certain that, according to the laws of gentle chivalry and of honour, he must make war upon them if he found them there upon his lands. And so must the Knight of Coucy, as being his cousin and ally. Only he could not do it if he had run a course with lances against her, because all the laws held that after such a deed the opposing knight must be allowed to depart whole and free, and with all his arms and all his friends and retainers, even though they were outlaws, as happened when a knight challenged another of another country with which his own was at war. He would have safe conduct for himself and his friends both in ingress and egress. So she was very glad that the Knight of Coucy had made her this challenge, and all she desired was to get the courses over. If she could do it she would unhorse him by a feat or a trick such as was permissible, but so seldom practised, because of its difficulty, that the Knight of Coucy would hardly expect it at her hands. To him she must appear such a novice as to be little more than a sucking child. But she had such a very good horse that she could well adventure upon it. So the trumpet blew.

The Knight of Coucy rode gently, and smiled within his helmet. It pleased him to see what a knightly figure this woman made as she put down her spear and came towards him, and he was very well minded to let her off lightly, with only a good fall and a broken limb, if that did not come by chance. For he was ready to consider himself beholden to this lady, since by her action his wife's leg was very well broken. And so during the winter months he might live in good peace in his castle, and go to devise and sport with his leman in the city of Salisbury when and as often as he would, until, the winter being over, the well-heads would no longer be frozen, roads would be passable, and he could ride abroad again. And for the next year he would ride into France or Almain, for he was determined never again to ride against the Scots. Against them he had done little or nothing, for they had seen not so much as the tail of the Scots' army. These things were in his mind as he rode along, bending gradually lower, so that most of his body should be behind his great shield. The Lady Dionissia was riding not so very fast, but she was come almost up to him. Then he felt upon his shield such a blow as was not very formidable, but yet it was more than he awaited, and as he felt it so he delivered his own thrust, leaning heavily forward. And his spear gave and broke, so that the Lady Dionissia did not come down from her saddle, and he perceived that her horse was checking and he checked his.

And then suddenly upon the side of his helmet that was farther away from the barrier he felt a great and heavy stroke. "*Die mercy!*" he exclaimed. "*Le coup de Guet!*"

And then he knew very well, for he could see nothing, that as she passed him the Lady Dionissia had dropped her spear and, seizing her axe, had struck backwards. This was a blow so seldom attempted that the Knight of Coucy had never thought upon it. For if the blow failed, so the knight who had attempted it was held much disgraced, and could take no more part in that tournament; but if it succeeded it was much honour to him. And as he felt that blow, which was heavy and tremendous, so with the weight of it he felt his stirrup leather break on the right-hand side. And because he was pressing hard upon the stirrup to draw in his rein, so there was nothing for him to do but to topple sideways and to fall from his horse. So he lay on his back for a moment.

"*Die mercy!*" he said again within his helmet. "I have deserved this." And then again he laughed, for he thought this was a pleasant adventure. And at first he thought he would lie there, and let her set her foot upon his throat. But then he considered that that would be too great a complaisance. So, just as he heard the ruler of that tournament say to the Lady Dionissia that she should get down from her horse and do that thing, he rolled sideways, scrambled to his knees, and so got to his feet. Then he stamped and moved his arms to feel that nothing was broken, and he felt that all was well with him. And by that time the Lady Dionissia was come almost up to him, on foot. Then the Knight of Coucy put up his visor and smiled broadly at her.

"No, no, gentle knight," he said, "for that I will call you, and a good one, you are not soon enough to set your foot upon my throat. If you would do that you must fight with me with swords and axes upon foot until you have me down again. But for me, you have given me a very good blow so that my head sings. And I am very well content that you shall have this course and this day for your own."

Then the Lady Dionissia put up her visor.

"Nenny!" she said. "I am very glad to have this day and to let it go at that, and I take no great credit from this adventure, which came about only by the breaking of a stirrup-strap."

"Nenny! Gentle knight," the Knight of Coucy said, "the shame is mine and the credit yours, for it is a discourteous thing to come into a tournament with an old stirrup-strap. And this I have done now to my great discredit. So the day is yours, and I am glad of it, though little had I thought to see the day when a woman should put me down, or any knight either. For I think that I am the best knight in Christendom, and you have put me down. So you may tell it to your children's children as a thing much to your credit. Yet, now strongly would I rede and advise you to depart and what you have won of me, that will I send after you, being £100 in gold and a chaplet of great pearls. But I think this is not a very safe place for you to abide in."

"So I think too," the Lady Dionissia said; "and when I have thanked you, so I will depart as quickly as I may."

Then she held her axe over her head to show that she claimed that victory, and when Sir Ygorac had given it her by calling on her trumpeter to blow, all the people there cried out and were joyous and amazed.

So was ended this singular and famous tournament, and of this the chaplain of the Dean of Salisbury says in his chronicle that there was never such another one in Christendom. But in this he errs. For there was one between ladies somewhere in the South of France, but I have forgotten the place and the name. The chaplain of the Dean of Salisbury says in his chronicle that this was a shameful and an immodest thing in the Lady Dionissia, so to put on men's attire; but in his day he found few to agree with him. For it was told of many ladies that they put on the armour of knights and went to find their true loves and did feats of arms, and sometimes they found their loves faithful to them and sometimes unfaithful, as in the story called *La Demoiselle Cavalière* which was told by Monseigneur de Foquessoles before the Dauphin of France. And so you may read it in the book called *Les Cent Nouvelles Nouvelles*. But the chaplain of the Dean of Salisbury thought, nevertheless, that this was a great shame. Nevertheless, he comforts himself, saying that there is no evil so great but some good must come of it, since in this tournament one woman had a broken leg and sustained other injuries so that she lay for three months in bed. And this, says the chaplain, is a very good and joyous thing, for by so long was at least one woman mewed up and rendered incapable of doing the works of Satan. For all women are the emissaries of the devil for the confusion and temptation of mankind. But, on the other hand, many ladies in that country took this text for sermons to their lords, telling them that so it showed that ladies, if they would, were as good as knights or better.

But the Lady Dionissia and her friend and her four women and her ten men-at-arms, with their pack-horses and their hutches, rode away south from the Plain and no one hindered them, and the Knight of Coucy helped them as much as he might.

THE DUSK WAS FALLING WHEN THEY APPROACHED THE LITTLE castle of Winterburne St Martin, the little castle that the old knight had said was no bigger than a house of stone. Yet it was certainly bigger. They had travelled over many bridges and across many valleys, so that sometimes they had seemed to have the whole world below them, the Plain stretching out behind like a sea of purple wine, and before them the New Forest with its great sea of dark tree-tops. Many of the hills up which they had travelled had been very steep, and they had gone slowly, accommodating their pace to that of the men-at-arms and the pack-horses which were burdened with their hutches. In the front there rode the Knight of Winterburne and the Lady Dionissia, keeping always a little ahead, for they had many things to talk of. Then behind them came the four ladies—Amoureuse, Blanchemain, Cunigunde, and Amarylle. They laughed all and were very joyous, for the ladies of the Lady Dionissia loved her very well, and those of the Lady

Blanche, even the little Lady Blanchemain whom she had favoured, were glad to leave her. And they all rejoiced to ride upon an adventure. Behind them came the Welsh men-at-arms, urging on the pack-horses. They passed no villages and few people, for this was a very wild and deserted country.

Now they were in a broad valley, that was all grass, and, as the sun set, they perceived the castle standing upon the hillside by itself, for the church and the little village which belonged to it were over the hill. Up to the castle there led a little road which had not been much used of late, so that it was nearly all overgrown with grass. That day there was a new moon, and it shone tremulously above the little castle that had a very high-pitched roof, running along the whole length, whilst round it went the battlements. Round this castle there was a moat, so they rode over the drawbridge, that was down, and at the other end of the drawbridge a very old and stupid man met them and gave up to them the keys. They could make nothing of him, for he could not understand the speech they spoke. He was of Hampshire, and those of them who spoke any English at all spoke it in the manner of Wiltshire, which was very different. So they laughed and let him go.

Now they must be very busy with torches lit, going from room to room to see where they should be housed. The horses must be taken to their stables, which lay round a courtyard, though it was all encompassed by the moat and a wall with towers and bastions, but they were small ones.

To house all these people was not a very easy thing, for no one there had been in a castle of that shape. It was very old, and the oldest part of it was a dwelling-house that had been built before the Normans had come into that countryside. Upon one side of the arch at which they had ridden in there was a great hall. And this they judged to be the dining-hall, for along its walls there lay boards and trestles; in one corner was a plough and several bill-hooks and scythes. And in this room there was no fireplace. Over against it, on the other side of the arch, there was such another hall, of the same size, but cut in half by a wall of plastered laths. Beyond this wall there was a chamber that they judged must be my lady's bower, for it had a closet of boards that had been painted, and in this closet they found pegs on which to hang clothes or armour, and perches for hawks or parrots. Above these were three fair rooms, where they might harbour guests. Above this was the great roof-chamber that ran all along this part of the building. Now if the ladies slept in the upper rooms, where should the guests sleep? And if the men-at-arms slept in the roof-chamber that would not be good husbandry, for how could they defend the gate if any sudden attack should be made upon it? And again, how could my lady call her ladies if by chance she fell ill at night? So they went walking about with their torches and laughing. And at last they found that, round the courtyard where the stables were, were many more rooms, so that there was a great kitchen, an armoury, butteries, a great cellar and fourteen rooms, where men or women could sleep. Then they all laughed gaily and made merry.

So then they went back to the smaller hall, and there the Lady Dionissia made a reverence to the Knight of Winterburne, and asked him to command how he would have all his servants to sleep. He said to her:

"Gentle friend, this bower with the closet shall be your bower, and the more so in that I have perceived that a little door in the closet leads into the large room that is behind it in the courtyard. And this room again has a door into another large room. I will let your ladies sleep in the first of these two rooms, so that they may come to you the more easily through the little door in the closet. Then in the second of these rooms shall sleep the pages, when we get them. And in this room, where we stand, I will sleep myself until we are married, which I hope may be soon. And for the men-at-arms, they shall sleep in the large room that is behind the banqueting hall. But one shall keep watch from the battlements by day, and one shall keep the drawbridge. And two shall stand beneath the arch all night to be on the watch. And when we have cooks and grooms and hinds and other servers, I will allot to each kind their rooms."

Then everyone said that the new knight had spoken very well, and the Lady Dionissia that she was very glad that now they knew their places. For she had ridden all that afternoon in armour, though without her helmet, so great had been their haste to get them gone from the neighbourhood of Tamworth.

The new knight bade the men-at-arms bring in the Lady Dionissia's hutch and her bed, and set them down in that room. Then the Lady Dionissia went in with her own two ladies, and the new knight said that he would have the men-at-arms strew rushes on the floor after she was come out again. So then the new knight very courteously begged the Ladies Amoureuse and Blanchemain that they would go into the banqueting hall and, taking with them two of the men-at-arms, would see to the setting up of the boards, and covering them with cloths and so making things ready for supper. And they should see that rushes were thrown upon the floor and torches set in the rings on the wall that they might have light by which to eat. Then he commanded two others of the men-at-arms to see to bringing in the hutches and the bedsteads of those ladies and of himself, and sacks, baskets of food, and skins, and such barrels of wine, ale, metheglin, and mead as they had had time to bring with them. So, having set all these people to work, he went away himself with the four men-at-arms that remained, bearing torches because it was quite dark.

It was his will to go to the priest of that village and to pray him to tell them where they might find such as owed him service, so that that night they might have lads for servers and some young girls for servants, and old women to see to the rushes on the floors. For fortunately they had discovered in the courtyard a great provision of rushes, and, for the matter of servants, these should have been there, awaiting them by the rights of it, the children of his villeins coming with their parents to ask what was desired of them. But the Knight of Winterburne judged that they had been too frightened or too wary to come, and he was determined to begin at once in the way that it was his intention to pursue. For now he felt himself to be a knight and the lord of that manor. The Ladies Amoureuse and Blanchemain said that all this was very well thought out by the knight, who was likely to make a good master if he continued as he had begun.

So he went over the hill with his men, and saw in the starlight and in the moving light of torches for the first time the village that he possessed. Here there were as many as fifty houses, with mud walls whitened, and with thatches of straw. They ran in a straggling street down a gentle hill. Behind the cow-yards they perceived, black and looming, a church tower, and beside it a small stone house, which was the only one that had lights in it. There undoubtedly dwelt the priest. So they knocked upon his shutter and he came out, and was glad to see them, and ready to do what he could to help them, for he foresaw that he would have from henceforth meals and good cheer in the little castle. So they went with their torches from house to house, and it was not long before they went

[323]

back up the little hill, driving before them seven lads, four young girls, and five cows to give them milk next morning. Some of these peasants' children wept and cried, and some were sullen. For, as is the nature of peasants, they had hoped that their duties would die out through disuse. But the girls for the most part were contented to escape from the surveillance of their mothers. They thought that life would now be more joyous for them, and they would be better fed and lodged. As for hard work, they had had it all the time.

So they all went in to the little castle under the archway, and, the priest having come with them, said grace and blessed that house and board. The peasants served them as best they might, and, for the food, it was all of it brought from Stapleford. So they contrived to be merry, and to eat and drink well. And when the boards were drawn, the new knight set all his household various tasks of sweeping and making the beds ready, and bringing in brushwood for the fires. The priest went away back to his little stone house, and it was about nine o'clock at night, and all the doors of the castle stood open, with men going in and out upon their errands.

So the Knight of Winterburne and the Lady Dionissia were at peace in the smaller hall on the left of the archway. In the corner of this room there was a fireplace, and here now a great log threw up loud flames. Two torches were in rings upon the walls; the floor was thick with rushes and their sweet scent. They had two stools before the fire, and the bed with its hutch at the foot was made, and had a coverlet of foxskins that was pretty to see in the firelight. The Lady Dionissia sat before the fire with a distaff, and twisted the wool from it in her fingers. The Knight of Winterburne walked up and down in the rushes near her.

"Now, God be thanked, gentle friend," he said, "I have all

things that I desire, save the one that we may be married soon, and I think that life will now be more pleasant and more gay than I had ever thought men's life could be."

The Lady Dionissia, looking down in the ground, crossed herself, and said:

"Give thanks to God and his little angels, and all the saints."

"Why, so I do," the knight said; "and very well I think I ought to do so."

Then the Lady Dionissia said:

"I think you have done very well this day, so that it is a marvel how you have directed all these people."

"Why, I had directed many people in my day," the knight answered; "I think it is what I do best and most gladly. And very gladly I have done it this day, for I have grown tired of being at all times a looker-on."

"Nevertheless," the Lady Dionissia said, "that time was not all lost. For in looking on you have used your eyes to good purpose, so that you can comfort yourself very well as a gentle and terrible knight should. Certain strangenesses you have that one may mark, but in this country, where all men are from different parts, some being from France, some from Normandy, some from Britain, some from the North, and some, like myself, from the West, it would be strange if all knights did not show differences of conduct. So I am very proud of you, for nothing makes a woman more glad than to have a well-seen husband."

"Well, all this has come very easily to me," the new knight said, "for I have travelled in many lands and seen many people. Moreover, it is said that the English, above all other nations, have the power to adopt strange manners and to settle easily in far countries. And I am English more than most people."

So he let himself down by her side in the rushes. He

[325]

stretched out his feet towards the fire, and leaned his back towards her skirts. And so he sat looking at the fire, and playing with his right hand amongst the little pearls that were sewn on to her shoes.

"Yes," he said, "in this autumn and winter that are coming I will set myself diligently to the husbandry of this my manor. I will study very carefully what are my rights and what are the peasants', and which are my lands and where they have the right to plough. And in these months too I will get hawks and dogs, and so we will ride hunting and hawking, so that I may perfect myself in these noble arts of falconry and venery, and this will be for your pleasure too. And from the gentle knight Sir Ygorac, who dwells not so far from here, I will take lessons in the arts and laws of chivalry and of heralds. And, if I may come to it, I will practise myself with spear and sword and heavy armour. But I think I am too old for these things; nevertheless, I will try it."

So the Lady Dionissia let down her hand that had been twisting wool from the distaff and let it rest upon his shoulder.

"All this I am very glad to hear," she said.

"And when the winter is over and the spring well advanced so that the crops and seedlings show in our lands that we may know the harvest will be good, then we will ride abroad into far countries and see the great forests and the broad rivers, the vast plains, the mighty cities, and the puissant kings that you have desired to see. And this I should wish to do at once, for I know that would be to your greater pleasure, gentle friend. But already summer is spent, and the leaves are turning yellow upon the hills, and for journeying in the winter that is nothing. And I think, too, wisely we must wait for news of what answer shall be made to our petition in Rome, so that we may be married the sooner."

"Ah, gentle friend," the Lady Dionissia said, "your plan is much the better, and in all things you are discreet and most wise. So it is more well with me that I can utter."

She put her distaff down beside her in the rushes, and with both her hands drew up his face that lay in her lap. And for long she kissed him on the mouth, and so afterwards sat with her cheek upon his forehead, gazing at the fire and thinking upon the journeys that they would make. Her dress was all of green cloth, being very long, and the long sleeves sewn with yellow silk, and her hennin was very broad and white, for she loved this fashion of head-dress better than any other, though new fashions were constantly arising. And the Knight of Winterburne was all in brown cloth with a great hood cast back. And his shoes of brown leather were very long, but were not tied up to the knee, for in such shoes you cannot ride. So they sat in the firelight and devised of the summer days that lay before them.

. . . . . .

Upon the valley track in the starlight a man came riding furiously upon a light horse in the fashion of a hackney. It was all dark where he rode, and there was danger from the roughness of the way, but he cared nothing because of the black rage that was in his heart. For that day, in the city of Salisbury, his leman had left him. She had gone away with a richer man who had seen her at a window and had promised her many dresses and a painted bower of her own in the town of London. But who this was he did not know, nor could he find any trace of where they had gone. And so he ridden very fast to the castle of Stapleford, leaving all his men masterless and forlorn in the city.

Being come to Stapleford, he learnt the news from his cousin the Lady Blanche, lying abed with her leg broken, raging and cursing God. And from her he learnt that all the evil that had fallen upon them came from this stranger who had come with the magic cross and from his half-wife, the Lady Dionissia, who was a very evil witch from the marches of Wales. And it was these two without doubt who had spirited away his leman Gertrude. The Lady Blanche whispered these things into his ears until he was frenzied, bidding him revenge himself. His cousin of Coucy would have given him better counsel, but that knight was down by the riverside seeing how his men folded up his pavilions and took down the lists, for here was much wood cut that would make good firing in the oncoming winter. So the Young Knight had ridden furiously, having drunk much wine and mead, through all these men at the riverside, paying no heed to them, neither could anyone overtake him, for his horse was very fast and enduring, being an Arab that his brother the Old Knight, now dead, had brought from the Holy Land. It was dusk when he passed his great castle of Tamworth, and night fell dark whilst he climbed the great hill behind the town of Wiley.

And all the while as his horse scrambled up the hill or galloped down valleys there ran in his muddled and agonised mind two only thoughts: the one that he would force these bitter sorcerers to conjure his Gertrude back as they had conjured her away; or else he would seize the cross which gave that wizard his power and so he himself would force her to come back. So he thought over and over again as he rode through the night, and his bitter tears fell down because his leman had left him. And he was fully convinced that this had been done by sorcery, so often had the Lady Blanche, lying in her bed, declared this to be the case.

So at last in the black night he perceived the torches of people going about on the hillside like moving stars and the lights of the little castle showed black against the sky. With no thought of the danger that he ran, entering alone and un-armed, he rode in over the drawbridge that was down and threw himself, beneath the archway, from his horse. The horse ran on into the courtyard, and he pushed open with vio-lence a door that was upon his right-hand side. He staggered into a large hall, and at first he could not see because of the bright light. Then there screamed out the Lady Amoureuse, and ran past him through the archway and into another door. So he turned and followed her. He came into this room cov-ered with sweat and mud and with his eyes staring. The Lady Dionissia was rising from her stool, the Lady Amoureuse was crouching back against the wall at the far end of the room with her eyes very large and full of fear. The new Knight of Winterburne was sitting on the rushes and looking back over his shoulder. Towards him the Young Knight ran, and cried out in a lamentable manner:

"Give me back my leman. Give me back that I love."

The new knight turned him slowly round in the rushes.

"Ah, gentle knight," he said, "what is this?"

"Give her back to me! Give her back!" the Young Knight cried out.

The Lady Dionissia went quickly into her bower to fetch from it some weapon, for all her harness had been put in her closet. But because it was dark in that room she could not well find the latch of the door of her closet, so she lost some time.

The new knight was drawing in his legs to rise from the rushes, and before him the Young Knight exclaimed perpetu-ally:

"Give me back my leman that you have taken."

And then suddenly he changed his cry, and said:

"Give me the cross that I see at your throat."

[329]

The new knight covered the cross with his hand. He was upon one knee now, and had the other foot upon the rushes ready to stand up.

"Nay, gentle knight," he said, "I do not know if I should give you this cross or no. For it was given me in trust by a lady the wife of an Egerton of Tamworth. That is true, and if you had a wife I would give it to her. But I think your only wife is Lady Dionissia, and yet it is not right for me to give this cross to her, for that would make it soon my own, and I think I have no right to it, but am only its guardian."

"Thou fool!" the Young Knight screamed out, "the only wife I have is this Gertrude, for I married before a hedge priest in Derby. I thought, fool that I was, that this would tie her to me."

And suddenly he began to sob and cry and hit his chest with his immense and knotted right hand. But his news had been so astounding that the new knight was struck perfectly still where he was, with one leg bent and the other stretched out behind him as he was rising from the floor. He could find no words to speak, for in his astonishment he had no thoughts to utter. Then a new and violent gust of rage came over the Young Knight, and without more words he sprang at the throat of the Knight of Winterburne to wrench from it the golden cross that he coveted. He fell upon the new knight with an enormous force, for he was considered to be the strongest man, whether in Christendom or in Heathernesse, of that day. But because the new knight was only half risen to his feet, so before this shock he overbalanced backwards and fell his full length. His head struck the stone of the wall and came forward upon his chest, and he lay stone still with his eyes shut. Then the Young Knight sprang down upon his hands and knees at the throat of the Knight of Winterburne to have the cross. But so firmly was the head of this body pressed down upon the chest that he could not come to the chain of the cross because it was under the chin. So he began to wrestle this body away from the wall. The Lady Amoureuse screamed:

"Ha, murder!"

She ran across the room and over the Young Knight's back set both her hands round his soft throat. And so great was the strength that God and love gave her that moment, that when she pulled the Young Knight off the dead man's body he staggered half across the room, turning round as he went. And there against him stood the Lady Dionissia coming out of the doorway of her room, the long dagger in her hand. Her eyes were enormously large and stared hardly, like two blue stones; her mouth was stretched tight open as if she desired to scream but could not. The Young Knight stared at her stupidly, for he did not know who she was.

She raised the dagger and drove it through his throat with such force that it stuck in the bones of his throat behind, so that she could not draw it out again. He clasped his hands over his eyes and spun round upon one leg, the other being drawn up in agony. Cry out he could not, for the dagger was through his throttle. Then a great fountain of blood poured from his throat, his mouth and nose, and so he fell down.

L'ENVOI

I

He was in darkness and voices spoke from outside it.
Arrogant and distant voices of people who were in light . . .
A curtain must be drawn back.

A bare white room. The pain: So much light that it hurt;
shining white walls; a shiny white ceiling; an overpowering,
hateful odour. He struggled with his hands. He must get
back.

A woman stood looking at him from the foot of his white
bed—with an impassive face and pursed, thin lips. She must
be in power over him. Her hands were folded before her. His
eyes rolled in agony. . . . Par pitié et amours de Die!

She was in a blue print dress. He had to see to the watch-
men. The blue print dress was almost covered by a white
apron with great pockets. Those women had stopped screaming in the dark. She turned and walked to the wall. Upon it
there was nailed a square of paper. It was divided by rec-
tangular lines and across it ran a black zigzag. Up and down.

She surveyed this for some moments holding to her lips a metal pencil case.

All serious knights at this season stocked their castles with brandwood and salted meats. . . . Were there then felling and slaughtering axes amongst the ploughs in the hall?

He could not lie here. That must be seen to.

A man looked out of a sort of cupboard. He had on a white linen coat that covered him from his chin to his feet. He looked at Mr Sorrell: he had a hard, keen expression, and he was pulling off his hands very thin, brown, viscous gloves that stuck gummily to his skin. These seemed to Mr Sorrell to be disgusting—like an obscene insult. The man nodded to the woman, who was looking at him over her shoulder. She had on a white linen cap, folded like a coif that hid all her hair. The man went into the cupboard again, sideways, withdrawing his head last of all.

The woman continued to look at the paper with the squares and the zigzag. She raised to it slowly the hand holding the silver pencil. She made a round mark at the end of the zigzag line. Then he heard his own voice say distinctly:

"Temperature chart!"

The nurse said: "Hush!"

She went towards the window. Most of the light was excluded. She closed a curtain or shutter. He could not see which. She told him he must not talk. He must sleep.

He said:

"A quoi bon? Qui surveillera les vassaux?"

She shrugged her shoulders. . . . But it was evident that all those women could not be in that little castle with no man to command the hinds.

"Wasn't there another?" he asked. "Another nurse?"

She looked towards him through the twilight.

[336]

"So you *can* speak English," she said. "For heaven's sake speak it. I haven't the patience of nurse Morans." She seemed to dislike him. She added: "Yes, there was another. You drove her into a breakdown with your French lingo and restlessness. But you can thank her that you're here. . . . And of course God," she finished perfunctorily.

"I don't thank them," he answered passionately. "It's as if there were a curtain. It must be drawn back at once." His hands struggled feebly on the counterpane. The nurse went quickly towards the door of the washing cupboard. She said into it:

"He's off again. He'd better have the draught at once."

2

Sir William Sorrell sat at his large desk in the great room that looked down on Covent Garden. The desk was covered with an entanglement of letters and agreements. A thin young man with a blue-shaven face, lantern jaws, large hollow eyes and carefully oiled black hair, was gathering the letters into packets.

"It's a comfort to have you back sir," he was saying. "These past four months have been a heavy responsibility."

It was two months since Sir William had first recovered consciousness and four since the accident. He thought he had grown older, slower and more morose. Heavier even, though that was unlikely considering hospital diets and masseurs. There were heavy creases under his eyes.

Two clerks came in, bearing the ledgers. He looked down columns. . . .

"The Claflin figures?" he asked.

"They're of course not all complete," the young man said, "It's still selling . . . Well!"

[338]

He looked at a slip of paper.

"I thought you would be interested in that, sir." . . . They had done eleven thousand sets in parts and . . .

Sir William said: "Ah! . . ." bitterly.

"It's not so bad, sir," the young man pleaded . . . "If you'd listen to all the figures, sir." He went on more earnestly. "It's better than we ever sold a thing in parts . . . And the book orders are heavy. . . ."

Again Sir William uttered his "Ah!" and the young man winced. The telephone rustled slightly. Sir William clutched at the receiver and said:

"Oh, damn, McCrackan, take this blasted thing."

He lunged up from his desk and began to pace up and down whilst McCrackan stood with the receiver to his ear, attentive. Like a sentry with a cunning face.

"What's all this?" Sir William muttered. "What is the good of all this? Any fool could do it. . . . This anaemic slave gets better results than I."

What then was he there for? What in Hell was he there for?

A ground glass door opened. This was young Lee-Egerton. . . . Honest eyes: mouth weak, naturally. He had a book under his arm.

"Mother's got you the R. O. Report on the Egerton-Morane Manuscripts," he said.

McCrackan said from the telephone:

"This johnnie wants to know whether we'll do any exchanges from our *Commercial Enterprise* with the *Waterbury Monitor*."

Young Lee-Egerton continued:

"It's mostly the report of a law-suit between a Lady Dionissia de Morant and a Gertrude de Egerton. It's rather sporting reading."

A page-boy announced that Mr Bunter wanted to speak to Sir William Sorrell.

Lee-Egerton said that Sir William's friend the Greek Slave disappeared clean and the Knight of Egerton too. That was the evidence. After years and years of suing the son of the Lady Dionissia was declared heir to all the lands and fined eleven thousand pounds.

Sir William said:

"She had a son?"

"There were doubts about the father," the boy answered. "That was why the son was fined." But according to Burke that son had been the founder of all the families of Egerton. " 'Of whose chief branch,' " the boy quoted, " 'the last descendant is Charles Lee-Egerton, Esq.,' " and he added "That's me!"

Along the front of the XVIII century room with its famous plaster-work ceiling ran three very tall windows that gave a dim, drizzling view of the Market with yellowing cabbage-leaves stamped everywhere into the wet and greasy cobbles. The three high walls were covered with tall, glass-fronted book-cases of mahogany. They contained books published by the House of Sorrell in the last forty years. The great, scarlet and blue carpet was Persian and of the thickest imaginable pile. . . . Chaste, that was what it was. . . . No, not chaste. . . . Monumental.

In the centre of the carpet was the great table-desk with, beside it, McCrackan holding the telephone to his ear. . . . Smiling slightly and looking half-starved. . . . And frightened out of his poor, faithful wits.

Once this great room had seemed like a Prime Minister's office. In it he, Sir William—then Mr—Sorrell had been used to sit like the head of a kingdom. His uncle was dead. Of the shock of hearing of his accident. So now he paced up and down there and owned the whole thing.

He had not any use for it.

His eyes looked musingly all over the young Lee-Egerton. . . . He was tall, slight, fair—very much like what Sir William himself must have looked like at that age. . . . But with a weak chin and no air of purpose. . . . Of ferocity! You had to be ferocious to succeed in these days. . . . Twice as ferocious and more savage than the Young Knight of Egerton. . . . With a chin and air like that you were bound to do nothing better than get into scrapes at Cambridge.

Something would have to be done for him if he was Dionissia's last descendant. . . . That sounded like madness but it appeared to be the truth. . . . Or what was truth? Had he himself ever been in the little castle? That was preposterous.

But it would be even more preposterous to say that he hadn't. . . . This was the dream. . . . This place was so tenuous that he could see through it the brightness of the Wiltshire hills in the sunlight. Where he would be before the sun set on them. . . . Where he was now. Certainly he wasn't here.

But something would have to be done for the boy. He was as unreal as that blue-grey cavern. . . . Yet a current seemed to proceed from him. . . . To him, Sir William. . . . The aura of paternity perhaps. . . . They talked a lot of nonsense. . . . What he needed, that boy, was a faithful slave. . . . To keep away the dragons whilst he slept in the desert. To give moral support.

You didn't have faithful slaves now. . . . Or hadn't you? Thin fellows with lantern jaws and oiled black hair. . . .

McCrackan was just the stuff to give moral support to a boy with a weak chin: the hard-bitten, industrious Scotsman. He might have taken the boy on himself but he was going. Out of here. Anywhere. . . . To Wiltshire?

To the Caucasus! Why not to the Caucasus? He could not expect them to get up another war so that he might have a good time. But no doubt the Soviet Republic or Darghestan.

. . . or Tcherkestan or Azerbeijan would let him work for them. They were said to want mining engineers. . . .

McCrackan said from the telephone:

"This persistent joker wants a set of *C. E.* sent to the Savoy. He wants to do a trade with us and won't take no. . . ."

"Send him three sets," Sir William said. "Send him twenty. Cut him off. I want to talk to you."

. . . Azerbeidjan was probably to the South by Baku. He didn't want to go where there was oil. The Soviet Republic of Tcherkestan was probably round Novo-Tcherkassk. In the territory of the Cossacks of the Don. The country for horses, if you liked. . . .

Mr Bunter was in front of him. A sallow man of perhaps fifty, with dyspeptic eyes, a stiff brown moustache and long, thin, cigarette-stained fingers. This author wrote twice each year for Sir William's firm, a volume of salacious memoirs. He said:

"Hallo!" in a voice so savage and sharp that he appeared to be snapping at something. "Nearly got you, didn't it?"

He sank into the divan near Sir William and looked with sardonic gloom at the carpet. The young Lee-Egerton said:

"It's odd what strikes people. The chaplain johnnie who wrote these chronicles of Tamworth—what struck him most about the miracles the Greek slave did was that he cured the chickens of some old abbess."

Sir William said:

"The chaplain considered that miracles are worked by God.

[342]

He would consider it odd that God should take the trouble to perform miracles for fowls that have not got souls."

Mr Bunter gave a curious, sideways glance at Sir William whom he considered to be a sort of moron.

"And of course," Sir William continued, "the affair of the chickens wasn't rightly speaking a miracle at all. Very likely God would not work miracles for chickens which must be the most soul-less of all animals. . . . The chickens of the convent were on the north side of the south wall, shut up. Forty of them in a filthy condition. All that was needed was to make a hole for them in the wall, so that they could get out into the sunlight. So he . . ."

"Who?" Mr Bunter asked.

"The pilgrim," Sir William answered.

"I thought he was a faithful slave of my ancestor's . . ." the young Lee-Egerton said.

Sir William said that perhaps that hadn't really been his ancestor. It had been held that in all probability the faithful slave was his ancestor. "In any case," he concluded, "you may take it that he was as faithful a slave as . . . as McCrackan there. And as much a pilgrim as I . . . and I've roulé ma bosse un peu partout, you know."

All this was very unreal. . . . There were perhaps real places left somewhere. Even today. Azerbaijan was obviously still going. . . . Probably Prince Diarmidov had been executed and his little castle razed to the ground. He had been one hell of a feudal overlord. Or maybe he was driving a taxi-cab in New York. A fine looking man and when he was in Caucasian costume with his knout . . . But perhaps they would have kept the castle intact. They might still want fortifications against rebel tribes. Or perhaps they were too efficient now. This all wanted looking into. . . .

Mr Bunter said bitterly as if some one had insulted him:

"What are you all talking about?"

McCrackan was still standing patiently by the desk. Sir William asked him what salary he got. He slowly rubbed his right palm on his well-oiled black hair and answered:

"Eight pound fifteen a week, Sir William."

Sir William said:

"You run this whole show for months at a time for £8.15 a week—and so as to make it shew a bigger profit than ever I did. . . ."

McCrackan exclaimed: "Oh, well, Sir William . . ." His employer appeared to him to be dangerously bitter. He might be jealous enough to throw him out. Such things had been known to happen in the City.

"And you never felt any temptation to draw out all our balance and cut off to the Argentines?" Sir William asked. "I'm damned if I should not have . . . I don't know that I'm not going to."

Mr Bunter said sardonically:

"I didn't come here to listen to metaphysical discussion. I have discovered that one of Margaret of Anjou's bastard daughters . . .

"We're not buying books to-day," Sir William said. "We're thinking of a reorganisation."

Mr Bunter said:

"We'll make this the book of the world." His "Love affairs of Ninon de l'Enclos" had done six thousand. This one would do forty. He would give them mediaeval love.

Sir William said to McCrackan:

"I'm done with this show."

He was going to turn the business into a public company. It was his to do what he liked with. He would look after Mc-

Crackan as he deserved. McCrackan in turn could look after
Lee-Egerton . . . As a dud secretary. The place was vulgar.
And the time. And the language. But if you had to stick there
you must make the best of it. He himself had been knighted—
under chloroform—for selling bum cyclopaedias. So he could
afford to roll his hump some more.

He was going to.

That was what they knighted you for, these days. Because
you sold things that were atrophied. Atrophied knowledge,
atrophied faith, atrophied courage! He would bet that if Mc-
Crackan cared he would get a peerage for selling pornography
. . . Atrophied too. He had been knighted. Think of that . . .

He addressed McCrackan with violence:

"What can you do?" he asked. "What do you know? Can
you kill an ox? Or throw an axe? Or spear a salmon? Or
make anything? A boot? A boat? Can any of us so much as
black our own boots or roast a duck or adze a bit of oak
board? Do you believe in God? Would you die for any principle? I don't mean you only . . ."

McCrackan said modestly that he had been trench-mortar
officer in the late war.

Sir William said:

"Yes, yes, you're a good fellow. But what does it do for you
here? This civilisation is so atrophied that it has hindered you.
It would be a hindrance to you here if you were a golf-
champion. Or a University don. Or even a first class conver-
sationalist. . . . Suspect! That's what you would be. . . ."
He added sharply:

"Trench mortar officer! Yes! But could you cast a trench
mortar? Or make the charge? Or even say what is the chemi-
cal composition of the charge? Where would you be if you
were thrown back into the Middle Ages? You'd probably keep

chickens in your back garden. You think that if you went
back to 1326 you'd be lord of the earth. With planes and, yes,
trench mortars and poison gas. And you'd invent bathrooms
. . . Bathrooms! . . . I'll tell you what you'd do . . . You'd
work a miracle by curing the chickens of a mitred abbess
. . . There's glory for you."

In Henrietta Street he stopped suddenly to inspect young
Lee-Egerton.

He passed his hand down his face.

"Get me to Salisbury," he said. "Cable them to have two
horses . . . Up to fourteen stone . . ."

He felt better when they were riding along Fisherton Street
beneath the spire. They got onto the Plain above the little
church of Bemerton. Sir William was looking for a long,
shallow valley . . .

There was however no castle. In its place stood a farm-
house of stone with many stone out-buildings and here and
there a green mound. Of Tamworth there was even less than
of Stapleford. Upon a knoll half a dozen stone cottages huddled together where the stables had been. On Wiley Hill Sir
William pointed a little way off the road to a circular clump
of dark pines.

"There used to be a gallows here," he said. "I hung Hugh
FitzGreville on it and his body could be seen from three
counties."

"You seem to know a lot about this part of the world," the
young Lee-Egerton said. "But you're one of the Shropshire
Sorells aren't you?"

"It's changed," Sir William answered. "It's all changed . . .
Let us get on."

They went up the hill, straight over the tough brown grass.
The road climbed slanting . . . They galloped. It was more

than the young man's wind could stand and his horse was not as good as Sir William's.

But he contrived to keep him in sight. He was convinced that Sir William was on the verge of insanity. His mother, Mrs Lee-Egerton, said he wasn't the same man . . . It had been one hell of a lick on the skull . . .

He caught the fellow up. A long way off was the church tower of a little village. A church and a cluster of buildings with patches of trees round them. They peeped like observant hares above a low hill.

Sir William was sitting perfectly still. His horse was grazing the roadside, its reins on its neck. They slipped onto the turf. Sir William said:

"It's no use going there . . . It would not be really going back."

"I don't know what you want to go back for," the young man said. "A man who can ride as you do can't be called used up."

A bicycle bell drilled behind them. Young Lee-Egerton shot off his horse and grabbed Sir William's reins.

"You'll have your neck broken," he grumbled. "It's you who need the faithful slave."

A girl coasted down past them, going very fast. She was noticeably fair, in a dress of green and white chequered print. A white linen coif hid all her hair.

"That's your old nurse, Dionissia Morant," the boy said. "*She* looked after you. . . ."

Sir William was off down the road. It turned immediately and mounted the hill towards the cluster of old and falling buildings. He turned his horse loose in the stockyard. One half of the house had fallen years before. The other still stood, the arched windows in its immensely deep walls, filled here and

[347]

there with lattice and in places with boards. Wallflowers, house-leeks, rushes and grass grew out of all the joints in the stones. It was so old that you could hardly recognise it for a house.

On the front door was a placard announcing that the materials of the house together with those of the hamlet of Fordingbridge were to be sold by auction at Salisbury in three days' time. By order of the War Office.

The living-room was large, long and low, part of a much longer hall that had been partitioned off. There was nothing on the great stone flags, but beneath a window, a pile of hay, some horse-blankets, a couple of old green coats and a sheep-crook with a long handle. A shepherd had slept there.

This was the little castle of Sir Ygorac. It was behind that festering pile of coats that his head had struck. What did you know about that?

A thin lath wall divided that long hall. The girl appeared. In a green and white chequered dress. A white coif hid her hair. She said:

"You are Sir William Sorrell. I am Dionissia Morane." She was singularly fair; her eyebrows were a dark brown. Her blue eyes had an absent expression as if she were trying to look beyond a curtain. She said:

"I was born in this room. We farmed here for six centuries. Now it is to be an air station. Nothing can stop it."

"Nothing can stop these things," he confirmed.

"It was a little old, lost place," she said. "You would have thought they could have spared it. In the summer it was pleasant. The birds sang and we walked in the gardens. In the winters we stayed in by our fire and friends came and we talked . . . It is still called Morant's Castle . . ."

He said:

"Don't you suppose that somewhere . . . if one had the whole world before one? . . ."

"You'd find another little castle?" she asked slowly. "I don't know. If one got somewhere where they were beginning. . . ." She added: "Beginning all over again. Inspired of course with faith."

He said:

"I once saw on the side of a valley in the Russian Caucasus . . . I was prospecting. I thought one day I would go back. That was in '13. I prospected for the Imperial Government."

"If you saw a little castle then," she said, "it would be a ruin now . . . But of course *they're* beginning."

He said:

"Yes, beginning. You'd get primitive conditions all right. But you have been ill . . . You could not stand . . ."

She said:

"You're extraordinarily like what I thought you were. I'm not ill by nature. I used to think and think . . . And read about battles. In chronicles . . ."

He said:

"Above my body . . . You used to imagine me doing things . . . They call it trying it on the dog . . . It got through. Your book had '*1325 to 1400*' in indented gilt, on the cover."

"As for not standing things!" she said. "Look what a great girl I am naturally. A regular pilgrim mother."

He said:

"Stamps . . . Crushers, you know. . . . For ore. Worked by water power. In the bottom of a valley. You're snowed in all the winter . . ."

It was certainly as if she were trying to look through a curtain.

"It seems good enough for me," she said.

He exclaimed:

"But if the . . . the fourteenth century is there. Behind a curtain . . . Beginning a new civilisation and certainly with brilliant faith. Then there's a new factor in psychics. . . ."

She said:

"I know what you mean . . . But it's really all one which beginning of which civilisation you take a hand in . . . As long as your stamps crush your ores. . . . And as long as we have faith . . ." she added. "That's what I've thought out during *my* illness. It's one thing to read Froissart and Commynes . . ."

He said:

"You read the *Chronicon* too . . ."

She exclaimed:

"Let me finish . . . It's one thing to read them and . . . and daydream. But if one's full-blooded one wants to take an actual part. Haven't you faith enough? . . . Even if we went back to those beginnings we'd have to go forward again. And only reach here. Happiness or any other human value— they're things you can't put in a bank."

She flushed and passed her hand over her eyes. "I talk too much," she said. "But I don't talk often," she went on. "It's getting back to a beginning of everything that matters. It doesn't matter where or even when. Then you can go forward with courage. That's what's the matter with to-day and here. We go forward into doubt because there's nothing but doubts into which to go forward. Faith is a thing you cannot borrow. Not even the Jew Goldenhand from whom they used to borrow can lend you that. It comes from your surroundings. From hard, unatrophied things and minds . . . After they trepanned you for the first time you stretched out your hand to me and said: 'Es-tu là?' I took your hand because no one was allowed to speak then. I said to myself that all was very well to me. My mind was full of old phrases like that from old English and the old French and I thought you were re-covering. But you grew worse . . . It was then that that idea was born to me—that the real problem was to go forward from now. I could tell from your mutterings, all day and all night, that your thoughts were—Oh, following mine . . . And it had seemed to me that if you came back we could together . . . Oh, restore this place . . . And only dress in homespuns . . . That sort of physical and moral deflatism."

She looked at him for a long time. She must have been try-ing to discern to what extent he followed her. For when she began again she said:

"After all, one could say that you have gone through the same . . . mental processes. There's no doubt a mental link between us . . . For when they—an irresistible force like the War Office—served me with notice that they would take this place . . . Of course that was bitter. A hospital nurse even is human . . . And at almost the same moment you were given over . . . Because they gave you over . . . It came into my head that I had been day dreaming all wrong . . . I should have been thinking into tomorrow. Not six hundred years ago. So I came to this village. Have always had a room here. Then I heard you had recovered . . . I am going back to-morrow. That is why I came here to-day."

He exclaimed:

"You are never going back."

She looked at him for a long time.

"Then you must never go back either," she said at last. She added: "What we have to do is to go forward—don't they say: over the graves?"

Carcassonne, Nov. 1910.
New York, Dec. 1934.